THE HISTORY OF HUMAN SOCIETY

General Editor: J. H. Plumb, LITT.D.
Christ's College, Cambridge

THE PORTUGUESE SEABORNE EMPIRE 1415–1825

THE HISTORY OF HUMAN SOCIETY

General Editor: J. H. Plumb

FIRST TITLES

Prehistoric Societies *Grahame Clark and Stuart Piggott*
The Dutch Seaborne Empire 1600–1800 *C. R. Boxer*
The Spanish Seaborne Empire *J. H. Parry*
Pioneer America *John Alden*
The Greeks *Antony Andrewes*
The Portuguese Seaborne Empire 1415–1825 *C. R. Boxer*

IN PREPARATION

The Romans *Donald Dudley*
The Jews *Cecil Roth*
The British Seaborne Empire 1600–1800 *J. H. Plumb*
The French Seaborne Empire 1600–1789 *Leo Gershoy*
Nineteenth Century France *Charles Morazé*
The Medieval Mediterranean World *Arthur Hibbert*
India and the West *Anil Seal*
Imperial China *Raymond Dawson*
China and the West *Jerome Ch'en*
Japan *Marius Jansen*
Africa *J. D. Fage*
Britain, the Industrial Empire *John Vincent*
The Delta Civilisations *Jacquetta Hawkes*

THE PORTUGUESE SEABORNE EMPIRE 1415-1825

C. R. BOXER

Hutchinson of London

HUTCHINSON & CO (*Publishers*) LTD
178–202 Great Portland Street, London W1

London Melbourne Sydney
Auckland Bombay Toronto
Johannesburg New York

★

First published 1969

This book has been set in Garamond, printed in Great Britain on Antique Wove paper by Anchor Press, and bound by Wm. Brendon, both of Tiptree, Essex

09 097940 0

Acknowledgements

GRATEFUL THANKS are due to Mr. Fred Hall and the authorities of the Newberry Library, Chicago, for permission to reproduce the Portuguese *Náo* or 'Great Ship' from the atlas attributed to Sebastião Lopes (*c.* 1565) which is in the Ayer Collection there. The Secretaries of the Hakluyt Society kindly gave permission for the reproduction of the sketch-map of the *Carreira da Índia*, and for the quotations in the text from *The Travels of Peter Mundy*, *The Tragic History of the Sea*, *The Travels and Controversies of Friar Domingo Navarrete, O.P.*, and other works published under that imprint. The Witwatersrand University Press likewise gave leave for the inclusion in this book of some passages from my *Four Centuries of Portuguese Expansion, 1415–1825: A Succinct Survey*, first published at Johannesburg in 1961, and reprinted in 1963, 1965 and 1968.

The Librarian and staff of the Lilly Library, Indiana University, generously allowed me unrestricted access to their treasures and gave permission to quote from the unpublished correspondence of the Spanish Augustinian missionaries in South China, 1680–1720, and other original sources. A general acknowledgement to the directors and staffs of the Portuguese and Brazilian archives where I have worked at different times and places is made in the Bibliography (p. 392). I must make special mention of the authorities of the Ashridge branch of the Public Records Office, London, for facilitating my consultation of the correspondence of the British envoys and consuls at Lisbon between 1660 and 1750. Also of Senhor Alexandre Eulálio Pimenta da Cunha and Senhora Nellie Figueira of the Biblioteca Nacional, Rio de Janeiro, for kindly supplying me with a set of the reproductions of the coloured drawings by Carlos Julião *c.* 1785, from which Plates 13, 14 and 15 are taken.

Finally, my thanks to David Hoxley who drew the maps, and Professor J. D. Fage for allowing me to base maps 4 and 5 on material from his *Atlas of African History*, published by Edward Arnold.

Contents

APPENDICES

List of illustrations and maps

MAPS

Preface

As C. R. Beazley observed some seventy years ago, the first of modern colonial empires, the dominion of the Portuguese on the coasts and seas of Africa and Asia, is in one sense more interesting than any of its successors. For it was, as he stated, essentially and peculiarly connected with the beginnings of that maritime expansion of Europe and Christendom which, above all else, marks off the modern from the medieval world. Since Beazley's day it has also become apparent that the first of modern colonial empires bids fair to last the longest, as it is still going strong in Tropical Africa whence all the others have withdrawn. But the existing Portuguese African empire is mainly a development of the last two or three generations, and its story requires separate treatment. The present book attempts to summarise the vicissitudes and the achievements of the old Portuguese seaborne empire as manifested from the Maghreb to the Moluccas and to the Mato Grosso, prior to Portugal's recognition of Brazilian independence in 1825. It also attempts to keep constantly in view the interactions between the principal portions of this furtherest flung of empires and the home country poised precariously on the western rim of Europe. By so doing it will, perhaps, help to explain not only how Portugal pioneered the overseas expansion of Europe, but how she managed to retain so much of her shoestring empire when other and stronger powers appeared on the scene.

Introduction

BY J. H. PLUMB

I

OVER THE LAST fifty to a hundred years, man's belief that the historical process proved that he was acquiring a greater mastery over Nature has received a brutal buffeting. In his early youth H. G. Wells, a man of vast creative energy, of rich delight in the human spirit, and of all-pervading optimism, viewed the future with confidence; science, born of reason, was to be humanity's panacea. When, in the years of his maturity, he came to write his *Outline of History,* his vision was darker, although still sustained with hope. World War I, with its senseless and stupid slaughter of millions of men, brought the sickening realisation that man was capable of provoking human catastrophes on a global scale. The loss of human liberty, the degradations and brutalities imposed by fascism and communism during the 1920s and 1930s, followed in 1939 by the renewed world struggle, these events finally shattered Wells's eupeptic vision, and in sad and disillusioned old-age he wrote *Mind at the End of its Tether*. His hope of mankind had almost vanished. Almost, but not quite: for Wells's lifetime witnessed what, as a young writer, he had prophesied—technical invention not only on a prodigious scale but in those realms of human activity that affected the very core of society. And this extraordinary capacity of man to probe the complexities of Nature and to invent machinery capable of exploiting his knowledge remained for Wells the only basis for hope, no matter how slender that might be.

If the belief of a man of Wells's passionate and intelligent humanism could be so battered and undermined, it is not surprising that lesser men were unable to withstand the climate of despair that engulfed the Western World, between the two World Wars. The disillusion of these years is apparent in painting, in music, in literature—everywhere in the Western World we are brought up sharply by an expression of anguish, by the flight from social and historical reality into a frightened self-absorbed world of personal feeling and expression. Intellectual life, outside science, has pursued much the same course as artistic life, although it has shown greater ingenuity and a tougher-minded quality. Theology, philosophy and sociology have tended to reduce themselves to technical problems of exceptional professional complexity, but of small social importance. Their practitioners have largely ceased to instruct and enliven, let alone sustain the confidence of ordinary men and women.

In this atmosphere of cultural decay and of professional retreat, history and its philosophy have suffered. As in so many intellectual disciplines its professional workers have resolutely narrowed the focus of their interests to even more specialised fields of inquiry. The majority of historians have withdrawn from general culture in order to maintain, at a high intellectual level, an academic discipline. They have left the meaning and purpose of history to trained philosophers and spent their leisure hours tearing to shreds the scholarship of anyone foolish enough to attempt to give the story of mankind a meaning and a purpose: writers, as diverse as H. G. Wells and Arnold Toynbee, have been butchered with consummate skill. The blunders of scholarship and the errors of interpretation have counted everything; intention nothing. Few academic historians, secure in the cultivation of their minute gardens, have felt any humility towards those who would tame the wilderness. In consequence, an atmosphere of anarchic confusion pervades the attitude of Western man to his past.

A hundred years ago, in the first flood of archaeological discovery, scholars possessed greater confidence: the history of mankind seemed to most to point to an obvious law of human progress. The past was but a stepping-stone to the future. First adumbrated by the philosophers of the late Renaissance—Bodin in France and Bacon in England—the idea of progress became an article of common faith during the Enlightenment. And progress came to mean not only the technical progress that had preoccupied Bacon but also moral progress. By the nineteenth century the history of man demonstrated for many an improvement in the very nature of man himself as well as in his tools and weapons. Such optimism, such faith in man's capacity for rational behaviour, was shaken both by discoveries in science and in history as well as by events. By the middle of the twentieth century man's irrational drives appeared to be stronger than his intellectual capacities. Freud and Marx laid bare the hollow hypocrisy of so-called rational behaviour either in individuals or in society. Also, the rise and fall of civilisations, laid bare by the spade, seemed to point to a cyclical pattern in human destiny which made nonsense of any idea of continuous progress; and this naturally attracted the prophets of Western doom. Yet more persuasive still, and, perhaps, more destructive of confidence in human destiny, was the utter loss of all sense of human control brought about by global wars and violent revolutions. Only those men or societies who felt life was going their way, the revolutionaries and, above all, the Marxists, believed any longer in the laws of historical progress. For the rest, retrogression seemed as tenable a thesis as progress.

This disillusion in the West suited academic historians. It relieved them of their most difficult problems. If they happened to be religious they were content to leave the ultimate meaning of history to God; if they were rationalists, they took refuge either in the need for more historical knowledge or in the philosophic difficulties of a subject that by its very nature was devoid of the same objective treatment that gave such authority to scientific inquiry. In the main they concentrated upon their professional work. And this was an exceptionally important and necessary task. What the common reader rarely recognises is the inadequacy of the factual material that was at the command of a historian one hundred years ago or even fifty years ago. Scarcely any archives were open to him; most repositories of records were unsorted and uncatalogued; almost every generalisation about a man or an event or an historical process was three-quarters guesswork, if not more. Laboriously, millions of facts have been brought to light, ordered and rendered coherent within their own context. Specialisation has proliferated like a cancer, making detail livid, but blurring the outlines of the story of mankind, and rendering it almost impossible for a professional historian to venture with confidence beyond his immediate province. And that can be very tiny—the Arkansas and Missouri Railway Strike of 1921; the place-names of Rutland: seventeenth-century Rouen; the oral history of the Barotse; the philosophy of Hincmar of Rheims. And so it becomes ever more difficult for the professional historian to reach across to ordinary intelligent men and women or make his subject a part of human culture. The historical landscape is blurred by the ceaseless activity of its millions of professional ants. Of course, attempts at synthesis have to be made. The need to train young professional historians, or the need to impart some knowledge of history to students of other disciplines, has brought about competent digests of lengthy periods that summarise both facts and analysis. Occasionally such books have been written with such skill and wisdom that they have become a part of the West's cultural heritage. A few historians, driven by money or fame or creative need, have tried to share their knowledge and understanding of the past with the public at large.

But the gap between professional knowledge and history for the masses gets steadily wider: professional history becomes more accurate, more profound, whilst public history remains tentative and shallow.

This series is an attempt to reverse this process. Each volume will be written by a professional historian of the highest technical competence; but these books will not exist *in vacuo,* for the series is designed to have a unity and a purpose. But, perhaps, first it is best to say what it is not.

It is not a work of reference: there are no potted biographies of the Pharaohs, the Emperors of China or the Popes; no date lists of battles; no brief histories of painting, literature, music. Nor is this series a Universal History. All events that were critical in the history of mankind may not necessarily find a place. Some will; some will not. Works of reference, more or less factually accurate, exist in plenty and need not be repeated. It is not my intention to add yet another large compilation to what exists. Nor is this a 'philosophic' history. It does not pretend to reveal a recurring pattern in history that will unveil its purpose. Fundamentally philosophy, except in the use of language, is as irrelevant to history as it is to science. And lastly this series will not cover all human societies. There will be two volumes devoted to Russia, none to Germany. There will be histories of China and Japan but not of Indonesia. The Jews have a volume to themselves, the Parsees do not. And so on. Yet the series is called *The History of Human Society* for very good reasons. This history has a theme and a position in time.

The theme is the most obvious and the most neglected; obvious because everyone is aware of it from the solitary villagers of Easter Island to the teeming cities of the Western World; neglected because it has been fashionable for professional and Western historians to concern themselves either with detailed professional history that cannot have a broad theme or with the spiritual and metaphysical aspects of man's destiny that are not his proper province. What, therefore, is the theme of *The History of Human Society?* It is this: that the condition of man now is superior to what it was. That two great revolutions—the neolithic and the industrial—have enabled men to establish vast societies of exceptional complexity in which the material well-being of generations of mankind has made remarkable advances; that the second, and most important, revolution has been achieved by the Western World; that we are witnessing its most intensive phase now, one in which ancient patterns of living are crumbling before the demands of industrial society; that life in the suburbs of London, Lagos, Jakarta, Rio de Janeiro and Vladivostok will soon have more in common than they have in difference: that this, therefore, is a moment to take stock, to unfold how this came about, to evoke the societies of the past whilst we are still close enough to many of them to feel intuitively the compulsion and needs of their patterns of living. I, however, hope, in these introductions, which it is my intention to write for each book, to provide a sense of unity. The authors themselves will not be so concerned with the overriding theme. Their aim will be to reconstruct the societies on which they are experts. They will lay bare the structure of their societies—their economic basis, their social organisations, their aspirations, their cultures, their religions and their conflicts. At the same time they will give a sense of what it was like to have lived in them. Each book will be an authoritative statement in its own right, and independent of the rest of the series. Yet each, set alongside the rest, will give a sense of how human society has changed and grown from the time man hunted and gathered his food to this nuclear and electronic age. This could only have been achieved by the most careful selection of authors. They needed, of course, to be established scholars of distinction, possessing the ability to write attractively for the general reader. They needed also to be wise, to possess steady, unflickering compassion for the strange necessities of men; to be quick in understanding, slow in judgement, and to have in them some of that relish for life, as fierce and as instinctive as an animal's, that has upheld ordinary men and women in the worst of times. The authors of these books are heart-wise historians with sensible, level heads.

The range and variety of human societies is almost as great as the range and variety of human temperaments, and the selection for this series is in some ways as personal as an anthology. A Chinaman, a Russian, an Indian or an African would select a different series; but we are Western men writing for Western men. The westernisation of the world by industrial technology is one of the main themes of the series. Each society selected has been in the main stream of this development or belongs to that vast primitive ocean whence all history is derived. Some societies are neglected because they would only illustrate in a duller way societies which appear in the series; some because their history is not well enough known to a sufficient depth of scholarship to be synthesised in this way; some because they are too insignificant.

There are, of course, very important social forces—feudalism, technological change or religion, for example—which have moulded a variety of human societies at the same time. Much can be learnt from the comparative study of their influence. I have, however, rejected this approach, once recorded history is reached. My reason for rejecting this method is because human beings experience these forces in communities, and it is the experience of men in society with which this series is primarily concerned.

Lastly, it need hardly be said that society is not always synonymous with the state. At times, as with the Jews, it lacks even territorial stability; yet the Jews provide a fascinating study of symbiotic social groupings, and to have left them out would be unthinkable, for they represent, in its best form, a wide human experience—a social group embedded in an alien society.

As well as a theme, which is the growth of man's control over his environment, this series may also fulfil a need. That is to restore a little confidence in man's capacity not only to endure the frequent catastrophes of human existence but also in his intellectual abilities. That many of his habits, both of mind and heart, are bestial, needs scarcely to be said. His continuing capacity for evil need not be stressed. His greed remains almost as strong as it was when he first shuffled on the ground. And yet the miracles created by his cunning are so much a part of our daily lives that we take their wonder for granted. Man's ingenuity—based securely on his capacity to reason—has won astonishing victories over the physical world—and in an amazingly brief span of time. Such triumphs, so frequently overlooked and even more frequently belittled, should breed a cautious optimism. Sooner or later, painfully perhaps and slowly, the same intellectual skill may be directed to the more difficult and intransigent problems of human living—man's social and personal relations—not only directed, but perhaps accepted, as the proper way of ordering human life. The story of man's progress over the centuries, studded with pitfalls and streaked with disaster as it is, ought to strengthen both hope and will.

Yet a note of warning must be sounded. The history of human society, when viewed in detail, is far more often darkened with tragedy than it is lightened with hope. As these books will show, life for the nameless millions of mankind who have already lived and died has been wretched, short, hungry and brutal. Few societies have secured peace; none stability for more than a few centuries; prosperity, until very recent times, was the lucky chance of a small minority. Consolations of gratified desire, the soothing narcotic of ritual, and the hope of future blessedness have often eased but rarely obliterated the misery which has been the lot of all but a handful of men since the beginning of history. At long last that handful is growing to a significant proportion in a few favoured societies. But throughout human history most men have derived pitifully little from their existence. A belief in human progress is not incompatible with a sharp realisation of the tragedy not only of the lives of individual men but also of epochs, cultures and societies. Loss and defeat, too, are themes of this series, as well as progress and hope.

2

Portugal and its empire are one of the great enigmas of history. By 1480 the Portuguese had reached down the coast of Africa, as well as across the wastes of the Atlantic to colonise the Azores; maybe its intrepid fishermen were already perched with Basques and Bretons on the rocky, fish-invested seas of Newfoundland. India seemed destined to be theirs and America too; indeed, had the Portuguese only listened to Columbus, they would have had three great continents in their coils before any other nation of Europe. Columbus and Spain denied what Fate seemed to have decreed for them, yet the Portuguese by the middle of the sixteenth century dominated more of the world and more of its trade than any other country. Africa, with the strings of trading posts and forts that reached up the East as well as down the West coasts: their hold on great ports at Ormuz and Goa gave them control of the rich trade of the Persian Gulf and Indian Ocean. Factories in Ceylon and Indonesia put the spice trade in their hands. Established firmly in China and Japan, they brought their ships home stuffed with oriental luxuries—silks, porcelain, lacquer. The dream that had haunted men in the days of Prince Henry the Navigator had come true. Those early fumbling probings, fraught with danger and interlaced with death, had blazened the great trade routes along which larger and larger ships crammed with people and piled high with goods made their stately way through tempests and calms to the great Eastern empires. But they had awakened Europe, and the Dutch and the British were within a hundred years of their discoveries yapping at their heels, wolfish with greed. They glutted Europe with spices and the Portuguese empire shrivelled. What had risen like a meteor, fell like one. Soon they were left with unprofitable patches of East and West Africa and a handful of trading stations —Luanda and Moçambique in Africa, Goa in India, Timor in Indonesia, Macao hard by Canton.

Brazil, the one great territory that remained to them, went in the nineteenth century, Goa scarcely a decade ago, and the rest remain. Of all the great empires of the West, more of the Portuguese endures. In this century Portugal has voluntarily given up none of its possessions; even the Indians had to use force to turn them out of Goa. And Portugal once more is the largest empire in Western Europe. It was the first; it is the last. Inertia and continuity through vast social and political upheavals is a rare phenomenon in human history. But this quality of survival is not the only strange feature of the Portuguese seaborne empire. Indeed the Portuguese empire poses a whole series of awkward questions for the historian. Why was this small, rather poor, culturally backward nation, perched on the south-west coast of Europe, so dramatically successful in that great century of enterprise that started about 1440? Again, why did this achievement fade to a shadow of itself with a span of a mere fifty years? And, even more enigmatic, why did possession of empire fail to act as a catalyst in Portugal? In the Netherlands, in Britain, in Spain and in France, the possession of empire worked like yeast, not only on the economic and political life of the nation, but also on its cultural life, on its literature, science and art. In Portugal, Lisbon fattened, and Camões wrote the *Lusiads*. Certainly there was greater prosperity than there would have been had Portugal been dependent on her wines and fish. But apart from Camões there are few writers, architects, painters or scientists whose names would be known except to the specialist. The cultural impact of the Portuguese empire, although not negligible, remains oddly slight. And, as one reads the haunting story of Portuguese enterprise, so brilliantly expounded by Professor Boxer, these insistent whys become louder and louder.

Of course, Portugal possessed some natural advantages. Throughout her existence she had lived by harvesting the sea. Her rocky coast, hammered by the Atlantic towards which her rivers run from her mountainous hinterland, had always been her gateway to a wider world, breeding a tough, skilful race of sailors who were not daunted by the tempests of the ocean. Trade and profit were from the earliest times seaborne, and with the Mediterranean dominated by Venetians, Genoese, Catalans and Arabs, the Atlantic remained the one vast area open to the Portuguese. With the crumbling of Arab power due to the hammer blows inflicted by the Spaniards, opportunities increasingly arose in the fifteenth century for the enterprising Portuguese to exploit the trade with the north-west African coast. However, that exploitation from the very first was encased in religious zeal and, without doubt, sustained too by genuine scientific curiosity. The latter should not be underestimated—curiosity is a compelling force once aroused, and curiosity, combined with competition betwixt the sea captains, drove them ever further south. This fascination is reflected in the men it drew to the Portuguese enterprises—Italians, Jews from Majorca, and even an occasional Scandinavian. But it was this mixture of the deeper passions—greed, wolfish, inexorable, insatiable, combined with religious passion, harsh, unassailable, death-dedicated—that drove the Portuguese remorselessly on into the torrid, fever-ridden seas that lapped the coasts of tropical Africa and beyond. The lust for riches and passion for God were never in conflict with each other, nor were they unconscious drives: in some men, as with Prince Henry the Navigator, religion was more important than trade, yet he wanted gold, trafficked in slaves and did not despise the wealth that he regarded as God's blessing. As with Prince Henry, so with the rest: the Portuguese pioneers plucked the naked blacks out of their canoes, traded their horses for nubile young women and shipped them back to Lisbon's slave market where they found eager buyers. This combination of greed and godliness has always been regarded as the major driving force not only of the Portuguese, but of the Spanish too; even to a lesser extent of the British, French and Dutch: indeed its repetition has so domesticated the concept that it is easy to underestimate the ferocity, the savagery, the compulsion that drove these remorseless men.

Unfortunately for the East, the Portuguese were heirs of the long accumulation of the technical skill of the late Middle-Ages. The Arabs and the Jews had endowed them with astrolabes and maps; the shipbuilding skills which had been sharpened by the great ocean whose challenge had produced the ships which, if cumbersome by the standards of the seventeenth century, were marvels of manœuvrability that made short work of the junks and dhows of the Indian Ocean, armed as they were with the best artillery that Europe could produce. Also, and the importance of this cannot be overstated, the fascination with exact observation can be found in most of the great Portuguese pioneers. They plotted and mapped their routes with astonishing exactitude: they noted with care the animals, vegetables, minerals and the strange new people as they voyaged down the Africa coast. There was nothing haphazard about their path-finding. It was deliberate, well-planned, daringly executed: high technical intelligence was placed at the service of God and profit. And the result was as savage, as piratical an onslaught on the dazzlingly rich empires of the East as the world has ever known. It was not one, however, that seems to have stirred the conscience of any Portuguese commander. For these Orientals were heathens, blacks, Moors, Turks, containing, as one of them wrote, 'the badness of all bad men'.

Hence the Portuguese had no shame in telling the stories of their pillage. As they relate, they bombarded on the slightest pretext the rich and prosperous ports of Africa, Persia and India, firing the houses, plundering the warehouses, slaughtering the inhabitants. They butchered crews of captured Moslem dhows, slinging some from the yardarm for target practice, cutting off the hands and feet of others and sending a boatload of bits to the local ruler, telling him to use them for a curry. They spared neither women nor children. In the early days they stole almost as often as they traded. They destroyed the long established routes that had bound the Far East and the Moslem World in a web of mutually profitable and largely peaceful commerce. And the children of Christ followed the trade of blood, setting up their churches, missions and seminaries, for, after all, the rapine was a crusade: no matter how great the reward of Da Gama, Albuquerque, Pacheco and the rest might be in this world, the next would see them in greater glory.

Although most of the clergy and missionaries who followed in the wake of the captains of the ocean were content to set up churches, receive their dues and dispense charity without keeping too sharp or too disapproving an eye on the sexual indulgence of their military masters, the same harsh zeal that drove the captains never entirely deserted the men of God either at Lisbon or in the East. The Kings of Portugal wasted men and treasure in the inhospitable wastes of Abyssinia in the hope of reconciling the Coptic Abyssinians to the Roman Church, but the inflexibility of their attitude, combined for once with a patchy military performance, quickly dispelled that dream. For a time they had more success, through the fanatical dedication of the Jesuits both in Japan and Brazil: in the former the Christian doctrines served a political and social purpose, which gave the Jesuits something of a mass base amongst the Japanese, whereas in the latter the Jesuits' protection of the converted Indians is one of the few luminous situations in the story of the Portuguese empire. The Jesuits, trained by their admirable education, pursued with avidity the intricacies of the alien cultures which they discovered in both the Far East and South America. And if their contribution was never so great to Oriental studies as that made by the French Jesuits who followed in their footsteps, it was far from despicable and their journeys of geographical discovery have been underestimated since the day that they were made. Antonio de Andrade penetrated into Tibet, Bento de Goes took five years to make his way from Goa to China, whilst Father Lobo, nearly two hundred years before Livingstone, plodded across Africa. Indeed the greatest intellectual contribution which the Portuguese brought to Europe through their seafaring was geographical knowledge and navigational exactitude. Their charts and sailing directions became the finest in the world. The Portuguese were, indeed, the path-finders of Europe's seaborne empires. Even more clearly than Spain they demonstrated to Europe the effectiveness of a sailing ship armed with cannon, not only against primitive native people of Africa, but also against the well-fortified ports and empires of the East. And so the Orient lay at Europe's mercy. The carracks, piled high with loot—pepper, cinnamon, mace, silks, pearls, rubies—aroused the lust of Europe. The Portuguese made the breach through which the jackals raced to get their fill. Few European historians will face up to the consequences of the murderous Western onslaught on India and the East, which broke not only webs of commerce but of culture, that divided kingdoms, disrupted politics and drove China and Japan into hostile isolation. Although one cannot fail to admire the heroism and endurance of many of the Portuguese captains, which Professor Boxer's lucid narrative demonstrates time and time again, one should not either overlook his account of the blood and carnage that followed in their wake.

Disastrous for the East, a vicious example of piracy too quickly followed by their European admirers, the possession of empire did little enough for Portugal itself. It enriched the monarchy, gave Lisbon a quiet prosperity that it was never to lose again, and provided sometimes a career and often a graveyard for the sons of the gentry. But its days of greatness were soon over. The epic days of plunder gave way to a settled and inefficient exploitation that grew ever more inert as decade followed decade and century century. Even in navigation and shipbuilding, the Portuguese were surpassed first by the Dutch, then the British: the rest of Western Europe followed. The Portuguese stayed faithful to their ancient carracks, making them ever larger and ever more cumbersome: and so the cruel sea took its harvest. Deepening conservatism, deepening reluctance to adjust to a changing world became the hallmark of the Portuguese. The Spanish empire may have grown arthritic, but the Portuguese possessed the rigidity of a corpse. In that first heroic age of adventure, in which the curiosity and the crusade were more evident than the cruelty, Prince Henry the Navigator drew about him some of the liveliest intellectuals of his age: some were Jewish, others had mozarabic connections; so long as they were gifted in navigation, cartography and mathematics they were welcomed to his councils and became recipients of his patronage. The same mild liberality, particularly with regard to the Jews, persisted even into the days of King Manuel, but inexorably the forces of the counter-reformation, particularly the Inquisition, eradicated anyone tainted with Jewish belief and locked the iron shutters on men's minds.

Rigid, orthodox, decaying, mouldering like an antique ruin in the tropical heat, the Portuguese empire slept on. As it moved into the turbulence of modern times, it found apologists because they thought that they discovered one feature, more liberal by far than could be discovered in the other great and more flourishing empires. The Portuguese empire might be moribund, decaying, corrupt, but, at least, it was free from racial prejudice. Historians pointed with pride to the mixture of races in Brazil, the coloured seminarists in Goa, the domestic bliss of Portuguese officials, rutting in the backlands of Mozambique and Angola. And the great Brazilian historian, Freyre, helped to fortify this legend in his great book on slavery in Brazil, but, alas, Professor Boxer shows just how false this belief is. His documentation is massive and conclusive. The Portuguese were intensely racist in

Africa, in Goa, in Brazil: indeed, in Goa, even a native wet-nurse was thought to contaminate an infant whom she suckled. And it should be remembered that in the sixteenth century Portugal possessed in the homeland far more slaves than any other European country; perhaps as much as ten per cent of Lisbon's population was servile. Certainly it contained the most active slave market in Europe. This is a fact, not a moral condemnation: the attitude of the rest of Europe, of Africa, of Asia, of the settled peoples of America, differed little on such questions. What the Portuguese empire reminds us of so forcibly in Professor Boxer's excellent and scholarly book is the cruelty and barbarity of life in the sixteenth-century world. Life was desperately cheap, the after life desperately real, the poverty of the world so great that luxury and riches inebriated the imagination and drove men mad with lust to possess. The one great difference between that Europe of which Portugal was the harbinger and the world that it enslaved was the intense certainty and exclusiveness of its religious convictions—Catholic or Protestant. In some, as in St. Francis Xavier, the lust for souls was as avid as the lust for gold and spices in Da Gama: but to kill the unconvertible, to punish the heathen, was always righteous: other races were base, slavery for them just. Neither can one stress often enough that an impervious rectitude sheathed these men of iron in moral steel, enabling them to forge those blood-red links that were to bind the rest of the world in Europe's chains for hundreds of years. And yet from this gross exploitation arose the surplus wealth, the opportunities, the stimulus, the intellectual challenge that were to be instrumental in enabling the whole of mankind to develop a totally new way of life. The possession of world markets helped to tip commercial Europe into its industrial future.

At a terrible cost Portugal opened the doors to a wider world, one that she could neither dominate nor control; with history's usual malice she was quickly overtaken and left moribund, a pensioner in the world stakes; possessing enough for survival, too little for glory. And, like the aged, she still clings desperately and meanly to all that she possesses, hoping to outlive the times—an unlikely prospect. And yet indelibly her name is written across the world's history: an extraordinary achievement for so small, so poor a country.

PROLOGUE

The Western Rim of Christendom

THE Spanish chronicler, Francisco López de Gómara in the dedication of his *General History of the Indies* to the Emperor Charles V in 1552 described the Iberian seafarers' discovery of the ocean routes to the West and East Indies as being 'the greatest event since the creation of the world, apart from the incarnation and death of Him who created it'. Just over two centuries later the Scots political economist, Adam Smith, stated virtually the same thing when he wrote: 'The discovery of America and that of a passage to the East Indies by the Cape of Good Hope are the two greatest and most important events recorded in the history of mankind.'

Even in this age of Space travel many people—including some who are not Christians—may think that López de Gómara and Adam Smith were not far wrong. For the most striking feature of the history of human society prior to the Portuguese and Spanish voyages of discovery was the dispersion and isolation of the different branches of mankind. The human societies that waxed and waned in the whole of America, and in a great part of Africa and the Pacific, were completely unknown to those in Europe and Asia. Western Europeans, with the exception of some enterprising Italian and Jewish traders, had only the most tenuous and fragmentary knowledge of the great Asian and North African civilisations. These on their side knew little or nothing of Europe north of the Pyrenees and of Africa south of the Sudan (save for the fringe of Swahili settlements along the East

African coast) and they knew nothing whatever about America. It was the Portuguese pioneers and the Castilian *conquistadores* from the western rim of Christendom who linked up, for better and for worse, the widely sundered branches of the great human family. It was they who first made Humanity conscious, however dimly, of its essential unity.

We are often told that the peoples of the Iberian peninsula—and particularly the Portuguese—were peculiarly fitted to inaugurate the series of maritime and geographical discoveries which changed the course of world history in the fifteenth and sixteenth centuries. Among their assets in this connection are commonly listed their geographical position in Europe's most advanced window on the Atlantic and certain national characteristics evolved in eight centuries of struggle with the Moors. The famous Brazilian sociologist Gilberto Freyre and his disciples have stressed that the long Moorish domination in the peninsula accustomed many of the Christian inhabitants to regard the swarthier Moor or Arab as a social superior. The brown Moorish woman was also seen as an enviable type of beauty and sexual attractiveness, as evidenced by the continuing popularity of the folk-tales of the *Moura Encantada*, or enchanted Moorish princess, among the illiterate Portuguese peasantry. From this, these sociologists allege, it was but a short step to tolerating half-breeds and mixed bloods. Hence the tendency of the Portuguese—and to a lesser degree of the Spaniards—to dispense with the colour-bar. Admittedly, the centuries during which Christians and Muslim struggled for the mastery of the Iberian peninsula were not unchanging epochs of unremitting religious intolerance and strife. The Castilian champion, *El Cid Campeador*, and his Portuguese equivalent, Geraldo *Sem Pavor* ('the fearless'), both served under Christian and Muslim rulers as occasion offered. There was even a time in the thirteenth century when Christian, Muslim and Jewish rites were amicably celebrated in the same temple—the Mosque of Santa Maria la Blanca at Toledo.

There is obviously some substance in these arguments, but they are usually pushed too far. In the first place, many, and in some regions a majority, of the 'Moors' who occupied the Iberian peninsula for so long were no darker than the Portuguese, since they were Berbers and not Arabs nor 'Blackamoors'. The people of North Africa were white, forming part of the great Mediterranean unity. Secondly, even if the bitter struggle for the hegemony of the peninsula was punctuated by spells of mutual tolerance, these respites were over by the fifteenth century. The years when the three rival creeds were celebrated on an equal footing at Toledo had no more permanent result than had the remarkable Christian-Muslim *rapprochement* achieved in Sicily under the rule of the Norman kings and their Hohenstaufen successor Frederick II, '*Stupor Mundi*', in 1130–1250. By the fifteenth century, at any rate, the average Iberian Christian, like his French, German or English contemporaries, seldom referred to the Muslim and Jewish faiths without adding some injurious epithet. Hatred and intolerance, not sympathy and understanding, for alien creeds and races was the general rule; and the ecumenical spirit so fashionable today was conspicuous by its absence. 'Moors' and 'Saracens', as Muslims were termed, Jews and Gentiles were all popularly regarded as doomed to hell-fire in the next world. Consequently, they were not likely to be treated with much consideration in this one.

Religious intolerance was not, of course, limited to Christians, though it was, perhaps, more deeply rooted among them than among most peoples of other faiths. But the orthodox Muslim regarded with horror all those who would 'give associates to God', and this was just what the Christians did with their Trinity, their Virgin Mary, and (to some extent) with their saints. Saint-worship, and belief in omens, superstitions and miracles, were indeed widespread in the Muslim world by the fifteenth century, particularly among the adherents of the Sufi orders, or mystic confraternities, to whom these practices made a great appeal. But the veneration of saints and of their sepulchres never attained in Islam the excesses to which the cult of the saints and their images was often carried in Christendom.

Medieval Europe was a harsh and rugged school, and the softer graces of civilisation were not more widely cultivated in Portugal than they were elsewhere. A turbulent and treacherous nobility and gentry; an ignorant and lax clergy; doltish if hard-working peasants and fishermen; and an urban rabble of artisans and day-labourers like the Lisbon mob described by the greatest of Portuguese novelists, Eça de Queiroz, five centuries later, as 'fanatical, filthy and ferocious' (*essa plebe beata, suja, e feroz*); these constituted the social classes from which the pioneer discoverers and colonisers were drawn. Anyone who doubts this need only read the graphic pages of Fernão Lopes—'the greatest chronicler of any age or nation', as Robert Southey described the official historian of the long reign of King Dom João I (1385–1433)—which witnessed the beginnings of Portuguese expansion.

With the capture of Silves, the last Moorish stronghold in the southernmost province (or 'kingdom' as it was technically called) of the Algarve in 1249, Portugal attained what for practical purposes are her present national boundaries. She was thus not only the first of the modern European nation-states, but she had expelled the Muslim invaders from her soil over two centuries before the conquest of Moorish Granada by Ferdinand and Isabella (1492) set the seal on Castile's predominance over the rest of the Iberian peninsula. During the later Middle Ages most of the land in Portugal was still uncultivated, and much of it is still uncultivated for the same basic ecological reasons. Two-thirds of the Portuguese soil is either too rocky, too steep, or too stony to be cultivated at all, or else the poor soil yields only uncertain and inferior crops. The extreme irregularity of the rainfall, which is apt to alternate between excessive or unreasonable quantities and totally insufficient amounts, is another natural drawback. Few of the rivers are navigable for any length, and the violent oscillations in their water levels (sometimes nearly 100 feet between flood and low water) are among the greatest in the world. The roads were wretchedly bad, even by medieval standards; and the towns or villages were relatively few and far between, situated on hill-tops or in clearings amid the vast expanses of scrub, heath, waste and woodlands.

The population probably totalled about a million at its maximum in the late Middle Ages. In Portugal, as elsewhere, the Black Death of 1348–9 took a severe toll; and the long-drawn-out war with Castile in 1383–1411 must have had an adverse effect on the population of the frontier regions. But human resilience from such national disasters is well attested, and the million mark was probably reached and passed again by about 1450. The only cities of any size to the north of the river Tagus were Oporto, Braga, Guimarães, Coimbra and Bragança, the first-named being by far the largest with a population of about 8,000. The region south of the Tagus, which had been more densely settled in Roman and Islamic times, boasted a good many more urban centres, but most of them were very small. Lisbon, with some 40,000 inhabitants, was by far the largest city in the kingdom, the other towns and villages (with the exception of Oporto) containing anything between 500 and 3,000 souls. Although Lisbon was the capital city of Portugal in more ways than one, the King and the Court did not always reside there. Like most medieval and Renaissance monarchs, the Portuguese kings were often on the move, and they frequently ranged as far afield as Evora down to the end of the dynasty of Aviz in 1580.

The economy was still largely on a barter basis in the countryside, but the collection of taxes and land-rents in coin rather than in kind was increasing the general use of money. No gold coins were struck in Portugal between 1385 and 1435, although foreign ones, including English nobles, had circulated freely at the time of Dom Fernando's accession (1367), when the country was relatively prosperous. The subsequent wars with Castile, with the revolution of 1383–5 and its aftermath, resulted in numerous successive debasements of the coinage by King Dom João I, despite frequent remonstrances by the Cortes or parliament of the three estates, which met twenty-five times during his reign. Silver money was also uncommon; and the coinage consisted chiefly of a base metal called *bilhão* (Spanish *vellon*), an alloy of silver and copper with the latter heavily predominating. The overwhelming majority of the population were peasants, growing cereals (chiefly wheat and millet) or producing wine or olive oil, according to the nature of the land they cultivated, while fishing and the extraction of salt gave employment to the population of the littoral. A modest but expanding maritime trade was based on the export of salt, fish, wine, olive-oil, fruit, cork, scarlet-in-grain, and hides to Flanders, England, the Mediterranean and Morocco; and on the importation of wheat, cloth, iron, timber and bullion from northern Europe and gold coins from Morocco.

The 'Three Estates' represented in the Cortes were the nobility, the clergy and the people (*povo*); but the last-named category did not comprise direct representatives of the working classes, save in so far as the guilds were represented in the delegations from some towns. These three main categories each comprised numerous classes and subdivisions. The nobility and the clergy as a whole were privileged classes, enjoying varying degrees of immunity from taxation and from arbitrary arrest and imprisonment. They also exercised certain rights over the commonalty in the case of great territorial magnates like the Duke of Bragança, who possessed a measure of jurisdiction over their vassals or tenants, although Pedro I (1357–68) had successfully established the Crown as the final court of appeal and enforced the submission of many private and local jurisdictions to the royal authority. Below the higher nobility came the gentry or knights and squires (*cavaleiros* and *escudeiros*). During the fourteenth to fifteenth centuries the word *fidalgo* (*lit. filho d'algo*, 'son of a somebody'), which was indicative of real or alleged gentle blood, became a synonym for *nobre* (noble), as *fidalguia* did for *nobreza* (nobility). The *cavaleiro*, originally a belted knight, likewise became in this period a purely honorific social category, but slightly inferior to that of *fidalgo*. The *fidalgo-cavaleiro* was a knight of gentle or noble blood, whereas the *cavaleiro-fidalgo* was a person of simple blood who had been knighted for services to the Crown. By 1415, the members of the *nobreza* were not so much a feudal knighthood, deriving their position from their prowess on the battlefield, as persons who were 'living nobly' (*vivendo à lei da nobreza*), that is, in manor houses on their own land and with 'servants, weapons and horses' at their disposal.

The clergy likewise did not form a homogeneous class, varying as they did from mitred prelates of royal blood to the sometimes barely literate village priests. There were also obvious differences between the regular clergy of the religious Orders and the secular clergy, the former being, for the most part, of higher social status. As elsewhere in Europe at this period, ecclesiastical standards left a good deal to be desired in many instances. Clerical concubinage was widespread, if we may judge from the fact that between 1389 and 1438 two archbishops, five bishops, eleven archdeacons, nine deans, four chanters, seventy-two canons and about 600 priests received official permission to legitimise their bastard children. These figures do not include those clerics in minor orders and others who did not bother to apply. A mediocre standard of ecclesiastical morality was accompanied by a low level of clerical learning. The university (*Studium Generale*) founded by King Dom Dinis at Lisbon in 1290 failed for over two centuries to attain the desired standards. Pope Nicholas IV expressly prohibited the teaching of theology there, and though this ban was not strictly observed, Pope Clement VII in 1380 denied Lisbon-trained theologians the customary licence to teach anywhere (*facultas ubique docendi*). Many friars of the Mendicant Orders, as likewise the Cistercian monks of Alcobaça, Portugal's most famous monastery, certainly studied at Lisbon; but no Portuguese friar was accepted by the foreign members of his own Order as a properly trained theologian unless he had first studied and graduated outside Portugal. One reason for this state of affairs was the very defective knowledge of Latin among many of the Portuguese priests, monks and friars. The result was that the Mendicant Orders sent their most promising friars to be trained (or at least to graduate) at foreign universities, including Oxford and Paris. The Lisbon University authorities complained of this practice in 1440, but it lasted until well into the next century. Furthermore, the Crown's tendency to move the university back and forth between Lisbon and Coimbra did not make for the maintenance of consistently high academic standards. The intellectual level of this sole Portuguese university, which only became permanently established at Coimbra in 1537, was admittedly inferior to those of Paris, Oxford, Salamanca, and Bologna.

Below the privileged clergy, *fidalgos*, knights and squires, but above the great mass of the unprivileged peasants and artisans, were the somewhat intermediate classes including merchants, lawyers, physicians and Crown officials. None of these groups was as yet numerous, but the merchants had attained considerable influence and importance in the two chief maritime cities of Lisbon and Oporto. The Portuguese traders had to contend with privileged groups of foreign merchants in these two places, especially at Lisbon, but they did so with a fair measure of success before the early sixteenth century. Magalhães Godinho has shown recently that between 1385 and 1456, out of a total of forty-six ships engaged in the maritime trade between Portugal, England and Flanders, which were captured by corsairs or confiscated in harbours, 83 per cent belonged to Portuguese, 15 per cent to foreigners, and 2 per cent were of mixed ownership. Out

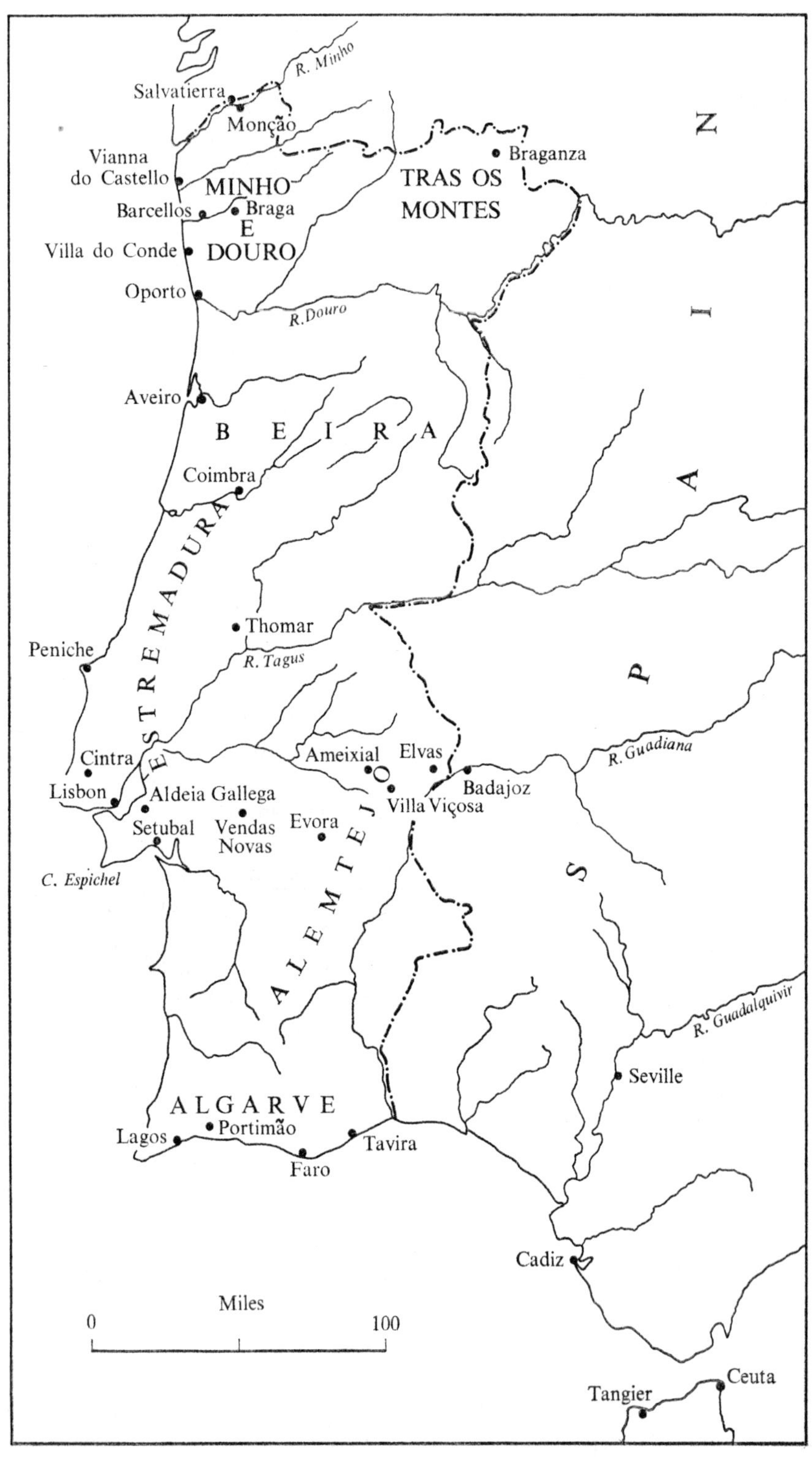

1 Portugal in the sixteenth to eighteenth centuries

of twenty instances in which the origin of the cargoes of these vessels is known, 55 per cent belonged to Portuguese, 20 per cent to foreigners, and 25 per cent was owned jointly. Nevertheless, it is an exaggeration to write of Portugal (as another authority has recently done) as possessing 'a powerful commercial class largely emancipated from feudal control' in 1415, unless with the caveat that this class was virtually limited to Lisbon and Oporto.

Physicians, lawyers, notaries, judges, municipal councillors, and Crown officials of various kinds probably did not total more than about a thousand individuals at the end of the fifteenth century, apart from the peripatetic Court and its hangers-on. Crown officials were paid a monthly or yearly monetary salary, supplemented in many cases by portions of textiles and cereals. Their hours of work naturally varied, but were often brief enough. The officials of the royal exchequer (*Casa dos Contos*), for example, had office hours from 6 to 10 a.m. in the summer and from 8 to 11 a.m. in the winter. In this, as we shall see, they had a great advantage over the artisans.

In Portugal, as in all other European countries, the great majority of the population were peasants (*lavradores*). They were divided into various categories ranging from the comparatively well-to-do men who farmed their own land and employed labour, to the landless rural proletariat, dependent on seasonal labour and odd jobs. Those who farmed their own land were not very numerous, and most peasants cultivated land which did not belong to them, paying rent in kind (or else in money) to the landlord, whether the Crown, the Church, or a private individual. Many of these peasants had relative security of tenure, in that they held the land which they cultivated on long lease; but, even so, the rent varied from one-tenth to one-half of the annual produce. In addition there were often feudal or semi-feudal dues to pay, and, above all, the tithe to the Church, which had precedence over all other payments. In some instances the peasant might have to hand over as much as 70 per cent of what he produced. Another vexatious imposition, which was not abolished until 1709, was the obligation laid on ordinary people to provide free board and lodging for the great ones (*poderosos*) of the land. Last not least, the peasants were often (though not always nor everywhere) liable to give their labour free for one, two or even three days a week in the service of the Crown or of their landlord. This forced labour might take the form of public works, transporting goods or produce, or engaging in field or domestic service for the landlord. There was also a general (and largely theoretical) obligation for all able-bodied peasants and artisans to be called up by the Crown for military service if the kingdom was invaded. This general liability to military service is one of the features which distinguished the Portuguese form of feudalism from that in vogue elsewhere in Western Europe.

Partly as a result of the devastation caused by the Black Death, agricultural day-labourers were able to demand and to secure higher wages than hitherto. The Crown and the small proprietors and landlords who served on the municipal and rural councils and who fixed the local wage-scales endeavoured to keep wages down by stabilising local prices and wages and by legally tying the labourer to the soil. These restrictions were increasingly evaded, and there remained a tendency for the peasants to emigrate from the countryside to the towns—above all to Lisbon and to Oporto. Those who stayed on the land often preferred to hire their services by the week or by the month, instead of on a yearly basis, as was the traditional practice. Still, the principle of free bargaining over conditions of labour and employment was not yet accepted in theory outside of Lisbon and its immediate neighbourhood.

By the end of the fourteenth century the artisans and the urban labourers had been grouped into a vocational hierarchy of guilds, with the goldsmiths at the top of the social scale and the cobblers at the bottom. Carpenters, shipwrights and weavers, for example, had a higher status than armourers, tailors and butchers. In accordance with the usual late medieval practice, the artisans, shopkeepers and stallholders were often grouped together in streets or wards, according to their respective professions. Hence the names of 'goldsmiths' street', 'coopers' street', 'cobblers' street', 'bakers' street', etc., which still survive in many towns. This grouping of arts, crafts and 'mysteries' (to use the Old English term corresponding to the Portuguese *mesteiraes*) in guilds suited all parties. The artisans, craftsmen and tradesmen could keep an eye on each other's prices and on the quality of the goods offered, besides having a sense of solidarity and mutual protection against possible violence and abuse. The buyers knew where to find what they were looking for, and they could easily compare prices and quality from their standpoint. The municipal and government authorities also found it easier to levy taxes and to make assessments on this basis. As a royal decree of 1385 noted approvingly, this practice redounded to the 'good administration and greater beauty and nobility of the city' of Lisbon. Each place of work was self-contained, with apprentices and journeymen working under the eye of a qualified practitioner or foreman. The hours of work were long; from sunrise to sunset, with only a half-hour break for the noonday dinner in many instances. But these long hours were offset to some extent by the frequent religious high-days and holidays, while Sunday was generally (though not invariably) observed as a day of rest. In Portugal, as elsewhere, the peasants and artisans comprising the *povo*, or people, bore the greatest share of the burden of taxation.

Despite the drift from the countryside to the towns, the artisans and urban labourers formed a very small percentage of the population in comparison with the peasants. Lisbon had a thriving maritime trade in the middle of the fifteenth century, but the city did not contain more than fifty or sixty caulkers at that period. Guimarães, which was still a relatively important city in the third quarter of the preceding century, had then fewer than fifty qualified artisans and craftsmen. In other and smaller towns the proportion of workmen to peasants was probably something between 5 per cent and 10 per cent. Owing to the important part played by the urban workers of Lisbon and Oporto in the revolution of 1383–5, the guilds became much more powerful and influential in these two cities than they had been hitherto, and to a lesser extent in the country towns also. Jews and Moors formed minority groups in some places but their numbers and importance were far less than in neighbouring Spain. During the late Middle Ages, the Jews in Portugal, as elsewhere, were forced to wear distinctive badges on their clothing, to live in ghettos, and to pay heavier taxes than Christians. They were subjected to occasional and small-scale pogroms, but their condition was relatively better than in most other European countries. Jewish tax-gatherers, physicians, mathematicians and cartographers were patronised by Portuguese kings despite periodic protests by the third estate (*povo*) in the Cortes. Jewish artisans and craftsmen predominated in some industries and trades, including those of tailor, goldsmith, blacksmith, armourer and cobbler. Jewish peasants, sailors, and men-at-arms were naturally few and far between; but in 1439 a Jewish goldsmith of Evora claimed and received a reward for having served in the capture of Ceuta and the abortive expedition to Tangier with his 'horse, weapons, and two foot-soldiers'. On the very rare occasions when Jews were voluntarily converted to Christianity, they were absorbed and assimilated into the Christian community without any difficulty. Until the mass immigration of the Jews from Spain after Ferdinand and Isabella's decision to expel them in 1492, the children of Israel did not form a major problem in Portugal. The Moors had by this time been absorbed in the mass of the population, save for a small trickle captured in the wars with Morocco and who were used as slaves.

If Portugal never had a *Morisco* problem after the final conquest of the Algarve (1249), whereas Spain had one for over a century after the capture of Granada (1492), yet Moorish influence in Portugal was hardly less evident in several cultural and material ways. Many words which are used to designate agricultural implements, techniques, weights and measures, which are of Romance origin in northern Portugal, are of Arabic origin in the south. The Moors also introduced some new plants, and they greatly extended the cultivation of others which they found in the peninsula: the carob-tree, the lemon, the bitter orange, and (perhaps) rice. They much improved the cultivation of the olive, as evidenced by the fact that although the word for the tree is of Latin origin (*oliveira*), the fruit and the oil extracted therefrom are of Arabic (*azeitona*, *azeite*). Many substantive nouns and several economic, military, and administrative terms are likewise of Arabic origin, to say nothing of numerous place-names in the south, where the Moorish-Berber occupation lasted much longer. This difference between north and south is also reflected in the regional domestic architecture, where Moorish influences are clearly discernible in the southern region, particularly in the Algarve, the 'sunset land' which was the last stronghold of Islam.

The differences between the north and the south of Portugal were (and are) reflected in other ways besides the climate and the etymology. Smallholdings predominated in the fertile and over-populated northern province of Minho, typified by the anecdotal saying that if a man puts a cow out to pasture in his own field her dung falls in his neighbour's field. Large estates and *latifundia* were common in the sparsely populated plains and wastes of the southern province of Alentejo. Geographical and geological differences between northern and southern Portugal were also reflected in the use of different building materials. Whereas stone predominated in the rocky and mountainous north, houses of *taipa* (tramped earth) and clay were more common in the south. The poor, of course, lived in mere shacks or hovels; or in loosely built stone dwellings roofed with slabs (or with thatch) in the remote highlands of Tras-os-Montes, as some of their descendants do to this day. It was of such humble habitations that the chronicler Gomes Eanes de Zurara was thinking when he described the astonishment of the Portuguese invaders at the beauty and richness of the Moorish mansions which they sacked at Ceuta in August 1415, 'for our poor houses look like pigsties in comparison with these'.

Apart from the very rough contrasting divisions which are made of Portugal as between north and south, or Roman and Arabic-Moorish, or Atlantic and Mediterranean (from the climatic point of view), there is another obvious subdivision—littoral and hinterland. The claim is often made that Portugal was pre-eminently a maritime nation. In a sense this is obviously true, for it was Portugal which led the way 'to track the oceans none had sailed before' (*por mares nunca dantes navegados*) in Camoens' famous lines. But in other ways the claim is more contestable. We shall see in the course of this work that deep-sea sailors were always in short supply in Portugal, and for long periods there was an acute shortage of them. The Portuguese coast has very few good natural harbours, Lisbon and Setubal being the only two natural ports of a spacious size. There are no off-shore islands to break the force of the Atlantic gales, nor are there sheltered deep-water estuaries, rivers, inlets and creeks, which are easy of access and where shipbuilding can easily be developed. The coast is often low, sandy and windswept, or else forbiddingly rocky and abruptly steep. The fishing villages are mostly situated in open roadsteads, whence the small craft in use could not put to sea save when wind, tide and weather were exactly right.

Admittedly, the sea off the Portuguese coast is rich in fish; and as long ago as the late Middle Ages Portuguese fishermen were fishing off the coast of Morocco. But it is virtually certain that a much higher proportion of the population is nowadays engaged in the fishing industry than was the case for most of the four centuries with which we are concerned. In recent years some 38,300 men, or about 1·2 per cent of the active population, were wholly or mainly engaged in fishing. This figure is certainly much more impressive than those which are available for the sixteenth to eighteenth centuries, as we shall see in due course (pp. 114, 211, 226).

In any event, as Orlando Ribeiro has pointed out, the seagoing occupations, however important they are (or appear to be) in the framework of the Portuguese national economy, can only be classified as limited, fragmentary, and intermittent in comparison with the permanent agricultural labour of the fields. Even a few miles inland from the coast many people are quite uninfluenced by the nearness of the sea. The inhabitant of the Alentejo, Portugal's largest province, has no dependence on the sea, either for his food or for his work. The peasant in the fields around Lisbon is only conscious of the Atlantic Ocean when trying to protect his vines from the strong sea breezes and the particles of salt which they bring. In some respects the sea has certainly played a more important part in the history of Portugal than any other single factor. But this does not mean that the Portuguese were a race of adventurous seamen rather than one of earth-bound peasants. Three or four centuries ago the proportion of men who 'went down to the sea in ships' for their livelihood in Portugal was almost certainly much less than it was in regions like Biscay, Brittany, the northern Netherlands, southern England and some of the Baltic lands.

PART I · VICISSITUDES OF EMPIRE

CHAPTER I

Guinea gold and Prester John 1415-99

THE Portuguese voyages of discovery in the Atlantic Ocean seem to have begun in or about the year 1419, four years after the capture of Ceuta from the Moors. For practical purposes the first stage of the overseas expansion of Europe can be taken as beginning at either of these dates. This stage can likewise be regarded as having ended with the return of Vasco da Gama to Lisbon in July 1499, some six years after the completion of Christopher Columbus' epic voyage of discovery to the Antilles.

The Portuguese and Spaniards had their (more or less isolated) precursors in the conquest of the Atlantic and the Pacific Oceans, but the efforts of these remarkable adventurers had not changed the course of world history. Carthaginian coins of the fourth century B.C. have been found in the Azores, and Roman coins of a later date in Venezuela, in circumstances which suggest the possibility of their having been brought there by storm-driven vessels in classical times; but, if so, there is nothing to suggest that these vessels ever returned to Europe with the news. Vikings had voyaged from Norway and Iceland to North America at intervals in the early Middle Ages, but the last of their neglected settlements in Greenland had succumbed to the rigours of the weather and the attacks of the Eskimo by the end of the fifteenth century. A few Italian and Catalan galleys from the Mediterranean had boldly ventured into the Atlantic on voyages of discovery in the thirteenth and fourteenth centuries. But though they probably sighted some of the Azores and Madeira, and though they certainly rediscovered the Canaries (the 'Fortunate Isles' of Roman geographers), these isolated voyages were not systematically followed up. Only a vague memory remained of the Genoese brothers Vivaldi, who had set out in 1291 with the evident intention of rounding southern Africa and reaching India by sea, but who had disappeared after passing Cape Nun on the Moroccan coast. Similarly, although the occasional storm-driven Chinese or Japanese junk may have involuntarily reached America, and although the Polynesian 'Argonauts of the Pacific' from Hawaii colonised islands as far distant as New Zealand, such feats did not affect the basic isolation in which America and Australia remained with respect to the other continents.

On the Euro-Asian land mass of the Medieval World, Marco Polo and other travellers—nearly all of them Italians—had journeyed overland from the shores of the Black Sea to those of the China Sea during the years (*c.* 1240–1350) when the Mongol Khans imposed their *Pax Tartarica* over Central Asia and far beyond. But these European travellers' accounts of the wonders and marvels of the East were either disbelieved by their compatriots or else they were too highly coloured and fragmentary to give an accurate idea of Asia to the Western World. It is significant that the fabulous 'letter of Prester John', and the fantastic travels of the (non-existent) Sir John Mandeville, proved far more popular with the European reading public than did the more factual narratives of Marco Polo and Friar Odoric de Pordenone—though even these contained plenty of exaggerations and misunderstandings.

Some Catalan and Majorcan maps of the fourteenth century, such as that made for Charles V of France about 1375, show a surprisingly accurate knowledge of the western Sudan region and the routes followed by the merchant caravans from North Africa on their way across the Sahara 'to the land of the Negroes in Guinea'. This geographical information was derived from Jewish merchants who could travel with relative freedom in the Muslim lands. It was not based on first-hand knowledge by European Christians, nor was there any information about the West African coast below the Gulf of Guinea. Roughly speaking, most medieval maps reflected either the Ptolemaic belief that the Indian Ocean was a landlocked sea or else the Macrobian conception of an open seaway to the Indian Ocean round a (highly distorted) southern Africa. Only after the Portuguese had worked their way down the West African coast, rounded the Cape of Good Hope, crossed the Indian Ocean and established themselves in the Spice Islands of Indonesia and on the shore of the South China Sea; only after the Spaniards had attained the same goal by way of Patagonia, the Pacific Ocean and the Philippines—then and only then was a regular and lasting maritime connection established between the four great continents.

Why did the Iberians succeed where their Mediterranean predecessors had failed? Why did Portugal take the lead when the Biscayan seamen and their ships were as good as any in Europe? What were the motives which impelled the leaders and the organisers of Portugal's maritime expansion? Were those leaders following a consistent and carefully considered plan, or were they prepared to adapt their aims and their methods to changing circumstances? Did the original inspiration and guidance come mainly if not entirely from the Infante Dom Henrique (alias Prince Henry the Navigator) and/or other members of the royal house of Aviz? Or was the propelling force provided by an emergent mercantile middle class whose influence had greatly increased after the revolutionary crisis of 1383–5, when the great majority of the old nobility were killed, dispersed or destroyed, for having taken the side of the Castilian invaders who were decisively defeated at Aljubarrota (14 August 1385)? How far was the piecemeal knowledge of North Africa (including the western Sudan), India and the Far East, which is reflected in the mappae-mundi and manuscript travel literature emanating from Arab, Jewish, Catalan and Italian cartographers and merchants, available to Prince Henry and to other interested persons in Portugal; and what (if any) use did the Portuguese make of this information?

Historians are still far from agreed on the answers to these questions; but the main impulses behind what is known as the 'Age of Discovery' evidently came from a mixture of religious, economic, strategic and political factors. These were by no means always mixed in the same proportions; and even motives primarily inspired by Mammon were often inextricably blended with things pertaining to Caesar and to God—as instanced by the medieval Italian merchant of Prato who headed all the pages of his ledgers with the invocation: 'In the name of God and of Profit.' At the risk of over-simplification it may, perhaps, be said that the four main motives which inspired the Portuguese leaders (whether kings, princes, nobles, or merchants) were in chronological but in overlapping order and in varying degree: (i) crusading zeal against the Muslims, (ii) the desire for Guinea gold, (iii) the quest for Prester John, (iv) the search for Oriental spices.

An important contributory factor was that during the whole of the fifteenth century Portugal was a united kingdom, virtually free of civil strife, save for the tragic episode of Alfarrobeira in 1449 when the ex-regent, Prince Pedro, fell a victim to the intrigues and the ambitions of the ducal house of Braganza. The reader will hardly need reminding that for most of that century the other countries of Western Europe were either convulsed by foreign or by civil wars—the Hundred Years War, the Wars of the Roses, etc.—or else they were preoccupied by the menace of the Turkish advance in the Balkans and in the Levant. More particularly, Castile and Aragon experienced a 'time of troubles' verging on ruinous anarchy before the reign of Ferdinand and Isabella. These internal broils went a long way towards preventing the Spaniards from competing as effectively with the Portuguese as otherwise they might have done (though they did eventually drive them out of the Canaries).

The Portuguese capture of Ceuta in August 1415, and, more important, its retention, were probably inspired mainly by crusading ardour to deal a blow at the Infidel, and by the desire of the half-English princes of Portugal to be dubbed knights on the battlefield in a spectacular manner. Admittedly, this traditional explanation as put forward by the chroniclers does not satisfy some modern historians. They argue that economic and strategic motives must have played a much larger part, since Ceuta was (apparently) a thriving commercial centre, a Muslim naval base, and a bridgehead for an invasion across the straits of Gibraltar. It has been further suggested that the (allegedly) fertile corn-growing region of the hinterland formed an additional attraction for the Portuguese, whose own country was even then normally deficient in cereals. This suggestion is discounted by the fact that a Muslim description of Ceuta written shortly before its capture states explicitly that the city had to import corn from elsewhere, although it was stored there in large granaries. Ceuta was likewise one of the terminal ports for the trans-Sahara gold trade, though how far the Portuguese realised this before their capture of the city is (like much else about the origins of the expedition) quite uncertain.

In any event, the occupation of Ceuta undoubtedly enabled the Portuguese to obtain some information about the Negro lands of the Upper Niger and Senegal rivers where the gold came from, if they were not aware of this already from such sources as the 'Catalan map' of 1375 and the reports of Jewish traders. Sooner or later they began to realise that they might perhaps be able to establish contact with those lands by sea, and so divert the gold trade from the camel caravans of the western Sudan and the Muslim middlemen of Barbary. They had the greater incentive to do this since there was a great demand for gold during the last two and a half centuries of the Middle Ages in Western Europe. During this period gold coinage was adopted by one city, region, and country after another, largely inspired by the striking of the Florentine gold florin in 1252 and the Venetian gold ducat in *c.* 1280. Portugal had had no gold currency of its own since 1383, and it was one of the few European kingdoms in this position.

The crusading impulse—which, in so far as the Portuguese were concerned, was exclusively directed against the Muslims of Morocco—and the search for Guinea gold were soon reinforced by the quest for Prester John. This mythical potentate was originally and vaguely located by Europeans as the ruler of a powerful realm in 'the Indies'—an elastic and shifting term which often embraced Ethiopia and East Africa as well as what was known of Asia. More specifically, Nearer or Lesser India meant, approximately, the north of the sub-continent; Further or Greater India meant the south between coasts of Malabar and Coromandel, and Middle India meant Ethiopia or Abyssinia. But few people in the early fifteenth century had such a clear-cut definition of 'the Indies'; and the terms 'India' and 'the Indies' were often vaguely applied to any unknown and mysterious regions to the east and south-east of the Mediterranean.

The passage of time, romantic travellers' tales, and the circulation of a highly embellished but widely publicised forged letter purporting to be from Prester John, all combined with Western European credulity and wishful thinking to build up the late medieval belief that this monarch was a mighty (if possibly schismatical) Christian priest-king. His realm was believed to lie somewhere in the rear of the Islamic powers which occupied a wide belt of territory from Morocco to the Black Sea. It was originally thought to be vaguely in Central Asia, and in course of time its location was gradually shifted to Ethiopia (Abyssinia).

From 1402 onwards a few Ethiopian monks and envoys reached Europe (via Jerusalem) from this ancient and isolated Christian Coptic kingdom in the highlands between the Nile and the Red Sea. At least one of these envoys got as far as Lisbon in 1452; but it is obvious from subsequent developments that the Portuguese, like other Europeans, only obtained a hazy idea of what or where his country was. The more extravagant forms of the legend of Prester John, such as the statement that 30,000 persons were entertained at his table made of emeralds, while twelve archbishops sat on his right hand and twenty bishops on his left, do not seem to have circulated as widely in Portugal as they did in some other European countries. But it was undoubtedly believed in Portugal, as elsewhere, that this mysterious priest-king, when once definitely located, would prove an invaluable ally against the Muslim powers, whether Turks, Egyptians, Arabs, or Moors. So far as the Portuguese were concerned, they hoped to find him in an African region, where he would be able to help them against the Moors.

The mixed motivation behind the Portuguese discoveries is clearly apparent from the wording of the Papal Bulls which were promulgated during the lifetime of Prince Henry and his immediate successors. It has been established that the wording of these documents closely follows that of the preliminary requests for their promulgation made by the Portuguese Crown. They thus reflect the attitude and the aspirations of the King, or of those who petitioned the Papacy in his name. The three most important Bulls were the *Dum diversas* of 18 June 1452; the *Romanus Pontifex* of 8 January 1455, and the *Inter caetera* of

13 March 1456. In the first the Pope authorises the King of Portugal to attack, conquer and subdue Saracens, pagans, and other unbelievers who were inimical to Christ; to capture their goods and their territories; to reduce their persons to perpetual slavery, and to transfer their lands and properties to the King of Portugal and his successors. Some modern authorities argue that this Bull was intended to apply only to the Portuguese campaigns in Morocco, where fighting had been going on ever since the Portuguese capture of Ceuta, but the wording of the Bull neither states nor implies any such limitation. Moreover, by 1452 the Portuguese were well aware that the population of Morocco was exclusively Muslim. The reference to pagans and other enemies of the name of Christ must surely refer to the population of the Saharan littoral and to the Negroes of Senegambia with whom the Portuguese were already in contact.

The second Bull, *Romanus Pontifex*, was even more specific, and it has been rightly termed the charter of Portuguese imperialism. The Bull begins by summarising the work of discovery, conquest and colonisation accomplished by Prince Henry since 1419. His apostolic zeal as a true soldier of Christ and defender of the Faith is lauded in eloquent terms. He is praised for his desire to make known and worshipped the glorious name of Christ, even in the remotest and hitherto undiscovered regions, and to compel the Saracens and other unbelievers to enter the fold of the Church. The Bull further recalls his colonisation of the uninhabited islands of Madeira and the Azores, and his efforts in the conquest and evangelisation of the Canaries. It specifically credits him with the intention of circumnavigating Africa, and thus making contact by sea with the inhabitants of the Indies, 'who it is said, honour the name of Christ', and, in alliance with them, prosecuting the struggle against the Saracens and other enemies of the Faith. The Prince is authorised to subdue and to convert pagans (even if untainted by Muslim influence) who may be encountered in the regions lying between Morocco and the Indies.

For the last twenty-five years, the Bull proceeds, Prince Henry has not ceased to send his caravels southwards to explore the west coast of Africa. They have reached Guinea and have discovered the mouth of a great river which seems to be the Nile [actually, the Senegal]. By trading and fighting, the Portuguese have secured a large number of Negro slaves and have brought them to Portugal, where many have been baptised and embraced the Catholic Faith. This gives hope that entire native populations, or at least many individuals, may be freely converted in the near future. The Crown of Portugal has in this way become the owner of an extensive maritime domain, and is anxious to retain the monopoly of the navigation, trade and fishing in those regions; lest others should come to reap where the Portuguese had sown, or should try to hinder the culmination of their work. Since this work is one which forwards the interests of God and of Christendom, the Pope, Nicholas V, here decrees and declares, *motu proprio*, that this monopoly does in fact apply not only to Ceuta and to all the present Portuguese conquests but likewise to any that may be made in future, southward of Capes Bojador and Nun, and as far as the Indies. The legitimacy of any measures taken by the Crown of Portugal to safeguard this monopoly is explicitly recognised by the Pope.

The Portuguese are further given Papal permission to trade with the Saracens, where they should find it expedient to do so, always provided that they do not sell weapons or war material to those enemies of the Faith. The King [Affonso V], Prince Henry, and their successors are authorised to build churches, monasteries and *pia loca*, and to send priests to administer the sacraments therein; although there is no specific mention of sending missionaries to preach the gospel to the unbelievers. Finally, all other nations are strictly prohibited from infringing or interfering in any way with the Portuguese monopoly of discovery, conquest and commerce. The importance of this last clause was underlined by the solemn proclamation of this Bull in Lisbon cathedral on 5 October 1455, in the original Latin and in Portuguese translation, and before a congregation which included representatives of the foreign communities in the Portuguese capital—French, English, Castilians, Galicians and Basques—who had been specially summoned for the occasion.

By the Bull *Inter caetera* of 13 March 1456 Pope Calixtus III confirmed the terms of the *Romanus Pontifex*, and at the request of King Affonso V and his uncle, Prince Henry, conceded to the Order of Christ, of which the latter was administrator and governor, the spiritual jurisdiction of all the regions conquered by the Portuguese now or in the future, 'from Capes Bojador and Nun, by way of Guinea and beyond, southwards to the Indies'. The Bull declared that the Grand Prior of this Order (founded in 1319 after the suppression of the Templars) would be empowered to nominate incumbents to all benefices, both of secular and of regular clergy; to impose censures and other ecclesiastical penalties, and to exercise the powers of an Ordinary within the limits of his jurisdiction. All these regions were declared to be *nullius diocesis*, or belonging to no diocese. Once again, however, no specific provision was made for the dispatch of missionaries as such.

I have analysed these Bulls at some length because they clearly mirror the spirit of the 'Age of Discovery', and because they established guide-lines for subsequent European behaviour (or misbehaviour) in the Tropical World. There is a passage in the Koran which states: 'Woman is thy tilth; plough her as thou wilt.' The cumulative effect of these Papal Bulls was to give the Portuguese—and in due course the other Europeans who followed them—a religious sanction for adopting a similarly masterful attitude towards all races beyond the Pale of Christendom. The contemporary court chronicler, Gomes Eanes de Zurara, writing (in 1450) of the doubts expressed by some people as to the justification of aggressive wars against Muslims, dismissed such critics as being 'little better than heretics'. The King Dom Duarte (1433–8) took a very similar line in his moral treatise, 'Loyal Councillor', as did the theologians consulted by Dom João I before the expedition to Ceuta. Jan Huigen Van Linschoten, a Netherlander who lived at Goa for six years in the last quarter of the sixteenth century, was very critical of the 'filthy pride and presumptuousness' of the Portuguese in India, 'for in all places they will be lords and masters, to the contempt and embasing of the inhabitants'. What Linschoten could hardly be expected to know when he wrote these words in 1596 was that the Dutch and English successors of the Portuguese in Monsoon Asia would, by and large, behave in a very similar way. The Bulls also reflect the initiative taken by the Crown of Portugal, and by Prince Henry and the other princes of the House of Aviz, in directing and organising the work of exploration, conquest, colonisation and exploitation. As to the meaning of the term 'the

Indies', in these Bulls, this expression was perhaps primarily meant for the realms of Prester John in East Africa, but it may have included parts of Asia and India proper as well.

There is thus good resaon to believe that crusading and religious motives as well as an intelligent (but hardly 'scientific') curiosity fortified Prince Henry's persistence in sending his ships and caravels southwards beyond Cape Nun; but economic motives also played their part, even though they were probably not so important in the early stages. Nevertheless, these voyages were extremely expensive, or so Prince Henry claimed in 1457. Moreover, the Prince maintained a large household of knights and squires, and he was a generous host to many foreign visitors. The revenues which he derived from a wide variety of sources, including lands of the Order of Christ and from soap and fishing monopolies, were never sufficient to cover his expenses and he died deeply indebted. This being so, it is very likely that one of his captains, Diogo Gomes, was correct when he told Martin Behaim of Nürnberg that Prince Henry, at the time of the conquest of Ceuta, gained information from Moorish prisoners and others, which led him to try to reach the gold-producing lands south of the Sahara by sea, 'in order to trade with them and to sustain the nobles of his household'. The chronicler João de Barros implicitly confirms this in his *Decada I* (written in 1539). Gold-dust was first obtained by barter from the natives (Touaregs in this instance) in 1442, and we do not know how much was brought from West Africa to Portugal in the remaining eighteen years of Prince Henry's lifetime. It must, however, have been a substantial quantity, particularly in his last years. For in 1457 the Lisbon mint resumed the issue of a gold coinage with the striking of the *Cruzado* ('crusade', significantly enough), a coin of almost pristine purity, which underwent no debasement until 1536.

The development of the slave trade also helped to finance the cost of the Portuguese voyages down the west coast of Africa after about 1442. The slaves were originally obtained by raiding first the Touareg encampments along the Sahara littoral, and then the Negro villages of the Senegal region. These raids, often directed against unarmed family groups or undefended villages, were written up by the Court chronicler, Gomes Eanes de Zurara, as if they were knightly deeds of derring-do, equal to any feats on the battlefields of Europe—and they were in fact so regarded by the great majority of his contemporaries. At one time the Portuguese indulged in slave-raiding against the Berber Guanches of the Canary Islands, and they were accused by the Papacy of sometimes enslaving those who had already been converted to Christianity. But after a few years of contact with the Negro peoples of Senegambia and Upper Guinea the Portuguese realised that slaves could be obtained more easily and conveniently by peaceful barter with the local chiefs and merchants. There was never any lack of Africans who were willing to sell their fellow-creatures, whether these latter were condemned criminals, or prisoners of war, or victims of witchcraft, to the European traders then and later.

For some years the Portuguese were content to conduct their slave-raids, or to drive their peaceful trade, from their ships as they sailed down the coast, anchoring off suitable roadsteads or estuaries. This use of the ship as a floating base always remained in vogue, but it was supplemented by the establishment of 'factories' or trading posts ashore. The first of these *feitorias* was established at Arguim (below Cape Blanco) about the year 1445 in an effort to tap the trans-Sahara trade of the western Sudan. A castle was built here some ten years later, where the Portuguese exchanged horses, cloth, brassware and corn, for gold-dust, slaves and ivory. Arguim thus became the prototype of the chain of fortified factories, which the Portuguese later established along the African and Asian coasts as far as the Moluccas. With the arrival of gold, slaves, and ivory in Portugal in considerable quantities, the West African expeditions organised by Prince Henry began to show a profit, if not for the Prince himself, at any rate for some of the participants. The merchants and ship-owners of Lisbon and Oporto, who had shown little interest in the voyages to the barren shores of the Sahara, now became anxious to participate in those to Senegambia and below. Several leading merchants and nobles, as well as members of Prince Henry's household, were allowed to do so under licence from the Prince, or from the Crown.

It may be useful at this point to recall, very briefly, what the work of discovery carried out in Prince Henry's lifetime amounted to. When these voyages began in or about the year 1419, the known southern limit of the Atlantic Ocean and West African coast was in the region of Cape Bojador, just below latitude 27° North, in what is now the Spanish Saharan territory of Rio de Oro. This Cape projects twenty-five miles westwards from the mainland. The violence of the waves and currents on its northern side, the shallows which exist near it, the frequency of fog and mist in the offing, the difficulty of returning northwards on account of the prevailing winds, were all seen as confirming the stories about the 'Green Sea of Darkness', as the Arab geographers called it, from which, it was popularly believed, there was no possibility of return. Some twelve or fifteen unsuccessful attempts were made (allegedly) over as many years, before one of Prince Henry's ships finally rounded this Cape in 1434, thus breaking not only the physical but the even more forbidding psychological barrier which had hitherto prevented voyages of discovery down the West African coast. This feat was, perhaps, Prince Henry's greatest achievement, since it was only accomplished by patient determination and a readiness to expend large sums of money on voyages from which no immediate return could be expected.

Once the dreaded Cape was rounded, further progress was relatively rapid, although interrupted periodically by Prince Henry's enthusiasm for crusading expeditions in Morocco. These enterprises diverted his attention, his men, and his ships thither at intervals, on one occasion at least with most disastrous results. An expedition under his command which was mounted against Tangier in 1437 was surrounded by the Moors and only allowed to retire to the ships after Prince Henry's younger brother, the Infante Dom Fernando, was left in Moorish hands as a hostage for the promised surrender of Ceuta. For reasons of state this promise was never implemented, and Dom Fernando, 'the holy Infante' as posterity christened him, was left to die in a dungeon at Fez, despite his piteous appeals to his brothers that they should exchange him for Ceuta as agreed. Prince Henry also made strenuous, if ultimately unsuccessful, efforts to challenge the position of the Castilians in the Canary Islands. Nevertheless, despite these major distractions, his ships had got as far south as Sierra Leone by the time of his death in 1460.

A very important accompaniment to this roughly 1,500-mile

advance down the West African coast was the simultaneous discovery (or rediscovery) of Madeira (*c.* 1419) and the Azores (*c.* 1439), followed in due course by the discovery and colonisation of the Cape Verdes (1456–60). Unfortunately, we have no reliable information about the motives which inspired these westward voyages of discovery, but it is clear that they were carried out mainly under Prince Henry's auspices, though on occasions with the co-operation of some of his brothers and leading members of the nobility. The settlement of these uninhabited islands initiated the Portuguese into the practice of overseas colonisation, and the settlers were literally pioneers in a New World. This was something of which they were naturally conscious, as shown by the fact that the first boy and girl born on Madeira were aptly christened Adam and Eve. The earliest settlers were probably drawn mainly from the Algarve, as Prince Henry's caravels sailed chiefly from the ports of that province, but they were soon reinforced by emigrants from elsewhere in Portugal and from as far afield as Flanders—the Azores for many years having the alternative name of 'the Flemish Islands'. By the time of Prince Henry's death, Madeira was producing substantial quantities of sugar and the Azores of corn.

Although we know virtually nothing about the conduct of these early voyages of discovery beyond the names of a few of the leaders who took part in them, and who included Flemings and Italians as well as Portuguese, it is obvious that the experience gained in them must have made the Portuguese familiar with the wind system of the North Atlantic and, in due course, of that in the South Atlantic. The experience gained in these voyages also enabled them to develop (though we do not know exactly when) a new type of ship, the lateen-rigged caravel, which could sail closer to the wind than any other type of European vessel. The use of the caravel in its turn facilitated their voyages of discovery; and it was by sailing in Portuguese caravels that Columbus attained at least some of his skill in high-seas navigation. The practical experience gained by the Portuguese in the Atlantic likewise enabled them to lay the foundations of modern European nautical science. By the end of the fifteenth century their best navigators could calculate fairly accurately their position at sea by a combination of observed latitude and dead-reckoning, and they possessed excellent practical sailing directions (*Roteiros*, hence the English 'Rutters') for the West African coast. Their principal instruments were the mariner's compass (probably derived from the Chinese through Arab and Mediterranean sailors) and the astrolabe and quadrant in their simplest forms. They also possessed some reasonably adequate nautical charts, which were based in part on latitudes calculated by observations made on shore as well as at sea. The so-called Cantino planisphere of 1502, copied by (or for) an Italian spy from a lost Portuguese original, gives a remarkably accurate outline of the coast of Africa, particularly of the West African coast north of the river Congo. But many of their deep-sea pilots continued to rely largely on their knowledge of Nature's signs (*conhecenças*), such as the colour and run of the sea, the kinds of fish and sea-birds observed in different latitudes and localities, the varieties of seaweed which they encountered, and so forth.

Although it is uncertain how far the search for gold was one of the original motives of the Portuguese voyages of discovery down the West African coast, the lure of the yellow metal certainly played a predominant part in their development after 1442. The Portuguese never succeeded in finding the elusive source of West African and Sudanese gold, which, as we now know, was mostly mined in the region of Bambuk on the Upper Senegal river, at Mali on the Upper Niger, and at Lobi on the upper reaches of the Volta. This gold, mostly in the form of gold-dust, was originally taken by bearers through the kingdoms of Mali and Ghana (no connection with the modern republic of this name) as far as Timbuktu. It was there traded to Arab and Moorish merchants, who carried it by camel caravan across the Sahara to the Islamic states of North Africa, whose ports were frequented by Jewish, Genoese, and Venetian traders amongst others. In the second half of the fifteenth century, by means of their fortified *feitoria* at Arguim, and by other unfortified *feitorias* in the coastal region of Senegambia, the Portuguese were able to divert a considerable proportion of this trans-Sahara trade to their own ships and establishments on the coast. This diversion was intensified when Dom João II ordered the erection of a castle at São Jorge da Mina (El Mina) on the Gold Coast in 1482. 'Saint George of the Mine', whose trade rapidly surpassed that of Arguim, was able to tap not only the gold trade of the western Sudan but that derived from the river-washings on the Gold Coast itself. This castle was supplemented by another and smaller one erected at Axim some twenty years later.

By this time the Portuguese were making a sustained and systematic effort to divert the gold trade to the coast, and their emissaries had penetrated, even if only fleetingly, as far as Timbuktu. The Portuguese never succeeded in establishing any of their *feitorias* in the interior for any length of time, and they were compelled to rely on Negro intermediaries to supply them with the gold which they could not mine for themselves. But the struggle of the Portuguese caravels against the Moorish camel caravans of the Sahara did result in the predominance of the former in the gold trade for a period of about 100 years, *c.* 1450–1550. During the reign of Dom Manuel I (1496–1521) an annual average of 170,000 *dobras'* worth of gold was imported from São Jorge da Mina alone, and in some years much more. While slaves and gold continued to be the principal products sought by the Portuguese in Senegambia and Guinea, other West African products, such as a pepper-like spice called *malagueta* or 'grains of paradise', and monkeys and parrots, found a profitable market in Portugal.

Down to his death in 1460 Prince Henry was the concessionary of all trade along the West African coast, but this does not mean that he actually engrossed the whole trade to himself. On the contrary, he could and often did license private traders and adventurers to make voyages, on condition that he was paid a fifth, or some other agreed share, of the profits. It is not certain how the trade was carried on in the decade following Prince Henry's death, but at the end of 1469 it was awarded by the Crown on a monopoly-contract basis to a rich Lisbon merchant, Fernão Gomes, the Crown reserving the right to monopolise a few valuable commodities. Gomes made a handsome profit on his contract, and he also discovered nearly 2,000 further miles of West African coastline for the Crown. On the expiration of this contract in 1475, King Affonso V entrusted the direction of the trade to his son and heir, the Infante Dom João, and it became and remained a directly administered Crown monopoly on the latter's accession to the throne in 1481.

King Dom João II, 'the perfect prince', was an enthusiastic and far-sighted imperialist who had a veritable passion for Africa and its products, whether human, animal, vegetable or mineral. He took a keen personal interest in the direction of the trade, reserving for the Crown the monopoly of importing gold, slaves, spices and ivory, and of exporting horses, carpets, English and Irish textiles, copper, lead, brass utensils, beads and bracelets. Private traders were allowed to import on payment of a licence such less valuable articles as parrots, seals, monkeys, cotton and raffia textiles, etc. Subsequently the Crown leased the rights to import slaves and ivory to certain favoured individuals, but it always retained a strict monopoly of the gold. In reality, of course, this monopoly was nothing like as rigid and effective as it appeared to be on paper. It was impossible to prevent the crews of the ships from trading privately on their own account, to say nothing of the royal officials and agents themselves, and the inhabitants of the Cape Verde islands. This West African trade had originally been driven mainly by ships equipped at Lagos and other ports of the Algarve. But by the end of the fifteenth century it was concentrated at Lisbon, where it was channelled through the *Casa da Mina* (House of the Mine). This establishment was a Crown office and warehouse situated on the ground floor of the royal palace by the waterfont on the river Tagus, where the King could personally watch the loading and unloading of the ships.

The commodities with which the Portuguese acquired the African slaves and gold were largely of foreign origin. Wheat often came from Morocco, the Atlantic islands, and northern Europe. Cloth and textiles were imported from England, Ireland, France and Flanders, though some Portuguese manufactured cloth was also used. Brass utensils and glass beads were imported from Germany, Flanders and Italy, and oyster-shells from the Canaries. Many of the imports from West Africa were likewise re-exported from Portugal. Much *malagueta* went to Flanders, and many of the slaves went to Spain and Italy before the discovery and exploitation of America diverted the slave trade almost wholly to the other side of the Atlantic. What was, perhaps, of most consequence was that a great quantity of the Guinea gold which entered Lisbon and was there coined into *cruzados* was re-exported to pay for the corn and manufactured goods which Portugal needed. Thus Portuguese gold of West African origin helped to put Portugal on the currency map of Europe, so to speak. Certain types of gold coins in northern Europe were called 'Portugaloisers' for centuries, though struck in places like Zwolle and Hamburg.

The effect of this trade on West Africa is more difficult to assess. Something like 150,000 Negro slaves were probably secured by the Portuguese between 1450 and 1500, and as these slaves were often obtained from the inter-tribal wars in the interior, the growth of the slave trade presumably worsened the existing state of violence and insecurity—or at any rate did nothing to help lessen it. The African chiefs and headmen were those who benefited most from trading with the Portuguese, and (as mentioned above) most of them were always willing partners in the slave trade. In Upper Guinea, which may be roughly defined as the region between the river Senegal and Cape Palmas, Portuguese traders and exiled criminals (*degredados*) frequented many of the rivers and creeks, often penetrating a considerable distance into the interior. Many of them settled in the Negro villages, where they and their Mulatto descendants functioned as principals or as intermediaries in the barter trade for gold, ivory and slaves, between black and white. Those of them who went completely native, stripping off their clothes, tattooing their bodies, speaking the local languages, and even joining in fetishistic rites and celebrations, were termed *tangos-maos*, or *lançados*.

The kings of Portugal did not object to this miscegenation so much as they objected to these *lançados* evading the taxes which the Crown imposed on all overseas trade. For this reason the death penalty was enacted against them in 1518, but although this law remained on the statute book for many years, it was seldom if ever applied, since the Portuguese Crown exercised no effective jurisdiction in West Africa outside the walls of its *feitorias*, or the immediate neighbourhood of the castles of Mina and Axim. Through the medium of these *lançados* and *tangos-maos* Portuguese became and for centuries remained the *lingua-franca* of the coastal region of Upper Guinea. Portuguese relations with the different peoples of this part of West Africa naturally varied as between one tribe or area and another. But armed conflicts were relatively few, and contacts on the whole remained friendly, since the conduct of the slave trade involved the active participation of the African chiefs and the co-operation of the *lançados* as intermediaries.

On the Gold Coast of Lower Guinea the Portuguese relied not only on peaceful contacts but on a display of power and force, as exemplified by their castles at Mina (1482) and Axim (1503). These were founded with the dual object of defending the gold trade against Spanish and other European interlopers, and of overawing the coastal Negro tribes through whom the gold was acquired. This last objective did not escape the intuition of the local Negro chief when Diogo de Azambuja came ashore with a richly clad and a well-armed suite to lay the foundation stone of Mina Castle in January 1482. This chief pointed out that the only Portuguese he had met hitherto were those who came annually in the caravels to barter for gold. These sailors, he said, 'were ragged and ill-dressed men, who were satisfied with whatever was given them in exchange for their merchandise. This was the sole reason for their coming to these parts, and their main desire was to do business quickly and return home, since they would rather live in their own country than in foreign lands.' He added that the Portuguese and the Negroes got on all the better for seeing each other at regular intervals, instead of living as close neighbours, and it would therefore be better if the trade was carried on by visiting ships as hitherto. Azambuja, who had orders from Dom João II to build the castle with or without the chief's consent, persisted in his demand and he eventually extorted a reluctant agreement. But if the coastal chiefs were not strong enough to prevent the building of European forts on the shore, they were strong enough to prevent the Europeans from penetrating into the interior in search of the coveted gold. The Portuguese, like their Dutch and English successors, had to remain in their forts, bartering brass bowls, bracelets, beads, textiles and other trade goods for the gold, ivory and slaves brought by itinerant African traders from the hinterland. There were no *lançados* and *tangosmaos* on the Gold Coast. Benin was the most important of the coastal states of Lower Guinea in the late fifteenth century. Portuguese visitors to Benin City commented admiringly on its great size, the neatness of its streets and houses, and on the huge royal palace with its magnificent brass figures and plaques.

With the resources derived from the flourishing gold and slave trades with Guinea, Dom João II was now in a position to prosecute the search for Prester John, which had evidently become something of an obsession with him. Vague though their notions were about the situation of this kingdom, the Portuguese knew that it was somewhere beyond the river Nile, which was then regarded by learned Europeans as forming the boundary between Africa proper and 'Middle India'. They hoped at first to get access to Prester John by way of the Senegal, the Gambia, the Niger, and finally the Zaire (or Congo) rivers, each of which they successively mistook for a tributary or branch of the Nile when first encountering their respective outlets into the sea. The discoverers were duly disillusioned in each case; but as they worked further down the coast of West Africa the prospect that this continent might be circumnavigated, and the way opened by sea to the kingdom of Prester John and the Indies, became more plausible. It was also in the reign of Dom João II that the quest for Prester John became coupled with the search for Asian (as distinct from African) spices.

This king took the decisive steps by sending out carefully organised reconnaissance expeditions to seek for Prester John and spices by land and sea in the mid-1480s. The chief maritime voyage of discovery was commanded by Bartholomeu Dias who left Lisbon in 1487. He first rounded the Cape of Good Hope early in 1488, and after voyaging for some distance up the coast of southern Africa returned with the news that the sea route to the Indies was evidently open. Most of the agents who were sent overland seem to have miscarried, but one of them, an Arabic-speaking squire named Pero de Covilhã, who left Lisbon in the same year as Bartholomeu Dias, reached the west coast of India proper in 1488. He then visited the Persian Gulf, and the Swahili coast of East Africa as far south, probably, as Sofala. This adventurous journey, which lasted for over two years, gave him a very good idea of the trade of the Indian Ocean in general, and of the spice trade in particular. On his way back to Portugal at the end of 1490 he found in Cairo a messenger from the King, ordering him to proceed to the kingdom of Prester John, which was by now localised in the highlands of Abyssinia. This he did, having first sent to the King from Cairo a detailed report of all his findings. He was honourably received by the Emperor of Ethiopia or Negus of Abyssinia, but he was not allowed to leave this kingdom, being given a wife and lands, and detained there till his death over thirty years later.

It is uncertain whether Covilhã's report of 1490–1 ever reached Portugal, for the evidence on this point is conflicting. If it did, then Dom João II had at his disposal a first-hand report about the spice trade in the Indian Ocean, and this would help to explain why Vasco da Gama was ordered to make for Calicut, then the most important Indian entrepôt of the spice trade, on his voyage to India seven years later. On the other hand, Da Gama and his men were very surprised at the high degree of civilisation attained by the Swahili city-states of Moçambique, Mombasa and Malindi, which they visited on their epic voyage; whereas if Covilhã's report had reached Lisbon the Portuguese should have had ample information about these places. Similarly, Da Gama on his arrival at Calicut was unable to distinguish between Hindu temples and Christian churches, something which Covilhã must surely have done—and reported—after his lengthy visits to the trading ports of Malabar. Finally, Da Gama was provided with the most trumpery presents for the ruler of Calicut and the most unsuitable trade goods—cloth, brass utensils, beads and the like—to barter for the pepper and other spices which he sought; whereas Covilhã would certainly have reported that these could only be purchased with gold and silver specie.

Whether the King of Portugal received Covilhã's report or not, it is certain that it was only during the 1480s that the Portuguese first became seriously interested in the possibility of tapping the Asian spice trade at its source, or somewhere very near it. Till then their relatively modest demand for Asian spices had been satisfied by those which they got (like the rest of Europe did) from the Venetians, who purchased them from the Muslim merchants of the Mameluke empire in Egypt and Syria. We have insufficient information about the prices of these spices in the second half of the fifteenth century to enable us to know exactly when and why Dom João II conceived the plan of breaking the Venetian-Mameluke spice monopoly, but the fact remains that he did. The instructions given to Pero de Covilhã in 1487 and to Vasco da Gama in 1497 are clear proof of this. It seems likely that once he was convinced that the sea route to India could be found, then the King would naturally have considered the possibility that the Asian spice trade (or some of it) could be diverted from its overland routes to the Atlantic Ocean, in much the same way as the gold trade of Guinea had been largely diverted from the camels of the Sahara to the caravels of St. George of the Mine.

However that may have been, the wording of the 'speech of obedience' made by the Portuguese envoy, Vasco Fernandes de Lucena, to the Pope in December 1485 showed that Dom João II was even then, *before* the voyage of Bartholomeu Dias and the journey of Pero de Covilhã, convinced that the opening of the sea route to India was a virtual certainty in the very near future. In this speech the envoy informed the Pope on behalf of his master that the Portuguese ships of discovery were expected shortly to enter the Indian Ocean and to make contact with Prester John and other Christian kings or peoples who were confidently believed to exist in those admittedly very obscurely known (*obscurissima fama*) regions. No mention was made of spices, but this was natural enough; even if Dom João II was already contemplating an attack on the Venetian-Mameluke monopoly, it would have been the height of folly to advertise the fact at a much publicised Papal audience in Rome.

Dom João II's long-standing interest in Prester John and his new-found interest in Asian spices were both inherited and continued by his successor on the throne, Dom Manuel I. When Vasco da Gama left on his famous voyage in July 1497 he was provided with letters of credence addressed to Prester John and to the Raja of Calicut, together with samples of spices, gold and seed-pearls. He had orders to show these commodities to the inhabitants of all the undiscovered places at which he might call along the African coast, in the hope that those peoples might recognise these valuables and indicate by signs, or through interpreters, where they might be found.

Vasco da Gama did not start on his voyage until nine years after Bartholomeu Dias had returned to Lisbon with the news that he had rounded the Cape of Good Hope. In the interval Columbus had returned from his epoch-making voyage in March 1493, with the claim that he had discovered some islands on the fringe of east Asia, and Dom João had died in 1495. These two events do not, in themselves, account for the lengthy delay in following up Bartholomeu Dias' remarkable voyage, particularly when we recall that in 1485 the King had publicly informed the Pope that his ships were on the eve of opening up the sea route to India. Various conjectures have been advanced by historians to account for this delay, such as the distracting turn of events in Morocco, the death of Dom João's son and heir in July 1491, and the King's subsequent illness. Some of the royal councillors were openly against prosecuting the design for the discovery of India, arguing that Portugal's economic and demographic resources were too limited for this little country to exploit a large region so far distant. They stressed that it was better to develop the existing and highly profitable gold and slave trades with West Africa and to let well alone.

All or any of these reasons may have affected Dom João to some extent; but he was not the type of man to be for long deterred from doing something on which he had set his heart. A more plausible supposition is that during those years the Portuguese were making secret voyages in the South Atlantic in order to familiarise themselves with the sailing conditions there, and to find a better way round the Cape of Good Hope than Dias' course of beating down the south-west coast of Africa in the teeth of the contrary south-east trade winds. This would explain why Vasco da Gama took the course which he evidently did, and which was essentially that followed by Portuguese East-Indiamen for centuries. It involved crossing the equator on the meridian of Cape Verde and picking up the steady westerly winds after working south-east in the zone of the variables of Capricorn. This route was completely different from Dias' outward-bound course in 1487, and it can only have been evolved (one may surmise) from the experience gained in other voyages of which no record has survived.

There is no need to repeat the oft-told tale of Vasco da Gama's famous voyage in 1497–9. The point to emphasise here is that although we are uncertain about the original motives prompting the first Portuguese voyages of discovery, by the time of Prince Henry's death (1460) they were mainly inspired by the search for Prester John and Guinea gold; and during the reign of Dom João II these motives were reinforced by the quest for Asian spices. Many readers will be familiar with the well-authenticated story that when the first man from Da Gama's crew reached Calicut he was accosted by two Spanish-speaking Tunisians. They asked him: 'What the devil has brought you here?' to which he replied: 'We have come to seek Christians and spices.' Equally significant is the fact that a couple of days after the return of the first of Da Gama's ships to the Tagus in July 1499 King Manuel wrote a jubilant letter to Ferdinand and Isabella of Aragon-Castile, announcing that the discoverers had reached their goal and had found great quantities of cloves, cinnamon and other spices, besides 'rubies and all kinds of precious stones'. The King likewise stated, with manifest exaggeration, 'that they also found lands in which there are mines of gold'. He further announced his intention of following up this voyage of discovery and wresting the control of the spice trade in the Indian Ocean from the Muslims by force, with the aid of the newly discovered Indian 'Christians'. In this way the existing Venetian-Muslim monopoly of the Levant trade in spices and in Asian luxury goods would be replaced by a Portuguese monopoly exercised via the sea route round the Cape of Good Hope. Writing a few weeks later to the Cardinal-Protector of Portugal at Rome, the King urged him to obtain from the Pope confirmation of the existing Bulls and Briefs by which 'the suzerainty and dominion' over all these new-found lands had been granted to the Crown of Portugal in perpetuity. In this letter to Rome, dated 28 August 1499, King Manuel entitled himself *inter alia* 'Lord of Guinea and of the conquest of the navigation and commerce of Ethiopia, Arabia, Persia and India'.

The wording of King Manuel's letters to the Spanish sovereigns and to the Papacy, taken together with his precipitate assumption of the overlordship of the Indian Ocean at a time when there was not a single Portuguese ship in that region, show clearly two things. Firstly, that he was determined to establish Portuguese control of the Asian spice trade by force of arms; and secondly that he counted on the help of friendly (though not rigidly Roman Catholic) Indian 'Christians' to do so. In this second premise he was mistaken, although contact was at last made with the elusive Prester John shortly before King Manuel's death. Nevertheless, the lure of the profits to be gained from the projected Portuguese spice monopoly, and the belief that Christian allies could be found in some of the lands bordering on the Indian Ocean, enabled King Manuel to overcome the hesitations of several of his counsellors, and to launch his little kingdom on its spectacular career of militant enterprise in Monsoon Asia.

CHAPTER II

Shipping and spices in Asian seas 1500-1600

A DISTINGUISHED Indian historian, the late K. M. Panikkar, observed in his popular book *Asia and Western Dominance* (1949) that the pioneer voyage of the Portuguese to India inaugurated what he termed the Vasco da Gama epoch of Asian history, 1498–1945. This period may be defined as an age of maritime power, of authority based on the control of the seas by the European nations alone; at any rate down to the emergence of America and Japan as major naval powers at the end of the nineteenth century. In the history of these 400 years nothing is more remarkable than the way in which the Portuguese managed to secure and retain for virtually the whole of the sixteenth century a dominant position in the maritime trade of the Indian Ocean and an important share of the seaborne trade to the east of the straits of Malacca.

Admittedly the Portuguese reached India at a singularly fortunate time for themselves, as may be seen by taking the briefest possible survey of the Asian scene at the turn of the fifteenth and sixteenth centuries. This is best done by dealing with the countries concerned from west to east, roughly in the order in which the Portuguese came into contact with them. The East African littoral is here included in the term Asia, since then and for long afterwards the Swahili coast from Somaliland to Sofala was closely connected with Arabia and India, politically, culturally and economically. The Portuguese used the expression *Estado da India* (State of India) to describe their conquests and discoveries in the maritime regions between the Cape of Good Hope and the Persian Gulf on the one side of Asia, and Japan and Timor on the other. Confusingly enough, the Portuguese also used the word 'India' to denote sometimes the Indian sub-continent and sometimes the narrow strip of land between the Western Ghats and the sea.

The most important of the chain of Swahili city-states strung along the East African coast in 1500 were Kilwa, Mombasa, Malindi and Pate. They had attained a high degree of cultural flowering and commercial prosperity, although their degree of Islamisation varied from the thinnest veneer to the austerely devout. Their culture was predominantly Arab, though a Persian (Shirazi) origin was claimed by many, and Swahili society as a whole was deeply Africanised through generations of marriage and concubinage with Bantu women from the interior. Gold, ivory, and slaves were the principal products which these Swahili settlements secured from the Bantu, or Kaffirs ('unbelievers') as they called them. These were exchanged for beads, textiles and other commodities brought by Arab and Gujarati traders from the Persian Gulf, the Red Sea and India.

Disregarding the Coptic Christian kingdom of Abyssinia in its highland fastness, we come next to the Mameluke empire, comprising Egypt, Syria and the Hejaz, which was then still outwardly prosperous. Its commercial prosperity was largely due to the tolls which the Mameluke rulers levied on the overland spice trade routes to Europe, respectively from the Persian Gulf via Aleppo and Alexandretta, and from the Red Sea via Suez, Cairo, and Alexandria. Most of Arabia was a barren waste inhabited by roving Bedouins, and fringed from the southern boundary of the Hejaz to the head of the Persian Gulf by a number of states and tribes, of which some on the north coast owed a shadowy allegiance to the Shah of Ormuz. This potentate claimed to rule over the Persian and the Arabian coasts opposite the little island at the entrance to the Gulf on which his capital city stood; but in effect his authority was limited to this barren islet and to the neighbouring one of Kishm (Queixome). Ormuz city was one of the richest entrepôts in the world, although the island on which it was situated produced nothing save salt and sulphur. But nearly all the trade between India and Persia was channelled through it, apart from its large share of the commerce in Indonesian spices and Arabian horses. Its coins, the gold *ashrafi* (*xerafim*) and the silver *larin*, were current in all the Indian, Persian and Arabian seaports and as far east as Malacca. In Persia proper, the founder of the Sufi (Safavid) dynasty, Shah Ismail I, was expanding his dominions in all directions, and was on the verge of coming into collision with the Ottoman Turks on his western borders. The clash, when it came in 1514, was exacerbated by the fact that the 'Grand Sophy' was an ardent Shia, whereas the 'Great Turk' was a fanatical adherent of the Sunni form of Islam.

India, then as now, was deeply divided between Hindus and Muslims. The so-called Moguls or Mughals (in reality, Central Asian Turks) had not yet crossed the Hindu Kush to invade the plains of Hindustan; but much of northern India had been conquered by previous Muhammadan invaders, whose descendants ruled powerful principalities in Gujarat, Delhi and Bengal. Nevertheless, northern India, though politically ruled by Muslims, save for the powerful Rajput confederacy, contained a numerous Hindu population which passively resisted all the attempts of its conquerors to impose their creed. The same was true, to some extent, of the Deccan, where five Muhammadan sultanates warred with each other and with their southerly neighbour, the great Hindu empire of Vijayanagar. This empire, known to the Portuguese as Bisnaga, was the largest and most powerful Indian state at the time of Vasco da Gama's arrival. But it had no direct access to the sea on the west coast, whereas one of the Deccani kingdoms, Bijapur, had a flourishing port at Goa. The Canara and Malabar coastal regions to the south of this place were largely secluded from the interior by the Western Ghats. They were divided among a number of independent petty Hindu rajas, of whom the Samorin (sea-raja) of Calicut was the most important. If southern India was politically Hindu, in contrast to the Muslim centre and north, there were many peaceful communities of Arab and other Muhammadan traders scattered throughout the Hindu states, where they were greatly respected and wielded considerable influence. It may be added that Ceylon, mainly peopled by Buddhist Sinhalese, included the Hindu Tamil kingdom of Jaffna in the north of the island. A Muslim power had never invaded Ceylon, but there were a number of Muhammadan merchants of Indian or Arab origin established at Colombo and elsewhere on the coast.

The regions corresponding to present-day Burma, Siam, and Indochina were occupied by a number of warring states whose kaleidoscopic shifts of fortune cannot be followed even in outline here. The Hinayana form of Buddhism was dominant in Pegu (Lower Burma), Siam and Cambodia, but it was tinged with many Hindu practices, particularly in Cambodia, where the Brahmin influence was still very strong. The Khmer empire in Indochina was a thing of the past, and Angkor an overgrown ruin in the jungle. Champa was steadily yielding ground to the southward advance of the Annamites (or Vietnamese) down to the east coast. The latter were much more influenced by Chinese than by Indian cultural and religious contacts; but they were unwilling to accord more than a purely token overlordship to the occupants of the Dragon Throne at Peking.

Coming down the Malay peninsula towards the Indonesian archipelago we find the kingdoms of Patani, Singora, and Ligor under Siamese political influence, but also affected by Chinese cultural and commercial contacts. Malacca was the seat of the wealthiest sultanate in the peninsula, and a great emporium for the spice trade with the Moluccas, ships coming from places as far away as the Ryukyu Islands and Arabia. Its rulers had gone over to Islam in the fourteenth century, but Hindu Tamil traders from Coromandel were made as welcome in the port as were Muslims from Gujarat, Java and Sumatra. Europeans who visited Malacca at the height of its prosperity just before the Portuguese occupation wrote lyrical accounts of this thriving port which were echoed by Tomé Pires in his *Suma Oriental* of 1515. 'No trading port as large as Malacca is known, nor any where they deal in such fine and highly prized merchandise. Goods from all over the East are found here; goods from all over the West are sold here. It is at the end of the monsoons, where you find what you want, and sometimes more than you are looking for.' Ormuz at one end of the Indian Ocean and Malacca at the other were the two great Asian entrepôts for the collection and distribution of luxury goods, including the Indonesian spices which eventually reached Europe via the Levant.

Sumatra, the second largest island of the Indonesian group, was divided into a varying number of petty states, most of them Islamised by this time. Achin, spreading outwards and downwards from the north-west tip of the island, became much the most important Sumatran kingdom in the second half of the sixteenth century. Pepper, benzoin, and gold were the most valuable commodities exported from this island to Malacca, India and China; but forest products and foodstuffs were readily available in many of the Sumatran ports. The Javanese Hindu empire of Madjapahit, which at one time (1330–1400) had controlled most of the Indonesian archipelago, was now reduced to a steadily declining kingdom in central and east Java. It had not yet been supplanted by the rise of the Muslim empire of Mataram, but Islam was extending its influence rapidly on this island, particularly in the coastal kingdoms. The lesser Sunda islands were of small importance to the outer world, save for the sandalwood of Timor which was a prized commodity in China. The Muslim sultans of Ternate and Tidore, 'whence merchants bring their spicy drugs' (*pace* Milton), competed for the suzerainty of the clove-bearing Moluccas and the adjoining islands from Celebes to New Guinea, the Sultan of Ternate being rather more powerful than his opponent. Borneo boasted of a small civilised state in the sultanate of Brunei on the north coast, but most of the island was more or less virgin jungle inhabited by head-hunting tribes uninfluenced by Islam. Muslim traders working their way up from the Islamised states of Indonesia had already reached the island group now known as the Philippines, where they had converted the inhabitants of several of the islands. Their further progress northwards was soon (1565) to be blocked by the settlement of the Spaniards at Cebu and Luzon.

This political bird's-eye view of early sixteenth-century Asia may be concluded with a brief reference to China and Japan. The Ming dynasty had given up its earlier overseas expansion policy, and Chinese fleets no longer visited the Indian Ocean as they had done as far as the Persian Gulf and Somaliland in the days of Marco Polo and the celebrated eunuch admiral, Cheng Ho. The reasons for the abandonment of this adventurous maritime policy are not altogether clear, but constant attacks by Japanese pirates on the east coast and the perennial menace of the nomadic Mongols and Manchus on China's northern marches may have had much to do with it. Chinese merchants and mariners from the coastal provinces of Fukien and Kwangtung, with or without the connivance of the local officials, continued to trade with some of the islands in the Philippines, in Indonesia and, on occasion, as far west as Malacca. But it was not on any very extensive scale, and their activities were either ignored or disowned by the Imperial government. Korea was vegetating in a peaceful seclusion typified by its later sobriquet of 'The Hermit Kingdom', and its rulers acknowledged the suzerainty of China. Japan was in the throes of the *sengoku-jidai*, or 'country at war period', with the authority of the nominal Emperor and of the Shogun (Generalissimo) both reduced to zero, while the unruly feudal nobility (*daimyo*) struggled among themselves for land and power.

Fortunately for the Portuguese at the time of their appearance in Asian waters, the empires of Egypt, Persia and Vijayanagar had no armed shipping in the Indian Ocean, if indeed they possessed any ships at all. Even the wealthy entrepôts of Ormuz and Malacca, whose prosperity entirely depended on their seaborne trade, possessed no ocean-going warships. The Malay vessels were mostly of the type known as *lanchara*, a small single-sail and square-rigged vessel steered by two oars mounted in the stern, save for a few large merchant-junks which were built at Pegu and Java. But the Javanese, though good shipbuilders and navigators, who had at one period sailed as far as (and partially colonised) Madagascar, now restricted their seaborne trade to the Indonesian archipelago and its immediate vicinity. The Arab, Gujarati, and other Muslim-controlled shipping which dominated the trade of the Indian Ocean comprised large ocean-going vessels as well as small coastal ships; but even the largest were not provided with artillery, and no iron was used in their hull construction. They were therefore relatively much more frail than the Portuguese carracks and galleons which they had to encounter.

The Portuguese habit of describing all the Muslims they met from Morocco to Mindanao as 'Moors' (*Mouros*) tends to obscure the fact that when they reached the Indian Ocean the Arabs no longer dominated the seaborne trade of Monsoon Asia from Ornuz to Canton, as they had done much earlier. Arab ships and seamen were still very important in the western half of the Indian

Ocean; but their place in the eastern half had been taken over almost entirely by Indian Muslim traders and seafarers from Gujarat, Malabar, Coromandel and Bengal. The Hindu Tamil merchants of Kalinga and Coromandel, known to the Portuguese as Klings, still had a good share of the Indian textile trade with Malacca, to which port they sailed in their own ships. But elsewhere the Hindu merchants remained shore-based, and they shipped their goods in Muslim vessels. This was the result of certain socio-religious caste taboos which had not, apparently, been operative in earlier centuries, when the Chola kings of southern India mounted impressive seaborne expeditions against the Sumatran empire of Çrivijaya. But by 1500 crossing the ocean was in itself considered as a defilement by many high-caste Hindus, after which inconvenient and expensive purification ceremonies had to be performed. Moreover, if they embarked their persons, as distinct from their goods, on board Muslim- (or later European-) owned and manned vessels, they equally incurred defilement through unavoidable contact with ritually unclean individuals. Apart from these prejudices, many of the originally Hindu coast-dwelling peoples of India from Gujarat through Malabar and Coromandel to Bengal had been converted to Islam by the fourteenth century.

The domination of the seaborne trade of the Indian Ocean, first by the Arabs and later to a large extent by Muslims of Indian origin, chiefly Gujaratis, was achieved in both cases quite peacefully. People engaged in oceanic trade did not travel with their families, least of all Muslim men with rigorous ideas about the seclusion of women. The Arab, Gujarati, and other merchants and mariners who traded to Ceylon, Malacca and Indonesia inevitably took wives, temporary or otherwise, from among the women of the ports where they stayed while awaiting the favourable monsoons for their return voyage. Their children were almost invariably raised as Muslims; and when they grew up they in their turn helped to spread the faith among their mothers' compatriots. These various Muslim trading colonies grew and flourished; and their richest and most influential traders were sooner or later granted the right to build mosques in the ports where they lived. They then sent for *Mullahs*, or religious teachers, who in their turn helped to attract many other Muslims from elsewhere and to propagate Islam locally. In this way the followers of the Prophet spread their creed and their trade to the Swahili coast of East Africa and to the Spice Islands of Indonesia, without their ever having to employ the militant methods which had characterised the original expansion of Islam from the Arabian desert to the Pyrenees and to the Himalayas. The fact that, on the west coast of India in particular, they co-operated closely and cordially with wealthy Hindu merchants and rajas without either party trying to convert the other, cemented this Muslim monopoly of the trade of the Indian Ocean. The Portuguese immediately realised that they could only break it by brute force and not by peaceful competition.

This they proceeded to do with complete ruthlessness and astonishing speed. In order to achieve their aim they needed a few fortified harbours to serve as naval bases and commercial entrepôts. These key points were secured during the governorship of Afonso de Albuquerque (1509–15). The landlocked island of Goa was wrested from the Sultan of Bijapur on St. Catherine's Day (10 November) 1510, and 'Golden Goa' soon supplanted Calicut as the principal trading port between Cambay and Cape Comorin. The harbour was also particularly well situated to function as the transhipment port for the lucrative Arabian-Persian horse-trade with the Hindu kingdom of Vijayanagar. Albuquerque made Goa the Portuguese headquarters, and he gained the support of its Hindu inhabitants. Control of the Persian Gulf was secured by the seizure of Ormuz in 1515, the Shah becoming a Portuguese vassal and puppet. Albuquerque's capture of Malacca four years earlier gave the Portuguese the major distributing centre for Indonesian spices, as well as a naval base which controlled the bottleneck between the Indian Ocean, the Java Sea and the South China Sea, for the alternative route through the straits of Sunda was rarely used.

These exploits of Albuquerque were made possible by his predecessor Franciso de Almeida's prior destruction of a makeshift Egyptian-Gujarati fleet off Diu (February 1509), thus avenging his own son's defeat and death at the hands of the same opponents in the previous year at Chaul, and thus eliminating the only Muslim naval force capable of meeting the Portuguese warships on something approaching equal terms. Portuguese naval supremacy on the East African coast was already assured by their construction of forts at Sofala (1505) and Moçambique (1507) and by their alliance with the Sultan of Malindi. The one major setback in this remarkable success story was their failure to close the spice route through the Red Sea by securing a stronghold at its entrance which would form a counterpart to Ormuz in the Persian Gulf. The island of Socotra, which they first occupied for this purpose, proved to be too distant and too impoverished to serve as a naval base, and it was abandoned in 1510. Albuquerque narrowly failed in his subsequent attempt to take Aden by storm (March 1513); and though the Portuguese then and subsequently entered the Red Sea briefly, they never achieved anything of lasting importance there. This sea remained, in effect, a Muslim lake after the first occupation of Aden by the Turks in 1538. The presence or the threat of Portuguese ships cruising off the straits of Bab-el-Mandeb helped to disrupt this spice-trade route for two or three decades, but it was then re-established, as we shall see below.

While full credit should be given to Albuquerque for his seizure of Goa, Malacca and Ormuz, when the fleeting opportunities for doing so occurred, it is a mistake to credit him with the entire inception and execution of a vast strategic plan methodically involving these moves. The plan to close the mouth of the Red Sea was early formulated at Lisbon, while the capture of Goa was suggested to him by a Hindu corsair, Timoja; though Albuquerque deserves great credit for adopting it and for insisting on retaining Goa in the face of doubts subsequently expressed by the government at Lisbon. Similarly, the importance of Malacca had been recognised in King Manuel's instructions to the commanders of the fleets which left Lisbon in 1509 and 1510, though it fell to Albuquerque to achieve the actual conquest.

The three key strongpoints of Goa, Ormuz and Malacca, which ensured Portuguese control of the major spice-trade routes in the Indian Ocean, save for the Red Sea gap, were soon supplemented by many other fortified coastal settlements and trading posts (*feitorias*) from Sofala in south-east Africa to Ternate in the Moluccas. In addition, the Portuguese were allowed to form a number of unfortified settlements and *feitorias* in some regions where the Asian rulers permitted them to enjoy what amounted to a limited form of extraterritoriality—a common and long-standing practice as exemplified by the Indian and Javanese mercantile communities at Malacca, the Muslim traders in Malabar, and Persians and Arabs in South China. Portuguese settlements of this type were São Tomé de Meliapor on the Coromandel coast, Hughli in Bengal, and Macao in China. Having smashed the virtually unarmed Muslim monopoly of the spice routes in the Indian Ocean by force of arms and having seized three of its principal entrepôts, the Portuguese then tried to enforce a monopoly system of their own, as implied in King Manuel's grandiloquent title of 'Lord of the conquest, navigation, and commerce of Ethiopia, India, Arabia, and Persia', which the Portuguese Crown retained for centuries. Trade with certain ports and in certain commodities (spices being the chief) was declared to be a Portuguese Crown monopoly, and such trade was carried on for the benefit of that Crown or of its nominees. On the whole, however, Asian shipping was allowed to ply as before, provided that a Portuguese licence (*cartaz*; compare the British *navicert* of 1939–45) was taken out on payment by the ship-owner or merchants concerned, and provided that spices and other designated goods paid customs dues at Goa, Ormuz or Malacca. Unlicensed ships in the Indian Ocean were liable to be seized or sunk if they met Portuguese ships, particularly if the former belonged to Muslim traders.

The Portuguese monopoly of the seaborne trade of the Indian Ocean was not, of course, a fully effective one, even though their possession of Moçambique, Ormuz, Diu, Goa and Malacca did enable them to regulate the course of maritime trade in that region to a very considerable extent for almost the whole of the sixteenth century. East of Malacca there was never any question of the Portuguese being able to channel all the trade through the ports which suited them, or of their effectively enforcing the *cartaz* system on the multifarious shipping which plied the seas lying between Java and Japan. Dom Franciso de Almeida's destruction of the Egyptian-Gujarati fleet off Diu in 1509 had its counterpart in the Portuguese destruction of the Javanese war-fleet of large junks off Malacca in January 1513. The Portuguese carracks could sail unchallenged by any Indonesian warships to fetch their cargoes of cloves from Amboina, Ternate and Tidore, and of mace and nutmegs from the Banda Islands; but Portuguese shipping in this region was merely one more thread in the existing warp and woof of the Malay-Indonesian interport trade. When they tried to apply in the South China Sea the strong-arm methods which had served them so well in the Indian Ocean, they were decisively defeated by the Chinese coastguard fleets in 1521 and 1522. Though they subsequently gained admission to the coveted China trade, it was on the terms laid down by the Chinese authorities and not on those imposed by themselves.

Nevertheless, when all is said, the Portuguese achievement in establishing a seaborne empire in Monsoon Asia was no less remarkable than that of the Spaniards in establishing their land-based empire in America. Perhaps even more so, when we consider that the population of Portugal in the sixteenth century probably never exceeded about a million and a quarter souls; that there was a perennial shortage of Portuguese shipping; that Goa was the only Portuguese port in Asia with adequate dockyard facilities; and that the Portuguese had many other commitments in Morocco and West Africa, to say nothing of their efforts to colonise the Brazilian coast from 1539 onwards. Moreover, the technological gap between the Portuguese and the majority of their Asian opponents was much less than that between the Spaniards and the Amerindians of the New World. Diogo do Couto (1543–1616) and other contemporary Portuguese chroniclers were fond of pointing out that their compatriots in Asia had to contend with well-armed opponents who were as skilled in the use of firearms and cannon as they were themselves; whereas the Castilian *conquistadores* of Mexico and Peru had to overcome primitive warriors armed only with stone and wooden weapons. In these circumstances it is worth briefly considering some factors which contributed to the spectacular rise of the Portuguese Eastern empire and to its comparatively long duration, despite the slender demographic and economic resources of Portugal itself.

The admitted superiority of the relatively well-armed Portuguese ships over the unarmed Muslim merchant-vessels of the Indian Ocean was reinforced by a tenacity of purpose on the part of the European intruders which was largely lacking in their

Asian opponents. As Sir George Sansom has pointed out in his discussion of this problem in *The Western World and Japan*: 'The Portuguese went into Asia in a spirit of determination to succeed, which was stronger than the will of the Asian peoples to resist. Even the Muslim power in the Indian Ocean, which stood to lose so much by Portuguese success, did not bring to the defence of its own interests the continuous and whole-hearted energy displayed by its European rival.' It is often forgotten that the Portuguese attacks on Goa, Malacca and Ormuz all failed or else proved abortive at the first attempts; and it was only through Albuquerque's tenacity in trying again that they eventually succeeded. Secondly, many Asian rulers shared the conviction of Bahadur Shah, the King of Gujarat, that 'wars by sea are merchants' affairs, and of no concern to the prestige of kings'. Thirdly, the Asian countries against which Portuguese enterprise was directed were often riven by internal or distracted by external rivalries, which prevented them from uniting effectively against the Portuguese, at any rate for any length of time. A few examples will suffice to illustrate this point.

The long-standing rivalry between Mombasa and Malindi in East Africa enabled the Portuguese to establish their power on the Swahili coast by allying themselves with the latter. The age-old enmity between the Samorin of Calicut and the Raja of Cochin enabled the Portuguese to get their first firm foothold in India by supporting the latter against the former. It also gave the Portuguese a strong position in the Malabar pepper trade, just as their exploitation of the endemic enmity between the Sultans of Ternate and Tidore enabled them to achieve a commanding position in the clove trade of the Moluccas. At the time of their arrival in Ceylon, the 'Supremely Beautiful Island' was divided between three weak and mutually hostile kingdoms which were contending for supremacy, and this rivalry greatly facilitated the establishment of Portuguese power. The bitter enmity between Sunni Turkey and Shia Persia, and the frequent warfare between the Muslim and Hindu states of India, likewise hampered effective Asian opposition to Portuguese aggression and expansion. Achin and Johore, the most dangerous enemies of Malacca, were often at odds with each other. The reluctance of the Imperial government at Peking to have any commercial or other dealings with the Barbarians from the Western Ocean was frequently circumvented by the desire of the officials and the merchants of the Chinese coastal provinces for contraband trade with the said Barbarians. The Portuguese did not, of course, create these rivalries, but they naturally exploited those which they found. In this respect their progress in Asia recalls the even more spectacular feats of the Spanish *conquistadores* in America. As Padre José de Acosta, S.J., pointed out in 1590, if the Spaniards had not exploited the enmity between the Aztecs and the Tlaxcalans in Mexico, or the rivalry between the Inca half-brothers Atahualpa and Huascar in Peru: 'Cortez and Pizarro could hardly have maintained themselves ashore, although they were excellent captains.'

The most striking feature of the Portuguese seaborne empire, as it was established by the mid-sixteenth century, was its extreme dispersion. In the East it was represented by a chain of forts and factories, extending from Sofala and Ormuz on the western side of Monsoon Asia to the Moluccas and Macao (in 1557) on the edge of the Pacific. On the other side of the world it was equally extended with a few strongholds in Morocco (Ceuta, Tangier, Mazagão), with some *feitorias* and a few forts between Cape Verde and Luanda (in 1575) on the west coast of Africa, with the islands in the Gulf of Guinea, and with some struggling settlements along the Brazilian littoral. Lisbon had regular maritime connections with Antwerp, which was a major distributing centre for the Asian spices and other colonial products. The Portuguese fished off the Newfoundland Banks in considerable numbers, until their fishery was reduced to insignificance in this region by aggressive English competition at the end of the sixteenth century. Among the important products of this far-flung empire were the gold of Guinea (Elmina), of south-east Africa (Monomotapa) and of Sumatra (Kampar); the sugar of Madeira, São Tomé, and Brazil; pepper from Malabar and Indonesia; mace and nutmegs from Banda; cloves from Ternate, Tidore and Ambonia; cinnamon from Ceylon; gold, silks and porcelain from China; silver from Japan; horses from Persia and Arabia; cotton textiles from Cambay (Gujarat) and Coromandel. The various kinds of merchandise originating in Asia were either bartered in the inter-port trade of that continent or else they were taken round the

Cape of Good Hope to Lisbon, whence they were redistributed to the Mediterranean and Atlantic worlds in exchange for the metals, cereals, textiles, naval stores and other manufactured goods on which Lisbon largely depended for its function as the nerve centre of a seaborne empire. Pepper was the principal commodity imported from the East, and silver bullion was the principal export to 'Golden Goa'.

To enable these channels of maritime trade to flow smoothly from Brazil to Japan, the Portuguese needed large numbers of men and ships, both of which were, inevitably, in short supply. In the first place, as indicated above (p. 4–5), the population of Portugal itself was not large, though some contemporaries professed to believe that it was. So far as can be deduced from the census returns of the year 1527, which were taken on a basis of hearths (*fogos*) or households, the population must have been something between 1,000,000 and 1,400,000. It can be estimated with reasonable accuracy that during the sixteenth century approximately 2,400 people left Portugal yearly for overseas, the great majority of them being able-bodied and unmarried young men, bound for 'Golden Goa' and further east, relatively few of whom ever returned. The annual drain on Portuguese adult manpower was thus considerable; and it was certainly far greater than that in neighbouring Spain, where, out of a population variously estimated at some seven or eight million, only about 60,000 people had emigrated to America by 1570—an average of just under 1,000 a year. Moreover, Portugal was at a disadvantage in another respect. Whereas most of the Spanish emigrants went to the healthy uplands of Mexico and Peru after the conquest of those regions, the vast majority of the Portuguese went to the malarial and fever-stricken tropical coasts of Africa and Asia. Finally, many more of the Portuguese who embarked at Lisbon for Goa died on the six-, seven- or eight-month voyage to India than was the case with the Spaniards who embarked at Seville for the relatively short and speedy Atlantic crossing to Vera Cruz.

Afonso de Albuquerque, the chief architect of *India Portuguesa* in 1510–15, had alleged that the Eastern empire could be made secure 'with four good fortresses and a large well-armed fleet manned by 3,000 European-born Portuguese'. He secured three of the four fortresses; but the *desideratum* of a powerful fleet manned by 3,000 Europeans was only once fleetingly achieved—in the armada of eighteen 'tall ships' and twenty-five smaller vessels, which relieved Malacca in 1606. During the sixteenth century circumstances conspired to make the Portuguese over-extend themselves by maintaining a chain of forts and coastal settlements between Sofala and Nagasaki, which numbered more than forty and not merely four. This wide-ranging dispersion aggravated the perennial manpower problem to such an extent that the viceroys could seldom muster more than a thousand white men for any expedition, however important. Very few women emigrated from Portugal to Asia, and an outward-bound Indiaman which carried 800 or more men would only have some ten or fifteen women on board, and often none at all. Once they had reached Asia, many of the Portuguese men cohabited with slave-girls in droves, as the scandalised Jesuit missionaries constantly complained; but the death-rate from battle, disease and misadventure was so high among the Portuguese males in the East that it is doubtful if there were ever as many as 10,000 able-bodied Europeans and Eurasians available for military and naval service between Moçambique and Macao. Typical of the reiterated official complaints in this respect was the statement of the Archbishop of Goa in 1569. He alleged that although there were then some 14,000 or 15,000 names of men entitled to draw service-pay on the central *matricola* or muster-roll, not more than 3,000 of these really existed, and only a few hundred of them could be mobilised at Goa at any given time.

It is true that despite the heavy annual emigration of able-bodied men to the tropical world, and despite the ravages of plague, famine and other natural disasters which afflicted Portugal at intervals during the sixteenth century, the population as a whole does not seem to have declined very much, though exact figures and hence reliable deductions are lacking. But it is certain that vast tracts of Portugal itself were still seriously under-populated, and that much potentially viable agricultural land was left uncultivated for want of labour. The regions that supplied the bulk of the emigrants and adventurers who went overseas in the sixteenth to eighteenth centuries were the northern province of Minho and Douro, the populous capital of Lisbon, and the Atlantic islands of Madeira and the Azores. In the Minho, as

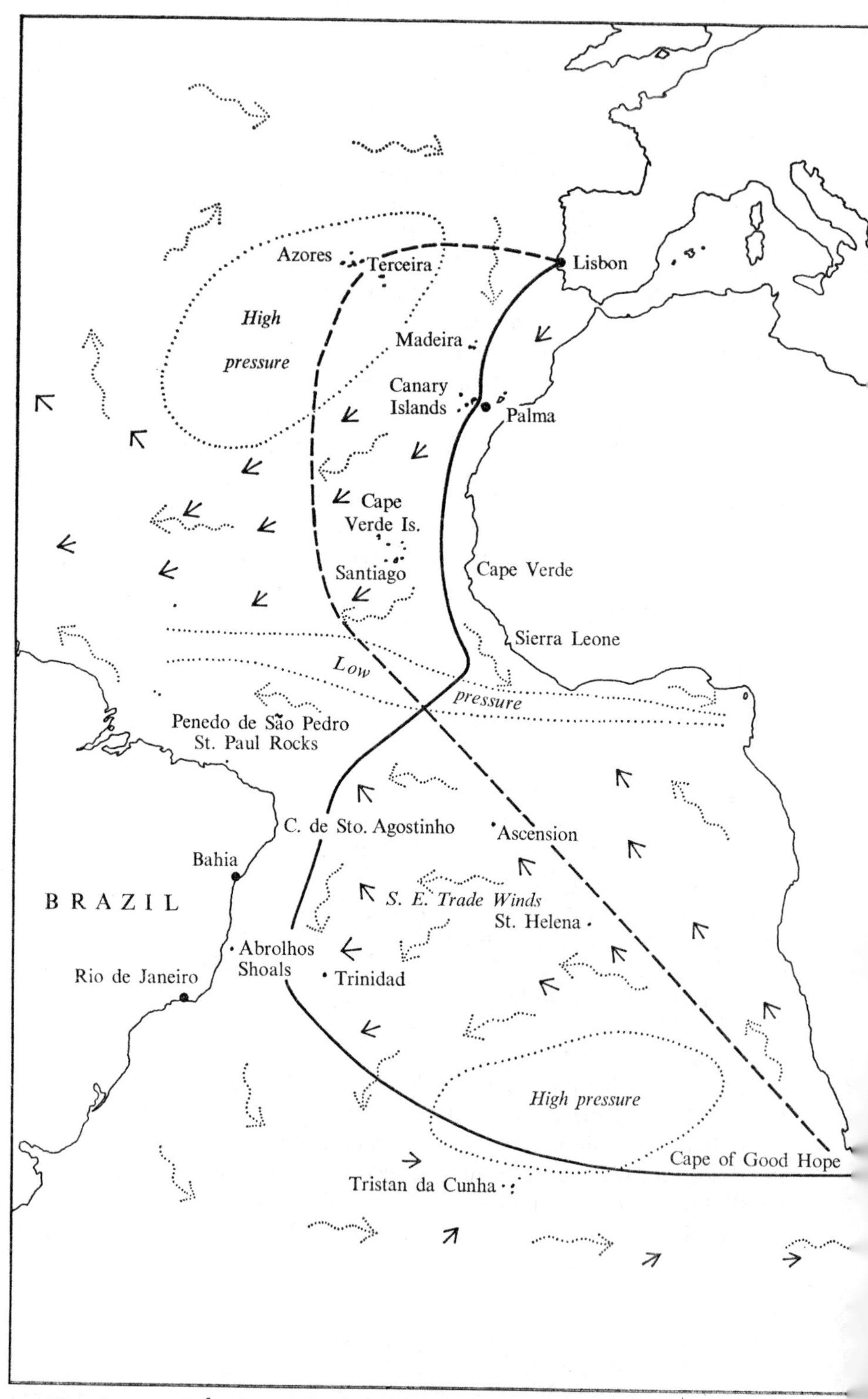

2 The *Carreira da Índia*, sixteenth to eighteenth centuries

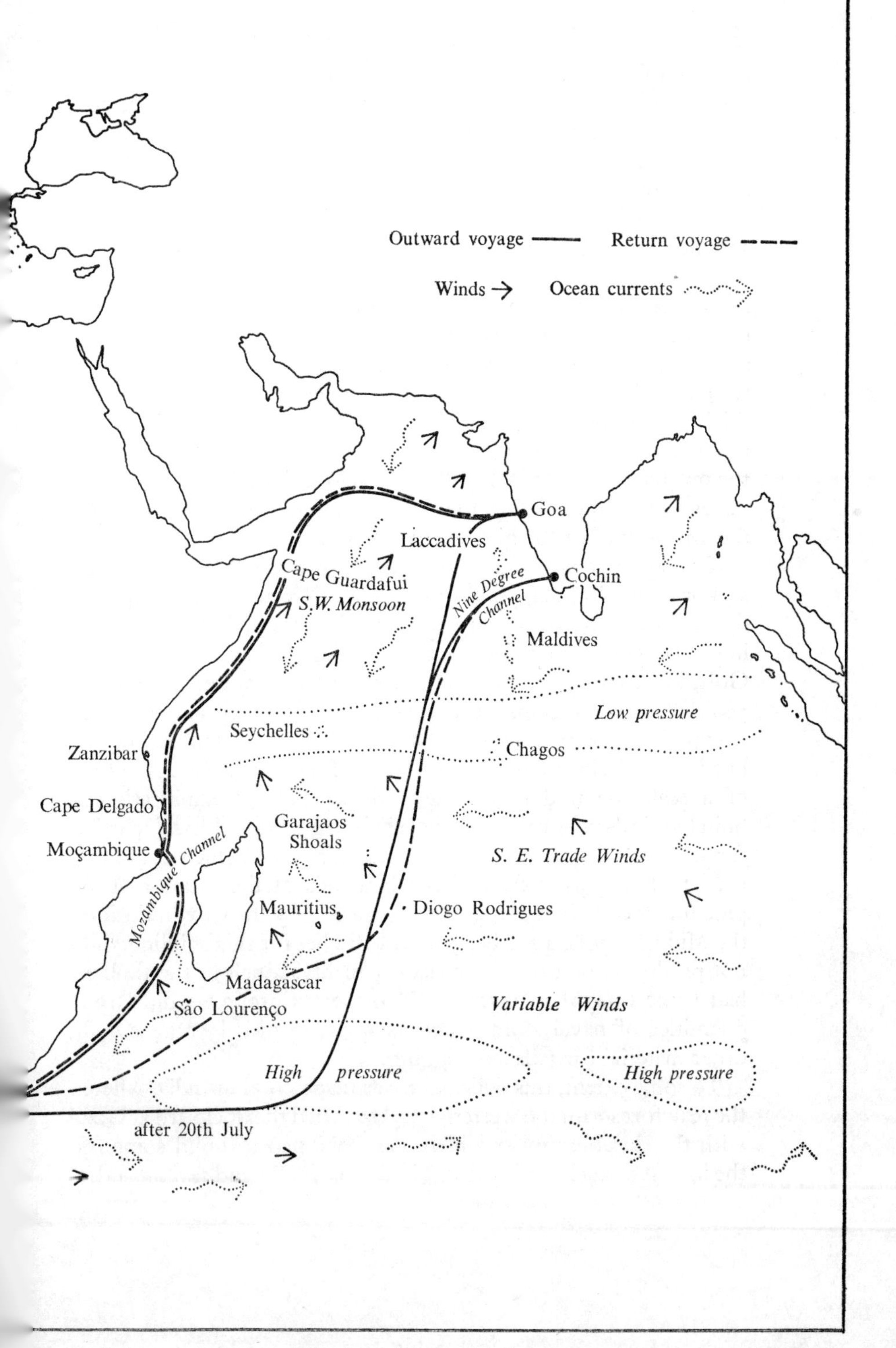

Outward voyage
Return voyage
Winds
Ocean currents
Goa
Laccadives
Cochin
Cape Guardafui
S.W. Monsoon
Nine Degree Channel
Maldives
Low pressure
Seychelles
Chagos
Zanzibar
Cape Delgado
Garajaos Shoals
Moçambique
Mozambique Channel
S. E. Trade Winds
Mauritius
Diogo Rodrigues
Madagascar
São Lourenço
Variable Winds
High pressure
High pressure
after 20th July

indicated above (p. 13), small-holdings and large families were the general rule, so there was every incentive for younger sons to emigrate. A similar situation prevailed in Madeira and the Azores, where the fertile volcanic valleys were thickly populated, and the terraced hillsides carefully cultivated, but where the population quickly reached saturation point. The large quota of emigrants supplied by Lisbon was due to the busy capital acting as a Mecca to the starving and the unemployed, just as London, Paris and Amsterdam later did in England, France and Holland. Many of these destitutes were unable to find work after their arrival, and so they either volunteered or were forced to emigrate as a last resource. When contemporaries claimed that Portugal was thickly populated (as some of them did), they were thinking of these relatively favoured regions. They forgot or they ignored the much larger regions, like the Alentejo and the Algarve, which never had the population they were capable of supporting until the second half of the nineteenth century.

If manpower was one perennial problem in the Portuguese seaborne empire, shipping was another. We have no complete figures for Portuguese shipping at this period, but two well-informed contemporaries, Garcia de Resende and Damião de Gois, both state that Portugal did not possess more than about 300 ocean-going ships at the height of its maritime power, *c.* 1536. This figure is an impressive one for such a small country; but it was obviously totally insufficient for the adequate support of a seaborne trading empire with world-wide ramifications. Suitable timber was not easily available in Portugal itself, partly for want of adequate roads and navigable rivers which could be used to transport it from the oak woods of the interior. The pine forest of Leiria, planted near the coast by the Crown during the Middle Ages expressly to provide timber for shipbuilding, did not produce wood of a very lasting quality. Much of the timber had to be bought in Biscay and northern Europe, as did large quantities of naval stores, such as spars, ironwork, canvas and other material for sails and rigging.

To some extent, this deficiency was made good in India, where the teak forests on the western coast supplied the dockyard at Goa with the durable timber which was fashioned to build some of the largest carracks and galleons in the sixteenth- and seventeenth-century world, as we shall see in Chapter IX below. The shipwrights of the royal yards at Lisbon and Oporto also turned out some very fine vessels, which aroused the admiration of their European contemporaries, but these great ships were slow and expensive to build, and difficult to replace. India, Malaya and China admittedly furnished an unlimited supply of wood for building small coastal vessels of the types known as galliots, *manchuas*, *fustas*, *fragatas*, etc., which could easily be replaced when lost, but here again the manpower problem made itself felt, as explained in Chapter IX. Consequently, Portuguese shipping in the interport trade of Asia was increasingly operated, from the days of Albuquerque onwards, by Asian seamen working under a few white or Eurasian officers. Even the great carracks of 1,000–2,000 tons which plied between Goa, Macao and Nagasaki might be entirely crewed by Asians and Negro slaves, save for the ship's officers and fifteen or twenty Portuguese soldiers and gunners. In the Portuguese ships plying the Indian Ocean interport trade, the captain or master was sometimes the only white man on board; for even the pilot and boatswain as well as the sailors were often Muslim Gujaratis. As early as 1539 we find that D. João de Castro, when organising an expedition to the Red Sea, found that none of the Portuguese pilots were familiar with the straits of Bab-el-Mandeb, or had any adequate charts of that region. He was forced to rely on 'Arab, Gujarati and Malabar pilots' with their own types of nautical charts.

For obvious reasons Portuguese maritime power was most effective in the seas in the immediate vicinity of their principal bases—Goa, Diu, Ormuz, Malacca and Moçambique. Even so, the inherently brittle superstructure of their maritime dominance was shown by the sweeping successes achieved by two weak Turkish raiding flotillas in 1551–2 and in 1585–6 respectively. On the former occasion the Turkish admiral, Piri Reis, with twenty-three galleys from the Red Sea, first sacked Muscat and then besieged for some weeks the Portuguese castle at Ormuz, although by all accounts his force was markedly inferior in numbers to the defenders. On the second occasion an adventurer named Mir Ali Bey, with one crazy ill-gunned ship, swept the Portuguese from the whole of the Swahili coast, save only Malindi, capturing twenty Portuguese prizes and a vast booty with no loss whatever to himself. At the other end of the Indian Ocean, Malacca was frequently reduced to severe straits by the action of blockading Javanese or Achinese fleets; and the Malays sometimes scored substantial successes against the Portuguese when operating with oared craft in the confined waters of rivers and estuaries, where carracks and galleons could not manœuvre or else became becalmed. Even almost within gunshot of the outlying forts of Goa, the Moplah corsairs of Malabar periodically wrought great havoc on the Portuguese coastal trade by intercepting the *cafilas* or convoys of small vessels laden with rice and provisions for the colonial capital.

Nevertheless such reverses, serious as they sometimes were, did not destroy the foundations of Portuguese maritime power in the Indian Ocean. Turkish, Egyptian, Malabar or Malayan corsairs in oared galleys and single-masted foists could not effectively challenge on the high seas the great carracks and galleons which formed the core of Portuguese naval strength. Only the Chinese war-junks could (and did) do this; and the operations of the Chinese coastguard fleets were strictly limited to their provincial waters by order of the Imperial government. As a broad generalisation it can be said that the Portuguese *did* more or less effectively dominate the maritime trade of the Indian Ocean for most of the sixteenth century. The losses which they suffered from Malabar and other corsairs who preyed on their coastal commerce did not affect the real sinews of their sea-power; just as the much greater damage done by French corsairs and privateers to English seaborne trade during the War of the Spanish Succession failed to sap the power of the British Navy.

It must also be remembered that on the only occasion when the Muslim powers of India and Indonesia agreed to co-operate in a combined attack on the Portuguese strongholds of Goa, Chaul, Malacca and Ternate they were decisively defeated in all save the last-named. And if Ternate eventually had to be abandoned to Sultan Baab in 1575, this was mainly because of the incompetence of the local Portuguese commander. The other three places were held against great odds; and the successful defence of Goa and Chaul in 1571 was rightly regarded by contemporaries as the Portuguese equivalent in the Indian Ocean of

Don Juan de Austria's victory over the Turks at Lepanto in the same year.

Portuguese plans to establish an effective monopoly of the Asian spice trade were thwarted by other factors besides shortages of shipping and of manpower. Although they dominated maritime trade in the Persian Gulf, thanks to their strongholds at Ormuz and Muscat, they could not close this route completely to Muslim traders, since for most of the sixteenth century they had to keep on good terms with Persia, whose friendship was necessary to them as a counterweight to the Turkish menace. The Ottoman Turks had conquered Syria and Egypt between 1514 and 1517, and they occupied most of Iraq in 1534–5. They took Aden in 1538 and Basra in 1546. The spice trade to the Levant through the Red Sea, which had never been entirely closed by the Portuguese for any length of time, revived markedly from about 1540 onwards, although the Persian Gulf route and that round the Cape of Good Hope both retained their importance.

The production of spices in Asia and the demand for them in Europe roughly doubled during the second half of the sixteenth century, and prices likewise increased two- or even threefold. The global amounts of the cargoes carried by the Portuguese round the Cape have been estimated at an annual total of between 40,000 and 50,000 *quintals* in the first third of the century and between 60,000 and 70,000 *quintals* later on.[1] The proportion of pepper in these cargoes oscillated between 10,000 and 45,000 *quintals*, but for a long time averaged about 20,000–30,000. The other spices—cinnamon, cloves, mace, nutmegs, ginger, etc.—accounted for between 5,000 and 10,000 *quintals* in these yearly shipments. By the end of the century the Portuguese share of the pepper exports to Europe had dropped to about 10,000 *quintals*, and greater quantities were reaching Europe by the overland routes to the Levant. It was stated in 1585, by a Portuguese official in a position to know, that the Achinese were exporting (mostly in Gujarati ships) some 40,000 or 50,000 *quintals* of spices to Jidda each year. The great bulk of these cargoes certainly consisted of pepper, but we do not know how much was destined for the European market and how much was consumed in the Turkish empire. With the

[1] The *quintal* was the Portuguese hundredweight of *c.* 130 lb. avoirdupois or 51.405 kg.

dawn of the seventeenth century and the arrival of the Dutch and English in the East, the Portuguese position deteriorated still further. But as late as 1611 it was officially stated at Lisbon that pepper was still the basic commodity of the Portuguese India trade, and the only one which yielded a satisfactory profit to the Crown.

The pepper laden in the homeward-bound Portuguese Indiamen came chiefly from Malabar, where the Crown agents had to buy it on the open market in places like Cochin and Cranganore, and in competition with Indian merchants. As noted above, large quantities of pepper were also produced in Sumatra and Western Java, but much of this was absorbed by the Chinese market. This Indonesian pepper was cheaper than the Malabar variety and of equally good (or better) quality; but owing to Achinese and Chinese competition the Portuguese were never able to secure enough to bring down the price of pepper in Malabar. For most of the second half of the sixteenth century the Malabar pepper traders refused to accept payment in anything but gold; but the Portuguese never had to send from Lisbon as much gold specie as the Venetians employed in their spice purchases in the Levant. Unfortunately, the records of the Indo-Portuguese mints at Goa and Cochin have not survived, and the figures for the amounts of specie sent annually from Lisbon to India are far from complete. But taking one thing with another, it seems clear that the greater part of the gold required by the Portuguese for their purchases in Malabar was obtained from south-east Africa, Sumatra and China from about 1547 onwards. In that year (or the next) the Goa mint commenced the issue of the *São Tomé*, a gold coin which held its own for centuries alongside the ever-popular Venetian ducat (*zecchino*), the *ashrafi* (*zerafim*) of Ormuz, and the Turkish sequins, Vijayanagar pagodas, Moghul mohurs and other gold coins which circulated throughout the East.

Originally the sale of pepper at Lisbon was free to all comers, but after 1503 all imports were sold through the intermediary of the *Casa da India* (India House). In 1530 the Crown decreed that the Casa should only sell spices in gross (one *quintal* and above), save for the small amounts needed to replenish apothecaries' medicine chests. Portuguese and foreign merchants both participated in the purchase of pepper at Lisbon, one of the earliest large-scale entrepreneurs in the spice trade being the Florentine merchant-banker, Bartholomé Marchione, who had already contracted for a large share of the Guinea trade in the reign of Dom João II. For most of the sixteenth century Antwerp was the principal entrepôt for the Lisbon pepper, whence it was redistributed to the various countries of north-west Europe. German and Italian merchant bankers, the Fuggers, the Affaitadi (Lafetá as they became known in Portugal), the Giraldi among others, competed with each other or else combined together to buy pepper and other spices from the Portuguese Crown on short- or long-term contracts. Up to 1549 the Crown maintained its own agency (*feitoria*) at Antwerp, but it was withdrawn in that year as the local factors could not compete with the more sophisticated Flemish, German and Italian traders. During the last quarter of the sixteenth century, these foreign pepper contractors were allowed to station their own representatives at Goa and Cochin, in order to supervise the purchase and shipment of the spices for which they had contracted; but owing to shipwrecks and other causes the contractors were seldom if ever able to deliver the stipulated amounts at Lisbon.

Apart from pepper, the Portuguese imports of mace, nutmegs, cinnamon and ginger increased somewhat in the second half of the sixteenth century, since their value roughly trebled during that period. The Crown did not ultimately derive much profit from the cloves and nutmegs, owing to the great cost of fitting out the annual carracks or galleons sent to fetch these spices from the Moluccas and from Banda, respectively, and owing to the cost of maintaining the precariously held forts at Ambonia, Ternate and Tidore. Smuggling and contraband trade likewise flourished in these remote islands to an even greater extent than elsewhere. The Crown Factor at Cochin in 1568 alleged that two galleons which came from the Moluccas loaded with cloves brought only six *bahares* (*one bahar*=400 lb. avoirdupois) for the account of the Crown, although both ships had been fitted out and manned at the expense of the King. Most of the Indonesian spices secured by the Portuguese were sold at Malacca, Goa and Ormuz to Asian traders, and only relatively small amounts were sent round the Cape to Europe, despite the increased demand for them there. By the end of the sixteenth century the Portuguese had abandoned their efforts to enforce the official monopoly of the clove trade, under which one-third of the total export crop was reserved for the Crown. When the Dutch admiral Steven van der Hagen captured Amboina in 1605 he found that the Portuguese allowed Muslim merchants from all over Asia, and even from Turkey itself, to buy cloves in this island. A similar state of affairs prevailed at Ormuz where, during the last quarter of the century, Persian, Turkish, Arab, Armenian and Venetian merchants frequented the island to buy spices from the Portuguese officials and private traders, in complete disregard of the Iberian Crown's theoretical monopoly.

The prosperity of Ormuz at this period was attested by Ralph Fitch, the Elizabethan merchant-adventurer who visited it in 1583:

> Ormuz is an island in circuit about 25 or 30 miles and is the driest island in the world: for there is nothing growing in it but only salt; for their water, wood or victuals and all things necessary come out of Persia, which is about 12 miles from thence. All thereabouts be very fruitful, from whence all kind of victuals are sent into Ormuz. In this town are merchants of all nations, and many Moors and Gentiles. Here is very great trade of all sorts of spices, drugs, silks, cloth of silk, fine tapestry of Persia, great store of pearls, which come from the isle of Bahrein, and are the best pearls of all others and many horses of Persia, which serve all India. They have a Moor to their King which is chosen and governed by the Portugals.

As regards cinnamon, the Portuguese were able to exercise a more effective monopoly in this than in any other spice, since the best variety grew only in the lowland districts of Ceylon which were under Portuguese control, and the Sinhalese had no merchant shipping of their own. Inferior varieties were grown in Malabar and in Mindanao, but, as Linschoten observed in 1596, 'the cinnamon of the island of Ceylon is the best and finest in the world, and is at least three times dearer in price'. The Crown should therefore have profited greatly from the royal monopoly in this spice, but in actual practice the chief profits were reaped by the governors and officials who embezzled or traded in cinnamon, despite all the legislation enacted at Goa and Lisbon to prevent such malpractices. The fame of cinnamon as a valuable and coveted spice was reflected in the verses of the poet Sá de

Miranda (*c.* 1550), who complained that Portugal was being depopulated by the numbers of men who left Lisbon for the East 'at the scent of this cinnamon'.

The deterioration of the Portuguese position in the Spice Islands after their loss of Ternate in 1575, was largely offset by their virtual monopoly of the valuable carrying trade between China and Japan which they achieved about this time. Their first attempts to establish themselves on the shores of the south China coast had failed, partly through their own mismanagement and partly through the reluctance of the Chinese imperial bureaucracy to take any official cognizance of unwanted barbarian intruders from the Great Western Ocean. But a precarious smuggling trade was connived at by the coastal officials of Kwangtung and Fukien provinces for their own profit. This eventually led to the Portuguese securing a footing at Macao (*c.* 1557), which was reluctantly sanctioned by the Emperor at Peking when he belatedly discovered the existence of this settlement after some twenty years. Owing to the constant friction prevailing between China and Japan at this period, and to the Ming dynasty's prohibition of trade with the 'dwarf-robbers' of the island-empire in either Chinese or Japanese shipping, the Portuguese of Macao were able to secure a more or less official monopoly of the trade between the two countries. This trade was essentially based on the exchange of Chinese raw and manufactured silks and of gold for Japanese silver bullion. Of course, the Ming prohibition of direct Chinese trade with Japan was not always rigorously enforced; but it was sufficiently effective to ensure that the most valuable part of the trade was left in the hands of the Portuguese. The political unification of Japan by Toyotomi Hideyoshi and his subsequent invasion of Korea (1592–8) greatly stimulated the Japanese demand for gold in the last quarter of the sixteenth century. Moreover, although Japan was a silk-producing country, the Japanese much preferred Chinese silk, whether raw or woven, to their own as it was of superior quality.

The round voyage between Goa and Nagasaki (terminal port of the Japan trade after 1570) took anything between eighteen months and three years, depending on the length of the ship's stay at Macao (and/or Nagasaki) if she missed the monsoon. This voyage, which originally had been open to all and sundry, was soon limited to an annual *náo*, or carrack, under a captain-major appointed by the Crown. The grantee could either make the voyage himself or sell the right to do so to the highest bidder. The actual silk trade was largely in the hands of the merchants and the Jesuits at Macao, who operated a system of imports arranged on a quota basis among all those who had a share in providing the cargo. The captain-major got a handsome rake-off from most items in the cargo, in addition to the profits of his own private investment. Linschoten, writing in 1596, estimated the profits at 150,000 or 200,000 ducats on the round voyage; and one such voyage was often enough to enable the captain-major to retire with a fortune.

Both Macao and Nagasaki rose from being obscure fishing villages to flourishing seaports by the end of the sixteenth century as a result of this mutually profitable trade. The privileged position attained by the merchants from Macao at Nagasaki was thus described by an envious Dutch visitor in 1610:

> The ship coming from Macao usually has about 200 or more merchants on board who go ashore at once, each of them taking a house wherein to lodge with his servants and slaves. They take no heed of what they spend and nothing is too costly for them. Sometimes they disburse in the seven or eight months that they stay in Nagasaki more than 200,000 or 300,000 [silver] taels, through which the populace profit greatly; and this is one of the reasons why the local Japanese are very friendly to them.

During the last decade of the sixteenth century the Portuguese monopoly of Japan's overseas trade and the Jesuit monopoly of the Japan mission founded by St. Francis Xavier in 1549 were alike threatened by the appearance of Spanish traders and missionary friars from the Philippines. These Iberian rivals caused the Portuguese considerable jealousy and concern, but their activities did not, in the upshot, greatly reduce the profits of the Macao-Nagasaki trade. Despite the union of the two Iberian Crowns in the person of Philip II in 1580, the government at Madrid accepted, by and large, the Portuguese contention that Japan lay within their sphere of influence (as demarcated by the Treaty of Tordesillas in 1494) and that the Japan trade should be monopolised by Macao rather than by Manila.

CHAPTER III

Converts and clergy in Monsoon Asia 1500-1600

THE importance of Japanese silver, Chinese silks, Indonesian spices, Persian horses and Indian pepper in Portuguese Asia should not obscure the fact that God was omnipresent as well as Mammon. As Padre António Vieira, the great Portuguese Jesuit missionary, observed in his *History of the Future*: 'If there were not merchants who go to seek for earthly treasures in the East and West Indies, who would transport thither the preachers who take heavenly treasures? The preachers take the Gospel and the merchants take the preachers.' If trade followed the flag in the British empire, the missionary was close behind the merchant in the Portuguese empire. Admittedly, if Vasco da Gama's men said they had come to India in search of Christians and spices, the quest for the latter was prosecuted with much more vigour than the care for the former during the first four decades of Portuguese activity in the East. Until the Jesuits arrived with new men and new methods at Goa in 1542, relatively few missionaries had been sent out, and they had achieved relatively little. Most of them made no effort to learn any of the Oriental languages, and they depended upon interpreters who were naturally better acquainted with market prices and bazaar gossip than with subtle theological arguments. Nor did these missionaries and their better qualified Jesuit successors for a long time take the trouble to study the sacred books and basic religious beliefs of those whom they wished to convert, whether Muslim, Hindu or Buddhist, being inclined to dismiss them all as the works of the Devil.

Moreover, some of the pioneer secular clergy were more interested in serving Mammon than God, as typified by the group of worldly clerics who told the scandalised Vicar of Malacca in 1514: 'That the chief reason why they had come out to the East was to amass a fortune in *cruzados*; and one of them said that he would not be satisfied unless he had secured 5,000 *cruzados* and many pearls and rubies within the space of three years.' Such converts as these worldly clerics made were, for the most part, either Asian women living (in wedlock or otherwise) with Portuguese men, or household slaves, or the starving poor and outcasts who became 'rice-Christians'. There were exceptions, of course, and the mass conversion of the Parava pearl-fishers in southern India, superficial as it must have been in the first instance (1537), subsequently gave lasting results. But it was the Company of Jesus, in its role as the spearhead of the Church Militant, which made the struggle for souls as intensive and wide-ranging as was the competition for spices. The sons of Loyola set and maintained much higher standards than did their predecessors; and the remarkable development of the Portuguese missions between 1550 and 1750 was mainly their work, which frequently elicited glowing tributes from otherwise hostile Protestants.

By a mixture of carrot-and-stick methods, in which the stick sometimes predominated, many of the Asians in the immediate vicinity of the Portuguese strongholds were converted to Christianity, particularly along the west coast of India and in lowland Ceylon. Beginning with the mass destruction of Hindu temples at Goa in 1540, the Portuguese authorities, mainly at the promptings of local ecclesiastics or of the Crown, enacted a large number of harsh and oppressive laws with the object of preventing the public practice of Hinduism, Buddhism and Islam in Portuguese-controlled territory. These laws were supplemented by a number of others which were enacted for the express purpose of favouring converts to Christianity at the expense of their compatriots who declined to be converted. The main lines of missionary policy were laid down by successive Ecclesiastical Councils periodically celebrated at Goa from 1567 onwards. This pioneer Council of 1567 was a particularly important one, as the post-Tridentine church was then in the first flush of its confident strength, and the decisions then taken were reaffirmed with only slight modifications in the subsequent Councils. Its deliberations were guided by three main considerations, the last of which proved in practice to be difficult (if not impossible) to reconcile with the first two:

1. All religions other than the orthodox Roman Catholic faith as defined at the Council of Trent were intrinsically wrong and harmful in themselves.
2. The Crown of Portugal had the inescapable duty of spreading the Roman Catholic faith, and the secular power of the State could be used to support the spiritual power of the Church.
3. Conversion must not be made by force, nor threats of force, 'for nobody comes to Christ by faith unless he is drawn by the Heavenly Father with voluntary love and prevenient grace'.

The injunction that converts must not be made by force, or the threat of force, was largely nullified in practice by various other decisions of the Council, which received the sanction of law by a viceregal decree promulgated on 4 December 1567. This decree enacted, *inter alia*, that all heathen temples in Portuguese-controlled territory should be demolished; that the name of the Prophet Muhammad should not be invoked in the Muslim call to prayer from a mosque; that all non-Christian priests, teachers and holy men should be expelled; and that all their sacred books, such as the Koran, should be seized and destroyed whenever found. Hindus and Buddhists were prohibited from visiting their respective temples in the neighbouring territories, and even the transit passage of Asian pilgrims to such places was forbidden. A ban was also placed on that ritual bathing which is such a feature of Hinduism.

The public celebration of non-Christian marriage ceremonies and religious processions was strictly forbidden. No conversions were allowed from Islam to Hinduism or to Buddhism, and *vice versa*, but only from these religions to Christianity. Monogamy was decreed for everyone, irrespective of their religion. Men who were already living with more than one wife (or cohabiting with more than one concubine) were ordered to dismiss all save the one whom they had first married (or to make a lawful wedded wife of one of the concubines). All orphaned Hindu children were to be taken, if necessary by force, from the relatives with whom they were living and were to be handed over to Christian guardians or foster-parents and prepared for baptism by Catholic priests. If either of the partners in a pagan marriage was converted, the children and the property were to be given into his (or her) keeping. Christians were not allowed to live or lodge with non-Christians, nor the former allowed to have other than strictly business dealings with the adherents of other creeds. Nominal rolls were to be made of all Hindu families, and these latter were to be sent in groups of fifty to hear Christian propaganda in the local churches and convents on alternate Sundays. A sharply increasing scale of fines was levied on those who tried to evade these obligations. Non-Christians were to be officially and legally discriminated against, and converts equally favoured, in competition for such public offices and remunerative posts which were not reserved (as many were) for Christian converts only. Most of these regulations were tightened by the later enactments of successive Ecclesiastical Councils, though a few were relaxed. Nor was it long before Muslim mosques shared the fate of Hindu and Buddhist temples in places where they had not already been destroyed by the crusading fury of the original *conquistadores*, as many had been. Roman Catholic churches were built on or near the sites of the demolished mosques and temples, and the income derived from the lands belonging to the latter was transferred to the support and maintenance of the former.

It is obvious that these discriminatory and coercive measures, if they did not actually force people to become Christians at the point of the sword, made it very difficult for them to be anything else. Deprived of their priests, teachers, holy men, sacred books and public places of worship, not to mention the free exercise of their respective cults, it was confidently expected by the legislators of 1567 that 'the false heathen and Moorish religions' would wither and die on territory controlled by the Portuguese Crown. But, as those legislators sententiously observed, it was one thing to enact good laws and quite another to enforce them. In fact, their application varied widely according to place, time and circumstances, and more particularly according to the character of individual viceroys and archbishops, whose powers were very great.

The Council of 1567 itself specifically excepted the mosques at Ormuz from its anti-Muslim provisions, for even if the local Shah was a Portuguese puppet, the population was Muslim; and some regard had to be paid to the susceptibilities of the neighbouring and increasingly powerful Persians. The Hindu traders at Diu secured exemption for their own temples when the island-city was ceded to the Portuguese in 1537. This exemption was confirmed about a century later on account of the help the Diu Banyans had rendered to the Jesuit missionaries in Abyssinia, and similar privileges were given to the local Muslims. It was obviously impossible to interfere with the Chinese temples at Macao; and the Portuguese reluctantly tolerated Buddhist and Taoist street processions and celebrations there. The Dutch Calvinist, Linschoten, no friendly critic of the Portuguese, tells us that when he was at Goa in 1583–9, 'all sorts of nations as Indians, heathens, Moors, Jews, Armenians, Gujaratis, Banyans, Brahmins and of all Indian nations and people which do all dwell and traffic therein' were allowed freedom of conscience, provided they practised their marriage-rites 'and other superstitious and devilish inventions' behind closed doors.

Although the decree of 1567 ostensibly put an end to all social intercourse between Portuguese families and their non-Christian neighbours, we know that this continued. Successive Ecclesiastical Councils denounced not only the toleration of some heathen processions on Portuguese territory, but the practice of Christians lending their jewellery, finery and slaves to the participants. We also learn from these ecclesiastical fulminations that the Portuguese on occasion supplied cannon to fire salutes during the Muslim fast of Ramadhan. Far from enforcing the practice of monogamy on all and sundry, as the puritanical prelates of 1567 and later Councils decreed, many of the Portuguese men maintained seraglios wherever and whenever they could. Missionary reports from the time of St. Francis Xavier onwards are full of complaints concerning Lusitanian concupiscence on a staggering scale. Nautch-girls and temple-prostitutes from nearby Hindu territories were lavishly patronised by the Portuguese *fidalgos* of Goa and Baçaim, despite repeated denunciations by successive viceroys and archbishops. Last not least, the stipulation that official posts should be reserved for Christian converts wherever and whenever possible was frequently ignored in practice. Apart from other instances which could be mentioned, experience showed that only the Hindu Banyans possessed the financial acumen, resources and experience to act as receivers for the rents from Crown lands, collectors of customs and excise and so forth.

The Jesuit Provincial, António de Quadros, writing from Goa to the Crown in 1561, explained the results of the carrot-and-stick methods employed to evangelise that island and the surrounding districts under Portuguese control. Most of the Hindus were converted by the preaching of the Jesuit missionaries.

> Others come because Our Lord brings them, without anyone else persuading them; others come because they are persuaded to do so by their recently converted relatives, some of whom have brought three hundred, others a hundred and others less, each one as best he could; others, and these are the least numerous, come because they are constrained to do so by the laws which Your Highness has promulgated in these lands, in which Hindu temples are prohibited and Hindu ceremonies are banned, forasmuch as these people have been found guilty in this respect and imprisoned forthwith; and after being imprisoned, out of fear of punishment, they ask for the holy baptism.

The writer adds that when these terrified prisoners asked for baptism or catechism, the Jesuits took them to the college of St. Paul and gave them food to eat. Once they had eaten this food and touched the dishes in which it was served, they lost caste without (so he said) any hope of regaining it, since they were permanently defiled in the eyes of orthodox Hindus. They therefore made no further difficulties about becoming Christian converts.

The Provincial admitted that many of the Portuguese laymen at Goa severely criticised this procedure as tantamount to making converts by force. He denounced these critics as motivated by malice or by self-interest, particularly the Crown officials who relied on the expertise and co-operation of the Brahmins to make the financial side of the administration function smoothly; but there is plenty of other contemporary evidence to indicate that these criticisms were largely justified. One of the Crown officials, writing to the Queen of Portugal in 1552, alleged that the Jesuits were more concerned with the prestige than with the fruit of their conversion policy, using rough-and-ready methods to obtain the desired results.

1. *6,400* reis *of King John V, Rio de Janeiro mint, 1727*

2. São Vicente *of King John III,* c. *1555*

3. Dobra *of 12,800* reis, *Rio de Janeiro mint, 1729*

4. Moeda (*moidore*) *of 4,000* reis, *Bahia, 1695*

5. Cruzado *of King Manuel I, 1496–1521*

6. *400* reis *of King John V, Minas mint, 1733*

7. São Tomé pardau d'ouro, *probably Cochin mint,* c. *1555*

1. *Gold coins from Portugal and her overseas possessions* (full size)

2. *Portuguese* Náo *(Great Ship) from the atlas attributed to Sebastião* Lopes, c. *1565*

> Besides other vexations and annoyances which they inflict upon the Hindus in order to constrain them to submit to being baptised, they forcibly shaved many of them, and compelled them to eat the flesh of cows and to sin against other of their superstitious and idolatrous rites; for which reason the majority of them have fled, and the Portuguese Christians complain because they cannot live without their services, both as regards the cultivation of their palm-groves and farms, as for other necessary tasks which are essential here.

The Ecclesiastical Council of 1567 also admitted that the Hindus often complained to the secular authorities at Goa that 'their children, or slaves, or retainers' had been made Christians by force, and such complaints recur at frequent intervals for centuries. No doubt some of these complaints were exaggerated, but many others were not. It is significant that a representation to the Crown drawn up at Lisbon in February 1563 by the Bishops of Ceuta, Lisbon, Tangier, Angra, Portalegre, Lamego and the Algarve categorically stated that there were great abuses prevalent in all of the Portuguese overseas mission-fields, including the use of force and the farcical mass baptism of uninstructed converts. It is unlikely that seven leading Portuguese prelates would have made such grave allegations without being quite sure of their facts. The extensive published documentation on the sixteenth-century Jesuit missions in Goa makes it abundantly clear that the missionaries used what was later euphemistically termed 'the rigour of mercy', when they could count on the support of such priest-ridden bigots as the Governor Francisco Barreto (1555–8) and the Viceroy Dom Constantino de Bragança (1558–61). During the viceroyalty of the last named, the exodus of Hindus from Goa to the mainland reached such alarming proportions that his immediate successors found it necessary to reverse his policy. Both the Count of Redondo (1561–64) and Dom Antão de Noronha (1564–8) gave the Hindus of Goa specific assurances that they would not be converted by force. A decree promulgated by the former Viceroy on 3 December 1561 announced that all Hindus who had fled from Portuguese territory to avoid religious persecution, and whose property and lands had been confiscated by order of Dom Constantino, would receive them back again if they returned to their villages within six months.

Perhaps it need hardly be said that although dubious methods were often used to obtain Indian converts to Christianity in the sixteenth century, the descendants of those converts became devout Christians in the course of time. This fact was realised by the Bishop of Dume, the pioneer prelate at Goa, when advocating (in 1522) the expulsion from Portuguese territory of all those Indians who would not accept conversion to Christianity. If they stayed and accepted baptism, he wrote, they could hardly be expected to become good Christians, 'yet their children will become so'. This is, in fact, exactly what happened. After the mass destruction of the Hindu temples in the 1540s and the mass conversions of the 1560s, Christianity took firm root in Portuguese territory in and around Goa and Baçaim. Just as in Europe the descendants of the Saxons, Teutons and Slavs, who in many cases were forcibly converted to Christianity, subsequently became fervent Christians, so the inhabitants of the Goa islands and the district of Baçaim in the course of two or three generations became profoundly attached to the religion which had been imposed, none too gently, on their forefathers.

A distinction must also be drawn between Portuguese policy and social attitudes towards the adherents of other religions in the first and second halves of the sixteenth century. By and large, once the Portuguese had grasped the fact that the Hindus were not Christians, they were at first prepared to tolerate and cooperate with them as a counterweight to the Muslims. It is true that Albuquerque had eventually to abandon his original plan of forcibly opposing the Muslims everywhere, and invariably favouring the Hindus at their expense, since he found that he could not do without Gujarati sailors and Muslim merchants under certain circumstances. Moreover, as Albuquerque wrote to King Manuel in October 1514:

> The Muslim merchants have their residences and settlements in the best ports of the Hindus. They have many very large ships, and they carry on a great trade, and the Hindu kings are very closely connected with them, owing to the yearly profit they derive from them. And the Banyans of Cambay, who are the principal Hindu merchants of these parts, rely entirely on Muslim shipping.

Albuquerque and his immediate successors, while equating

Hinduism with 'blind idolatry', did not systematically destroy Hindu temples or overtly interfere with the public Hindu rites and ceremonies (save for abolishing suttee or widow-burning) in the same way that they demolished Muslim mosques and banned Islamic practices wherever they had the chance. Similarly, the Portuguese pioneers in Asia and Abyssinia were not unduly perturbed by the Chaldean and Syriac rites of the St. Thomas Christians in Malabar, or even by the Monophysite Ethiopian Church when they at last made contact with Prester John. But the hardening of religious differences in Europe, resulting from the growth of Protestant heresies and from the Roman Catholic revival which goes by the name of the Counter Reformation, was clearly reflected in the East during the reign of Dom João III (1521–57), which ushered in what Professor Francis Rogers has termed 'The Age of Latin Arrogance'.

The Council of Trent, the establishment of the Inquisition (1536) and of a rigid ecclesiastical censorship in Portugal, were closely followed by the destruction of the Hindu temples at Goa, and by an increasing tendency to regard the St. Thomas Christians and the Abyssinians as obstinate heretics who must be brought back into the fold of the Church as soon as possible. In Europe, the principle that ruler and ruled should share the same faith—*cujus regio illius religio*—became widely accepted by both Catholics and Protestants; and it was inevitable that the Portuguese should try to apply the same principle to the places where they exercised effective control. In practice this amounted to their settlements on the west coast of India and lowland Ceylon. The penal laws which from 1540 onwards were enacted against the public profession of Islam, Hinduism and Buddhism, in some of Portugal's Eastern possessions, have their counterpart in the penal laws enacted in European countries against the profession of any forms of Christianity which the respective governments were pleased to consider as subversive and heretical. One need only recall the treatment of Roman Catholics in Britain and Ireland, and the humiliations inflicted on Jews everywhere. It has been said, no doubt rightly, that 'man is a religious animal'. It can be stated with equal truth that man is also a persecuting animal. The history of Christianity, professedly a pacifist religion of brotherly love, affords ample proof of this fact; and the

Portuguese in India were no exceptions to this general rule.

The position of the Roman Catholic Church in Portugal and her overseas empire was already a powerful one by 1550, and it was further strengthened by the Counter Reformation, to which Portugal gave immediate and unconditional adherence. The priests were to a great extent immune from civil jurisdiction; the Religious Orders and the Church owned about one-third of the available land in Portugal itself, and much of the best lands in Portuguese India; priests and prelates often stayed a lifetime in Asia, thus providing a continuing influence which contrasted with the triennial term of viceroys and governors as epitomised in the popular Goan jingle, *Vice-rei vá, vice-rei vem, Padre Paulista sempre tem* ('Viceroys come and go, but the Jesuit Fathers are always with us'). Above all, the Portuguese had a deeply ingrained veneration for the sacerdotal status, which was reflected in another popular saying, 'the worst Religious is better than the best layman'. These are some of the factors which help to explain why in a deeply religious age Portugal's seaborne empire in Asia can be described as a military and maritime enterprise cast in an ecclesiastical mould. When some of the Crown officials at Goa remonstrated with the Viceroy, Dom Constantino de Bragança, over his efforts to convert the local Banyans by hook or by crook, pointing out that the collection of the Crown revenues would be greatly hindered thereby, 'he replied, like a most Christian prince, that he would prefer for the honour of the royal estate and the glory of His Highness, the conversion of the poorest Canarim in this island to all the profits derived from the lands thereof and carracks laden with pepper, and that he would risk everything for the salvation of a single soul'. Nor were these idle words; for it was the same viceroy who rejected the King of Pegu's offer of a royal ransom for the sacred relic of Buddha's tooth, which he had captured at Jaffnapatam, and which was publicly pounded to smithereens with a mortar and pestle by the Archbishop of Goa.

If the forcible conversion of adults was forbidden in theory by the Crown, and by the responsible ecclesiastical and civil authorities, this restriction did not apply to the conversion of Hindu orphans in the territories of Goa and Baçaim, where the use of force was explicitly sanctioned by a series of royal and viceregal decrees beginning with one promulgated at Lisbon in March 1559. In this decree, the Crown ordained that:

all children of heathens in the city and islands of Goa . . . who are left without father and without mother, and without grandfather or grandmother or any other forebears, and who are not yet of an age when they have a proper understanding and reasoned judgement . . . should forthwith be taken and handed over to the College of São Paulo of the Company of Jesus in the said city of Goa, in order that they may be baptised, educated and catechised by the Fathers of the said College.

Legislation was subsequently enacted, both at Lisbon and Goa, specifically authorising the use of force in taking such orphaned children from their surviving relatives, guardians, or friends, and force often had to be used.

Nor did this coercive legislation stop there. While the wording of the original decree of 1559 made it clear that an orphan child was defined as one who had lost both parents and both grandparents, the practice quickly arose of defining an orphan as a child who had lost his (or her) father, even if the mother and the grandparents were still living. The excuse for this ruling was that the *Ordenações*, or Portuguese code of law, defined an orphan in this way; and that this definition was equally applicable in colonial as well as in metropolitan territory. This definition was abolished in 1678, when the more liberal terms of the 1559 decree were restored. The age under which orphans could be forcibly taken from their non-Christian relatives was not specifically stated in the decree of 1559; and in practice it varied widely before being finally fixed at fourteen years for boys and twelve years for girls by a viceregal decree in 1718.

The task of ferreting out Hindu orphans and securing them if necessary by force was entrusted to a priest, who was called the *Pai dos Christãos*, or 'Father of the Christians'. As such, he exercised a wide range of powers in protecting and favouring the spiritual and temporal interests of the converts. The *Pai dos Christãos* was usually, though not invariably, a Jesuit; and holders of this post were appointed not only in Goa, but in Baçaim, in Ceylon, and in several other places where the Portuguese exercised effective jurisdiction in the East. Not surprisingly, the relatives of these Hindu orphans often made every effort to conceal these children from the unwelcome attentions of the *Pai*, and from those of the Inquisition after the establishment of this tribunal at Goa in 1560. Here again, however, theory and practice often differed widely. The *Pai* and the minions of the Holy Office sometimes complained that not merely adult Hindus favoured the smuggling of such children to Hindu or Muslim territory, but even native Christians did so on occasion. Similarly, the ecclesiastical authorities frequently alleged that the representatives of the civil power were lukewarm, or even downright obstructive, when called upon to support them in such activities.

Many other instances could be given to show how the Portuguese sometimes used force, or the threat of force, at certain times and places in order to forward their conversion policy in the East, but one more example will suffice. Padre Alexandre Valignano, the great reorganiser of the Jesuit missions in Asia during the last quarter of the sixteenth century, wrote that the saintly Xavier:

realised with his spirituality and prudence how incapable and primitive is the nature of this people in the things of God, and that reasoning does not make such an impression on them as does force. Therefore he considered that it would be very difficult to form any Christian community among the Niggers,[1] and much more difficult to preserve it, unless it was under the rule of the Portuguese, or in a region whither their power could be extended, as is the case with the sea coast, where the fleets of His Highness can cruise up and down, dealing out favours and punishments according to what the people there deserve.

Valignano added that the spectacular success of Xavier's missionary methods on the Fishery Coast was largely due to his judicious mixture of threats and blandishments, 'and now with the favours that he promised them, and at times adding some threats and fears of the harm that might come to them if the [Portuguese] captain deprived them of their fishing and seaborne trade, and finally *compellendo eos intrare ad nuptias* as the Lord says, he influenced a great multitude of them to become Christians'. Even if Valignano exaggerated Xavier's advocacy of what was later known as the 'gunboat policy', the fact remains that such

[1] '. . . *entre los negros*', although he was here referring to Indians in general, and to those of the Malabar coast in particular.

views were widespread among Portuguese missionaries in the East. The Church Militant was no mere figure of speech.

Nor, for that matter, was the Church Mercantile. Apart from the worldly clerics who were more interested in amassing riches than in saving souls, the religious Orders often had to temporise with Mammon in order to secure, in whole or in part, the money which they required for the support of their missions. By the terms of the *Padroado*, the Crown of Portugal was supposed to provide the funds needed for this purpose; but with the enormous commitments of its seaborne empire, it was seldom able to do so adequately. The balance had to be made up by private alms and charitable bequests, and in places where these did not suffice, and where the native Christians were too poor to support their churches and those who ministered to them, recourse was necessarily had to trade. The Jesuits were those who, voluntarily or involuntarily, most often employed this method of supporting their missions, above all in Japan. There was a popular if cynical saying in Portuguese Asia that payments made by the Crown were received either late, in part, or never (*tarde, mal, e nunca*). Although viceroys, governors and captains constantly complained that the Crown gave priority to payments for the ecclesiastical branch, rather than to naval, military or civil needs (as indeed it usually did), the royal exchequer was often empty and everyone had to go short.

When Padre Alexandre Valignano, S.J., was taxed by his superiors at Goa with having traded unlawfully in Chinese gold and silks with Portuguese India he retorted angrily from the Japan mission-field in 1599:

> By the grace of God I was not born the son of a merchant, nor was I ever one; but I am glad to have done what I did for the sake of Japan, and I believe that Our Lord also regards it as well done and that he gives and will give me many rewards therefor. Because if His Divine Majesty had not prompted me to do what I have done for Japan, it might very well be that Japan would now be in the throes of a still worse crisis without any hope of remedy. Wherefore, my friend, he who is well fed and wants for nothing, cannot be a good judge of the difficulties which beset those who are dying of hunger in great want. And if any of your Reverences could come here and see these provinces at close quarters, with their vast expenses and their miser-

ably small income and capital, and this latter derived from such uncertain and dangerous means, I can assure you that you would not peacefully sleep your time away . . . wherefore Your Reverence and the Father-Visitor should favour us in this matter, and not argue against us.

Valignano's logic was irrefutable, and it is not too much to say that without the aid provided, directly or indirectly, by Mammon, the Church in the Asian mission-fields would not have been able to function as effectively as it did.

By the end of the sixteenth century the Portuguese had largely abandoned the *conquistador* attitudes and mentality which had inspired them in the first decades of their expansion in Asia; and they were primarily concerned with peaceful trade and with keeping what they had already got. This pacific outlook was denounced by the more bellicose Spaniards at Manila, where a swashbuckling Dominican friar, Diego Aduarte, wrote in 1598: 'It is certain that neither the Royal Crown nor the Faith will be greatly increased by the Portuguese, since they are quite satisfied with holding the ports which they already have, in order to secure the sea for their trade.' A similar view was propounded a few years later by Hugo Grotius, who observed in his celebrated *Mare Liberum* (1609): 'The Portuguese in most places do not further the extension of the Faith or, indeed, pay any attention to it at all, since they are interested only in the acquisition of wealth.' It would be easy to multiply such unfavourable contemporary criticisms, not least from Portuguese sources; but in point of fact God was not everywhere subordinated to Mammon, as these derogatory remarks imply. On the contrary, even a cursory survey of 'Portuguese Asia' at the end of the sixteenth century reveals an impressive and a continuing achievement by the missionaries of the *Padroado* in general and by the Jesuits in particular.

Admittedly, no accurate assessment of the number of Christians in Asia at this period is possible. The writers of missionary reports had a fondness for round figures and for the multiplication-table which make many—perhaps most—of their reports suspect. Often no distinction is made between those people who were practising Christians with a fair knowledge of their faith, and those whose Christianity was merely nominal. Mass conversions were apt to be followed sooner or later by mass apostasies in regions where the Portuguese secular power could not be used to support the spiritual, or where the ruler (or the landowner) decided to persecute his Christian subjects (or tenants). The estimates which follow are inevitably loose approximations and are subject to revision in the light of further research.

Then, as now, Christian converts in Muslim lands were very few and far between, being mainly limited to women living with Portuguese men and to the children of these (usually illicit) unions, to runaway slaves, and to social outcasts. From Sofala to Pate in East Africa there can hardly have been more than a few hundred of these, though there may well have been a few thousand Christian converts among the Bantu Negroes including the slaves in the same area. The Portuguese possessions in the Persian Gulf contained even fewer indigenous Christians, for obvious reasons, nor were there many in Diu, where (as we have seen) Hinduism and Islam were officially tolerated. On the west coast of India the coastal strip between Damão and Chaul known as the 'Province of the North' probably contained something between 10,000 and 15,000 Christians, mainly in and around Baçaim. Goa and its adjacent islands, together with the mainland districts of Salcete and Bardez, may have contained some 50,000 or rather more; and Cochin, the Kanara and Malabar coastal settlements a very few thousand, apart from the St. Thomas Christians. Estimates of the Christian population of the Fishery Coast vary between 60,000 and 130,000, and I would not like to suggest which figure is nearer the mark.

A figure of 30,000 for Ceylon may well be fairly reliable, although it is not clear whether this includes the Tamil kingdom of Jaffna and Manar in the north of the island, which was often regarded as a separate entity from the Sinhalese kingdom. There must have been a few thousand Christians in and around the Portuguese trading settlements on the Coromandel coast, in Bengal and in Arakan; but there were few Christians at this period in Malacca, Siam, Burma and Indochina. Something between 15,000 and 20,000 for the islands of Indonesia would be the most favourable estimate, most of these converts being concentrated in the Ambonia group and in Solor in the Lesser Sunda Islands. Macao had a population of some 3,000 Christian souls, but the

Jesuits' missionary work on the mainland of China, which had such spectacular results in the seventeenth century, was still in the embryo stage. Last not least, both for quantity and for quality, was the prized mission-field of Japan. Here the Christian community may have numbered as many as 300,000; most of them in and around Nagasaki, in the island of Kyushu, and in the capital of Kyoto and its immediate neighbourhood.

Excluding those of the St. Thomas Christians of the Syriac-Chaldean rite who were reconciled with the Church of Rome at the synod of Diamper in 1599, these (very rough) estimates give us a total of something between half a million and a million Roman Catholic Christians in the area from Sofala to Sendai, the real figure being probably nearer the latter total than the former. This may not seem very many in comparison with the teeming millions who adhered to their traditional faiths; but it is undeniably impressive when we consider that most of this harvest had been reaped between 1550 and 1599, and when we recall the relatively small numbers of missionaries active in the field.

Japan, the best and most promising mission-field, had only 137 Jesuit missionaries in 1597; and the (estimated) 16,000 Christians of the Moluccas had been ministered to by a mere fifty Jesuits between 1546 and the end of the century. Moreover, the wastage from death and disease among missionary personnel was inevitably high at a period when the scientific origins and cures of tropical diseases were virtually unknown. Thus fifty-eight Jesuits died in the Eastern mission-fields during the four years 1571–4, many of them prominent personalities. In some of the unhealthier stations, such as Zambesia and the Moluccas, there might be only five or six missionaries available to serve an enormous region at any given time. Nor was the work of conversion notably forwarded by the Gestapo-like activities of the so-called and self-styled Holy Office of the Inquisition; and the burning of Hindu widows in suttee was replaced by the roasting to death of Jews in the *autos-da-fé* celebrated at Goa.

One of the principal difficulties with which the missionaries had to contend was the suspicion of many Asian princes and potentates that those of their subjects or retainers who accepted Christianity tended to become more closely identified with the European intruders than with the land of their own birth. This was to some extent unavoidable, particularly in India, where the high-caste convert from Hinduism automatically became an 'untouchable', and so was compelled to rely on his European co-religionists for protection and support. In China, Indochina and Japan, suspicion that the Christian converts would form the nucleus of what is nowadays termed a 'fifth column' was widespread and not altogether unjustified. One need only recall the Jesuit Padre Alonso Sánchez' ambitious scheme for the conquest of China in 1588, with the aid of auxiliary troops recruited from Christianised Japanese and Filipinos. Sánchez' scheme was quickly repudiated by his more sensible colleagues; but it is significant that twenty years later a Jesuit chronicler could claim in his officially approved history of the Portuguese missions in Asia: 'As many heathen as are converted to Christ, just so many friends and vassalls does His Majesty's service acquire, because these converts later fight for the State [of Portuguese India] and the Christians against their unconverted countrymen.'

In view of the obstacles with which the missionaries had to contend, not the least of which was often their own ignorance of the religious beliefs of those whom they were trying to convert, it is in some ways surprising that they made as many converts as they did, particularly in places where (unlike Goa, or the lands of the Christian *daimyo* in Japan) the secular arm, or else commercial greed, could not be employed as a menace or as an attraction. God, moving in a mysterious way His wonders to perform, doubtless provides an answer which would satisfy the pious believer both then and now; but those of more mundane views might consider that there were some other factors at work. It is surely rather significant that in several of the Buddhist lands where the missionaries achieved their greatest success, notably in Ceylon and Japan, Buddhism was just then at a low ebb of spirituality and efficacy. In some ways it may not be fanciful to compare the decadent state of Buddhism in both those countries to that of the Roman Catholic Church in much of Western Europe on the eve of the Reformation.

Another factor which clearly operated in the missionaries' favour was the striking similarity of many of the outward manifestations of Hinduism and Buddhism (the use of images, incense and rosaries, orders of monks and nuns, the colourful ceremonies and temples) with those of the Roman Catholic Church. It is true that the missionaries usually did not see things in this light, and they often blamed the Devil for sacrilegiously grafting Catholic practices on to those Eastern religions in order to confuse the Faithful. But the subsequent experiences of the Calvinist and other Protestant missionaries in Asia clearly indicated that such superficial similarities made the transition from the indigenous religion to the Roman Catholic faith relatively easier than it did to the bleakly austere dogmas and practices deriving from Jean Calvin, Theodore Beza and John Knox. It is also worthy of remark that the Christian missionaries in Hindu and Buddhist lands often scored their greatest and most enduring successes among the fisher castes and classes. This was doubtless due, at least in part, to the deep-rooted conventional Buddhist and Hindu prejudice against the taking of animal life. The fishing castes and classes, who were despised by their co-religionists in Tuticorin, Manar and in Kyushu, found acceptance and an enhanced self-respect in Christianity. Even in Muslim Malacca the only section of the population which has remained Christian down to the present day is the fishing community.

Finally, it should be stressed that the influence of Christianity in sixteenth-century Asia was not confined to those who accepted conversion. There were Jesuit missionaries resident at the court of the Great Moghul, though their sanguine expectations of converting the Emperors Akbar and Jahangir were disappointed. There were also Jesuits at the court of the *Taiko* Hideyoshi, even in the period when Christian missionaries were ostensibly forbidden to live outside Nagasaki; and the Jesuit Visitor, Valignano, acted as envoy from the viceroy of Goa to the military dictator of Japan. Franciscan friars converted the last Sinhalese ruler of Kotte, who claimed the paramountcy over Ceylon, and who bequeathed that island to the King of Portugal (and Spain) in his last will and testament. The Shah of Persia received Augustinian friars in his capital, and the kings of Siam and Cambodia allowed Dominican and other missionaries in theirs, at any rate for a time.

Despite the cultural myopia which afflicted many missionaries, others were more perceptive, and they acted as cultural catalysts between Asia and Europe. The European paintings and engravings brought by the Jesuits to Akbar's court made a deep and lasting impression on Indian painters, as can be seen from the numerous miniatures which clearly reveal European influences and motifs. The Jesuits introduced the first printing press with movable types to India and (perhaps) to Japan, besides printing at Nagasaki (in 1599) a Japanese abridgement of the Dominican Luís de Granada's *Sinners' Guide* in a mixture of movable types and woodblocks. In Ming China the missionaries had already begun under Matteo Ricci's inspiration that tactful introduction of Western science which gave them such a privileged position in the following century. But, above all, they enormously enlarged the scope and depth of Europe's knowledge of Asia by the letters and reports which they sent from their mission-fields, and which were widely circulated through the medium of the principal European presses.

CHAPTER IV

Slaves and sugar in the South Atlantic 1500-1600

It is immaterial to us whether Brazil was discovered accidentally or of set purpose by the Portuguese of Pedro Álvares Cabral's outward-bound India fleet in April 1500, but the 'Land of the True Cross', as these discoverers christened it, was soon called 'Brazil' from the profitable red dyewood of that name which was found in some quantity along the littoral. Concentration on the India trade, on the gold of Guinea (Mina), and on the wars in Morocco, for many years prevented the Portuguese Crown from devoting serious attention to this newly discovered region, which seemed to contain nothing better than dyewood, parrots, monkeys and stark-naked savages of the most primitive kind. These Amerindians were of the linguistic family of Tupí-Guaraní, the men being hunters, fishers and food-gatherers, leaving to the women what little agricultural work they knew. Their wandering tribes or family groups knew the use of fire but not of metal, and the more settled tribes built stockaded villages containing a few large sleeping-huts made of stakes, woven grass and thatch. The manioc plant provided many of them with their staple food after its poisonous juice had been extracted; and some, but by no means all, of the tribes practised ritual cannibalism.

First impressions of these stark-naked Stone Age savages were very favourable. They were described as being innocent children of Nature, just like Adam and Eve in the Garden of Eden before the Fall. Pedro Vaz de Caminha, the eyewitness reporter of this idyllic encounter, wrote to King Manuel:

They seem to me to be people of such innocence that, if we could understand them and they us, they would soon become Christians, because they do not seem to have or to understand any form of religion. . . . For it is certain that this people is good and of pure simplicity, and there can easily be stamped upon them whatever belief we wish to give them. And furthermore, Our Lord gave them fine bodies and good faces as to good men, and He who brought us here, I believe, did not do so without purpose . . . there were among them three or four girls, very young and very pretty, with very dark hair, long over the shoulders, and their privy parts so high, so closed and so free from hair that we felt no shame in looking hard at them . . . one of the girls was all painted from head to foot with that [bluish-black] paint, and she was so well built and so rounded, and her lack of shame was so charming, that many women of our own land seeing such attractions, would be ashamed that theirs were not like hers.

This Portuguese anticipation of the eighteenth-century French *philosophes'* conception of the 'Noble Savage' is often cited by modern writers as evidence of the Lusitanian lack of a colour-bar and of the Portuguese proclivity for mating with coloured women. In point of fact it was merely the natural reaction of sex-starved sailors, and it can easily be paralleled by similar reactions on the part of eighteenth-century English and French seamen to the scantily clad Polynesian beauties of Tahiti and the Pacific Islands. Moreover, this flattering comparison of these Stone Age savages with the innocent inhabitants of an earthly paradise or a vanished golden age did not last very long—any more than did the similar reactions of Columbus and his Spanish mariners to the Arawaks of the Caribbean Islands discovered on his first voyage. The stereotype of the Brazilian Indian as an unspoilt child of Nature was quickly replaced by the popular Portuguese conviction that he was an irredeemable savage, '*sem fé, sem rei, sem lei*', without religion, king or law.

This change in attitude became much more pronounced and general—though it was never universal—after about the middle of the sixteenth century. It was largely the result of the substitution of sugar for brazilwood as the country's principal export, and the consequent need for a disciplined (or a slave) labour force. During the first three decades of this period Portuguese contacts with Brazil were virtually limited to transient traders and seamen who came to barter iron tools and European trinkets and baubles for brazilwood, parrots, monkeys, and such food as they needed during their stay. These activities did not involve any permanent settlement, though there were a number of castaways or runaways who 'went native' and became members of some Amerindian tribal group. This barter economy resulted in fairly easy and amicable race relations on the whole, though there were, of course, the inevitable misunderstandings and clashes. Moreover, French mariners and merchants from Normandy and Rouen likewise frequented the Brazilian coast for the purpose of obtaining brazilwood by barter during this period on as large, or possibly even greater, a scale than did the Portuguese. At first the Amerindians made no distinction between the two rival European nations; but by 1530 they had learned to do so. Their age-old inter-tribal rivalries were thenceforward further inflamed by some groups, chiefly the Tupinambá, supporting the French, and others, chiefly the Tupiniquíns, allying themselves with the Portuguese.

The growing menace that the French might settle permanently in this portion of South America, which had been assigned to the Portuguese Crown by the outcome of the Treaty of Tordesillas (1494), eventually induced King Dom João III systematically to promote the colonisation of Brazil. The system which he adopted in 1534 was to divide the coastline between the Amazon river and São Vicente into a dozen hereditary captaincies (*capitanias*) of a limited width varying between thirty and a hundred leagues, but with an indefinite extension into the interior. The four northerly captaincies, lying between Paraíba do Norte and the Amazon, were not occupied during the sixteenth century, though the *donatários*, or lords proprietors, to whom they had been allotted, vainly attempted to do so. Of the remaining eight, only Pernambuco in the north-east and São Vicente in the extreme south succeeded in overcoming the 'teething troubles' of their pioneer days, and they became relatively important centres of population and economic growth. The others were either abandoned as a result of Amerindian attacks or else vegetated in complete obscurity with a few settlers who maintained a precarious toe-hold at isolated spots on the coastal fringe. A further step was taken by the King in 1549, when a governor-general was sent out to establish a new and centrally situated captaincy at Bahia, which came under the direct administration of the Crown. He was accompanied by a number of Jesuit missionaries, who were charged with the tasks of converting the Amerindians and educating and reforming the morals of the colonists, many of whom at this period were exiled convicts or *degredados*. The French, who had meanwhile established themselves in Rio de Janeiro, were expelled from 'La France Antartique', as they ambitiously called it, in 1565. The Brazilian littoral was thenceforward under Portuguese control, though the only region where the settlers penetrated far into the interior was the southernmost district of São Paulo de Piratininga.

The *donatários* who took up the original grants in 1534 and their successors were not great nobles or wealthy merchants, but members of the gentry and lesser nobility. They had not, for the most part, the capital and other resources to enable them to develop their lands, despite the extensive juridical and fiscal privileges which they were granted by the Crown. These privileges included the right to found townships and grant municipal rights to them; the right of capital punishment over slaves, heathen and low-class Christian freemen; the right to levy local taxation, except as regards commodities (like brazilwood) which were Crown monopolies; and the right to licence buildings such as sugar mills, and to receive tithes on certain products such as sugar and fish. The *donatário* system, with its mixture of feudal and capitalistic elements, had previously been used successfully to develop the islands of Madeira and the Azores, and it was applied less successfully to the Cape Verdes and for a short time (in 1575) to Angola.

Whether they were ultimately successful or not, the institution of these captaincies, and the establishment of a central government authority at Bahia, brought thousands of Portuguese settlers to the Brazilian littoral, thereby leading to a marked shift in the hitherto rather casual relationship between Portuguese and Amerindians. The pioneer settlers (*moradores*) likewise depended at first largely on barter trade with the local Amerindians to supply them with food and labour, as the transient traders and loggers in brazilwood had done. But when the settlers began to cultivate allotments or clearings (*roças*) where food crops (chiefly manioc) were grown, and to lay out sugar plantations, as they did in Pernambuco and Bahia, they found it very difficult to secure an assured supply of sufficient Amerindian labour. The aboriginals were prepared to work intermittently for such tools and trinkets as they fancied; but they showed no disposition to labour for long periods, still less for a working lifetime in the back-breaking toil of farm, field and plantation.

On the other hand, the Portuguese who emigrated to Brazil, even if they were peasants from the tail of the plough, had no intention of doing any manual work, in what was represented to them as being a new promised land, if they could possibly avoid it. The inevitable result was that when they found that the Amerindians were unwilling to work for them as long-term agricultural labourers, or as bondservants, they tried to force them to do so as slaves. They secured such slaves partly by 'ransoming' or buying captives taken in the frequent inter-tribal wars, and partly by direct raids on Amerindian villages, which were actually or allegedly hostile to the settlers. The enslavement of the Amerindians was categorically forbidden by the Crown in 1570, save in cases where they might have been captured in a 'just war', or from cannibal tribes. This decree was not taken very seriously by most of the *moradores*, but other causes combined to reduce the numbers available for work on the plantations. With the decimation of many Amerindian groups through wars and the introduction of European diseases such as smallpox, and with a high death rate among Amerindian slaves who could not endure plantation servitude, the *moradores* were increasingly forced to seek an alternative supply during the second half of the sixteenth century.

This supply was secured through the expansion and intensification of the existing trade in Negro slaves with West Africa. These slaves had already had been used on an extensive scale to develop several of the Cape Verde Islands, and to a lesser extent in Madeira and in the southern regions of Portugal itself. Large numbers were also being exported to the Antilles and the Spanish empire in the New World by the middle of the sixteenth century. But the most spectacular and successful use of Negro slave labour was afforded by the islands of São Tomé and Príncipe in the Gulf of Guinea. Uninhabited when first discovered by the Portuguese about 1470, they were colonised by a mixture of white settlers sent from Portugal (including levies of Jewish children deported in the 1490s) and by a labour force of Negro slaves secured from a wide variety of tribes on the mainland, many of whom subsequently gained their freedom. The soil and climate of São Tomé proved to be very favourable for the cultivation of sugar, and the island experienced a remarkable economic boom for most of the sixteenth century with the rapid increase in the European demand for sugar. The São Tomé sugar industry was a flourishing one by 1530, and production increased from some 5,000 *arrobas* in that year to over 150,000 *arrobas* in 1550. The transplantation of sugar cultivation and of Negro slavery to Brazil, which began during those years, was a natural outcome of the example afforded by São Tomé.

The lush greenery of tropical shores was no novelty to the Portuguese pioneers in Brazil, as some of them had become accustomed to what was a superficially similar environment in their voyages of discovery and trade along the west coast of Africa. But if there were some similarities between the tropical lands on both sides of the South Atlantic, there were also marked differences. The Portuguese settlers soon found that there were many physical drawbacks and natural hazards in the vast and varied continent between the Amazonian jungle and the rolling plains of the southernmost region which now goes by the name of Rio Grande do Sul, even if these drawbacks were in some respects less inimical to white settlers than were the fever-stricken regions of West Africa. Numerous insect pests made any kind of agriculture a gamble in many regions of Brazil, even if the African tsetse-fly was not one of them. Droughts ravaged some parts of Brazil for years on end, especially in the hinterland of the north-east, where the ecology seems to have got worse rather than better during the last three centuries. Elsewhere, the capricious Brazilian climate was apt to alternate between excessive rains and floods on the one hand and totally insufficient rainfall on the other. Though the soil was rich enough in some districts, such as the sugar-growing regions of the *Recôncavo* of Bahia and the *Várzea* of Pernambuco, it was mostly very poor in organic chemical elements once the tropical jungle and vegetation had been cleared to make room for cultivation. The dearth of calcium was (and is) particularly serious, adversely affecting the nutritional value of such plants as did grow. With the notable exception of the Amazon and its tributaries, the rivers in Brazil did not afford easy access to the interior, as navigation upstream was blocked by rapids and falls within relatively short distances of the coastal estuaries. This physical handicap did not apply to the same extent in West Africa, where, however, the Negro societies, whether of Sudanese or Bantu origin, formed a more cohesive and stronger barrier to penetration of the interior than did the wandering Amerindians of Brazil.

On the other hand, as indicated above (p. 53), conditions in parts of Portugal were often such that many people had no alternative but to emigrate. Brazil, with all its drawbacks, gave them opportunities of a better life than they could hope to find at home. Portugal, no less than Brazil, suffered from capricious and ill-distributed rainfall, and from organic poverty of the soil in many regions. The mother country was severely ravaged by bouts of plague in the sixteenth and seventeenth centuries, something which did not occur in Brazil until the yellow fever visitations of the 1680s. Overpopulation and pressure on the land in certain fertile regions (Minho) in northern Portugal, and in the Atlantic islands of Madeira and the Azores, provided a constant stream of emigrants; and from about 1570 onwards increasing numbers of these people sailed for Brazil rather than for 'Golden' Goa and the East. *Degredados* or exiled convicts had formed 400 out of the original 1,000 settlers of Bahia in 1549; but thenceforward the voluntary emigrants heavily outnumbered those who were deported from their country for their country's good. Moreover, although there were naturally many more male emigrants than there were female, yet the proportion of the latter who accompanied their menfolk to Brazil was much higher than the tiny trickle of women who embarked for India.

Ambrosio Fernandes Brandão, a settler with wide experience of north-east Brazil at the end of the sixteenth century, divided the Portuguese immigrants into five categories. Firstly, the sailors and mariners who manned the ships sailing between Portugal and Brazil; though, strictly speaking, these men were not immigrants but transient visitors, even if they maintained the sailor's traditional wife or girl-friend in every port. Secondly, the merchants and traders, many of whom worked on a commission basis for principals in Portugal. Brandão accused these traders, rather unfairly, of doing nothing to enrich the colony, but on the contrary seeking to strip it of all the wealth they could. Thirdly, the craftsmen and artisans, working for their own account as stonemasons, carpenters, coopers, tailors, cobblers, goldsmiths, etc. Nearly all of these artisans relied on slave labour, once they had earned enough money to buy a slave (or slaves) whom they could train in their craft. Fourthly, those men who served others as salaried labourers, overseers or foremen on sugar plantations, or as stockmen on cattle ranches. Fifthly, the employer class, the most important of whom were the *senhores de engenho* or sugar mill and plantation owners. These planters already formed the local aristocracy and they gave themselves the airs of gentry and nobility, however humble or disreputable their social origins might have been. Brandão alleged that most men among all of these five classes were anxious to return to Portugal as soon as they had accumulated enough money to do so and retire in comfort. Here he was obviously exaggerating; and he admitted that in any case the great majority had to remain in Brazil where most of them married and raised families, thus contracting ties with the country and the people which they could not easily sever.

Padre Fernão Cardim, a Jesuit contemporary of Brandão, has left us another interesting eyewitness description of Brazil at this period, which was taken from him by English corsairs in 1601, and published by Samuel Purchas twenty-four years later. Since part of Cardim's original *Tratado* has been lost, I will quote from Purchas' translation where necessary, though modernising the spelling and punctuation. Cardim was frankly eulogistic about the climate of Brazil, which he extolled as being generally 'temperate, of good, delicate and healthful air', better than that of Portugal. He was struck by the longevity of the inhabitants, whether the indigenous Amerindians or the Portuguese settlers, as 'the men live long, even to ninety, a hundred, and more years, and the country is full of old men'. He was duly impressed by the 'very pure and clear' beauty of the tropical nights under the Southern Cross. But, like most of his contemporaries, he was obsessed with the medieval belief in the baleful influence of the moon, which, he wrote, 'is very prejudicial unto health, and corrupteth the things very much'. He noted the short dawns and twilights, and the fact that in the southern hemisphere 'their winter beginneth in March and endeth in August; the summer beginneth in September and endeth in February; the nights and days are all the year almost equal'. He made the rather curious comment that the country was 'somewhat melancholic', which he attributed to the heavy rainfall and the numerous flowing rivers. He noted the scarcity of building-stone in some of the coastal regions, and that the land lacked suitable primary materials for clothing with the exception of cotton. Cattle and sugar were the chief products in the settled districts; and in these regions 'the food and waters are generally healthful, light, and of easy digestion'.

In comparing Brazil with Portugal, Cardim considered that the former enjoyed a 'much more temperate and healthful climate, without great heats or colds, where the men do live long, with few sicknesses, as the colic, or the liver, the head, the breast, scabs, nor any other diseases of Portugal'. The sea off the Brazilian coast afforded an inexhaustible supply of edible and succulent fishes, and there was a welcome dearth of lice and fleas ashore. Admittedly, colonial houses were on the modest side, 'for most of them are of mud walls, and thatched, though now they begin to make buildings of lime and stone and tiles'. The chief shortages were of European clothing materials and manufactured goods, particularly in the poorer and sparsely populated southern captaincies. In Pernambuco and Bahia, on the other hand, 'they are provided with all kinds of clothing and silks, and the men go well apparelled, and wear many silks and velvets'. The relative absence of lice and fleas was offset by the presence of other insect pests, including stinging insects 'of so many kinds and so cruel and venomous, that stinging any person, the place swelleth for three or four days, especially in the fresh men, which have their blood fresh and tender, with the good bread, wine and delicate fare of Portugal'. It is rather curious that in his enumeration of the insect pests of Brazil, Padre Cardim does not mention the ubiquitous ant, which was christened by the exasperated sugar planters 'the King of Brazil' (*O Rei do Brasil*).

Father Cardim was extremely critical of the way in which the Portuguese settlers (*moradores*), or most of them, mistreated the Amerindians, killing and enslaving them with (and without) the slightest provocation, despite reiterated royal orders and official legislation prohibiting such atrocities. His eyewitness report is but one of many sixteenth- and seventeenth-century documents which describe in detail how the Amerindians were either killed or enslaved or exploited by the majority of the settlers and the Crown officials, while the Jesuit missionaries were virtually alone in trying to act as their friends and protectors. When due allowance has been made for exaggeration, and for the fact that the Amerindians did not always refrain from wantonly hostile acts, and that some of them were indeed cannibals, the weight of evidence makes it abundantly clear that 'the Black Legend' had a strong basis of truth in Portuguese as well as in Spanish America. Cardim gives several examples of how the settlers lured the Amerindians from their villages in the backlands (*sertão*) to the coastal region, where they then subjugated and enslaved them. On occasion, the slave-raiders even disguised themselves as Jesuit missionaries, complete with cassocks and tonsures, in order to win the confidence of the savages, since the Jesuits were, by and large, the only white men whom the Amerindians would trust.

Cardim's allegations concerning the ways in which the Portuguese settlers often acted on the principle later followed by the Anglo-Saxons in North America that 'the only good Indian was a dead one' are too numerous to reproduce here. It will suffice to quote one of his observations which stresses the gulf between royal precept and colonial practice that always bedevilled this problem from first to last.

As touching the justice that is used with the Indians, the King our lord is to understand that although His Majesty, as all the Kings his predecessors, do recommend always this matter of the Indians to the Governors above all as their principal duty, with very effectual words, notwithstanding the justice that until now hath been in Brazil towards them was none or very little, as it is plainly seen by the assaults, robberies, captivities and other vexations that always were done to them, and even now are done. Against the Indians was always a rigorous justice; they have already been hanged, hewn in pieces, quartered, their hands cut off, nipped with hot pincers and set in the mouth of cannon, for killing or helping to kill some Portuguese (who peradventure had well deserved it at their hands). But having persons, not a few in Brazil, as always there were, and yet there are, notoriously infamous for robbing, stealing, branding, selling and killing many Indians, never until this time was there any show of punishment; and it is to be feared, seeing it wanteth on earth, that it will come from Heaven on all the inhabitants of Brazil.

As indicated above and below, there is plenty of evidence to disprove the modern Portuguese claim that their colonisation of Brazil was a bloodless affair, marked by an instinctive sympathy for and an understanding of the Amerindians, which other colonising nations in America, whether Spaniards, English, French or Dutch, did not possess. But it would, of course, be equally erroneous to undervalue the very real achievements of the Portuguese in colonising Brazil, and to assert that the aboriginals were always and everywhere as ill-treated as Cardim and other contemporary critics alleged. If the settlers for the most part regarded the Amerindians as an exploitable and expendable source of forced labour, there was also a certain amount of intermittently peaceful inter-racial assimilation. In Pernambuco, for example, where two generations of the pioneer *donatário* family of Duarte Coelho had a hard time to establish their colony in the face of much opposition from some of the local tribes in 1540–70, these years of strife likewise witnessed the amorous exploits of the philoprogenitive *conquistador* Jeronimo de Albuquerque. He was described as being 'naturally of a mild and friendly disposition; and since he had many children by the daughters of the tribal chiefs, he treated the latter with consideration'. The 'Pernambucan Adam', as this patriarch was christened on account of his numerous progeny, acknowledged a total of twenty-four offspring in 1584, and many of the leading Pernambuco families at the present day are proud to claim descent from his Amerindian 'princess', Maria do Espirito Santo Arco-Verde, who is the Brazilian (and more fecund) equivalent of the Virginian Pocahontas.

The Jesuits tried to domesticate and Christianise the wandering Amerindians by gathering them in village mission settlements (*aldeias*), as their Spanish colleagues subsequently did with conspicuous success in the better-known Reductions of Paraguay. These *aldeias* were originally located fairly near the white settlements and townships, since the Jesuits were constrained to allow their charges to perform manual labour for the Portuguese

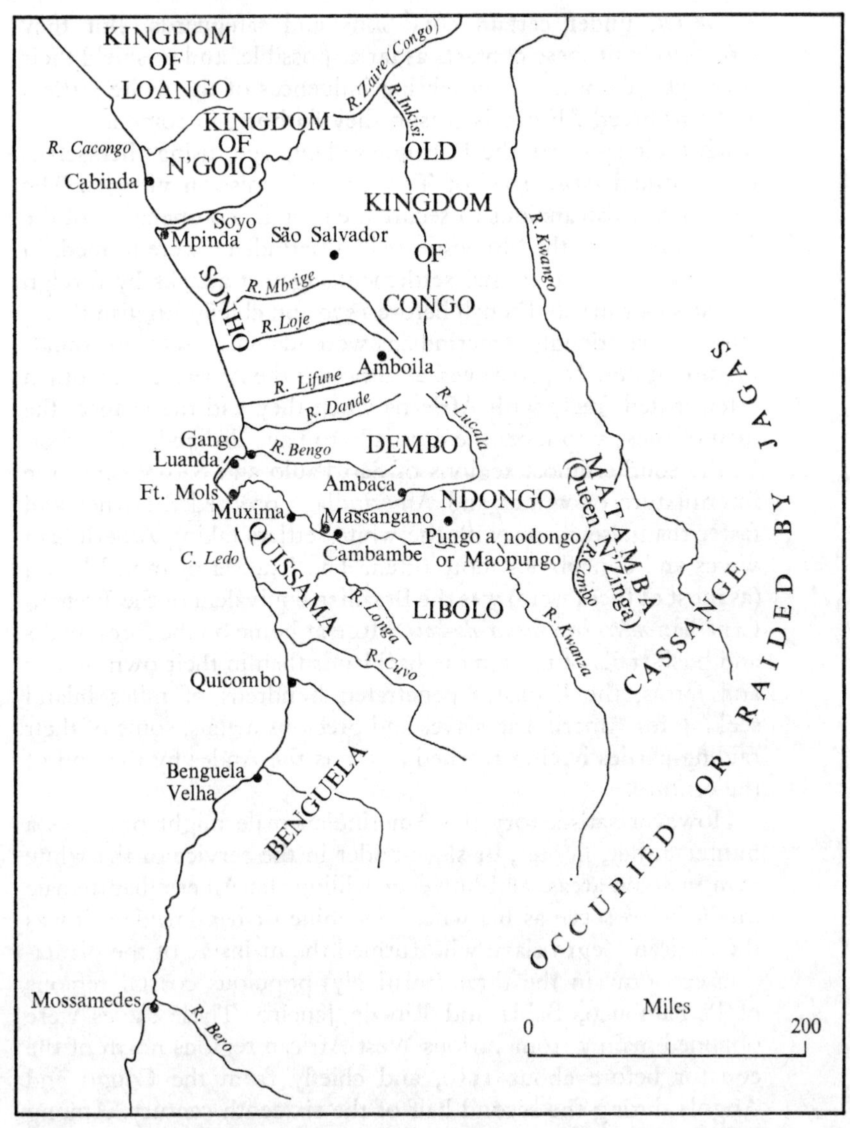

3 Angola and the Congo Kingdom, sixteenth to eighthteenth centuries

moradores, under certain conditions and safeguards. But they strove to limit these contacts as far as possible, and to shield their neophytes from the demoralising influences of the white settlers and half-breeds. For this reason they forbore, in some areas, to teach their converts the Portuguese language, using themselves the so-called *lingua geral* of Tupí in their mission villages. The Crown was also anxious to secure the friendly co-operation of the *Indios Mansos*, as the 'domesticated' Amerindians were termed, in the defence of the coastal settlements against attacks by foreign corsairs—primarily French before 1570 and chiefly English thereafter. These friendly Amerindians were likewise useful in rounding up fugitive Negro slaves, as although the Amerindian women often mated freely with Africans when they had the chance, the men of these two races seem usually to have disliked each other. In the southernmost regions of São Paulo and São Vicente the intermixture of whites and Amerindians proceeded farther and faster than elsewhere, with the white settlers taking Amerindian wives and concubines more often. The Paulista of mixed blood (as most of them were) was the Brazilian equivalent of the French-Canadian *métis* or *coureur-du-bois*. More at home on the forest paths and bush-trails of the remote backlands than in their own houses and farms, the Paulistas penetrated hundreds of miles inland seeking for Amerindian slaves and precious metals, some of their raiding-parties having reached as far as the Andes by the end of the century.

However satisfactory the Amerindian male might prove as a hunter, fisher, fighter, or slave-raider in the service of the white man in some areas, and however willing the Amerindian female might be to serve as his wife, concubine or handmaiden, it was the African Negro slave who formed the mainstay of the plantation economy in the three (relatively) populous coastal regions of Pernambuco, Bahia and Rio de Janeiro. These slaves were obtained mainly from various West African regions north of the equator before about 1550, and chiefly from the Congo and Angola during the second half of the sixteenth century. Among the west Sudanese groups from which slaves were originally received were the Jolofs and Mandinga of Senegambia, the Ardra and Yoruba of the slave coast in Lower Guinea, and the inhabitants of Benin and Warri in the Niger river delta. The islands of São Tomé and Príncipe, especially the former, soon became entrepôts where slaves from Lower Guinea, and later from Loango and Congo, were assembled prior to being traded for gold at São Jorge da Mina, or else dispatched for sale to Lisbon, to Brazil, or to Spanish America. A similar function was performed by the Cape Verde island of Santiago for many of the slaves originating in Senegambia. The slave trade of São Tomé, and consequently the development of sugar cultivation in that island, received a great stimulus after the Portuguese had established friendly relations with the Bantu kingdom of Congo in 1483. The story of the abortive attempt to implant the Christian religion and European civilisation in this African kingdom during the first half of the sixteenth century has often been told and need only be resumed in briefest outline here. It epitomises in the most striking way the dichotomy which bedevilled the Portuguese approach to the black Africans for so long—the desire to save their immortal souls coupled with the urge to enslave their vile bodies.

The core of the old kingdom of Congo lay in what is now northern Angola, centred on the city of Mbanza Kongo, which was later renamed São Salvador. It was bounded on the north by the river Zaire (Congo), on the south by the river Loje, and the eastern boundary ran roughly southwards from Stanley Pool and parallel to the river Kwango. Various states and tribes to the east and south of these boundaries intermittently recognised the overlordship of the Congo by the occasional dispatch of tribute and presents to the *Mani*, titular chief or king, at Mbanza Kongo. The southernmost of these rather tenuous tributaries was the *Ngola*, king or chief of Ndongo between the Dande and Kwanza rivers. The peoples of this savanna region south of the equatorial forest, including the Congolese and the Mbundu or Ambundu, practised shifting cultivation and the rotation of different crops. They knew how to work metals, including iron and copper, and they were fairly skilled potters. They wove mats and articles of clothing from raffia tissues or palm-cloth, and their skill in this respect excited the admiration of the Portuguese pioneers. They had domesticated several animals—pigs, sheep, chickens and in some districts cattle—though they did not use milk, butter, or cheese. They lived for the most part in huts or kraals constructed of flimsy materials and usually rectangular in shape. Their agricultural implements were limited to the hoe and the axe, but the millet, sorghum and beans which they cultivated were supplemented by the fruits of the forest and the products of the chase. Tribal law and custom regulated their daily lives, and their medicine-men or witch-doctors were held in high esteem. The Congolese did not know the art of writing; but the Portuguese considered that they were the most advanced of the Negro races whom they had hitherto discovered; and these iron-age Bantu were indubitably much more so than the Stone-age Brazilian Amerindians.

The Congolese monarchy was not an hereditary one. The king was usually succeeded by one of his sons; but the succession was generally contested, and the victorious claimant then killed his rivals and their principal supporters. Once established on the throne, the king theoretically enjoyed absolute power, but in practice he had to pay a good deal of attention to the opinions of the leading nobles. The most important of these were the governors of five of the six provinces into which the kingdom was divided (the central sixth province being governed by him personally). These governors or rulers were responsible for collecting and forwarding to the capital the provincial tributes of palm-cloth, ivory, hides, and slaves. Sea-shells called *nzimbu* were the most valued form of currency; and these were obtained exclusively from the island of Luanda, which was directly administered by a royal representative.

The Portuguese kings of the House of Aviz from 1483 onwards did not attempt to secure political control of the kingdom of Congo, nor did they try to conquer it by force of arms. They were content to recognise the kings of Congo as their brothers-in-arms; to treat them as allies and not as vassals, and to try to convert them and their subjects to Christianity by the dispatch of missionaries to the Congo and by educating selected Congolese youths at Lisbon. The early Portuguese embassies and missions to the Congo included not only priests and friars but skilled workers and artisans, such as stone-masons, bricklayers, blacksmiths and agricultural labourers. Two German printers at Lisbon emigrated voluntarily with their printing press to the island of São Tomé in 1492, presumably with the intention of working in or for the Congo kingdom, though nothing of whatever they may have printed has survived. Several Portuguese women were sent out to teach the local ladies the arts of domestic economy as practised in Portugal. One of the Congolese princes sent to Europe for his education was in due course consecrated titular Bishop of Utica, with the rather reluctant consent of the Pope, at the King of Portugal's insistence in 1518. The most ardent advocate of Western religion and civilisation in the sixteenth-century Congo was King Nzinga Nvemba, called Dom Afonso I after his conversion to Christianity, who ruled from 1506 to 1543. This monarch was a genuine, fervent and intelligent convert to Christianity, who did his utmost to implant the new religion by precept and example. Portuguese missionaries, traders and workers were warmly welcomed, and for a time at least the Congolese showed an enthusiastic willingness to adopt (or adapt) European patterns of life which anticipated that of the Japanese 350 years later. What, then, prevented this Bantu kingdom from becoming Westernised four and a half centuries ago, when King Manuel I of Portugal and King Afonso I of Congo both regarded this as a consummation devoutly to be wished?

In the first place there were never enough missionaries, instructors and artisans to teach the Congolese effectively. Dom Afonso repeatedly pleaded for many more to be sent him, but nothing like a sufficient number ever came. Many of those who did come soon died, as nothing was then known of the causes and cures of malarial fever and other tropical diseases. Secondly, many of the missionaries who came were of indifferent character with no true sense of vocation, for clerical morality in contemporary Portugal was at a very low ebb, as it was elsewhere in Europe. Thirdly, Portgual's vast and increasing overseas commitments from the Spice Islands to São Vicente, together with the continual warfare in Morocco, inevitably distracted attention and effort from the Congo. King John III of Portugal, who ruled from 1521 to 1557, unlike his two predecessors, showed relatively little interest in the promising Congo mission-field. He often left unanswered for years on end the repeated letters and messages from the king of Congo; and when he did send help or a reply of any kind it was usually too little and too late. The irruption of the cannibal Jaga hordes from central Africa into the Congo kingdom in 1568–73 devastated several regions for years on end before these savages were expelled by a Portuguese expeditionary force. But the chief reason for the ultimate failure of the promising start made by Western civilisation in the Congo was undoubtedly the close connection which speedily grew up between the missionary and the slave-trader. This connection was firmly established before the Jaga invasion.

As early as 1530 the annual export of slaves from the kingdom of Congo was reliably estimated at 4,000 to 5,000 *peças*. The *peça* or *peça de Índias* was a prime young male slave; all other slaves of both sexes counted less than a *peça*. This term might, therefore, include two or even three individuals, depending on their age, sex and physical fitness, children at the breast not counting separately from their mothers. At this period most of the slaves came from regions outside the boundaries of the Congo kingdom proper, being obtained chiefly by barter from the Teke and Mpumbu to the north-east, or by alternately raiding and trading with the Mbundu to the south. But King Afonso I and his successors increasingly complained that the Portuguese traders were securing Congolese as slaves; and the Jaga invasion was naturally accompanied by a great boom in the slave trade, which continued to flourish in Congo after their expulsion. The Congolese kings themselves sent occasional presents of slaves to the kings of Portugal; but it is clear from their correspondence that the growth of the slave trade made them very uneasy and they tried to limit it in so far as they could. The kings of Portugal were also disposed, intermittently at any rate, to co-operate in this respect with the Congolese monarchs; but their efforts were systematically sabotaged by the governors and planters of the island of São Tomé, who steadily intensified this traffic in conjunction with dealers on the mainland.

The better to evade compliance with inconvenient royal decrees and the payment of export taxes at the Congolese port of Mpinda, the slave-traders of São Tomé increasingly turned their attention to the Mbundu kingdom of Ndongo south of the river Dande. The Portuguese were aware of the existence of this recently established but growing Bantu state by the year 1520, when instructions were issued by King Manuel for two envoys to visit the 'King of Angola', as this potentate was called from his patronymic of Ngola. The envoys were informed that the Ngola's country was believed to be rich in silver, and that he himself had asked for missionaries to be sent him with a view to accepting Christianity. The results of this pioneer embassy are not known, but the quest for souls and silver continued to influence Portuguese policy in Angola for many years, although, as in the Congo, slaves proved to be the most immediate and the most enduring source of profit. Prior to the year 1571, the Portuguese Crown stipulated that slaves could only be embarked at the Congolese port of Mpinda; but from about 1520 onwards increasing numbers were fetched direct from the mouth of the Kwanza river in Angola, where the interloping slavers from São Tomé paid no export duty to the Crown.

In 1560 another attempt was made by the Portuguese Crown to open official relations with the Ngola; but the envoys, who included four Jesuit missionaries, were detained for several years at the Ndongo capital of Ngoleme, which was described as a city of some five or six thousand 'houses' (kraals) before its destruction by fire in 1564. Paulo Dias de Novais, who had escorted the Jesuits to this place, was released with some of his surviving companions by the Ngola in the following years; but the Jesuit priest Francisco de Gouveia remained in captivity until his death ten years later. Long before then he had become disillusioned with the prospect of painlessly converting the Mbundu to Christianity. Writing to the Crown of Portugal in 1563, he asserted that experience had shown that these Bantu were barbarous savages, who could not be converted by the methods of peaceful persuasion which were employed with such cultured Asian nations as the Japanese and Chinese. Christianity in Angola, he wrote, must be imposed by force of arms, although once the Bantu were converted they would make excellent and submissive Christians. This was, and for long remained, the general view among Portuguese missionaries and laymen alike. As another pioneer Jesuit missionary wrote from Angola twelve years later: 'Almost everybody is convinced that the conversion of these barbarians is not to be achieved through love, but only after they have been subdued by force of arms and become vassals of Our Lord the King.'

The advocacy of the Church Militant fitted in well enough with the proposals of Paulo Dias de Novais, who, after his return to Lisbon in 1565, urged the government to appoint him as *conquistador* and *donatário* of Angola, which could then be developed in a way similar to the more successful of the captaincies in Brazil. The charter which was finally given him by the Crown in 1571 envisaged the colonisation of at least a part of Angola by peasant families from Portugal, who were to be provided with 'all the seeds and plants which they can take from this kingdom and from the island of São Tomé'. But when Paulo Dias' expedition arrived off Luanda in February 1575 the slave trade was already firmly established there by the interlopers from São Tomé. Malaria and other tropical diseases proved an insuperable obstacle to large-scale white colonisation of the hinterland for the next three centuries, and the high ideals of the royal charter were soon abandoned for the unrestrained procurement of *péças*, whether by slave-trading or by slave-raiding. In the former instance slaves were usually obtained through the intermediary of *pombeiros*. These were traders, sometimes white Portuguese, but more often Mulattos, free Negroes, or even trusted slaves, who travelled to the *pumbos* or markets of the interior and brought caravans of slaves thence to the coast. The Portuguese also exacted tribute in the form of slaves from the *sovas* or tribal chiefs who submitted to them. When they went slave-raiding (as distinct from trading) they came to rely increasingly on the use of Jaga auxiliaries. These warriors formed the backbone of the *guerra preta* ('black war') and they were also called *empacasseiros* from a word meaning buffalo-hunters.

The people of the Pende tribe, who lived on the Angola coast in the sixteenth century but subsequently migrated inland to the Kasai river, have preserved an interesting oral tradition of the Portuguese conquest of their original homeland.

One day the white men arrived in ships with wings, which shone in the sun like knives. They fought hard battles with the Ngola and spat fire at him. They conquered his salt-pans and the Ngola fled inland to the Lukala river. Some of his bolder subjects remained by the sea and when the white men came they exchanged eggs and chickens for cloth and beads. The white men came yet again. They brought us maize and cassava, knives and hoes, groundnuts and tobacco. From that time until our day the Whites brought us nothing but wars and miseries.

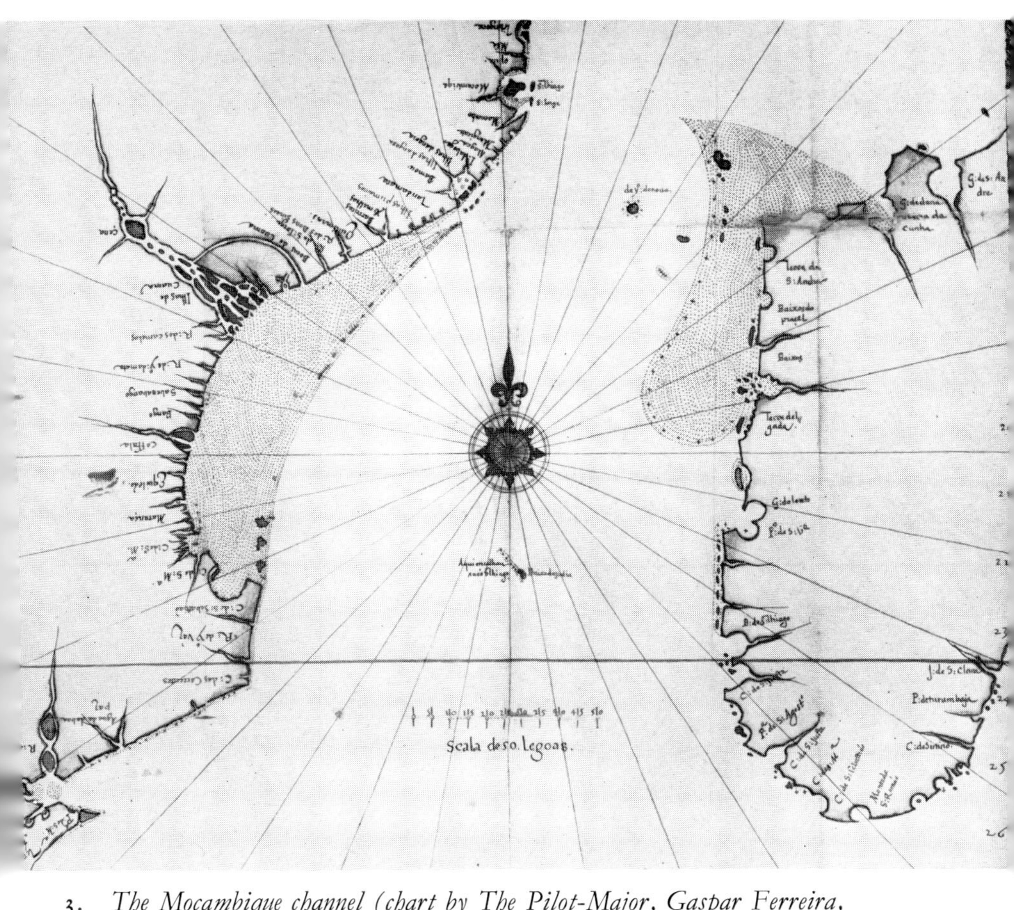

3. *The Moçambique channel (chart by The Pilot-Major, Gaspar Ferreira, 1612)*

4. *Diogo do Couto, 1542–1616*
(from an engraving in his Década *VII, 1616)*

When introducing the new crops the Europeans taught a prayer which had to be said for the crops to grow; and this prayer is still remembered in a garbled form by the Pende.

Although the Portuguese continued to export slaves from Mpinda and Loango to Brazil via São Tomé throughout the sixteenth century, Angola became the main source of supply after the foundation of Luanda in 1575. Reliable statistics for long periods are wanting, but a visiting official who inspected the books of the Luanda Customs House in March 1591 reported that a total of 52,053 *peças de Índias* had been exported since the year 1591. This figure is obviously too low for the West African slave trade as a whole, since it takes no account of the considerable contraband trade and of the slaves exported from other ports. Nor can we distinguish between the numbers exported to Brazil and those shipped for sale in the Spanish-American empire. The contractors and dealers who played the principal parts in this trade, and who were often Portuguese Jews, preferred to ship the slaves to the 'Indies of Castile' rather than to Brazil, even when the slave-ships were ostensibly cleared for some Brazilian port. The Spaniards paid in silver coin for their slaves, whereas the planters and settlers of Brazil paid in sugar, rum, and tobacco. Other contemporary but unofficial estimates place the number of slaves exported annually at about 23,000 individuals from Angola alone. This figure is undoubtedly too high, but the available evidence indicates that between 10,000 and 15,000 Negro slaves from West Africa were landed in Brazilian ports in an averagely good year, the great majority of them coming from Angola during the last quarter of the sixteenth century.

The distribution of the Negro slave population in Brazil in those years is also the subject of conflicting estimates, but it is indisputable that the majority were located in Pernambuco and Bahia. Between 1580 and 1590 these estimates range between 10,000 and 2,000 for Pernambuco and 3,000 and 4,000 for Bahia. The two extremes given for Pernambuco are certainly 'way out', but the higher is obviously nearer the true figure than the latter, as Pernambuco was then richer and more prosperous than Bahia. F. Mauro, who has analysed all the relevant figures, suggests that the Negro population of Brazil in 1600 amounted to some 13,000 to 15,000 souls, 70 per cent of whom were employed on a total

E

of 130 sugar plantations. He likewise calculates that each Negro produced eighty *arrobas* of sugar yearly in a total annual production of 750,000 to 800,000 *arrobas*. Calculating the working life of a slave at seven years, he estimates the maximum importation of West African slaves at 50,000 in thirty years, 'and this is a generous estimate'.

Estimates of the white population of Brazil are similarly incomplete, vague and contradictory, in the absence of any form of census. One estimate for the year 1584 which has gained fairly wide acceptance gives a total population of 57,000 souls of whom 25,000 were white, 18,000 domesticated Amerindians and 14,000 Negro slaves. Apart from the fact that this estimate is based on conflicting contemporary sources (Anchieta, Cardim and Soares), it takes no account of what proportion of these categories were of mixed blood, although miscegenation between the three races involved had been practised for nearly a century. Magalhães Godinho, accepting the total of 57,000 souls for 1583, estimates it at 150,000 in 1600, distributed between 30,000 whites and 120,000 slaves. But this calculation completely ignores the Amerindians and the mixed bloods, apart from the fact that it is unlikely that the population had virtually tripled in seventeen years. The most that can be said with certainty is that both the white and the black population of Brazil markedly increased in the last quarter of the sixteenth century; and the records of the visiting Inquisitors during that period indicate that a high proportion of the immigrants came from northern Portugal.

Whatever the real numbers may have been, there can be no doubt but that the rapid expansion of the Brazilian sugar industry in the years 1575–1600 was one of the major developments in the Atlantic world of that time. Pernambuco and Bahia remained by far the most important centres of production and population, for as late as 1585 there were only three sugar mills and 150 Portuguese householders in Rio de Janeiro, when Olinda and its district contained sixty-six mills and 2,000 Portuguese households. The allegedly luxurious dress and Lucullan banquets of the richest Pernambuco planters evoked some criticism from Jesuit moralists, Father Cardim observing that 'there was more vanity to be found in Pernambuco than in Lisbon'. But he also admitted that the planters were generous supporters of the Church in general and of the Jesuits in particular, sending their children to be educated at the Jesuit college of Olinda. Cardim tells us that in 1584 some forty ships were employed in the sugar trade between Recife and Lisbon, and the number had increased to 130 by the year 1618.

The prosperity and resilience of the sugar trade were convincingly proved by the repeated setbacks which it successfully overcame. In the three years from 1589 to 1591, for example, Elizabethan privateers captured sixty-nine ships engaged in the Brazil trade, the value of the captured sugar being worth at least £100,000 and rendering (as a Spanish spy reported) sugar cheaper at London than at Lisbon or at Bahia. French corsairs and Barbary rovers likewise took their toll of this shipping, to say nothing of natural hazards such as the great drought of 1583, which temporarily crippled the production of sugar in Pernambuco. But the ever-increasing demand for sugar in Europe and the expansion of the slave trade with Angola, together with such expedients as the freighting of neutral (Hansa) shipping, enabled the planters steadily to increase their production. By the end of the century one of their number could boast to the government at Lisbon that the sugar of Brazil was more profitable to the Iberian dual monarchy than all the pepper, spices, jewels and luxury goods imported in the Indiamen from 'Golden' Goa.

CHAPTER V

The global struggle with the Dutch 1600-63

WILLEM BOSMAN, author of a classic description of Guinea at the end of the seventeenth century, observed that the role of the Portuguese discoverers and conquerors in the colonial world was that of 'setting-dogs to spring the game, which as soon as they had done, was seized by others', the Dutch being the principal beneficiaries. This cynical observation had a large element of truth, for when the Dutch moved over to the offensive in their Eighty Years War of independence against Spain at the end of the sixteenth century, it was on the Portuguese rather than on the Spanish colonial possessions that their heaviest and most persistent attacks were concentrated. Since the Iberian possessions were scattered round the world, the ensuing struggle was waged in four continents and on seven seas; and this seventeenth-century contest deserves to be called the First World War rather than the holocaust of 1914–18 which is commonly awarded that doubtful honour. Obviously, the casualties suffered in the Dutch-Iberian conflict were on a much smaller scale, but the population of the world was much smaller at that period, and the struggle was indubitably world-wide. Apart from Flanders fields and the North Sea, battle was joined in such remote regions as the estuary of the Amazon, the hinterland of Angola, the island of Timor and the coast of Chile. The prizes included the cloves and nutmegs of the Moluccas; the cinnamon of Ceylon; the pepper of Malabar; silver from Mexico, Peru and Japan; gold from Guinea and Monomotapa; the sugar of Brazil and the Negro slaves of West Africa.

When we recall that the respective populations of the two small countries with which we are primarily concerned, the kingdom of Portugal and the Republic of the United Netherlands, probably did not exceed a million and a half, and when we remember that they were both deeply embroiled in Europe, the magnitude and range of the efforts which they put forth must compel our admiration. Moreover, this global struggle often involved third parties, such as the English, Danes, Congolese, Persians, Indonesians, Cambodians and Japanese at various times and places. Last not least, there was a strong religious element concerned, since the Romanist Portuguese and the Calvinist Dutch regarded themselves as champions of their respective faiths, and consequently as fighting God's battles against His enemies. To the adherents of the 'True Christian Reformed Religion' as defined at the Synod of Dort in 1618–19, the Church of Rome was 'the Great Whore of Babylon', and the Pope a veritable Anti-Christ. The Portuguese, on their side, were fully convinced that salvation was only obtainable through belief in the doctrines of the Roman Catholic Church as defined at the sixteenth-century Council of Trent. 'The Hollanders are merely good gunners and are otherwise fit for nothing save to be burned as desperate heretics', wrote a Portuguese chronicler who expressed the convictions of many of his compatriots in 1624.

The massive Dutch attack on the Portuguese colonial empire was ostensibly motivated by the union of the Spanish and Portuguese Crowns in the person of Philip II of Spain, against whose rule in the Netherlands the Dutch had rebelled in 1568. Ten years later the defeat and death of the childless King Sebastian on the field of El-Ksar el-Kebir in Morocco (4 August 1578) left the Portuguese Crown to the last monarch of the House of Aviz, the aged and ailing Cardinal-King Henry. He died in January 1580, and a few months later Philip, whose mother was a Portuguese princess, enforced his claims to the vacant throne with the aid of the Duke of Alva's veterans and of Mexican 'silver bullets', in a judicious combination which enabled him to boast of his new domain: 'I inherited it, I bought it, I conquered it' (*Yo lo heredé, Yo lo compré, Yo lo conquisté*). The Crowns of Spain and Portugal remained united for the next sixty years, a period which Portuguese patriots subsequently compared to the Babylonian captivity of the Jews. The Iberian colonial empire which lasted from 1580 to 1640, and which stretched from Macao in China to Potosí in Peru, was thus the first world-empire on which the sun never set.

Philip's seizure of the Portuguese Crown met with little more than token resistance in 1580, save only in the Azorean island of Terceira, where the Spaniards had to mount a major invasion. Most of the Portuguese nobility and the higher clergy were in favour of the union. The mass of the people and many of the lower clergy were sullenly opposed to it, but they were disorganised, dispirited and leaderless after the disaster of El-Ksar el-Kebir, which had further crippled the country's economy by the need to ransom the thousands of captives taken by the Moors. Nevertheless, Portuguese national sentiment was strong enough, and Philip himself was prudent enough to ensure that at the 1581 assembly of the *Cortes*, which gave legal sanction to his seizure of the Crown, it was agreed that the two colonial empires should remain separately administered entities. The union of these two Iberian Crowns was a personal one, like that of the United Kingdom of Scotland and England in the persons of the Stuart monarchs from the accession of James VI (and I) to the Act of Union under Queen Anne. King Philip II of Spain and I of Portugal swore to preserve Portuguese laws and language; to consult Portuguese advisers on all matters pertaining to Portugal and its overseas possessions, and to appoint only Portuguese officials in those possessions. Spaniards were expressly prohibited from trading or settling in the Portuguese empire, and Portuguese from trading or settling in the Spanish.

The Portuguese subsequently complained that the union of their Crown with that of Castile was the sole reason why their overseas dominions were attacked by the Dutch, and to a lesser extent by the English, in the early seventeenth century. These complaints, while natural enough, were hardly fair. The English had already challenged Portugal's claim to the monopoly of the Guinea trade in the mid-sixteenth century, and there is no doubt but that the two Protestant maritime powers would in any event have come into conflict with Portugal over the latter's claim that she was the sole mistress of the seas to the east of the Cape of Good Hope. Still, the fact remains that it was Philip II's efforts to suppress the revolt of the Netherlands, and his sporadic embargoes on Dutch trade with the Iberian peninsula and empire, which helped to involve the Portuguese in hostilities with the northern maritime powers earlier than might otherwise have happened. Moreover, once the Dutch had decided to carry the war overseas, and to attack their Iberian enemies in the colonial possessions which gave them the economic resources wherewith to wage war in Flanders and Italy, then Portugal, as the weaker partner in the union of the two crowns, inevitably suffered more than did Castile under the blows of superior Dutch sea-power. The colonial war began with attacks by Dutch warships on the islands of Príncipe and São Tomé in 1598–9. As the fighting spread in space and time, the Dutch tended more and more to concentrate on attacking Portuguese settlements in Asia, Africa and Brazil. These were nearly all situated on the exposed sea coasts, and hence they were far more vulnerable than the land-based Spanish viceroyalties of Mexico and Peru, which could never be reduced—nor even seriously threatened—by seaborne attacks alone.

The Dutch expansion on the Seven Seas during the first half of the seventeenth century was in its way as remarkable as the overseas expansion of Portugal and Spain 100 years earlier, but we are mainly concerned here with its devastating effect on the Portuguese empire. Nevertheless, while concentrating on this side of the story, we must not forget that the Dutch were often likewise making powerful attacks on the Spanish colonial world. Simultaneously with the Dutch West India Company's first attack on Brazil in 1624–5, another Dutch fleet of eleven ships and 1,650 men, equipped by the States-General and the Dutch East India Company, sailed via the Straits of Magellan into the Pacific, raided the coasts of Peru and Mexico, then crossed the ocean to the Moluccas and Batavia—an astounding feat of enterprise and organisation. Moreover, while the Dutch were attacking the Portuguese in their Asian possessions, they were launching frequent—if far less successful—attacks on the Philippines, until the treaty of Münster in 1648 ended the Eighty Years War between the northern Netherlands and Spain.

The Luso-Dutch struggle, which began with the raids on Príncipe and São Tomé in 1598–9, ended with the capture of the Portuguese settlements on the Malabar coast in 1663, although the terms of peace were not finally settled until six years later at Lisbon and The Hague. Up to the restoration of Portuguese independence with the proclamation of the Duke of Braganza as King John IV (1 December 1640) the Portuguese and Spaniards were allied against the Dutch, but for the next twenty-three years the Portuguese had to fight the Spaniards on the home front as well as the Dutch overseas. At the risk of over-simplification, it can be said that this lengthy colonial war took the form of a struggle for the spice trade of Asia, for the slave trade of West Africa, and for the sugar trade of Brazil. Similarly, it can be said that the final result was, on balance, a victory for the Dutch in Asia, a draw in West Africa, and a victory for the Portuguese in Brazil. In briefest outline the decisive events in this war can be summarised as follows.

The Dutch early achieved success in the East Indies by their capture of the principal Spice Islands in 1605, against strong Portuguese resistance at Tidore and against no resistance whatever at Amboina. The Spaniards from the Philippines staged an unexpected counter-offensive in the following year, which enabled them to seize and retain Tidore and a part of Ternate, until the threat of a Chinese attack on Manila forced them to recall their Moluccan garrisons in 1662, and to resign the clove monopoly to the Dutch. After their expulsion from the Moluccas the Portuguese established themselves at Macassar (south Celebes), which they used as a base for trading in cloves, sandalwood and other Indonesian products, under the protection of the tolerant Muslim rulers of Gowa and Tallo, and in defiance of the monopolistic claims of the Dutch East India Company with its headquarters at Batavia (Jakarta) since 1619. The Dutch were forced to mount two major expeditions against Macassar (in 1660 and 1667) before they finally secured the expulsion of the Portuguese, together with the representatives of the English and Danish East India Companies. Meanwhile the Dutch systematically harried the Portuguese interport trade of Asia from the Persian Gulf to Japan, and they reduced many of the long chain of Portuguese coastal settlements by picking them off one by one. Their blockade of the straits of Malacca in the years 1634–40 was particularly effective, and this stronghold—the Singapore of the sixteenth and seventeenth centuries—finally fell in January 1641. Between 1638 and 1658 they conquered the Portuguese settlements in coastal Ceylon; rounding off their Asian conquests with the capture of Cochin and the other Portuguese strongholds on the Malabar Coast in 1663.

In this way the Dutch East India Company, which had been founded in 1602, successfully gained control of the cloves, mace and nutmegs of the Moluccas, of the cinnamon of coastal Ceylon, and of the pepper of Malabar. By 1663 the Dutch had also displaced the Portuguese in securing the lion's share of the carrying trade in Asian waters between Japan and Arabia. The Dutch had secured a monopoly of European trade with Japan after the Portuguese had been expelled from the island empire by the ruling military dictator of the Tokugawa family for political and religious motives in 1639. The only places where the Dutch failed in their efforts to expel the Portuguese were Macao on the South China coast and in the outermost islands of the Lesser Sunda group (Timor, Solor, Flores) in Indonesia. They launched a powerful attack on Macao in June 1622, but it was repulsed with heavy loss by the defenders, and another expedition which they mounted in 1660 was diverted to Formosa. Their efforts to deprive the Portuguese of the sandalwood trade in the Lesser Sunda Islands failed in the long run, mainly because the inhabitants were inspired, led, and organised by the resident Dominican missionaries to oppose them. Unlike the Dutch, the English in the East for the most part contented themselves with a defensive attitude towards the Portuguese, although the Persians would not have captured Ormuz in 1622 but for the six stout Indiamen and the expert gunners which the English provided. The rapid progress made by the Dutch in the East alarmed the English almost as much as it did the Portuguese, leading to a *renversement des alliances* and to the conclusion of an Anglo-Portuguese Truce at Goa in 1635. Jealousy of the Dutch also brought about a working agreement between Danes and Portuguese in the East Indies after some sporadic and minor hostilities between them in 1619–31.

In East Africa the Dutch failed twice to take the Portuguese way-station of Moçambique Island (1607 and 1608), and this failure was one of the reasons which later induced them to found their own settlement at the Cape of Good Hope in 1652. It was, however, a long time before they penetrated any considerable distance into the interior, whereas the Portuguese at this period were extending their hold in the Zambesi river valley by raiding and trading into what is now Southern Rhodesia. In West Africa the Dutch established themselves on the Gold Coast as early as 1612 at Mouri (Fort Nassau), and they very soon managed to deprive the Portuguese of the greatest share in the gold trade. They failed disastrously in their first attempt to take São Jorge da Mina in 1625, but they succeeded with a better organised expedition thirteen years later. The Dutch forcibly occupied the coast of Angola and Benguela in August 1641, although they knew that Portugal had rebelled against the Spanish connection in the previous December, and that the overseas *conquistas* would in all probability follow the example of the mother country—as, indeed, they all did by 1645, with the sole exception of Ceuta. The Calvinist invaders of Angola established surprisingly cordial relations with the Roman Catholic King Garcia II of Congo and with the cannibal Queen Nzinga of the Jagas. In August 1648 these strangely assorted allies were on the point of annihilating the surviving Portuguese defenders of Angola in their three remaining strongholds in the Kwanza valley (Muxima, Massangano and Cambambe) when a Luso-Brazilian expedition from Rio de Janeiro recaptured Luanda and dramatically reversed the situation at the last minute of the eleventh hour. When peace was signed in 1663 the Dutch were left in possession of the former Portuguese strongholds on the Gold Coast, but the Portuguese retained control of Angola, Benguela, São Tomé and Príncipe, which they had regained in 1648–9.

In Brazil, after an ephemeral occupation of Bahia in 1624–5, the Dutch invaded Pernambuco in 1630 and fifteen years later they controlled the greatest and richest part of the sugar-producing north-eastern coastal districts. The inhabitants of this region rose against their heretic overlords in June 1645 and, after some preliminary hesitation on the part of King John IV, received substantial if unofficial help from Portugal in men and ships. Following nearly a decade of bitter warfare, Recife and the last Dutch strongholds capitulated in January 1654. The insurgents' original password for the rising was 'sugar', which indicates clearly enough one of the main causes (and prizes) of the war, though *odium theologicum* between Calvinists and Romanists, played an even greater role in the outbreak of rebellion. Both sides used Amerindian auxiliaries in this struggle, as had happened a century earlier in the fighting with the French, the bulk of the cannibal Tapuyá tribes joining the Dutch, whereas most of the Tupís remained loyal to the Portuguese. Many of the Luso-Brazilian forces in this campaign consisted of Mulattos, Negroes and half-breeds of various kinds. A full-blooded Amerindian chief (Camarão) and a full-blooded Negro (Henrique Dias) were among their outstanding regimental commanders, and the original leader of the revolt, João Fernandes Vieira, who fought from the first day to the last, was the son of a Madeira fidalgo and a Mulata prostitute. The natural chagrin of the Dutch at their loss of 'Netherlands Brazil' was greatly increased by their realisation that they had been defeated by what was in great part a coloured army. The sugar trade of Brazil was thus finally left in undisputed possession of the Portuguese; but improved methods of sugar cultivation and cane-grinding were introduced into the British and French West Indies during the Dutch occupation of Pernambuco, probably through the agency of Luso-Brazilian Jews.

The disasters which the Portuguese suffered at the hands of the Dutch during the first forty years of the seventeenth century formed one of the chief reasons why they rebelled against the Spanish Crown in 1640; but they were disappointed in their hope that the Dutch would cease their aggression against the Portuguese *conquistas* as soon as these and the mother country severed their connection with Spain. A ten-year truce between the two contestants was signed at The Hague in 1641, but it was only ratified a year later and it was not implemented in Asia until November 1644. In Brazil and Angola the truce was ill-observed, even before the full-scale renewal of the war with the outbreak of the Pernambuco revolt in June 1645. The intensification of hostilities outside Europe after the expiration of the truce in 1652 led to the Portuguese seeking the protection of an English alliance through Charles II's marriage to Catherine of Braganza in 1661. The peace which Portugal subsequently secured with Spain and the United Provinces (in 1668–9), partly through English mediation, was a peace of exhaustion in so far as Portugal was concerned. The sacrifice of Bombay and Tangier to the heretic English as part of Catherine's dowry was naturally resented by the fervently Catholic Portuguese, although there was no likelihood of their being able to develop those two possessions in the existing circumstances.

The reasons for the Dutch victory in Asia can be reduced to three main heads: superior economic resources, superior manpower, superior sea-power. The United Provinces of the Free Netherlands provided a richer home base than the impoverished kingdom of Portugal. The populations of the two countries were probably roughly equal (1,500,000 to 1,250,000 each); but whereas Portugal had to supply cannon-fodder in the service of Spain before 1640 and against her thenceforward, the Dutch could and did make extensive use of neighbouring German and Scandinavian manpower in their armies and fleets. The disparity in sea-power was even more striking, and was cogently expressed by the great Portuguese Jesuit, António Vieira, in 1649. He estimated that the Dutch possessed over 14,000 vessels which could be used as warships, whereas Portugal did not possess thirteen ships in the same category. The Dutch, he claimed, had a quarter of a million sailors available to man their shipping, whereas Portugal could not muster 4,000. Vieira was evidently exaggerating, but he was not exaggerating very much. A census taken at Lisbon of seamen available for manning the fleet in 1620 listed only 6,260 men for the whole country. At a meeting of the Viceroy's advisory council at Goa in November 1643 it was stated that there were not sufficient qualified pilots at Lisbon to navigate any ships to India, since all those with adequate qualifications (fewer than ten individuals) were then in the three Indiamen detained by the Dutch blockade at Goa. Shortage of deep-sea mariners was a perennial problem in the Portuguese empire, as we often have reason to recall (pp. 57, 212), but at no time was it more acute than in the lengthy crisis of the Dutch War.

Another reason for Dutch maritime successes in Asia was that the governor-generals at Batavia, and particularly Antonio van Diemen, who broke the back of Portuguese sea-power in the Indian Ocean between 1636 and 1645, possessed a much better grasp of naval strategy than did most of the Portuguese viceroys at Goa. Moreover, the Portuguese, with their almost exclusive reliance on *Fidalgos*, or gentlemen of blood and coat-armour, as naval and military leaders, were at a disadvantage compared with the commanders in the service of the Dutch East India Company, where experience and professional competence rather than family pedigree and social status were the main criterions for promotion. This fact did not escape the more intelligent Portuguese observers. One of them, writing in 1656, pointedly contrasted the aristocratic *fidalgos* who had lost Malacca and Ceylon with the humbly born Hollanders who had conquered those places. Other relevant factors were the better discipline and training of the Dutch sailors and soldiers, and the growing wealth of the Dutch East India Company contrasted with the declining economy of erstwhile 'Golden' Goa.

Padre Fernão de Queiroz, the Jesuit chronicler of the Luso-Dutch War in Ceylon, complained that 'the Hollanders said truly that our way of fighting was always a poor man's war' (*guerra de pobres*). An experienced Portuguese commander in India told the Viceroy in 1663: 'It is a well-known fact that the fortunes of war cannot be improved without men and money, and this is why we see so many disorders, so many tears and so many losses, because the King has only an empty treasury and his vassals have no capital to help him.' The next year another Portuguese commander on the Malabar coast wrote to the same Viceroy:

> Any Dutch captain has full powers and plenty of money to utilise on any occasion, and he is authorised to spend regardless when necessary. With us, we have to obtain permission from superior authority for the smallest thing, and such permission often arrives too late. Moreover, as we are ill-provided, we are always compelled to beg our way wherever we go, which in turn makes it impossible for us to accomplish anything, since nothing can be done without money, above all with these natives of India.

Dom Manuel Lobo da Silveira erred when he implied that the directors of the Dutch East India Company never grudged the naval and military expenditure in which the costly campaigns of their subordinates involved them. But his observation reflects the truism that in a war between rich and poor, where all other factors are roughly equal (morale, physique, equipment, training, tactics, etc.), the rich are bound to win.

Obviously, in the course of the long struggle between Portuguese and Dutch, these other factors were not always roughly equal. In two of them, physique and discipline, the advantage was, on balance, with the Dutch, especially in the Asian theatre of war. The soldiers of the Dutch East and West India Companies were, of course, mercenaries, and the rank and file comprised mainly Germans, French, Scandinavians and (before 1652) English, though there was a higher proportion of Netherlanders among the officers. The physique of these northern Europeans was a matter of envious comment among their opponents in Brazil and Ceylon; and if the former often grumbled about the inadequacy of their own rations, they were in fact almost invariably better fed than the Portuguese. The half-starved Portuguese soldiers in Ceylon complained in 1644, 'we are so thin and hungry that three of us are not equal to one Hollander'. The senior Portuguese officer present at the recapture of Bahia in May 1625 wrote of the defeated Dutch garrison: 'They were all youths, picked men who would shine in any infantry in the world.' One of the Portuguese defenders of Bahia on the occasion of the second Dutch attack in 1638 wrote in his diary after the repulse of the final assault: 'We counted their dead when we handed them over—327 of the finest-looking men who ever were seen; they looked like giants and they were undoubtedly the flower of the Dutch soldiery.'

On the other hand, the Portuguese soldiers who were sent out as cannon-fodder to the colonial battlefields during the whole of the seventeenth century were only too often forcibly recruited from gaol-birds and convicted criminals, as the reiterated complaints of the authorities at Goa and Bahia monotonously testify. Nor were the authorities in Portugal itself unaware of the disadvantages which this practice involved. Manuel Severim de Faria, the scholarly Canon of Evora, wrote in 1622 after receiving the news of the fall of Ormuz:

> Nothing better can be expected from the bad choice which is made in Portugal of the soldiers we send to India, by emptying the prisons of all the ruffians who are gaoled there because they do not know how to keep faith with God or Man. And therefore it is hardly surprising that those who misbehave in this way at home should act in the same way abroad.

An identical opinion was expressed some sixty years later by

Captain João Ribeiro, a veteran of the war in Ceylon between 1640 and 1658, apropos of the drafts of convict soldiers sent annually from the Lisbon prison of Limoeiro: 'For he who misbehaves in Portugal cannot behave in India.' No less numerous are the official complaints that far too high a proportion of the raw recruits shipped to the *conquistas* consisted of mere children—'soldiers' of twelve, ten or eight years being relatively common, and those of six being not unknown. Moreover, many of the better types of adult recruits promptly exchanged the soldier's sword for the friar's cowl, or the gown of the Jesuit novice, soon after their arrival at Goa. This practice was the theme of much acrimonious correspondence between the Crown, the viceroys, and the ecclesiastical authorities throughout the seventeenth century. The very persistence of this correspondence shows that the abuse was never eradicated despite all the royal and viceregal fulminations against it.

The want of strict discipline and of adequate military training in peacetime also put the Portuguese at a grave disadvantage with their Dutch opponents. This was especially so in Asia, where for reasons which are discussed in Chapter XIII the Portuguese for nearly two centuries deliberately refrained from organising any permanent military units. They practised no tactics other than a disorderly charge to the war-cry of 'St. James and at them!' (*Santiago e a elles!*). But even in Europe the Portuguese were always the last nation to adopt any innovations in tactics, training and equipment, as Dom Franciso Manuel de Mello, a literary luminary of considerable naval and military experience, stated in his *Epanaphoras* of 1660. This is all the odder since their Spanish neighbours has been in the vanguard of military progress during the whole of the sixteenth century. Consequently the Portuguese were the butt of much scornful criticism from their Castilian contemporaries in 1580–1640, on account of their 'complete ignorance of any form of military discipline'.

This lack of discipline and military training was allied to an overweening self-confidence, which rendered the Portuguese notoriously careless and negligent at critical times and places when great care and vigilance were necessary. Francisco Rodrigues da Silveira was writing from personal experience when he complained in 1595 that most of the soldiers of the Ormuz garrison habitually lodged and slept outside the castle, came on sentry duty two hours late, and when they belatedly reported for such duty they sent ahead a Negro (or even a Negress) slave carrying their weapons. Some Dutch sailors who landed near Damão in the truce-year of 1649 entered the city without meeting or being challenged by anyone, since the entire population (including the garrison) were soundly asleep during the four-hour *sesta* from noon to 4 p.m. Portuguese garrisons were also commonly ill-provided with sufficient weapons and when they had them they were often neglected, rusty and otherwise unserviceable, as a stream of complaints from the time of Afonso de Albuquerque onwards testifies. Innumerable other examples could be given of what Manuel Severim de Faria indignantly termed:

> this abominable negligence in which our Portuguese live beyond the bar of Lisbon, just as if they were safe at home in the interior of Portugal. This has often led to them suffering the most appalling reverses, since fighting unarmed against strongly armed opponents we must needs either be defeated or else escape through a miracle from Heaven.

As in all long-drawn-out wars, the course of the struggle between Portuguese and Dutch in the tropical world was embittered by mutual accusations of atrocities and of cruelties to prisoners of war. This was especially the case in the Pernambuco campaign of 1644–54, where each side accused the other of inciting their respective Amerindian auxiliaries to commit savage barbarities, and where leaders on both sides sometimes forbade their own men to give quarter. In the last stages of the fighting in Ceylon, Corporal Saar relates how he and some of his comrades, who had been badly treated when prisoners of the Portuguese, revenged themselves on the fleeing enemy after the battle of Paniture in October 1655.

> For although our officers cried out, 'Comrades, we are called merciful Hollanders, so let us show ourselves to be really so and give quarter!'—yet we acted as if we did not hear them, but lustily shot and cut down the fugitives so long as we could raise our hands and arms, laying low several hundred of them.

Odium theologicum likewise played its part in exacerbating mutual hatred, and the Portuguese complained that when they suffered at the hands of the Dutch, whether in Ceylon or in Brazil, their worst oppressors were usually the zealously Calvinistic Zeelanders, or 'Pichilingues' as they called them, from their mispronunciation of Vlissingen (Flushing).

In view of the advantages enjoyed by the Dutch, only a few of which I have enumerated here, it may be asked why they took some sixty years to conquer part of Portuguese Asia, and why they failed completely in Angola and Brazil after such a promising start. Among several reasons which can be suggested the following may be mentioned. Though there can be no doubt but that man for man the Dutch mercenaries were usually physically stronger than their Portuguese opponents, the latter were often better acclimatised in the tropics. This helps to account for the eventual Luso-Brazilian victory in Brazil, where the decisive battles of the Guararapes in 1648 and 1649 were won by men inured to the tropical sun and skilled in bush warfare against men who had learnt their trade on the cooler and more formal battlefields of Flanders and Germany. In tropical Ceylon, on the other hand, the final victory rested with the Dutch. Partly, no doubt, on account of the assistance which they received from their Sinhalese allies—though the Portuguese had their faithful Sinhalese *lascarins* or auxiliaries, too—but mainly because of the chronic incompetence of the Portuguese high command in that island. Contrariwise, in Pernambuco it was the Luso-Brazilians who eventually produced the most efficient leaders in the form of that remarkable triumvirate: João Fernandes Vieira (Madeira-born), André Vidal de Negreiros (Brazilian-born) and Franciso Barreto (Peru-born), ably seconded as mentioned above (p. 113) by the Amerindian, Felipe Camarão, and the Negro, Henrique Dias. It should be noted that the vicissitudes of the fighting on land contrasted strongly with the course of the struggle at sea, where the Dutch early established and subsequently maintained an overwhelming superiority, both in the Indian Ocean and in the South Atlantic. Even when they temporarily lost command of the sea with disastrous results to themselves, as at Luanda in August 1648 and at Recife in January 1654, this was not due to any naval defeat at the hands of their opponents, but to their own strategic miscalculations and administrative shortcomings, combined with the accidents of wind and weather.

Apart from such more or less technical considerations, the basic reason why the Portuguese retained so much of their ramshackle seaborne empire, in despite of the overwhelming superiority of the Dutch in several respects, was that the former, with all their faults, had struck deeper roots as colonisers. Consequently they could not, as a rule, be removed from the scene simply by a naval or by a military defeat, or even by a series of defeats, such as they sustained in north-east Brazil between 1630 and 1640, and in Angola between 1641 and 1648. Many of the Dutch were conscious of this fact, and it impressed such different observers as Governor-General Antonio van Diemen at Batavia, and Corporal Johann Saar in Ceylon. The former wrote to his superiors at Amsterdam in 1642:

> Most of the Portuguese in India [=Asia] look upon this region as their fatherland. They think no more about Portugal. They drive little or no trade thither, but content themselves with the interport trade of Asia, just as if they were natives thereof and had no other country.

Corporal Saar, after some years' service against the Portuguese in Ceylon, wrote of them twenty years later:

> Wherever they once come, there they mean to settle for the rest of their lives, and they never think of returning to Portugal again. But a Hollander, when he arrives in Asia, thinks 'when my six years of service are up, then I will go home to Europe again'.

Mutatis mutandis, similar criticisms could be (and were) applied to the temporary Dutch domination in north-east Brazil and along the coast of Angola and Benguela. Count Johan Maurits of Nassau, whose enlightened governorship of Netherlands-Brazil is still acknowledged by many Brazilians today, never ceased to warn his superiors at The Hague and Amsterdam that unless they would send out Dutch, German and Scandinavian colonists in large numbers to replace (or to mix with) the existing Portuguese settlers, the latter would always remain Portuguese at heart and would revolt at the first opportunity. And so it proved in June 1645. The celebrated Huguenot traveller, Jean-Baptiste Tavernier, wrote that 'the Portuguese, wherever they go, make the place better for those who come after them, whereas the Hollanders endeavour to destroy all things wherever they set foot'. Tavernier was grossly prejudiced against the Dutch, but it is true that, as Corporal Saar explained, when the Dutch took Colombo, Cochin and other well-built Portuguese settlements, they immediately dismantled many of the houses, walls and fortifications, contenting themselves with about one-third of the ground-space occupied by their predecessors. It is equally true that during the sixteenth century the Portuguese, directly and indirectly, spread the cultivation of the clove-tree more widely in the Moluccas, particularly in introducing it into Amboina. The Dutch, on the other hand, later cut down clove-trees on a massive scale rather than risk over-production, and they enforced (by means of the so-called *Hongi-tochten*) the sale of cloves to themselves alone, something which the Portuguese had never been able to do. The Portuguese had also stocked the uninhabited island of St. Helena with fruit-trees, pigs and goats, etc., so that it could serve as a way-station where fresh food could be obtained by their homeward-bound Indiamen in case of need. The Dutch cut down the trees and endeavoured to lay waste the island on their own early visits there, but they later changed this destructive policy and followed the Portuguese practice.

Although the Portuguese often enforced their claims to the monopoly of the 'conquest, navigation and commerce' of the Indian Ocean in a brutal manner, the Dutch were chagrined to find when they successfully challenged these monopolistic pretensions that the Indians 'were nevertheless more favourably disposed to the Portuguese than to any other Christian nation', as Gillis van Ravesteyn wrote from Surat in 1618. Forty-three years later Willem Schouten complained of the pearl-fishers of Tuticorin that they much preferred their Portuguese oppressors to their Dutch deliverers; and we find many similar statements by other Netherlanders who had wide experience in Asia. They are echoed in the encyclopaedic work of Pieter van Dam, compiled for the confidential information of the directors of the Dutch East India Company at the end of the seventeenth century. He stated that although the Portuguese often ill-treated and affronted the Indians, 'capturing and burning their ships, damaging and raiding their harbours, making their captives Christians by force, levying arbitrary taxes on the cargoes they send by sea, behaving proudly and arrogantly in their land', yet the Indians would rather deal with the Portuguese than with any other Europeans.

Many modern writers, particularly Portuguese, claim that this attitude of the Indians, which was shared by many other (though not all) Asians, was mainly due to the fact that the Portuguese intermarried with their women to a much greater extent than did the northern Europeans, and that they had no colour prejudice. Both of these explanations can be largely discounted, and they were not among those advanced in the seventeenth century. The Dutch and English merchants in the East likewise cohabited with Asian women, even if they did not marry them so often as did the Portuguese. Moreover, the women concerned were nearly always low caste or low class, or prostitutes, or converts to Christianity who were regarded as renegades by their respectable compatriots; and they exercised no influence whatsoever on political and economic policy. Far from being devoid of colour prejudice, the Portuguese exhibited it to a marked degree in several spheres, as explained in Chapter XI; quite apart from the fact that (as Linschoten noted with only mild exaggeration) 'in all places they will be lords and masters to the contempt and embasing of the inhabitants'.

Several of the more perceptive Dutch officials and merchants in the East observed that the Portuguese had a great advantage over the Netherlanders owing to the influence and prestige which the Roman Catholic missionaries had acquired in many regions. We have seen above (pp. 67–77) that Portuguese methods of propagating their faith were sometimes more coercive than persuasive in places where they exercised untrammelled political power, but where they did succeed in implanting Roman Catholicism it usually took firm root. Antonio van Diemen, one of the few zealously Calvinistic governor-generals of the Dutch East Indies, noted regretfully that in the field of religious proselytising the Portuguese missionaries 'are too strong for us, and their popish priests show much more zeal and energy than do our preachers and lay-readers'. Pieter van Dam, writing at the end of the century, ascribed the success of the Portuguese in holding on to their dangerously exposed positions in the Lesser Sunda

Islands mainly 'to their priests and clergy having got most of the natives on their side, and having thus secured a great advantage over us, they have then been able to reap the full benefits'. The Dutch came up against Roman Catholic-inspired resistance to their rule in coastal Ceylon and in southern India; and the Calvinist Scots 'interloper', Alexander Hamilton, complained that the Bantu of Zambesia and the Moçambique littoral 'would have commerce with none but the Portuguese, who keep a few priests along the sea-coasts, that overawe the silly natives and get their teeth [i.e. elephant-tusks] and gold for trifles'. It was the Jesuit missionaries at the court of Peking who were largely responsible for thwarting all the efforts of the Dutch to establish an officially recognised trade with China, although the provincial officials of Kwangtung and Fukien were on the whole in favour of admitting the 'red-haired barbarians' after the advent of the Manchu dynasty in 1644.

The close co-operation between the Cross and the Crown which was such a feature of the Iberian empires did not, of course, invariably work to the advantage of the Portuguese in their struggle with the Dutch. Fear of a Christian 'fifth column' was one of the principal reasons for the Japanese government's closure of the country to all Europeans save only the Dutch in 1639; and this fear, which had long been latent in the minds of Japan's military dictators, was deliberately exacerbated by the Protestant Dutch and English denunciations of Roman Catholic missionaries as dangerously subversive agents in the early seventeenth century. On the other side of the world, the Roman Catholic King of Congo and his native clergy, although they unhesitatingly rejected Dutch Calvinist attempts at propaganda, enthusiastically welcomed reports of Dutch victories. They even offered prayers in their churches for the success of Protestant Dutch arms against the Catholic Portuguese in Angola during the years 1641–8. Dom Matheus de Castro, titular Bishop of Chrysopolis and a Goan by birth, carried his dislike of his Portuguese co-religionists to the point of inciting both the Calvinist Dutch East India Company and the Muslim Sultan of Bijapur to attack Goa in the decade 1644–54. If Jesuit missionaries were often welcomed as envoys to the court of the Great Moghul, the 'Great Sophy' of Persia, Shah Abbas I, requested in 1614 that no more Augustinian friars or Jesuit priests should be sent to him in a diplomatic capacity, 'because a Religious out of his cell was like a fish out of water'. But the attitude of Shah Abbas was not widely shared in Asia. Brahmins in India and Buddhist priests in Japan were frequently employed as diplomatic envoys, and most Asian rulers saw nothing incongruous in Portuguese missionaries performing similar functions.

In any event, as the Dutch authorities ruefully admitted, their own Calvinist ministers or *predikanten* could never compete on equal terms with the Roman Catholic priests. During the Dutch occupation of Pernambuco (1630–54) many of the Netherlanders came over to or were reconciled with the Church of Rome; whereas converts from Catholicism to Calvinism were as rare as hens' teeth. It was a similar story in Asia in the Portuguese possessions which had been taken by the Dutch, or wherever a Roman Catholic community existed under their heretic sway. The Eurasians of Batavia, Malacca, Coromandel, Ceylon and Malabar, whenever they had the chance, and often at considerable risk to themselves, would leave the *predikant* preaching to empty pews while they sneaked off to hear mass said, or to have their children baptised, or their marriage solemnised by some passing Roman Catholic priest in disguise. With a few exceptions—of which Amboina is the chief—the Calvinist converts made by the Dutch in the former Portuguese possessions have left no trace in the tropical world at the present day, whereas the Roman Catholic communities planted by the Portuguese are still flourishing in many regions.

Another reason why the Asians—or many of them—preferred dealing with the Portuguese to either the English or the Dutch was explained by the chronicler, António Bocarro, writing of the European trade in Gujarat textiles in 1614. Whereas the poorest and most lowly Portuguese would employ some of the local natives to pack, carry, and ship anything which he bought ashore, the Dutch and the English East India Companies insisted on much of this manual labour being done by their own sailors and white employees. Besides being greater employees of local labour, the Portuguese were also content with making a smaller profit on certain commodities than were either the Dutch or the English at various times and places. Francisco Pelsaert, the Dutch Factor at

Agra, writing of the decline in the Portuguese trade with Gujarat in 1626, noted:

> Because of this decay, we are cursed not only by the Portuguese, but by the Hindus and Muslims, who put the whole blame on us, saying that we are the scourge of their prosperity; for, even though the Dutch and English trades were worth a million rupees annually, this cannot be compared to the former trade which was many times greater, not merely in India, but with Arabia and Persia also.

At the risk of some over-simplification it may, perhaps, be said that although the Dutch were at first warmly welcomed by many Asian peoples as a counterweight to Portuguese pride and pretensions, experience soon showed that those who fell into the sphere of the Dutch East India Company's monopoly had exchanged King Log for King Stork.

Apart from the straightforward fighting and the economic, political and religious rivalry between the Portuguese and Dutch, there was another aspect of this struggle which deserves a brief mention here. This was the battle between the two languages, and in this the Portuguese easily bore away the palm. Since the overseas expansion of Europe was pioneered by the Portuguese, their language (or some form of it) became the *lingua franca* of most of the coastal regions which they opened up to European trade and enterprise on both sides of the globe. By the time that they were challenged by the Netherlanders, their language had sunk roots too deep for eradication, even in the Dutch colonial conquests where they tried to replace it by their own. During the twenty-four years in which the Dutch held all or part of north-east Brazil the subjugated population obstinately refused to learn the language of their heretic overlords, and it is believed that only two Dutch words have survived in the popular language of Pernambuco. In Angola and the Congo, although the great majority of the Bantu rallied to the side of the Dutch between 1641 and 1648, their Negro slaves, auxiliaries and allies alike continued the use of Portuguese and they made no efforts to learn Dutch. In north-east Brazil, several of the Tapuyá chiefs' sons were sent to Holland for their education, where they acquired both the language and the religion. But these few swallows did not make a summer, and the Jesuit missionaries soon removed all traces of Dutch influence from the Amerindians of Brazil after 1656.

In Asia the Portuguese language, or rather the Creole forms thereof, resisted Dutch official pressure and legislation with even more remarkable success. The King (or Emperor) of Kandy in Ceylon, Raja Sinha II (1629–1687), though allied with the Netherlanders against the Portuguese, refused to accept letters or dispatches written in Dutch, and insisted on their being in Portuguese, which language he spoke and wrote fluently. The contemporary Muslim rulers of Macassar were likewise fluent in Portuguese, and one of them had even read all the works of the Spanish devotional writer, Fray Luís de Granada, O.P., in the original. In April 1645 Gerrit Demmer, the governor of the Moluccas, observed that Portuguese, 'or even English', seemed to be an easier language for the Ambonese to learn, and more attractive to them than Dutch. The most striking evidence of the victory of the language of Camoens over that of Vondel was provided by the Dutch colonial capital of Batavia, 'Queen of the Eastern Seas'. The Portuguese never set foot there, save as prisoners of war or else as occasional and fleeting visitors. Yet a Creole form of their language was introduced by slaves and household servants from the region of the Bay of Bengal, and it was spoken by the Dutch and half-caste women born and bred at Batavia, sometimes to the exclusion of their own mother tongue. There was much official criticism of this practice, but, as the Batavian authorities noted in 1647, most Netherlanders considered it 'as a great honour to be able to speak a foreign language'—unlike their Portuguese predecessors and their English and French successors as empire-builders. It was a similar story in many other places; and even at the Cape of Good Hope, where conditions favoured the development of white colonisation after the first difficult decades, Creole Portuguese long remained a *lingua franca*, and it was not without influence in the development of Afrikaans. As Governor-General Johan Maetsuyker and his council at Batavia explained to the directors of the Dutch East India Company in 1659:

The Portuguese language is an easy language to speak and to learn.

That is the reason why we cannot prevent the slaves brought here from Arakan who have never heard a word of Portuguese (and indeed even our own children) from taking to that language in preference to all other languages and making it their own.

CHAPTER VI

Stagnation and contraction in the East 1663-1750

PADRE MANUEL GODINHO, a Jesuit priest who made the overland journey via the Persian Gulf and Iraq from India to Portugal in 1663, began the account of his travels, which was published at Lisbon two years later, with the following lament for past glories and present miseries:

The Lusitanian Indian Empire or State, which formerly dominated the whole of the East, and comprised eight thousand leagues of sovereignty, including twenty-nine provincial capital cities as well as many others of lesser note, and which gave the law to thirty-three tributary kingdoms, amazing the whole world with its vast extent, stupendous victories, thriving trade and immense riches, is now either through its own sins or else through the inevitable decay of great empires, reduced to so few lands and cities that one may well doubt whether that State was smaller at its very beginning than it is now at its end.

After comparing the rise, growth, prosperity and decay of Portuguese India to the four ages of Man, the Jesuit concluded sadly:

If it has not expired altogether, it is because it has not found a tomb worthy of its former greatness. If it was a tree, it is now a trunk; if it was a building, it is now a ruin; if it was a man, it is now a stump; if it was a giant, it is now a pigmy; if it was great, it is now nothing; if it was the viceroyalty of India, it is now reduced to Goa, Macao, Chaul, Baçaim, Damão, Diu, Moçambique and Mombasa, with some other fortresses and places of less importance—in short, relics and those but few, of the great body of that State, which our enemies have left us, either as a memorial of how much we formerly possessed in Asia, or else as a bitter reminder of the little which we now have there.

Padre Godinho's jeremiad was echoed by many of his contemporaries, including the Viceroy, João Nunes da Cunha, who wrote to the Crown in June 1669: 'There are fewer Portuguese in the whole of this State than there are in Alhos Vedros', a small town south of Lisbon containing only 200 householders. Reckoning five or six people to a household, this would give a total of less than 1,500 of white Portuguese in all of the remaining Portuguese settlements from Sofala to Macao. The Viceroy must have been exaggerating, but he was not exaggerating very much. The official correspondence between Lisbon and Goa in the century 1650–1750 continually reflects concern at the inadequate numbers of European-born Portuguese in the East and the high mortality rates among them in unhealthy places like Goa and Moçambique Island. More particularly, the perennial scarcity of white women—there was only one at Muscat in 1553, and only one at Macao in 1636, for example—was aggravated by the fact that if we are to believe the Jesuit Padre Fernão de Queiroz, writing at Goa in 1687: 'Even nowadays the pregnancies of Portuguese women almost invariably terminate fatally for both mother and child.'

We have already seen (p. 53) that very few women left Portugal with their menfolk for the East during the sixteenth century, and this state of affairs continued for the next 200 years. The Portuguese Crown, unlike the Spanish, tended to discourage women from going out to the Asian and African 'conquests' (*conquistas*, as the colonies were officially termed for centuries), with the exception of the 'Orphans of the King'. These, as their name implies, were orphan girls of marriageable age, who were sent out in batches from orphanages at Lisbon and Oporto at the expense of the Crown. They were provided with dowries in the form of minor government posts for the men who might marry them after their arrival at Goa. The first contingent left Lisbon in 1546 and the system seems to have continued until the early eighteenth century. I do not think that more than about thirty girls ever went out in a single year, and between five and fifteen seems to have been a more general average. In some years none were sent at all, though Francisco Rodrigues de Silveira, who served in India from 1585 to 1598, was clearly exaggerating when he wrote: 'It shows in truth great negligence on our part that we send every year to India four or five great ships laden with men, but carrying no women whatever.' It must also be noted that not all of these orphan girls did find husbands when they reached 'Golden' Goa, as viceroys, governors, municipal councillors and the guardians of the Misericordia from time to time reminded the Crown. Some of the women were allegedly too old or too ugly; in other instances the official posts earmarked for prospective husbands were so poorly paid as to constitute no financial attraction. On several occasions the municipality of Goa petitioned the Crown not to send any more orphan girls from Portugal to India. The councillors claimed, no doubt correctly, that there were enough women and girls of marriageable age in India, daughters of respectable Portuguese citizens by Eurasian mothers, for whom provision should be made in the first place. The Crown temporarily stopped the dispatch of these girls in 1595, but soon revived the practice, though never on a scale sufficiently large to make any appreciable contribution to the demographic problem of 'Portuguese Asia'.

Apart from the 'Orphans of the King', some married Portuguese took their wives and female children with them to India, although in the vast majority of cases only the sons accompanied their fathers. Jorge Cabral, the Governor-General of India in 1549–50, was the first viceroy or governor with a European-born wife at Goa. This precedent was not followed for another two centuries, when the wife of the newly appointed Viceroy, Marquis of Tavora, insisted on accompanying her husband to India in 1750, despite the reluctance of the Crown to grant her the desired permission. The relatively few white women who accompanied their husbands to Asia scarcely made more difference than did the periodic levies of the orphan girls, as noted by the chronicler of the Goan Augustinian Convent of Santa Monica, writing at the end of the seventeenth century.

> Although the Portuguese have now frequented the Orient for nearly two hundred years and every year a great number of men and likewise a few women go thither; yet with all this multitude they have not

increased at all, nor is there direct descent from sons to sons for more than three generations, nor any natural increase of our nation that is worth mentioning.

Here again there is some exaggeration, as there were a few white families at Goa who could boast of an unbroken line of descent for more than three generations. But they were admittedly few and far between, and the overwhelming majority were Eurasians by the second or third generation.

Another reason for the failure of the Portuguese 'to increase and multiply' in their Asian andAfrican coastal settlements during the seventeenth and eighteenth centuries was the extreme unhealthiness of some of their most important strongholds, particularly Goa and Moçambique Island. The latter place was described as being a graveyard of the outward-bound voyagers to India as early as 1550, for the reasons which are mentioned on page 218 below. As regards 'Golden' Goa, the municipal council writing to the Crown in 1582 alleged that the colonial capital had become noticeably unhealthy after the great siege of 1570–1, and the position steadily deteriorated for the next two centuries. The two main reasons for this progressive deterioration were the porous nature of the soil, which allowed the drainage to seep into the wells whence the householders drew their drinking water, thus aiding the transmission of fecal-borne diseases; and the increase in the incidence of malaria, owing to the stagnant waters which formed breeding-grounds for mosquitoes in the wells, tanks, and bathing pools of the abandoned houses and gardens. But the causes of tropical diseases, such as dysentery and malaria, could not be diagnosed before the scientific discoveries of the nineteenth and twentieth centuries. Contemporaries were apt to blame the mortality on the allegedly unhealthy climate and on the air—especially on the 'night air'. The records of the Royal Hospital for Soldiers at Goa showed that 25,000 Portuguese had died there in the first thirty years of the seventeenth century, exclusive of those men who died in their billets, or when serving on board the fleets. Although long runs of reliable statistics are lacking, there is no reason to suppose that this wastage of manpower showed any relative decline for the next 150 years. Nor were the citizens much better off, since whole districts of the once populous capital became depopulated and reverted to the jungle during the same period, despite all the efforts of the municipal council to arrest this catastrophic decline. Old Goa was officially abandoned in 1760 for the healthier but much smaller site of Panjim, a few miles nearer the mouth of the river Mandovi.

A lesser but a contributory cause for the failure of the white and Eurasian population to reproduce itself in adequate numbers in Portuguese India during this period was the high incidence of desertion among the newly arrived drafts of raw recruits and the convict soldiers who formed such a large proportion of the garrison. Complaints of such desertions go back to the time of Afonso de Albuquerque, but in the years 1650–1750 they reach a crescendo for reasons which are discussed on pages 297–8 below. Here it will suffice to reproduce two typical observations on this evil. The first was made by Dom Christovão de Mello in the Viceroy's Council of State at Goa in August 1721, when the project of a combined Anglo-Portuguese expedition against Kanhoji Angria, the Maratha chief of Alibagh, was under discussion. Dom Christovão pointed out that the only European Portuguese troops available were the 700 men of the regiment (*terço*) of Goa, many of whom were physically unfit for active service.

> Most of the remainder [he added] cannot be depended upon, since experience has shown us how reluctantly and unreliably they serve. For although they are punctually paid and adequately fed, yet they desert without the slightest reason or excuse, preferring to act as slaves to Muslims, Hindus and heretics, rather than as vassals of their king. And this is something which we cannot easily avoid, since most of them come out in drafts from the kingdom as convicts exiled for infamous crimes, and thus neither courage nor zeal can be expected from such men in so difficult an undertaking.

Twenty-five years later the Viceroy Dom Pedro de Almeida, Marquis of Castelo-Novo, wrote to the Secretary of State at Lisbon that he was at his wits' end how to cope with the stream of deserters. He was well aware that the best way to prevent soldiers from deserting was to pay, clothe and feed them well, and not to exasperate them with brutal punishments. 'This is how those in this State are treated, yet in spite of everything desertions are so many and so frequent that I fear we shall shortly find ourselves without a single European soldier.' Of those men who did remain at Goa, a considerable number entered the religious Orders; and this again afforded a perennial subject of complaint in the correspondence of viceroys and governors with the Crown (p. 117) besides adversely affecting the potential birth rate.

The shortage of soldiers in Portuguese India during the second half of the seventeenth and the first half of the eighteenth centuries was all the more serious as the 'State of India' was engaged in almost continual warfare with the Arabs of Oman and with the Marathas of western India during this period. If the Portuguese had hoped for some respite from fighting at the end of the long-drawn-out and disastrous war against the Dutch in the East they were bitterly disappointed. 'Tell me, sirs,' wrote the soldier-chronicler, Diogo do Couto, in his *Dialogue of the Veteran Soldier* (1611), 'is there today in this world another land which is more of a frontier, and in which it is more necessary to go about with arms in the hand than in India? Most certainly not!' A century later the Overseas Councillors at Lisbon observed that 'the government of India is a completely military and warlike one' (*um governo totalmente militar e guerreiro*). In 1746 the Viceroy Dom Pedro de Almeida reminded King John V: 'This State is a military republic, and its preservation depends entirely on our arms by land and sea.' This frontier milieu of continuous warfare, which lasted with few intermissions until the end of the eighteenth century, helps to explain why so few Portuguese women went out to India in comparison with men; and why peasants emigrating voluntarily from Portugal and the Atlantic islands preferred to take their chance in Brazil, where some of the hostile Amerindian tribes might be cannibals but were not equipped with muskets and artillery, as were the Omani Arabs and the Marathas.

The coastal Omani had been a seafaring race for centuries before the Portuguese occupation of Muscat, but their shipping had been of the 'sewn' variety and thus was unable to stand up to the Portuguese guns on the high seas. In January 1650, however, these Arabs captured Muscat together with a number of Portuguese ships in the harbour. In a remarkably short space of time the Imams of Oman succeeded in forming and maintaining a navy which included well-gunned warships modelled on these and subsequent Portuguese prizes, and which fought the Portuguese high-seas fleet (*Armada de alto-bordo*) on more or less equal terms in the Indian Ocean between about 1650 and 1730. The meteoric rise of Omani sea-power from virtually nothing in the sixth decade of the seventeenth century requires much further investigation and research. We do not know to what extent the Omani relied on European deserters and renegades to man their guns and design their ships, nor where they obtained their shipbuilding timber from, or whether they relied entirely on ships which they secured by purchase or by capture. But the fact remains that they sent seaborne expeditions against Mombasa in 1660–1, sacked the town of Diu (where they obtained an immense booty) in 1668, and they narrowly failed to capture the fortress of Moçambique Island two years later. They repeatedly raided the smaller Portuguese possessions on the west coast of India, beginning with Bombay in 1661. By the end of the seventeenth century they had expelled the Portuguese from Mombasa and from all the Swahili island- or city-states along the East African coast (Pate, Pemba, Zanzibar, Malindi, etc.) over which they claimed suzerainty, north of Cape Delgado.

The Portuguese periodically sent fleets from Goa to relieve Mombasa before it fell in December 1698, and also to cruise in the Persian Gulf against their Omani enemies. Both sides claimed resounding victories in the numerous naval actions which ensued, but in reality the honours (such as they were) were fairly evenly divided. Alexander Hamilton's sarcastic summary of these inconclusive campaigns was not altogether unfair:

> The *Muskat* War (that has lasted since the *Arabs* took that city from them) tho' the longest has done them the least harm, for it obliges them to keep an Armada of five or six ships, besides small frigates and grabs of war, which gives bread to great numbers of people, who otherwise would be much more burdensome to the State, by crowding into churches. The *Arabs* and they have had many encounters, but no great damage done on either side. I was witness to one engagement near *Surat* bar, but it was not bloody.

Ovington, who visited Surat in 1689, was even more uncomplimentary, and he gave the balance of advantage to the Omani: 'The Portuguese generally endeavour to avoid them, and never dispute it with them but with great advantage on their side.' Both Ovington and Hamilton compared the treatment of prisoners of war by either side to the advantage of the Arabs.

The *Portuguese* use their captives with great severity, making them labour hard, and inure them to the discipline of the whip, but the *Arabs* use theirs with very much humanity, only making them prisoners at large, without putting them to hard labour and allow them as much diet-money as their own soldiers receive, and that is duly paid them twice a month. And if any of the *Portuguese* are artificers or mechanics, they may freely work at their trade, to earn money to redeem themselves.

The evidence of Ovington and Hamilton may be regarded as suspect, since both of them were staunch Protestants and apt to prefer Muslims to Roman Catholics; but the Portuguese failure to cope adequately with the Omani menace is equally apparent from the correspondence of the authorities at Goa with the Crown, and from the admissions made in the proceedings of the Council of State at Goa during those years. It should also be added that if the battle casualties were not very heavy, these campaigns were exceedingly costly both in men and money, particularly during the lengthy siege of Mombasa (March 1696 to December 1698). Belatedly reporting the fall of the fortress in a dispatch written at the end of 1699 the Viceroy added: 'I can assure your Majesty that this siege has caused immense harm to this State, for more than a thousand Portuguese men died in it, besides nearly ten thousand natives, all of them vassals of Your Majesty, and all due to the infected atmosphere.' There is no way of checking these figures, but it is quite clear from all the accounts of this epic siege that the overwhelming majority of the casualties were caused by disease; malnutrition and the plague carrying off scores of people for every individual who was killed in action. Dissensions between the Swahili of East Africa and their Omani overlords enabled the Portuguese to retake Mombasa in March 1728, and briefly to re-establish their suzerainty over the whole Swahili coast. But the fickle Sultan of Pate who had called them in changed sides again in the following year. Mombasa surrendered to some local insurgents in November 1729, and an expedition from Muscat quickly re-established Omani control over the coast north of Cape Delgado. The Omani control was almost as fragile as that of the Portuguese had been, and the authorities at Lisbon and Goa did not at once give up all hope of retaking Mombasa. But the rapid rise of the Maratha power on the west coast of India provided the Portuguese with an even more formidable enemy at closer quarters; and they were quite unable to take any advantage of the opportunities afforded by the increasing weakness and dissensions of the Omani after 1730.

The Marathas were already a menace to the Portuguese in the last quarter of the seventeenth century, and Goa was only saved from what appeared to be its inevitable capture by a victorious Maratha army in 1683 through the sudden and unexpected appearance of a Mughal army over the Western Ghats in their rear. The Maratha pressure reached its climax in 1737–40, when the city of Baçaim (Bassein) and the prosperous 'Province of the North' were taken by the Peshwa's armies after a series of hard-fought campaigns. The stubborn defence of Baçaim, which capitulated with the honours of war on 16 May 1739, aroused the admiration of the chivalrous Hindu victors, who coined a new proverb, 'warriors like Portuguese'. The 'Province of the North' comprised the Portuguese settlements along the sixty-mile stretch of the coast between Bombay (reluctantly ceded to the English in 1665) and Damão. It extended for some twenty or thirty miles inland in some districts, and it was the most productive part of what Indian territory was left to the Portuguese after their disastrous wars with the Dutch and the Omani. The proud and wealthy inhabitants of its capital city termed it 'Dom Baçaim'. Not only they, but many of the inhabitants of Goa were ruined in the war of 1737–40, 'the estates of the nobility and the clergy lying for the most part in the Province of the North', as the Viceroy told an English emissary from Bombay in October 1737. For that matter, Goa itself only escaped being occupied by the Marathas in 1739–40, through the payment of a large war indemnity, most of which was provided by forced loans and contributions extracted from the local Hindus, since the native Christians (and many of the Portuguese) were too impoverished to contribute anything substantial.

Apart from the progress which they made by land, the Marathas also developed into dangerous enemies by sea. The most formidable corsairs were those led by successive members of the Angria family in the first half of the eighteenth century. The original Khonaji Angria had been the commander-in-chief of the Maratha navy, but he broke away to found an independent principality in a stretch of territory measuring about 240 miles in length by forty miles in breadth between the sea and the Western Ghats from Bombay harbour to Wingurla. The Angria chiefs rejected the designation of 'pirates', which their European enemies bestowed upon them, but their formidable grabs, gallewats, ketches and other light but well-armed vessels attacked all merchant ships of any nationality wherever they saw the chance of doing so. The Angrias' prestige was greatly increased by their repulse of the Anglo-Portuguese attack on their main stronghold of Culabo (Colaba) in December 1721, and at this period some of the Portuguese traders from the Province of the North were even accepting Angrian *cartazes* or passports to secure their ships from molestation—a painful humiliation for the subjects of a monarch who still styled himself 'Lord of the Conquest, Navigation and Commerce' of the Indian Ocean.

The Culabo fiasco of 1721 further embittered relations between the English of Bombay and their Portuguese neighbours of Baçaim and Thana, which had never been cordial since the reluctant cession of the former island to the English as part of Catherine of Braganza's dowry on her marriage to Charles II. Boundary disputes over the limits of Bombay harbour frequently ended in armed clashes, and in the year 1722 these sporadic hostilities took the form of a local if not very deadly open war. A compromise peace was soon patched up, but mutual distrust prevailed for most of the eighteenth century. The English accused the Portuguese of having basely abandoned them in the expedition of 1721, and of subsequently supplying the Angria with arms and ammunition against them. The Portuguese priests were expelled from Bombay in 1720 and replaced by more amenable Italians. The Portuguese on their side were disgusted at the constant drunkenness, quarrelling and want of discipline among the English, and they accused them of supplying the Peshwa's armies with expert gunners and munitions of war in the fighting which led to the loss of the Province of the North. In point of fact, the English gunners who took service with the Marathas were deserters, and there was at least one such gunner with the Portuguese. It is also clear from the East India Company's records that their subordinates at Bombay sold provisions to the Marathas and gunpowder to the Portuguese, in both instances with reluctance, and in pursuance of their policy of strictly self-interested neutrality.

The loss of the Province of the North and the resultant cessation of boundary disputes over Bombay did not end friction between the Portuguese and English in Asia. The Viceroy Marquis of Alorna complained bitterly of the arrogance of English naval officers, especially Commodore Griffin and Admiral Boscawen, whom he accused of interfering with Portuguese merchant shipping in the Bay of Bengal, and of forcibly incorporating the old Portuguese settlement of São Tomé de Meliapur in the growing town of Madras. The same Viceroy also complained of similar high-handedness by the authorities of the Dutch East India Company against Portuguese shipping calling at Malacca; but as he explained in his instructions to his successor in 1750:

> I have acted towards these two nations with that prudence which is unavoidable on the part of one who has no strength wherewith to repel insults and violence; for it is not practicable to push matters to an open breach in the present state of affairs. I have referred the business to His Most Faithful Majesty, so that he can demand what satisfaction he requires from the two courts concerned, and take whatever decision he considers necessary.

It need hardly be added that subsequent Portuguese diplomatic protests at London and The Hague were equally unavailing, in view of the powerful influence exerted by the respective East India Companies in those two capitals.

Apart from the harm wrought to 'the State of India' through the wars with the Omani and the Marathas, the expansion of Portuguese power and influence in south-east Africa, which in the mid-seventeenth century bid fair to extend across the continent to Angola, was brought to an abrupt halt and severely contracted by the action of a Bantu warrior chief with the dynastic title of Changamire in 1693–5. Readers familiar with the history of Southern Africa will recall that the Spanish dream of finding El Dorado in South America had its African equivalent in the Portuguese quest for the gold and silver mines of Monomotapa, for long thought to be identical with the Biblical Ophir. Following in the wake of itinerant Arab and Swahili traders in gold, ivory and slaves, the Portuguese penetrated in the period 1575–1675 far up the Zambesi river valley into what is now

Southern Rhodesia, certainly as far as the Kariba gorge. The number of such adventurers was very small, though ambitious schemes were concocted at Lisbon for the despatch of European miners, peasants and artisans, accompanied by their respective families and provided with the tools of their respective vocations, to south-east Africa in 1635 and again in 1677. These colonisation plans proved to be much more modest in execution than they were in conception; and of the relatively few emigrants who reached East Africa, fewer still survived to make their way beyond the three fever-stricken minuscule settlements of Quelimane, Sena and Tete in the Zambesi river valley. But some of the luckier and hardier ones joined the ranks of the *prazo*-holders of Zambesia, either by marrying local heiresses or by carving out such extensive estates for themselves.

Taking advantage of the crumbling power of the Monomotapa, or paramount chief of the Makalanga (Wakaranga, va-Karanga) tribal confederacy, some Portuguese (and later, Goan) adventurers continued to occupy, by force or by agreement, the lands of various sub-chiefs, whose powers and jurisdiction they assumed. The Jesuit Padre Manuel Barreto, who knew the Zambesi region well, described the position as follows in 1667:

> The Portuguese lords of the lands have in their lands that same power and jurisdiction as had the Kaffir chiefs [*Fumos*] from whom they were taken, because the terms of the quit-rent [*foro*] were made on that condition. For this reason, they are like German potentates, since they can lay down the law in everything, put people to death, declare war and levy taxes. Perhaps they sometimes commit great barbarities in all this; but they would not be respected as they should be by their vassals if they did not enjoy the same powers as the chiefs whom they succeeded.

Padre Barreto added that these adventurers did not limit themselves to inspiring respect and fear, but were likewise famous for their prodigal hospitality and princely generosity. He instanced as an example Manuel Pais de Pinho, whose 'conduct of his household and person was that of a prince'. He maintained his prestige and reputation by being 'very lavish in giving and very fierce, even cruel, in chastising, which are two qualities that will make any man adored by the Kaffirs'.

Though these adventurers originally received their lands from the Monomotapa and later from the Portuguese Crown, the *prazos* were, in effect, virtually private principalities ruled by individuals of the 'robber baron' type. The *prazo*-holders maintained private armies composed of the free Negroes who lived on their lands with a hard core of more disciplined slaves. These armies were sometimes 10,000, 20,000 or 25,000 men strong when they took the field, though they were apt to dissolve as easily as they were formed if anything went wrong. The *prazo*-holders frequently feuded with each other, aside from being engaged in perennial warfare with unsubdued and hostile tribes. For these and other reasons the *prazos* changed in ownership and in extent very rapidly, and the *prazo*-holders themselves tended to become completely Africanised within two or three generations. With the object of averting this development and in order to bring these lands under the effective control of the Crown, the *prazos* were transformed into entailed estates which were granted by the Crown for three successive lives on payment of an annual quit-rent in gold-dust. Theoretically, they were granted to white women born of Portuguese parents. Male children of these unions were excluded from the succession, the *prazos* descending only in the female line, with the same proviso that the heiress must marry a white man. A *prazo da Coroa* (Crown *prazo*) was granted to a family on these conditions for three lives only, after which it was supposed to revert to the Crown. Failure to cultivate the land properly, the marriage of the lady owner with a coloured man, or her failure to reside upon the estate, likewise carried the penalty of the *prazo* reverting to the Crown. Some endeavours were also made to limit the size of the *prazos*.

In course of time all these conditions were increasingly disregarded. *Prazos* swelled to enormous proportions, rivalling those of the largest *fazendas* in colonial Brazil. The smallest *prazo* took a day to cross, and there were others which could not be crossed on horseback in eight days. The obligation to cultivate the land properly was generally ignored, as there was no market for an exportable agricultural surplus. The *prazo*-holders therefore contented themselves with growing enough food crops for their household and slaves. White men were so few in the Zambesi river valley, and their expectation of life was so short, that the *prazo* heiresses in the eighteenth century often

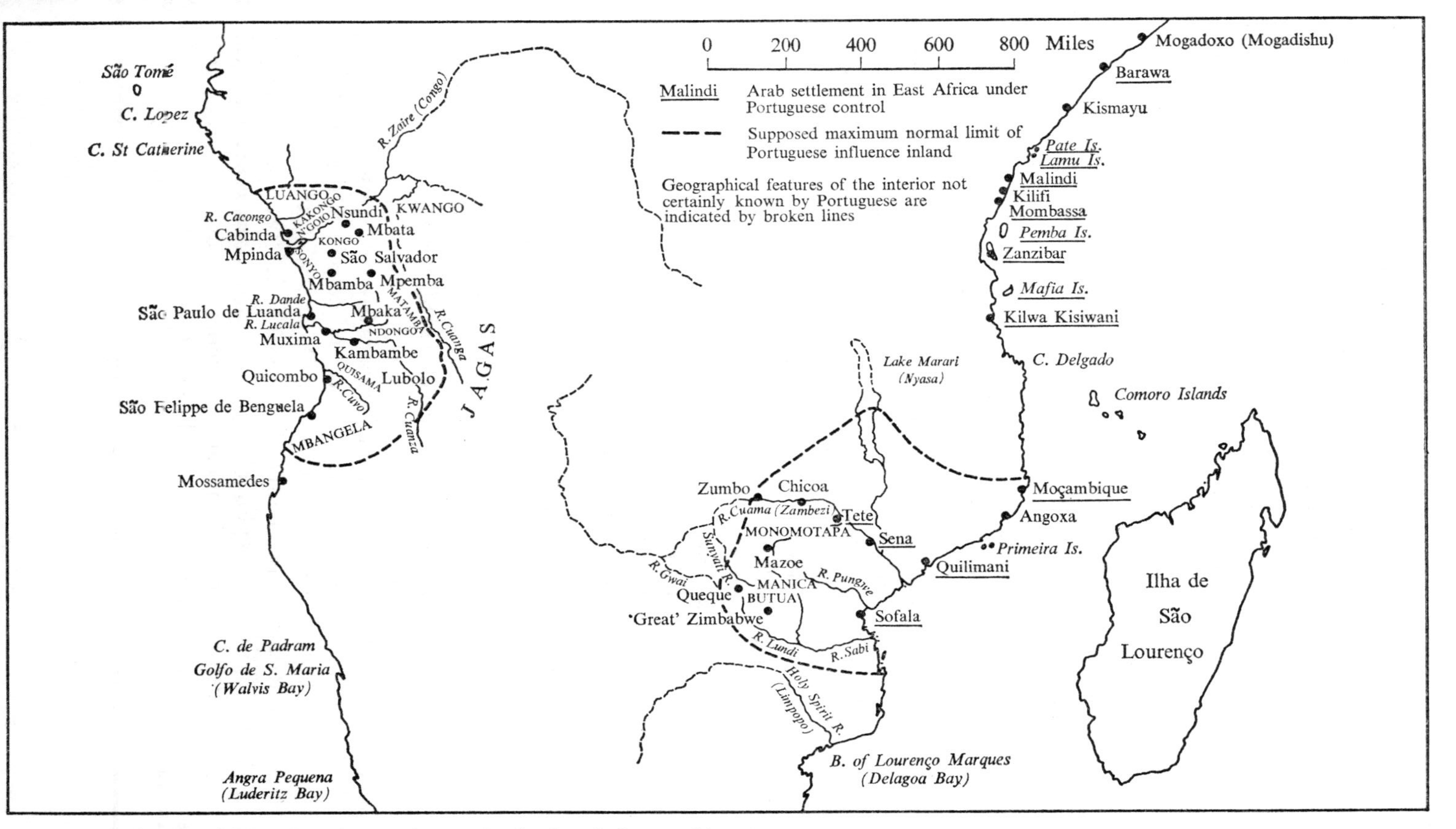

4 East and West Africa showing regions colonised or influenced by the Portuguese

married with the better acclimatised Mulattos, or with Indo-Portuguese from Goa. Nevertheless, many of the *prazos* flourished for a time, and many tales are told of the wealth and generosity of their owners, and of the vast fortunes in gold, ivory and slaves that some of them accumulated. The system also helped to maintain Portuguese power and influence in Zambesia, if at times in a very tenuous form. It was on the private armies of the *prazo*-holders that the Crown depended to fight its native wars, since the regular garrisons of Sena, Tete, Sofala and Quelimane seldom amounted to more than fifty or sixty fever-stricken convict-soldiers deported from Portugal and India. Shortage of European manpower was the basic reason why Portuguese East Africa was unable to make any material progress in the first half of the eighteenth century. The Viceroy reported to the Crown in 1744 that the Querimba Island group, which extended for a distance of some 300 miles between Moçambique Island and Cape Delgado, was garrisoned by a force of fifteen men and a sergeant, 'so there is not even one soldier for one island', as there were nineteen of the latter which were inhabited.

Though the Portuguese were very thin on the ground in south-east Africa, whether in the interior or on the coast, they had penetrated a remarkable distance inland, one of the most important trading-fairs which they frequented being that of Dambarare, which has recently been identified as a site near the Jumbo mine, about twenty miles north-north-west of the Southern Rhodesian capital of Salisbury. This *feira*, together with all the outlying posts visited by the Portuguese, was overrun in a widespread tribal rising, in which the reigning Monomotapa and Changamira temporarily co-operated, in the years 1693–5. One of the traders who survived this disaster some years later found the post at Zumbo, and thenceforward this place marked the western limit of Portuguese penetration along the Zambesi. The Jesuits and the Dominican missionary friars also possessed *prazos*, which did not, of course, involve any descent in the female line but belonged to their respective Orders. With the exception of the Jesuits, the standard of the regular and secular clergy was, for the most part, deplorably low; but they often exercised great influence over the Bantu among whom they lived, and they kept them at least nominally loyal to the Crown.

Two outstanding examples of this clerical influence in the first half of the eighteenth century were Fr. João de Menezes, O.P., in the Querimba Islands, and Fr. Pedro da Trindade, O.P., in the Zumbo district. The former, who died in 1749, was the virtual ruler of the northerly Querimba Islands, and a much more effective example of Portuguese authority than the wretched sergeant with his fifteen men. Fr. João ignored all the orders of his ecclesiastical superiors and of successive viceroys and governors to leave his fief and return to Goa, but he kept the Portuguese flag flying. He also carried on an active contraband trade with the French and English, and he died surrounded by a numerous progeny of sons and grandsons. His colleague of Zumbo, who died in 1751, apparently led a celibate life, but he traded on an extensive scale for gold, ivory, and slaves with tribal chiefs in the interior. His memory was for long revered among the local Bantu, to whom he taught various arts and crafts, including the use of some European agricultural implements. Both these friars maintained their own private armies of enslaved and free Negroes in the same way as the *prazo*-holders.

At the other end of Portugal's eastern empire, it was likewise the Dominican missionary friars who were mainly responsible for the fact that most of Timor, part of Solor, and the eastern tip of Flores (Larantuca) in the Lesser Sunda Islands still acknowledged the suzerainty of the Portuguese Crown. Admittedly, these friars only obeyed the Portuguese governors in so far as it suited them, and on at least two occasions they expelled the King's representatives in a most summary fashion. Lifao, on the north coast of Timor, was the nominal centre of Portuguese authority. When visited by William Dampier in 1699 it consisted of 'about forty or fifty houses and one church. The houses are mean and low, the walls generally made of mud and wattle, and thatched with palmetto leaves.' Dampier described the inhabitants as:

> a sort of Indians, of a copper-colour, with black lank hair. They speak Portuguese, and are of the Romish religion, but they take the liberty to eat flesh when they please. They value themselves on the account of their religion and descent from the Portuguese; and would be very angry if a man should say they are not Portuguese. Yet I saw but three white men here, two of which were Padres . . . and there are very few right Portuguese in any part of the island.

These conditions remained unaltered for the next half-century and more, the Viceroy Marquis of Alorna noting in his previously quoted report of 1750: 'There are only seven or eight Portuguese in that island, and several missionaries, whose fruit is not so much what they reap in the vineyard of the Lord, as in the liberty and licence in which they live.' Macao also had to weather some difficult years between 1660 and 1750, being repeatedly reduced to the verge of ruin by Chinese economic 'sanctions' (as they would be termed nowadays), which were imposed by the provincial authorities of Canton. But the 'City of the Name of God in China' had some useful friends at court in the persons of the Jesuit Padres at Peking, who often interceded successfully on the city's behalf with the occupants of the Dragon Throne.

Another reason which helps to account for the stagnation and decay of the Portuguese possessions in Asia and East Africa for most of this period was the maladministration of justice (*a falta de justiça*), which was the theme of continual complaints in both official and unofficial correspondence for several hundred years from places as far apart as Moçambique, Goa and Macao. Gaspar Correia, Afonso de Albuquerque's one-time secretary who spent a lifetime in the East, penned an eloquent denunciation of the lack of justice in his day, which was repeated in almost exactly similar terms by Diogo do Couto and by many other honest and upright men in the seventeenth and eighteenth centuries.

The greatest evil of all evils is when justice is not done to the people; because the captains of the fortresses of India are heads over the people, powerful owing to the powers given them by the King, and they take upon themselves still greater ones. They commit many evil deeds, as the King very well knows, such as robberies, injuries, murders, rapes, adulteries with married women, widows, virgins, orphans, and public concubinages; inflicting all these evils without fear of God and the King upon Christians, Muslims, Hindus, natives and foreigners. And as they behave like this, so do the Crown judges, the magistrates, the bailiffs and the Treasury officials. None of this would happen if only the King would order that a Governor of India should be publicly executed on the quay at Goa, with a proclamation to the effect that the King has ordered him to be beheaded because he had not done his duty as he ought to have done.

Allowing for some exaggeration in Correia's outburst, and

admitting that honest and conscientious officials were not unknown, even if they were few and far between, the fact remained that the *falta de justiça* always occupied a prominent place in the official correspondence between the authorities at Lisbon and Goa, and not least of the Goa Municipal Council.

This inveterate and deeply rooted abuse was also denounced in the First Ecclesiastical Council celebrated at Goa in 1567, and in the proceedings of subsequent councils. Even when judges and other officials might be honest, the complicated legal system which prevailed in Portugal and her empire gave infinite scope for delay in appeals, counter-appeals, challenging of witnesses, etc., of which lawyers (including the Christianised Indian Brahmins who were allowed to practise in the courts) took full advantage. The Jesuit Chronicler Padre Francisco de Sousa, writing at Goa in 1698, observed: 'The Portuguese may well despair of securing the favourable opinion of Oriental natives, in so far as our administration of justice is concerned, until we decide cases in the law-courts with greater brevity and dispatch, like the nations of the North do, who accordingly get on much better with the rural folk.' As the administration of justice by the English, Dutch, and French at this period left much to be desired in many respects, whether in the Metropolitan countries concerned or in their overseas settlements, it is significant that Padre Francisco de Sousa could still hold up these other European tribunals and judges as examples to the Portuguese.

In view of the overwhelming difficulties, aggravated in many instances by faults of their own making, which confronted the Portuguese for most of the seventeenth and eighteenth centuries, and in view of their own relatively exiguous demographic and economic resources, it may be asked how they survived in Asia and East Africa at all. Prophecies of impending doom for the hard-pressed 'State of India' were two a penny in this period. It was often characterised as being 'on its deathbed with a candle in the hand', though in the upshot the guttering candle was not forcibly extinguished until the unprovoked Indian invasion of Goa, Damão, and Diu in 1961. The Portuguese have for centuries displayed a remarkable ability to survive misgovernment from above and indiscipline from below, and in this particular period they were helped by some other factors.

In the first place their enemies usually had their own and even more acute dissensions. The Ya'arubi Imams, who ruled Oman from 1624 to 1738, were torn by internal feuds and factions to a degree almost unparalleled even in the fissiparous Arab world, and they were also preoccupied with fighting the Persians as well as the Portuguese for most of the time. The Marathas likewise seldom presented a united front for long, and they had other enemies to contend with in their rear. In any event, they were probably reluctant to give the *coup de grâce* to Goa when it was completely at their mercy in 1739, because they were becoming apprehensive of the growing English power in India, and they considered the Portuguese to some extent as a counterweight. The death of the victorious Changamire in 1695 probably prevented the Portuguese in Zambesia from being completely overrun, and none of his successors proved capable of uniting the hostile Bantu to the same extent. The endemic inter-tribal warfare which prevailed in the island of Timor from time out of mind until well into the nineteenth century meant that whenever some clans rebelled against the (largely nominal) overlordship of the Portuguese Crown, their jealous rivals could be depended upon to support the *partido real* (royalists). Even among the Muslims of East Africa, the princes of Faza (Ampaza) and the Queens of Zanzibar remained loyal to the Portuguese through thick and thin during the struggle for Mombasa in the 1690s. Moreover, the singular ineptitude of the Portuguese commanders in several campaigns was offset to some extent by the bravery and self-sacrifice of some of their subordinates.

But one main reason why the Portuguese retained as much of their shoe-string Eastern empire as they did, when they had to compete not only with formidable Asian enemies but with intensive commercial competition from the far wealthier Dutch and English East India Companies, was their own inherent tenacity and resilience. 'It's dogged as does it' sums up much of their otherwise unfortunate vicissitudes in this period. Disastrous as were many of their defeats by land and sea, humiliating as were the indignities to which they were sometimes subjected in places like Macao and Madras, the Portuguese in the East were always proudly conscious of what they considered as their glorious sixteenth-century past. They were convinced that as the descendants of Afonso de Albuquerque's *conquistadores*, and as the vassals of their 'mighty' king, they were *ipso facto* vastly superior to the upstart merchants of the European trading companies, however wealthy these might be. They were equally convinced of their superiority over the Asian peoples whom they had dominated in the Indian Ocean for so long—a conviction expressed by Padre Francisco de Sousa, S.J., when he referred in his *Oriente Conquistado* of 1710 to 'the Portuguese character, which naturally despises all these Asiatic races'. God, the Portuguese felt, was on their side in the long run, even if, as they frankly acknowledged, He was in the meantime punishing them for their sins by the loss of Malacca, Ceylon, Malabar and Mombasa.

The title of 'very high and very powerful' (*muito alto e muito poderoso*) which they applied to their kings in all their official correspondence was no mere figure of speech in so far as the Portuguese were concerned, even if it was singularly inapt in the view of the other Europeans when applied to the first three monarchs of the House of Braganza, who were hardly the equals of their Bourbon, Habsburg and Stuart contemporaries. As a French missionary working in Siam and Indochina (1671–83) observed: '*parler à un Portugais de la puissance et de l'autorité de son roi, c'est lui enfler tellement le cœur que, pour la soutenir, il n'ya a point de' excès où il ne s'abandonne.*' This pride was shared by all ranks and classes in Portugal, with the almost solitary exception of King John IV, who once confided to the French envoy at Lisbon that he would gladly abandon the heavy burden of trying to sustain Portuguese India if he could think of an honourable way of doing so. But he was the first and the last Portuguese monarch who made such an avowal, and his successors did not hesitate to make considerable sacrifices to keep the ramshackle 'State of India' afloat. The English governor and council of Bombay observed in 1737, correctly enough: 'The Crown of Portugal hath long maintained the possession of its territories in India at a certain annual expense, not inconsiderable; purely as it seems from a point of Honour and Religion.' Moreover, this attitude was endorsed even by the 'Enlightened' statesmen who criticised the follies and extravagancies of the 'Magnanimous' King John V, but who agreed with him that (in the words of Dom Luís da Cunha, the most experienced Portuguese diplomat of his time) 'the conquests are what honour us and what sustain us'. If Portugal still counted for something in the councils of the great powers of Europe it was primarily because of the importance of her overseas empire; and if by 1700 Brazil was clearly the most profitable jewel in the Portuguese Crown, India was still the most prestigious.

Lastly, it should be emphasised that the 'decadence' of Portuguese Asia, so much lamented by contemporaries at the time, and so much emphasised by historians ever since, was not equally obvious at all times and places, and there were intervals of relative calm and prosperity. Both the 'golden age' of the sixteenth-century *conquistadores* and the penury of many of their descendants tend to be exaggerated in retrospect. When Padre Manuel Godinho, S.J., boasted in 1663 that the State of India had at one time exercised sovereignty over territory including 8,000 leagues, twenty-nine capital cities and thirty-three tributory states (p. 128), he was indulging in a rhetorical flight of fancy rather than stating a sober historical truth. The figure of thirty-three kingdoms could only have been reached by including petty Indian coastal rajas and chiefs of Indonesian *kampongs* whose effective jurisdiction was limited to a few square miles. Similarly, when Alexander Hamilton sneered at the miserable poverty of the Portuguese 'everywhere in their colonies all over India' at the end of the seventeenth century, we find the Italian globe-trotter Gemelli Careri noting after his visit to Damão and Goa in 1695: 'The Portuguese live very great in India, both as to their tables, clothing, and the number of Kaffirs, or slaves to serve them.' There is plenty of other evidence by equally reliable eye-witnesses to the same effect. Apart from the numerous East African Negro slaves whom the Portuguese employed, Indian, Indonesian and Chinese free labourers were all available in large numbers and at exceedingly cheap rates. If there was undoubtedly (as Padre Francisco de Sousa, S.J., wrote in 1710) always a pullulating and impoverished proletariat in all the Portuguese Asian strongholds, rich merchants and wealthy captains were not wanting either. 'For the poor always ye have with you', as the Gospel tells us, but so for that matter are the rich.

The magnificent churches and the massive fortresses whose ruins from Moçambique to Macao still impress the twentieth-century traveller, were nearly all built (or at any rate extensively rebuilt) between 1600 and 1750, and not in the halcyon days of the sixteenth century, as is so often assumed. The gold and ivory of East Africa continued to come to Goa during the first half of the eighteenth century, even if the gold and pepper of Sumatra no longer did so. Goa was an important centre of the diamond trade in 1650–1730, more so, perhaps, than Madras; and the East Indiamen which sailed from the Mandovi to the Tagus were still usually very richly laden, even though there were only one or two sail a year instead of five or six. By 1725 the economic centre of the Portuguese seaborne empire had long since shifted from 'Golden' Goa to the City of the Saviour on the Bay of All Saints in Brazil, but the gentry or *fidalguia* of India still boasted that theirs was the only true nobility with style and panache, 'and that of Portugal is a mere shadow in comparison'.

CHAPTER VII

Revival and expansion in the West 1663-1750

THE economic revival of Portugal and her overseas empire, which had been expected to follow the definitive conclusion of peace with Spain and the United Provinces in 1668–9, largely failed to materialise during the next two decades. The Portuguese economy depended chiefly on the re-exportation of Brazilian sugar and tobacco, and on the exportation of Portugal's own products of salt, wine and fruit, to pay for the essential imports of cereals and of cloth and other manufactured goods. The value of those exports never sufficed to pay for these imports; and the country's balance of payments problem became increasingly critical with the rise of British and French West Indian sugar production in competition with the older Brazilian. 'Who says Brazil says sugar and more sugar', wrote the municipal council of Bahia to the Crown in 1662; and a couple of years later a visiting English seaman noted of Brazil: 'The country is much abounding with sugars, which is the best sugar for the most part that is made.' He added that Rio de Janeiro, Bahia and Recife 'all yearly lade many ships with sugar and tobacco and brazilwood for the merchants of Portugal, it being a great enriching to the Crown of Portugal, without which it would be but a poor kingdom'. But in 1671 the experienced English consul-general at Lisbon, Thomas Maynard, 'a very stirring man on his nation's behalf', reported to his government: 'All their sugars which are arrived this year, with all other commodities this kingdom affords to be exported, will not pay for half of the goods that are imported, so that their money will all be carried out of their kingdom within a few years.' The position was aggravated by the general economic depression which was then affecting much of Western Europe, and by a decline in the annual imports of silver bullion to Lisbon from Spanish America via Cadiz and Seville.

Nor did the situation look any more cheerful on the other side of Portugal's Atlantic empire. The correspondence of the municipal council of Bahia with the Crown in the last quarter of the seventeenth century is particularly valuable in this respect, as the council represented primarily the interests of the local sugar-planters (*senhores de engenho*). These planters continually complained—as did their French and English competitors in the Caribbean islands—that falling prices, poor trade, high taxes, costly and inefficient slave labour, all combined to render their occupation an extremely thankless and hazardous one. Their leading spokesman, João Peixoto Viegas, pointed out in 1687 that heavy duties had been laid on Brazilian sugar at Lisbon in the mid-seventeenth century, when its sale price in Europe was high; and these duties were maintained and even increased later, at a time when the European price of sugar was falling, owing to the increasing production of sugar in the English and French West Indies. Seven years earlier Peixoto Viegas, who was also a tobacco-grower and cattle-rancher as well as a sugar-planter, had complained that out of every hundred rolls of tobacco which he sent to Lisbon seventy-five went to defray the customs dues and freight charges. Peixoto Viegas, who wielded a singularly pungent pen, also claimed that quite apart from these man-made obstacles, the natural hazards of tropical agriculture were such that sugar-planting 'is just like the act of copulation, in which the participant does not know whether he has achieved something or whether the result will be a boy or a girl, or sound or deformed, until after the birth is achieved'.

Admittedly the planters were partly responsible for their own difficulties, owing to the extravagant and seigneurial way of life which they affected. Moreover, they nearly all bought their slaves and equipment on long-term credit at high rates of interest from their correspondents and merchants in the seaports, to whom they were usually heavily indebted. Bankruptcies were frequent, and relatively few plantations remained in the ownership of the same family for more than two or three generations. Both Brazil and Angola suffered from an acute shortage of coin at this period, since the merchants of Lisbon and Oporto now preferred to collect payment in specie whenever they could, instead of accepting the equivalent in sugar. The Governor-General of Brazil complained in the year 1690 that more than 80,000 *cruzados* had been exported recently from Bahia to Oporto alone, and that if Brazil's unfavourable balance of trade continued at this rate, her entire economy would soon collapse. The deteriorating economic situation of Portugal's Atlantic empire was worsened by the ravages of smallpox throughout Angola during the mid-1680s and by the simultaneous introduction of yellow fever into Brazil, where Bahia and Pernambuco suffered heavy mortality in 1686–91. Writing from Bahia to a friend at Lisbon in July 1689, Padre António Vieira, S.J., observed gloomily:

> This year many sugar mills ceased grinding cane, and next year only a few of them will be able to function. Prudent people advise us to dress in cotton, to eat manioc and to revert to using bows and arrows for lack of modern weapons; so that we will shortly relapse into the primitive savagery of the Indians and became Brazilian natives instead of Portuguese citizens.

There was obviously some exaggeration in these complaints, but there is plenty of other evidence to show that the economic depression in Portugal's Atlantic empire for most of the last quarter of the seventeenth century was both real and profound, even if it was not quite so catastrophic as the jeremiads of Padre Vieira and so many of his contemporaries implied. It is significant that Thomas Maynard, who was forecasting the proximate collapse of the Portuguese economy in 1671, could write twelve years later, when the depression was still in full swing, about the 'wonderful quantities' of Brazilian sugar which were habitually re-exported from Lisbon. But it is equally significant that the Lisbon municipal council, in a strongly worded remonstrance submitted to the Crown in July 1689, reiterated the complaints of the *Camara* of Bahia against the penal duties levied on sugar, tobacco and other primary products, which the councillors claimed had encouraged the English and French to develop their own crops in their own colonies. The Lisbon council also argued that experience had shown that the yield from taxation tended to decrease in proportion as the fiscal screw was tightened. If Peixoto Viegas had stressed the difficulties and uncertainties of agriculture in the tropics, the Lisbon councillors, quoting classical precedents for the peasants' plight in Portugal, reminded the Crown: 'Agricultural workers are subjected to unavoidable toil and to uncertain hopes; in barren years through the loss of their crops, and in good years through a glut and consequent fall in prices, and thus they inevitably have to endure one of these two calamities.'

These representations—and many similar ones from all corners of the far-flung Portuguese empire—were sometimes sympathetically received but were usually shelved by the King and his councillors. The basic reason for this evasive action was that the Portuguese Crown depended so heavily on the revenue from its Customs that it could not forgo the immediate yield for the uncertain prospect of a larger income in a distant future if taxation was drastically reduced. In 1715, for example, the duties levied on goods exported (or re-exported) to Brazil from Lisbon amounted in some instances to as much as 40 per cent. The home government was, of course, well aware of the gravity of the situation. It tried to avert disaster by a combination of stop-gap and more far-reaching methods, which did not involve any diminution of the Customs duties. Persistent efforts were made to foster the growth of the cloth industry in Portugal by protectionist legislation on Colbertian lines, and by contracting French and English skilled textile workers. Sumptuary laws were enacted against the importation of luxury goods, particularly those from France, such as lace and gold thread. In 1688 the nominal value of the gold and silver coinage in Portugal and her empire was increased by 20 per cent, while leaving its intrinsic value unchanged. In 1695 a colonial mint for striking provincial gold and silver coins was inaugurated at Bahia, the nominal value of this money being raised by an additional 10 per cent, and its circulation was restricted to Brazil alone. This mint was moved to Rio de Janeiro in 1698–9, to Recife in 1700–2, and finally back to Rio de Janeiro on a permanent basis in 1703. A copper coinage for Angola was authorised in 1680, although the first consignment of this money (which was struck at Lisbon) did not reach that African colony until fourteen years later. In 1680 a Portuguese settlement was founded at Sacramento on the northern branch of the Rio de la Plata opposite Buenos Aires, largely in the hope of diverting the stream of silver from Potosí through this back door of High Peru, as had happened in the period 1580–1640. Last but not least, the search for gold, silver and emerald mines in Brazil, which had been carried on intermittently ever since the mid-sixteenth century, was more actively stimulated by the Crown.

Not all of these measures were equally successful. The industrialisation programme was hampered by the unwillingness of the French and English governments to allow their skilled workers to emigrate and improve the technical knowledge of the Portuguese. The English envoy at Lisbon was told by his government in 1678: 'If you could learn the names of any of His Majesty's subjects that are now in the Portugal service of making manufactures, the severest course would be used for bringing them back again', presumably by reprisals on their families at home. In the upshot, it proved impracticable to prevent the emigration of such skilled workers if they left as individuals or in small groups. In this way nine weavers from Colchester and two English women arrived at Lisbon in 1677, 'to teach the Portuguese to card and spin in the English way'. A much more serious blow to the development of the Portuguese textile industry than this dog-in-the-manger attitude of foreign governments was the suicide of the third Count of Ericeira, the protagonist of Colbertian policies in Portugal, in May 1690. His successors were more interested in developing the wine trade, and this they were able to do owing to the Anglo-Dutch war with France between 1689 and 1697, which greatly increased the English demand for Portuguese wines and which hampered the seaborne export of French wines. The monetary devaluation of 1688 was most unpopular in Brazil, but the establishment of a colonial mint in 1695 was warmly welcomed. The colony of Sacramento, though it quickly became a centre of contraband trade with the viceroyalty of Peru, proved very expensive to maintain in the face of Spanish hostility.

The Brazilian sugar industry, which seemed to be on the verge of complete collapse in 1691, began to recover soon afterwards, probably because of increased demand in Europe, the exhaustion of stocks held at Lisbon, and because Brazilian sugar still retained its prestige as being of better quality than the West Indian varieties. At any rate, the observant circumnavigator William Dampier, who visited Bahia (Salvador) in 1699 and stayed there long enough to get a good idea of what was going on, noted: 'It is a place of great trade' with thirty-two large ships from Europe in the harbour, besides two slave-ships from Angola and an 'abundance' of coastal shipping. He added: 'The sugar of this country is much better than that which we bring home from our plantations, for all the sugar that is made here is clayed, which makes it whiter and finer than our *Muscovado*, as we call our unrefined sugar.' But the spectacular revival of the Luso-Brazilian economy which began in the 1690s was mainly due to the belated discovery of alluvial gold on a hitherto unprecedented scale in the remote and forbidding region some 200 miles inland from Rio de Janeiro, which was henceforward known as Minas Gerais, the 'General Mines'.

The exact date and place of the first really rich gold strike are uncertain. The traditional accounts vary, and the official correspondence of the governors of Rio de Janeiro and Bahia only tardily and inadequately reflects the finds of the first ten years. In the present state of our knowledge, it seems a fair assumption that alluvial gold was found on an unexpectedly profitable scale almost simultaneously by different individuals or by roving bands of Paulistas in the years 1693–5. They were ranging through the virgin bush and forest country of what is now Minas Gerais, looking not so much for gold as for Amerindians to enslave and for silver, which metal the Spaniards had found in such dazzling quantities in the uplands of Mexico and High Peru. As often happens, the Paulista pioneers who first struck it rich tried to keep the secret of the finds from the outer world, but inevitably they failed to do so for long. By 1697 even those people in the coastal cities who had been sceptical of the rumours about the first discoveries had come to realise that there was indeed 'gold in them thar hills' on an unprecedented scale. The first of the great modern gold-rushes had begun. Writing to the Crown in June 1697, the Governor of Rio de Janeiro reported that the Caeté diggings alone 'extend in such a fashion along the foot of a mountain range that the miners are led to believe that the gold in that region will last for a great length of time'. New and rich workings were discovered almost daily over wide areas, where every river, stream and brook seemed to contain alluvial gold.

The Paulista discoverers and pioneers were not left in unchallenged possession of the gold diggings. A swarm of adventurers and unemployed from all over Brazil and from Portugal itself quickly converged on the 'general mines' by the few practicable trails through the wilderness, leading respectively from Bahia, Rio de Janeiro and São Paulo. 'Vagabond and disorderly people, for the most part low-class and immoral', as the Governor-General at Bahia unflatteringly described them in 1701. A Jesuit eye-witness, writing about the same time, described the immigrants in less jaundiced terms.

> Each year crowds of Portuguese and of foreigners come out in the fleets in order to go to the Mines. From the cities, towns, plantations and backlands of Brazil, come Whites, Coloureds and Blacks together with many Amerindians employed by the Paulistas. The mixture is of all sorts and conditions of persons: men and women; young and old; poor and rich; gentry and commoners; laymen, clergy and religious of different Orders, many of which have neither house nor convent in Brazil.

The hardships endured on the trails to the diggings proved too much for many of the *Emboabas*, as the 'tenderfeet' from Portugal were called in derision by the Paulista backwoodsmen from the protective leggings of hides or skins which they wore in the bush. Some of these newcomers started out with nothing more than a stick in their hand and a knapsack on their back, not a few being found dead on the line of march 'clutching a spike of maize, having no other sustenance'.

The unruly crowds which poured into the gold diggings of Minas Gerais in the confident expectation of making their fortunes there speedily divided into two mutually hostile groups. The first comprised the original Paulista pioneers and their Amerindian auxiliaries, servants and slaves. The second comprised the newcomers from Portugal and from other parts of Brazil, together with their slaves, who were mainly of West African origin. What amounted to a small-scale civil war between these two rival groups broke out towards the end of 1708, and the subsequent fighting, or rather skirmishing, lasted with intervals for almost exactly a year. There was more sound and fury than death and destruction involved, as it is doubtful if over a hundred were killed on either side. But the result was a decisive victory for the *Emboabas* and their (mainly Bahian) allies, who expelled their Paulista rivals from most of the gold-fields of Minas Gerais. Henceforth the white population of this region was predominantly of Portuguese origin, chiefly *Minhotos* and men from northern Portugal. West African slaves were likewise numerous and a large Mulatto population developed from the concubinage of 'Mineiros' with Negresses.

The 'War of the Emboabas', as the civil broils of 1708–9 were called, enabled the Crown to assert its authority over the turbulent mining community for the first time. Both sides had appealed to Lisbon for support, and this gave the Crown the chance to send out a governor and to create a skeleton administration in Minas Gerais. Difficulties over the collection of the *quinto real*, or tax of the 'royal fifth' of 20 per cent on all gold mined, caused a great deal of discontent, which eventually culminated in a revolt against the authority of the Governor at Villa Rica de Ouro Preto, the principal mining town, in June 1720. The Paulistas, significantly, gave no help to the Emboabas who rebelled on this occasion, and the revolt was soon suppressed with a mixture of guile and force by the Governor. A regiment of dragoons (likewise mainly recruited in northern Portugal) was raised to reinforce the royal authority in Minas Gerais, which remained unchallenged for nearly seventy years. The Paulistas who had been expelled from this region by the victorious Emboabas in 1708–9 trekked ever westwards in the following decades and discovered successively the gold-fields of Cuiabá, Goiás, and Mato Grosso. During the late 1720s diamonds were also discovered in Minas Gerais, and in 1740 the so-called Diamond District was placed under a particularly strict and onerous Crown regime, unparalleled in the European colonial world. This regime virtually isolated the Diamond District from the rest of Brazil, and it could only be entered or left by persons holding written permits from the intendant in charge.

The discovery of gold and diamonds in Brazil and their exploitation on an unprecedented scale had several major repercussions in the Portuguese world. In the first place, and for the first time, it led to a large shift of population from the coastal regions of Pernambuco, Bahia, and Rio de Janeiro to the mining regions in the interior of Brazil. This movement was not like the slow and steady penetration already effected in some areas, such as the valley of the river São Francisco, by scanty groups of cattle rangers who were very thin on the ground, but it was an emigration *en masse*. Secondly, while greatly stimulating the colonial economy, and thus helping to solve one economic crisis, it started another by attracting labour, both bond and free, from the sugar and tobacco plantations and the coastal towns to seek more remunerative employment in the diggings and mines. A sharp rise in prices also resulted from a labour shortage coupled with a greatly increased production of gold. Thirdly, the increased demand for West African slaves in the mines and plantations of Brazil led to a corresponding increase in the slave trade with West Africa and a search for new slave-markets there. In Portugal itself, the exploitation of Brazil's mineral resources and the great revival of Portuguese trade with that colony enabled the mother country to settle its unfavourable balance of trade with the rest of Europe in gold. Brazilian gold and diamonds also greatly enriched the Crown, the Church and the Court, and gave King John V the wherewithal to avoid calling the Cortes and asking them for money during the whole of his long reign, 1706–50. This monarch is reported to have said in this connection: 'My grandfather feared and owed: my father owed: I neither fear nor owe.'

Presumably this proud boast was made some time after the War of the Spanish Succession had been wound up by the Treaty of Utrecht in 1715, for when King John came to the throne as a timid young man nine years earlier, Portugal was suffering severely through her involvement in that war, into which she had been dragged mainly by English pressure. In the light of hindsight, neutrality would have been the best solution for Portugal's delicate position between France and Spain on the one hand and the maritime powers and the Austrian empire on the other. The Duke of Cadaval, the premier noble of Portugal and one of King Pedro II's confidential advisers, saw this clearly enough without the benefit of hindsight, since he took a cynically realistic view of Portuguese resources and of the country's complete unreadiness for war. He observed in 1705 that far from allying herself with England and the United Provinces against France and

Spain, Portugal was not in a position to confront 'the most inconsiderable prince in Lombardy'. The war was also very unpopular with the common people, who had not yet recovered from the sacrifices imposed by the long struggles with Spain and with the Dutch, even after thirty-five years of peace. Although the Portuguese army and the allied British and Dutch forces managed to enter Madrid briefly on two occasions, the war as a whole brought Portugal nothing but humiliation and loss. It will suffice to mention the capture of Sacramento by the Spaniards (1705), the disastrous allied defeat at Almanza (April 1707) and the sack of Rio de Janeiro by Duguay Trouin in 1711, after an ill-organised attack by Du Clerc had been completely (if narrowly) defeated in the previous year. Even the millions in gold which were now reaching Portugal in the annual Brazil fleets could only help to pay for a fraction of the war, since most of it had to be sent to England to pay for essential imports. British and Dutch governmental subsidies were needed to maintain about half of the Portuguese armies as well as their own troops in the Iberian peninsula.

The European frontier rectifications, which Portugal had been promised as part of the price of her entry into the war on the allied side, were never seriously pressed by the British government in the negotiations preceding the Treaty of Utrecht. Portugal had to be content with the recognition of her rights as against French claims in the Amazon region, and with the restoration of the colony of Sacramento by the Spaniards on the final conclusion of peace. This experience confirmed King John V in his resolve to remain neutral in any future European conflict, though he sent a few warships to the Aegean to help the Papal and Venetian naval squadrons against the Turks in 1716–17. He also took violent umbrage with the Spanish Court over some trivial infringement of the diplomatic immunities of the Portuguese Embassy at Madrid, which led to mutual threats of war and to the severance of diplomatic relations between the two Iberian monarchies in 1735–7. But actual hostilities were confined to the Rio de la Plata estuary, where the elements caused more difficulties and more casualties to both sides than did the desultory and inconclusive fighting. King John V was the most punctilious as well as the most devout of the Portuguese monarchs, and his excessive preoccupation with his personal prestige led to very strained relations with the Papacy in 1728–32. But he was always prodigal in his expenditure on the Church, modelling the recently created patriarchate of Lisbon as closely as possible on the ritual splendour and etiquette of St. Peter's at Rome. He took the side of the Jesuits of the China mission in their disputes with the College of the Propaganda Fide over the celebrated 'Chinese Rites'; but the quantities of Brazilian gold which he sent to the Papal court and cardinals eventually earned him the title of 'Most Faithful Majesty' in 1748, thus fulfilling his long-cherished wish to equal the 'Most Christian' King of France and the 'Most Catholic' King of Spain.

King John V avowedly modelled himself in many ways on the 'Sun King' Louis XIV, and he strove to inaugurate a golden age of absolutism in Portugal, as Louis had done in France. To some extent he succeeded, for during his reign Portugal attained a position of international prestige and importance which she had not enjoyed since the reign of King Manuel I and the opening of the sea route to India. Lisbon was again one of the wealthiest cities in Europe, as it was likewise one of the most crowded and one of the most insanitary. If much—perhaps most—of the Brazilian gold which reached Lisbon was squandered on costly ecclesiastical establishments, on patriarchate prodigalities and on building the gigantic monastery-palace of Mafra (1717–35) as a rival to the Escorial and to Versailles, some of it went on more justifiable objects: the superb libraries at Coimbra, at Mafra, and the Lisbon Oratorian College; the scientific mapping of some regions in Brazil; and the gold coins which he gave to the poor and needy in the bi-weekly public audiences which he held for many years. One of the literally outstanding monuments of his reign is the cyclopean Aqueduct of the Free Waters, constructed essentially between 1732 and 1748 (though not finally finished until 1835), which brought drinking water to Lisbon for the first time on an adequate scale. This magnificent work was financed by a surcharge on the wine, meat, and olive-oil consumed by the inhabitants of the capital and its district, but John V deserves credit for insisting that the ecclesiastics, including those of the pampered patriarchate, paid their share of this tax when they displayed their habitual reluctance to do so on the plea of ecclesiastical immunity.

The Aqueduct of the Free Waters was of such obvious public utility that the working classes paid their share of taxation for it more or less uncomplainingly, but this did not apply to the building of Mafra, on which over 45,000 workmen were engaged at one time. Carts and pack-animals were requisitioned on a massive scale for the transportation of building materials and provisions, and trained artificers were compelled to work there if they showed any reluctance to go of their own accord. A disgruntled French consul complained in 1730 that it was impossible to find a single wheelwright in Lisbon to mend the broken wheel of a coach, thus compelling the owner to walk, however exalted his social status might be. The British envoy previously complained that he could not buy a bucket of lime to make whitewash for his house. As early as 1720 the French ambassador at Lisbon reported confidently to his king that the work would never be finished as the treasury was empty and all the money in the Iberian peninsula would not suffice to pay for it. But finished it was, even though the wages of the artists and artisans employed there were often in arrears for months or years on end. The Lisbon municipal council was bankrupted by the loans which it was forced to raise in order to help finance this work, and which the King failed to repay despite repeated reminders and reiterated promises. The Swiss soldier-naturalist, Charles Frédéric de Merveilleux, who visited Mafra in 1726, noted that virtually everyone complained about this costly extravagance, adding: 'It is certain that three-quarters of the King's treasures and of the gold brought by the Brazil fleets were changed here into stones.'

Nor was it only the building of Mafra which financially crippled the Lisbon municipal council, for the King compelled it to celebate the annual Feast of Corpus Christi on such a ludicrously lavish scale in 1719 that the council was never able to pay off the debts incurred on that occasion. The royal marriages between the ruling houses of Spain and Portugal in 1729 were mainly financed on the Portuguese side by a tax (euphemistically known as a *donativo* or free gift) levied throughout the whole of Portugal and her empire, and of which Brazil's share alone was assessed at 8,000,000 *cruzados*. This fiscal burden was also widely resented, particularly by the Luso-Brazilians who had to find the bulk of it. Remittances on this account were being made to Lisbon for many years after it was obvious that the (admittedly costly) dowries and expenses involved did not come to more than a fraction of that sum. By the time the 'Magnaminous Monarch', as his loyal subjects called him, died in 1750, he was a drooling bigot. Far from 'neither fearing nor owing', he was terrified of his approaching death and deeply indebted. There was not enough money in the royal treasury to pay for his funeral, and some of the servants of the royal household, including the Queen's coachman, had received no wages for five years. The pay of the army and navy, particularly that of the remoter colonial garrisons, was also often in arrears in whole or in part for lengthy periods.

It must, however, be admitted that the traditional view of King John V as the most sluggish and the most superstitious of the Portuguese kings, active only in his amours with nuns and in his prodigal expenditure on churches and music, is largely a caricature. Largely, but not entirely. He was a different man before the epileptic strokes which crippled him physically and mentally in the 1740s, transforming his always pronounced religiosity into something like religious mania. Before that time a British ambassador to Lisbon who knew him well considered that he had 'a piercing intelligence' and that he was 'extremely quick and lively' in the apprehension and dispatch of official business. This favourable assessment is borne out by a study of the King's state papers and private correspondence. These documents show that for much of the time he was an intelligent and conscientious monarch, though always liable to fits of backsliding and depression. Moreover his most obvious faults—if that is the right term—were shared by the great majority of his subjects. A few Portuguese who had lived long in Paris, Rome, London or The Hague and who had been markedly influenced by the ideas of the Enlightenment, might and did deplore King John's passion for gorgeous ritual in church services, his fondness for elaborate religious high-days and holidays, his patronage of the Inquisition and his exaggerated respect for priests, friars and ecclesiastics of all kinds. But most of his compatriots felt exactly the same way about these things, partly perhaps because the numerous religious festivals meant that there were only about 122 working days in the Portuguese year, as Dom Luís da Cunha alleged in 1736. In other words, as the late Jaime Cortesão wrote in his

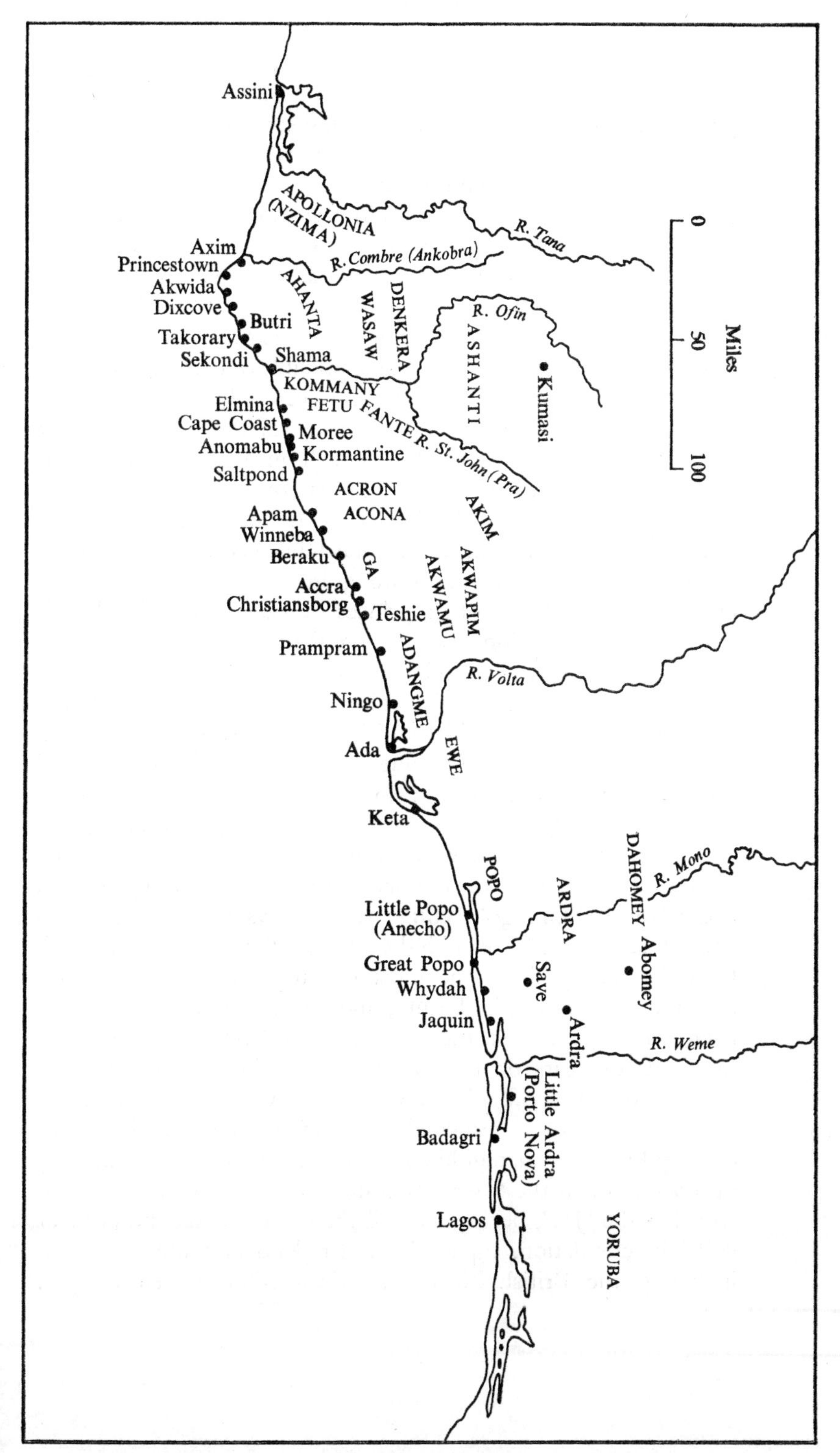

5 Area from which slaves were secured on the Guinea Coast

perceptive study of John V, if the King sinned in these respects, he sinned in company with the entire nation.

Writing towards the end of this long reign, the King's chronicler and panegyrist, Padre António Caetano da Sousa, described it as 'a happy reign, which could properly be called the Golden Age, since the mines of Brazil continued to yield an abundance of gold'. Nor was this mere hyperbole, though it may have been a slight exaggeration. The ostentatious extravagance of King John V, although it was often made possible only by withholding wages or by 'welshing' on his debts, certainly encouraged the general belief in Europe that the Crown of Portugal was much richer than it really was. The Rev. John Wesley echoed this widespread belief when he wrote in his *Serious Thoughts occasioned by the great Earthquake at Lisbon* (1755): 'Merchants who have lived in Portugal inform us that the King had a large building filled with diamonds, and more gold stored up, coined and uncoined, than all the other princes of Europe together.' This conviction—or illusion—concerning the Golden Age of King John V was the more readily accepted in England since Portuguese and Brazilian gold coins enjoyed an even wider circulation in some counties than did English sovereigns. They were legal currency everywhere, their values were listed in the local annual pocket-almanacs, and in 1713 an Exeter man noted: 'We have hardly any money current among us but Portugal gold.'

Apart from the mercantilist theories then in vogue, which placed such emphasis on the acquisition (or retention) of gold and silver bullion, gold coins have always exercised an irresistible fascination for mankind ever since they were first minted. Gold has always been the most coveted form of coinage on account of its rarity, its beauty, and because it retains its lustre even when buried in the ground or otherwise secreted for hundreds of years on end. People and princes would stop at nothing to get gold, observed José da Cunha Brochado, the Portuguese envoy in England, 1710–15. During the eighteenth century Luso-Brazilian gold coins, particularly the *moeda* (*moidore*) of 4,000 *reis* and the 6,400 *reis* coin, known in the Anglo-Saxon world as the 'Joe', became two of the most general and popular coins in circulation, especially in England and the Americas, including the British North American colonies before 1778.

Luso-Brazilian gold coins were also extensively counterstamped for use in other regions, such as the French West Indies down to the Napoleonic period. In so far as the European bullion markets were concerned, shipments of Brazilian gold from Lisbon to Amsterdam, Hamburg and elsewhere were usually made by way of England, because of the frequent availability of English shipping and the special facilities offered by English firms and houses. As late as 1770, when the production of Brazilian gold had declined disastrously, we find a merchant banker of St. Malo importing 'l'or de Portugal' from Lisbon via London and Calais. The export of gold from Portugal was strictly prohibited by law, but English warships, and the Falmouth packet-boat which maintained a weekly service with Lisbon from 1706 onwards, were officially exempted from search by the Portuguese authorities. Some discretion had to be exercised in getting the gold aboard these vessels, but the lengths to which the English were prepared to go in driving this contraband gold trade are clearly shown by the following extract from the journal of the purser of H.M.S. *Winchester* during her stay at Lisbon in August 1720:

For the twenty last days I have been highly caressed by Captain Stewart to use all my interest with the merchants of my acquaintance to get money upon freight for England; and in that time with no little trouble, fatigue and hazard, I received and carried on board several thousands of moidores [=*moeda*, Luso-Brazilian gold coin of 4,000 *reis* valued at 27*s.* 6*d.* in 1720]; particularly in one day I received upwards of 6,000 which I brought from the merchants (who are extremely cautious in sending them off with safety and privacy) in my own pockets at several trips to the pinnace which waited for me, the men being armed with muskets, pistols and cutlasses to oppose any of the Shurks (or Custom House) boats who should attempt to stop, molest or attack us (the carrying of money out of Portugal being prohibited upon pain of death), but I met with no disturbance. Each day I leave the boat armed as before mentioned and lying ready at either the King's Palace or the Remolares to receive me, and the moment I set my foot in her she puts off and makes all haste on board, where when I am unladen of my golden burthen, I am dispatched back to seek for more; being obliged to neglect my own business to attend the Exchange every noon and evening, to be at both the coffee houses every morning, to spend my own money to fetch the gold from the houses of the respective persons who send it off, to watch proper times to avoid being discovered with it about me . . . the merchant no sooner puts the money on board but by the first packet sends a bill of lading to his correspondents with advice of the day the ship will sail with it.

Some figures survive of the bullion brought by the packet-boats from Lisbon to Falmouth: between 25 March 1740 and 8 June 1741 it was valued at £447,347, while in the calendar years 1759 and 1760 it totalled £787,290 and £1,085,558 respectively. This certainly underestimates the total bullion flow to England in the first half of the eighteenth century, as warships were used on the scale indicated above and of which many other examples could be given. Captain Augustus Hervey, R.N., took home a freight of 80,000 moidores from Lisbon in 1748 and another 63,533 moidores in 1753, apart from 30,000 moidores from Lisbon to Gibraltar and Italy in 1752. Merchant ships were also used, and 'above a million of Portugal gold' was coined into English money by the London mint in the three years 1710–13 alone, while, as we have seen, Luso-Brazilian gold coins circulated as common currency in England, especially in the West Country with the facilities afforded by the Falmouth packet-boats. One must always be wary of figures in a trade where so much contraband was involved; but it is perhaps safe to estimate the value of annual flow of Luso-Brazilian gold into England during the reign of King John V as something between £1,000,000 and £2,000,000 sterling. A well-informed French resident at Lisbon estimated the average annual drain of Luso-Brazilian gold to England at 12,000,000 *cruzados* (£1,500,000) in the decade 1730–40. Needless to add that gold-smuggling was not confined to Lisbon, and its prevalence at Bahia and Rio de Janeiro is briefly discussed on pages 219–220 below.

The key role of Brazilian gold in the growth of English exports to Portugal in the reign of King John V was often emphasised by the English domiciled there. In 1706 the consul at Lisbon wrote that the English woollen manufacturers' trade 'improves every day, and will do more as their country grows richer, which it must necessarily do if they can continue the importation of so much gold from the Rio every year'. In 1711 the English merchants at Lisbon ascribed their growing business principally to the 'improvement of the Portuguese trade to the Brazils and the great quantity of gold that is brought from thence'. They added, correctly enough, 'as that trade goes on increasing, our woollen trade will probably also increase proportionably'. Four years later they unhesitatingly declared the Brazil trade to be 'the basis and foundation' of their whole trade. In 1732 Lord Tyrawly, the English envoy at Lisbon, asserted complacently: 'The English are the nation here of most considerable figure by far, both from our numbers settled here, our shipping and trade.' This fact was freely admitted by envious French and Dutch merchants at Lisbon, one of the former observing in 1730: 'The trade of the English at Lisbon is the most important of all; according to many people, it is as great as that of all the other nations put together.' Small wonder that the members of this 'jolly, free Factory', as Benjamin Keene termed the association of leading British merchants at Lisbon in 1749, waxed fat and kicked, or that their profits, their privileges and their arrogance were increasingly resented by the Portuguese.

A few of the more perceptive English visitors to Lisbon sympathised to some extent with the Portuguese point of view, as exemplified by the following extracts from the journal of Captain Augustus Hervey, R.N., after conversing with the special envoy, Lord Tyrawly, in the summer of 1752:

> Lord Tyrawly talked to me a good deal about the affairs here, and I found his tone very much altered with regard to the Portuguese from what it was in the voyage. He now condemned the Factory as a set of dissatisfied, restless, proud and extravagant fellows, and I had reason to think his old [Portuguese] friends here had got some ascendancy over him. In short, at last he grew outrageous with the Factory and abused them all. He obtained the redress to the complaints he was sent to enquire into, and was not long after recalled, going away with the contempt and curses of all the English, who I think are in general very unreasonable in their demands, and yet think in some things the Portuguese are endeavouring to prejudice the trade with them, but not more so to us than other nations; and who can blame them for wanting to save a very great part of the balance of that trade that is against them, if they do not favour any other country to our prejudice?

The flourishing state of Anglo-Portuguese trade in the first half of the eighteenth century was not primarily due to the famous Methuen Treaty concluded in December 1703, since the commercial privileges then granted to the English by the Portuguese government were soon extended to other nations, beginning with the Dutch in 1705. But this treaty certainly kept the way open for the spectacular increase in the importation of English cloth and other exports into Portugal, whence the bulk of them were re-exported to Brazil, and of Portuguese wines into Great Britain, where they eventually affected the traditional Scotch preference for claret, as a patriotic bard later lamented:

> Firm and erect the Caledonian stood,
> Good was his claret and his mutton good.
> 'Let him drink port,' the *British* statesmen cried.
> He drank the poison, and his spirit died.

In truth, the preferential duties on Portuguese wines went back to 1690, and the Methuen Treaty of 1703 confirmed them. It was the sweet Lisbon wines rather than the harsher Douro wines of the north which benefited immediately from that treaty, and the development of the port-wine trade came a good deal later. The light woollen and worsted textiles, suitable for the Brazilian market, in which the English cloth manufacturers specialised to a far greater extent than did their Dutch, French and German rivals, formed a prime factor in the ability of the English to exploit the expanding Luso-Brazilian market for clothing and furnishing needs. The prosperous English merchants established at Lisbon and Oporto, who could draw on the concentrated mercantile wealth of London, were also able to extend to their Portuguese—and through them to their Brazilian—customers longer and more plentiful credit than their foreign competitors were able to do.

The gold rush in Minas Gerais and the acute labour shortage which it created in Brazil led, as we have seen (pp. 157–8 above), to heavy emigration from Portugal and to a sharp increase in the transportation of Negro slaves from West Africa. The number of emigrants from Portugal and its Atlantic islands can only be guessed at, but there is no need to accept the inflated figures which are still widely current. It is doubtful if more than 5,000 or 6,000 people emigrated from Portugal to Brazil in a single year at the height of the gold-rush to Minas Gerais during the first two decades of the eighteenth century. Even so, it is rather surprising to find some of the King's councillors observing complacently in

1715 that despite the drain on manpower caused by emigration and the recent war, Portugal was so thickly populated that the loss was hardly noticeable. Five years later the councillors abruptly changed their tune, for the numbers of able-bodied men emigrating from the Minho alone induced the Crown to promulgate a decree (March 1720) drastically limiting emigration to Brazil, which thenceforth was only permissible with a government passport. Of course this decree was not always strictly observed, and in any event the overpopulated regions of the Minho, the Azores and the 'great wen' of Lisbon continued to provide the bulk of the emigrants. Able-bodied young men heavily predominated among them, and they all went out at their own expense or that of their families and friends. But there were not wanting councillors who urged on the Crown better balanced and more ambitious schemes for sending whole families of agricultural workers to Brazil, with assisted passages at the expense of the Crown. One such scheme was actually implemented in 1748–53 when groups of peasant families were sent from the Azores to Santa Catarina and Rio Grande do Sul. The projected total of 4,000 emigrant families was not attained, but sufficient numbers of both sexes arrived to give the Santa Catarina (modern Florianopolis) region a high proportion of white blood as compared with other parts of late eighteenth- and early nineteenth-century Brazil.

If the gold-rush in Minas Gerais was mainly responsible for the marked increase in white immigration into Brazil it was also the cause of an even greater intensification of the West African slave trade with the ports of Bahia, Rio de Janeiro, and (to a lesser extent) Pernambuco. In the year 1671 the Mbundu kingdom of Ndongo in Angola finally foundered between Portuguese pressure from the west and the attacks of the Imbangala kingdom of Kasanje from the east. One branch of the Mbundu had previously 'hived off' and founded the kingdom of Matamba under the famous Queen Nzinga (died 1663), which was able to maintain itself for a long time against both the Portuguese and Kasanje. The old kingdom of Congo likewise disintegrated after the defeat and death of King António I by the Portuguese at the battle of Ambuila (29 October 1665). During the course of the eighteenth century the focal point of the West Central African slave trade shifted beyond Matamba and Kasanje to the Lunda empire on the Kasai, while the densely populated Ovimbundu country in the hinterland of Benguela was increasingly tapped by the Portuguese slave-traders. The smallpox epidemic of 1685–7 brought great havoc among the Bantu tribes of Angola, and this demographic disaster gave an additional impulse to the revival of the Portuguese slave trade in the Gulf of Guinea, which had just got under way. This development was further accelerated by the demand for slave labour in the gold-fields of Brazil from 1695 onwards.

After the Dutch had driven the Portuguese from their Gold Coast forts in 1637–42, the latter had for some decades only a limited interest in this region. The Dutch found by experience, however, that the Negroes preferred Brazilian tobacco from Bahia to any other form of trade goods. They therefore allowed traders bringing tobacco from Bahia (but not other commodities from Lisbon) to obtain slaves at four ports along what is now the Dahomey but was then called the Slave Coast: Grand Popo, Whydah (called Ajuda by the Portuguese), Jaquin and Apa. The ships engaged in this trade were compelled to call at the Dutch West India Company's stronghold of São Jorge da Mina (Elmina), in order to have the nature of their cargoes checked, and to pay a tax of 10 per cent of the tobacco rolls which they brought from Brazil, on pain of confiscation of ship and lading by the cruisers of the West India Company if they failed to comply with this regulation. The Portuguese naturally resented this imposition, which they evaded whenever they could. But they badly needed the slaves of Sudanese origin whom they obtained at Whydah and who were more robust than the Bantu from Angola.

Moreover, the Bahia exporters found this market exceptionally useful, as the Negroes preferred the third-grade Bahian tobacco to any other, and the first and second grades were reserved for export to Portugal. This third-grade tobacco was formed of the rejected leaves of the superior qualities, which were rolled into the form of a thick rope, like the leaves of other grades, but were more liberally brushed with molasses. This process was never effectively imitated by the English, Dutch and French traders on the Guinea Coast, despite all the efforts they made to do so. The monopoly of this third-grade Bahian tobacco consequently gave the Portuguese an advantage over all their European rivals for the whole of the eighteenth century. As late as 1789 the Director of the French fort at Whydah reported: 'Brazilian tobacco is better twisted, that is to say more sugared, and the rolls weigh more than ours; it is prepared with pure syrup, while the tobacco we get from Lisbon is prepared with syrup and sea-water. This dries it out too soon, and the Negroes know it.' The growth of the Bahia-Whydah trade, despite the difficulties caused by Dutch exactions and by the frequent wars between the petty coastal states of Ardra, Whydah and Jaquin with Dahomey, which dominated them all by 1728, is shown by the fact that whereas eleven tobacco ships from Bahia had visited the Mina Coast in the five-year period 1681–5, this number had increased to 114 in 1700–10. Originally, the Portuguese exported some smuggled gold-dust from Guinea in this trade, the first gold coins issued by the mint at Bahia in 1695 being largely struck from gold obtained in exchange for tobacco; but after the exploitation of the mines of Minas Gerais this process was reversed. Thenceforward Brazilian gold was smuggled by the Bahian slave-traders into Whydah, despite all the efforts of the home government and the colonial authorities to stop this 'leak' and to confine the export trade to tobacco.

Writing to the Crown in 1731, the Viceroy Count of Sabugosa stressed the complete dependence of the Brazilian economy on the West African slave trade, and especially on that with Whydah. He estimated that between 10,000 and 12,000 slaves were imported yearly into Bahia alone from Whydah, adding that even this number was not enough for the mines and plantations. Angola provided about 6,000 or 7,000 slaves annually and these were distributed on a quota system between Bahia, Rio de Janeiro, Pernambuco and Paraíba. The Bantu from Angola were generally regarded as being inferior to the Sudanese from the Mina (or Slave) Coast, and numbers of the latter who were ostensibly imported to work on the sugar plantations and tobacco fields of Bahia were soon more or less clandestinely re-exported to the more lucrative markets of Rio de Janeiro and Minas Gerais. The Viceroy alleged that other actual and potential slave-markets in Upper Guinea, Senegal, Gambia, Loango, and even

Madagascar and Moçambique, had been tried as alternative sources, but they all had been found wanting for one reason or another, so that slaves from Whydah were irreplaceable. Seven years later his successor, the Count of Galveas, stressed that Whydah was still the best source of slaves for Brazil, both in quantity and quality. The West African slave trade was often subject to violent fluctuations, apart from variations in supply and demand, and in later years the Whydah trade fell off somewhat and the Angola-Benguela slave export (official) figures rose to about 10,000 a year.

This accelerated emigration from Portugal, the Atlantic islands and West Africa into Brazil during the first half of the eighteenth century probably brought the total population up to something like a million and a half, if the unsubdued Amerindian tribes of the interior are excluded. Despite the gold- and diamond-rushes which successively opened up parts of Minas Gerais, Cuiabá, Goiás and Mato Grosso, and despite the less spectacular but important development of cattle-ranching and stock-raising in regions as widely separated as Marajó Island, Piauí and Rio Grande do Sul, the old sugar-producing captaincies of Pernambuco, Bahia and Rio de Janeiro still retained in the aggregate more than half of the colonial population. The mining districts of the Brazilian far west were largely isolated from each other. Their communications with São Paulo, Minas Gerais and the coast involved long and complicated journeys by bush-trails and rivers through uninhabited stretches of country, or across regions infested by hostile Amerindians. It has rightly been observed that isolated settlements and so-called 'hollow frontiers' have typified Brazil from its colonial beginnings to the present day, when the lorry, the omnibus and the aeroplane are at last achieving what the Negro carrier, the pack-horse, the mule-train and the canoe inevitably failed to bring about—easy and rapid communication.

The racial composition of the country in 1750 is difficult to determine in the light of the relatively few reliable figures that we have, and which refer to widely scattered localities. The main classifications, ignoring the numerous subdivisions, were roughly as follows: *Brancos*, meaning 'whites' or at least persons socially accepted as such; *Pardos*, or dark-hued coloured people of mixed descent, including Mulattos, though these were sometimes classified separately; *Pretos*, 'Blacks', or Negroes, whether bond or free: the Christianised Amerindians. The northern State of Maranhão and Pará, which was administered separately from Brazil at this period, contained mainly Amerindians, with *mamelucos* or *caboclos* (mixture of white and Amerindian) in the second place, whites and Mulattos in the third, and Negroes last. The tropical rain-forest of the Amazon valley, though it provided an admirable fluvial highway to the interior, was ecologically unsuitable for white colonisation on a large scale; and even nowadays the vast Amazon jungle region (*selva*) has fewer inhabitants than the island of Puerto Rico. In the populous ports of Recife, Salvador (Bahia) and Rio de Janeiro, and their respective environs, Negroes, *Pardos* and Mulattos predominated, with pure (?) whites in the second place and *Caboclos* and Amerindians in the third. In the mining districts of Minas Gerais the number of Negroes (*Pretos*) probably slightly exceeded the whites and *Pardos* put together. In São Paulo the whites and coloured (largely *Mamelucos*) heavily outnumbered the Negroes, as they did among the cattle rangers and stockmen of Rio Grande do Sul. In other regions, such as the São Francisco river valley and in Piauí, the races were mixed to such a degree that coloured people were by far the most numerous. The actual situation is, of course, completely different, owing to the vast increase in European immigration during the nineteenth and twentieth centuries, coupled with the total cessation of Negro immigration after the effective suppression of the African slave trade with Brazil by 1860.

Successive epileptic strokes had left King John V virtually a speechless imbecile for some weeks before he finally expired on the evening of 31 July 1750. But if he had died in full possession of his faculties he might, perhaps, have felt moderately satisfied with the state of his Atlantic empire, at any rate in comparison with the places where the Portuguese flag still flew in Asia and East Africa. Of course, some of the problems which worried the Portuguese government in 1706 still persisted in 1750, but there were positive achievements to record as well. The drain of Brazilian gold to England was the cause of as much anxiety to the Portuguese authorities as it was of complacency to the English government and merchants, but this gold drain also ensured that

English naval support would be forthcoming if it appeared (as in 1735) that Portugal was seriously threatened by either Spain or France. Attempts made to develop new or languishing home industries (silk, glass, leather, paper, etc.) had for the most part ended in failure, but the Portuguese army was clothed in cloth manufactured at Covilhã, and a pragmatic of May 1749 ordained that all liveried servants must henceforth wear cloth made in Portugal. The vast amounts of foreign (mainly English) manufactured goods, corn, butter, meat and other provisions which were imported, and which were largely paid for with Brazilian gold, were intended almost exclusively for the thriving cities of Lisbon and Oporto and their immediate vicinities. Elsewhere, owing to the execrable roads (appalling by even eighteenth-century standards) and to the dearth of navigable rivers, the small local and regional industries of the interior successfully resisted foreign competition, since the imported goods could not bear the additional cost of inland transportation. An Italian traveller in Portugal observed with only mild exaggeration that it was easier to find at Lisbon a ship bound for Goa or for Brazil than a carriage for Oporto or for Braga.

The widespread belief that the Methuen commercial treaty of December 1703 killed these modest but essential cottage and home industries is grossly exaggerated where it is not quite unfounded. Moreover, even though Lisbon and Oporto were largely dependent on imports from abroad, in other ways they benefited from being the European entrepôts for the thriving Brazil trade, which was conducted almost exclusively by shipping from these two ports. The wine trade was flourishing, although it was common knowledge that the English merchants who handled the exports made much greater profits than the Portuguese growers. If most of the Brazilian gold which reached Portugal subsequently found its way to England, or was metamorphosed into the stones of Mafra, or was squandered on the Lisbon churches and patriarchate, some of it percolated into the countryside, as attested by the charming *quintas* and *solares* (manor houses) which were built or rebuilt in this period. If the high living of the prosperous English merchants at Lisbon and Oporto was what struck most foreign visitors to those places, there were also many Portuguese merchants and entrepreneurs who made their fortunes in the Brazil trade, as instanced on pages 331–2 below.

A balance-sheet struck in 1750 for Portugal's South Atlantic empire would also have shown more profit than loss, if the reign of King John V was taken as a whole. Admittedly the Governor of Angola in 1749–53 in his private correspondence denounced that colony as a corrupt and vicious settlement on the verge of total ruin, but in his official correspondence he claimed that the export of slaves to Brazil had markedly increased during his term of office. Whatever the moral shortcomings of the *moradores* of Luanda, enterprising slave-traders and military mobile columns penetrated further into the interior with the defeat of the kingdom of Matamba in 1744. This advance, however slow and irregular, contrasted favourably with the contraction of Portuguese power and influence in Zambesia and Moçambique on the opposite side of Africa. In Brazil, although several of the municipal councils of Minas Gerais informed the Crown in 1750–1 that the production of gold was disastrously on the down-grade, and that the number of Negro slaves imported into that captaincy had dropped alarmingly, the annual fleets from Rio de Janeiro were still very richly laden. Similarly, although the sugar-planters of Bahia and Pernambuco complained louder than ever of their economic woes, yet substantial cargoes of sugar were still being shipped to Lisbon in the fleets from Salvador and Recife. If the English market for Brazilian sugar had virtually ceased to exist by 1750, Italy and other Mediterranean countries still took sizeable quantities. The northern State of Maranhão-Pará, which had hitherto subsisted on a purely barter economy, received a regional metallic currency (struck at Lisbon) in 1749. The obvious prosperity of the Amazon entrepôt of Belém do Pará, with its well-built European-style houses, favourably impressed the French scientist, La Condamine, when he stayed there six years earlier.

The most convincing evidence of Brazil's development during the first half of the eighteenth century was afforded by the terms of the Treaty of Madrid (13 January 1750), which delineated the frontiers between Portuguese and Spanish South America Though not fully implemented on the ground, this treaty gave Brazil, in effect, roughly her present boundaries, and it secured the official Spanish renunciation of all claims to Brazilian territory arising out of the Treaty of Tordesillas, which was formally abrogated. Some daring Portuguese and Paulista adventurers had recently established direct communications between the Mato Grosso region of the Brazilian far west and the Amazon, by way of the Guaporé, Mamoré and Madeira rivers. Formal sanction for this accomplished fact was given by the Portuguese Crown in 1752. The Treaty of Madrid also ceded to this Crown seven Spanish Jesuit mission-stations along the river Uruguay in exchange for the cribbed, cabined, and confined Portuguese outpost of Sacramento on the Rio de la Plata.

This treaty was rightly regarded as a great diplomatic triumph for Portugal, since it was previously acknowledged that it would be easier to persuade the Spanish government to abolish the Inquisition than willingly to cede a foot of ground in America to any European people, 'and least of all people to the Portuguese'. Yet there were some influential persons in Portugal who could not stomach the surrender of Sacramento, and who were prepared to sabotage the implementation of the treaty, which was largely the work of King John's Brazilian-born secretary, Alexandre de Gusmão. One of these hostile critics was Sebastião José de Carvalho e Mello, a former Portuguese envoy at London and Vienna and a man who was about to make a greater impact on Portuguese history than anyone else has ever done.

CHAPTER VIII

The Pombaline dictatorship and its aftermath 1755-1825

THE biographical approach to history exemplified in the 'Life and Times of So and So' is generally admitted to be suspect, owing to the temptation to exaggerate the importance of the 'Life' in relation to the 'Times'. On the other hand, there are certain individuals—Oliver Cromwell in England, Louis XIV and Napoleon I in France, Peter the Great and Joseph Stalin in Russia—whose impact on their times and indeed on posterity has been so undeniably great that one is justified in referring (in a very general way) to Cromwellian England, Napoleonic France, and Stalinist Russia. Similarly, the twenty-two years of the virtual dictatorship of Portugal by Sebastião José de Carvalho e Mello, widely known by his title (conferred in 1770) of Marquis of Pombal, forms a period of Portuguese history which has left deep and enduring marks to this day. It would be absurd to deal with the history of Portugal in the second half of the eighteenth century, however briefly, without some consideration of this extraordinary Jekyll-and-Hyde character, who so profoundly affected his country for both good and ill. His ruthless suppression of the Jesuits, his barbaric executions of the aristocratic Tavoras and the crazy Padre Malagrida, his policy of regalism *à outrance*, his drastic reform of the educational system, and his attitudes to the English Alliance, to the Jewish problem and to the colour-bar, all had far-reaching repercussions in his own day and for long afterwards. He inaugurated a practice of violently polemical writing, which was followed by both his defenders and his detractors for successive generations. If French historiography concerning the Napoleonic period can be considered in terms of 'Napoleon, For and Against', there is an even more marked division in nineteenth- and twentieth-century Portuguese historical writing over Pombal. Moreover, Pombal is one of the very few Portuguese in history who is more than a name to the great majority of educated persons outside Portugal and Brazil—ranking in this respect with Prince Henry the Navigator, Vasco da Gama and (one may safely assume) Dr. António de Oliveira Salazar.

Born in 1699, his life-span lasted for over three-quarters of the eighteenth century. He came of a family of undistinguished rural gentry and he passed the first forty years of his life in relative obscurity. The possessor of a remarkable physique and an iron constitution, he was more than six feet tall and survived a very sedentary life and recurrent bouts of illness with his mental and physical faculties unimpaired until after his fall from power. His strikingly handsome features helped him to make a runaway match with an older aristocratic widow in 1733, but this marriage did not give him the position in high society which he coveted. King John V, divining the streak of sadistic cruelty in his character, refused to give him an important post in the government on the grounds that he had 'a hairy heart' (*cabellos no coração*). When appointed envoy to the Court of St. James in 1738 he possessed no diplomatic qualifications or experience of foreign countries, having studied law at Coimbra University, which was a singularly backward institution even in comparison with the intellectual torpor of contemporary Oxford and Cambridge. He never learnt English during the six years he spent in London, but he was remarkably fluent in French. He was apparently an avid reader of English books, state-papers and documents in French translation; but his prolix dispatches from London do not reveal any profound understanding of either English society or of the British economy. He was often affable and agreeably informal in his dealings with individuals, although foreign diplomats were apt to be bored by his loquacity and verbosity.

Pombal was greatly impressed by English commercial prosperity and maritime power. He was equally impressed by the glaring and gross inequality between the privileged position enjoyed by the English residents at Lisbon and Oporto and the scurvy way in which the few Portuguese who visited London were apt to be treated there. He complained that cockneys amused themselves by stoning inoffensive Portuguese sailors (in exactly the way satirised by *Punch* a little over a century later—' 'Ere's a foreigner: 'eave 'arf a brick at 'im'). This might be explained as the ignorant malice of gin-sodden watermen on Wapping Stairs, but Pombal added: 'Those better-class people who see these insults, although they do not encourage them with words, yet they condone them by their silence.' He claimed for himself, by virtue of Article XV of the Anglo-Portuguese Treaty of Alliance in 1703, tax-exemptions and fiscal immunities equal to the wide range of those enjoyed by the British envoys at Lisbon. Embarrassed and annoyed by Pombal's continual and prolix complaints, the Duke of Newcastle, Secretary of State for Foreign Affairs, took refuge in the contention that King John V, being an absolute monarch, was bound by the letter of the Anglo-Portuguese treaties, whereas King George II, being a constitutional monarch, might be compelled by Parliament to modify the details of their application The English government also showed their annoyance at Pombal's disconcerting insistence on Portuguese Treaty rights by meanly refusing to give him the customary present to a departing envoy when he was sent on a special mission to the Court of Vienna in 1745.

Pombal remained for four years at the Austrian capital, although he never achieved a diplomatic result of any importance. His first wife having died, he married the niece of Field Marshal Daun, and this marriage gave him access to the best society in Vienna. The bride was half his age, but the union was a life-long love-mtch The ruthless dictator was a model family man in private life, whose deep affection for his wife and children was fully reciprocated by them. Pombal returned to Lisbon shortly before the death of the (by now ailing) King John V. Thanks to his Austrian wife, he quickly won the favour of the Austrian-born Queen of Portugal and through her he got access to the heir to the throne, Dom José. As soon as this latter succeeded his father he made Pombal Secretary of State for War and Foreign Affairs, subsequently showing greater confidence in him than in any of his other ministers, whether old or new; but it was the great Lisbon earthquake of 1 November 1755 which accelerated Pombal's rise to the position of virtual dictator of Portugal for the next twenty-two years. There were several other high officials besides Pombal who acted with courage and decision in this unprecedented catastrophe, which laid over two-thirds of Lisbon in ruins and cost something between 5,000 and 15,000 lives; but it was to Pombal that King Joseph turned instinctively in this crisis, and it was Pombal who persuaded the wavering monarch to rebuild the capital on the same site and not transfer it to Coimbra or elsewhere, as was suggested. Within three weeks of the disastrous All Saints Day the British envoy at Lisbon was reporting to his government that Pombal was already discussing plans for the rebuilding of the stricken city, 'which may be very easily accomplished while the gold and diamond mines in the Brazils remain unhurt'.

The Lisbon earthquake made a profound impression throughout the whole of Europe, which did not fade for many years. Even if Dr. Johnson soon tired of hearing of its wonders, Voltaire made great use of it in *Candide*, and Goethe feelingly recalled in his *Dichtung und Wahrheit* the shock which it had given to childish trust in an All-Merciful God. The British community at Lisbon naturally suffered severely in the earthquake although their commerce was not so hard hit as they themselves complained in the immediate aftermath of the catastrophe. The chief loss sustained by the factory members was the unavoidable repudiation of their debts by many Lisbon shopkeepers to whom the English had sold goods on long-term credit and who were completely ruined by the disaster. But Edward Hay, the consul at Lisbon, wrote a few months later: 'As the Brazil merchants are many of them substantial people, there is great hope that most of these will pay, and I make no doubt that this considerable branch of our commerce will go on pretty much as usual.' Hay was right; and Voltaire was likewise not far wrong when he suggested cynically a few weeks after the earthquake that the English would make substantial profits from supplying materials for the rebuilding of the city. Despite the loud lamentation of the factory merchants that they were utterly ruined, and despite their churlish reluctance to pay their share of a tax on imports which was levied in order to provide funds for the rebuilding of the city, the volume of Anglo-Portuguese trade actually increased in the five years following the earthquake, and so did the balance in favour of the English. This can be seen from the relevant figures, expressed in £000 annual average:

Five-year period	*English exports to Portugal*	*English imports from Portugal*	*Export surplus*
1746–50	1,114	324	790
1751–5	1,098	272	826
1756–60	1,301	257	1,044

It is true that the volume of Anglo-Portuguese trade began to fall off sharply during the 1760s, English exports declining from an annual average of about £1,200,000 in the decade 1750–60 to a corresponding figure of about £600,000 in 1766–75. This decline was due to several causes, such as a steep fall in the production of Brazilian gold and to recurring crises in the sugar trade, in the slave trade and in diamond-mining. These developments considerably reduced the purchasing-power of people in Brazil, which in turn adversely affected Portuguese and English merchants engaged in that trade. The resultant severe and protracted economic depression was aggravated by Portugal's brief but unfortunate participation in the Seven Years War, which involved heavy military expenditure and the ravaging of many frontier districts, although the actual fighting was on a small scale.

The severe contraction of English exports to Portugal during this period was ascribed by the members of the Lisbon and Oporto factories to the malignant machinations of Pombal rather than to the more deep-seated economic causes mentioned above. Some colour was given to the English traders' assertions by the fact that Pombal was obviously anxious to curb their extensive privileges and their economic preponderance. Desirous of reducing the importation of foreign manufactured goods and primary materials, particularly with the fall in Brazilian gold production after 1760, he started or revived several regional industries and founded a number of chartered trading companies. Each of these had exclusive privileges of its own, which took precedence over those of the English factories at Lisbon and Oporto, where and when their respective interests conflicted.

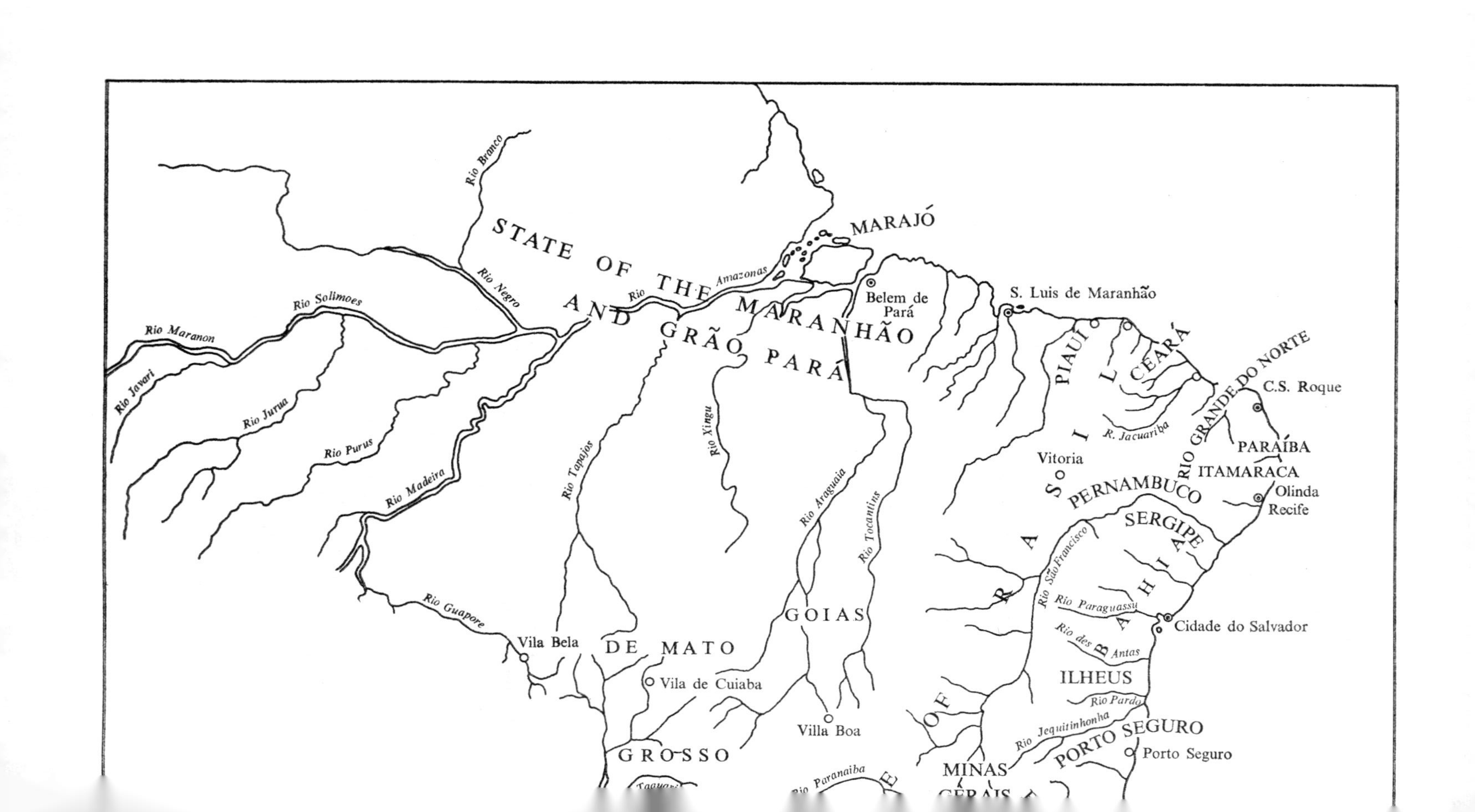
STATE OF THE MARANHÃO
AND GRÃO PARÁ
MARAJÓ
Belem de Pará
S. Luis de Maranhão
PIAUI
CEARÁ
RIO GRANDE DO NORTE
C.S. Roque
PARAÍBA
ITAMARACA
Olinda
Recife
PERNAMBUCO
SERGIPE
Vitoria
Cidade do Salvador
ILHEUS
PORTO SEGURO
Porto Seguro
MINAS
GOIAS
Villa Boa
DE MATO
GROSSO
Vila de Cuiaba
Vila Bela
Rio Branco
Rio Negro
Rio Amazonas
Rio Solimoes
Rio Maranon
Rio Javari
Rio Jurua
Rio Purus
Rio Madeira
Rio Guapore
Rio Tapajos
Rio Xingu
Rio Araguaia
Rio Tocantins
R. Jacuariba
Rio São Francisco
Rio Paraguassu
Rio des Antas
Rio Pardo
Rio Jequitinhonha
Rio Paranaiba

6 Brazil and the Maranhão-Pará in the eighteenth century

Two such chartered companies were founded to monopolise the trade of the Amazon region (Maranhão-Pará) and of north-east Brazil (Pernambuco-Paraíba) respectively, and a third as a competitor for the English wine-traders in the Douro region. These monopolistic companies were not welcomed by many Portuguese either, some of whom, such as the *comissarios volantes*, or peddling traders on a commission basis in Brazil, were more hard hit than the wealthy English merchants. But Pombal ruthlessly suppressed any manifestation of discontent from whatever quarter it came.

The Lisbon Chamber of Commerce (*Mesa do Bem Comum*), which ventured to criticise the formation of the Brazil companies, was abruptly dissolved by Pombal. Several of its leading members were exiled or imprisoned, and the others reorganised under stricter government control in the form of the *Junta do Comercio* (1755). At the other end of the social scale some working-class rioters who had demonstrated in a mildly drunken and disorderly way against the Douro Wine Company at Oporto, were punished with savage severity, seventeen of them being executed. Like all dictators, Pombal was convinced that he knew best what was good for the nation which he ruled in all but name. 'I find it absolutely necessary to bring all the commerce of this kingdom and its colonies into companies,' he wrote in 1756, 'and then all the merchants will be obliged to enter into them, or else desist from trading, for they certainly may be assured that I know their interests better than they do themselves, and the interests of the whole kingdom.'

Pombal unhesitatingly rejected numerous English protests concerning the real or alleged grievances of the factories at Lisbon and Oporto. Nevertheless his anti-British policy was carefully confined to his manifestations of economic nationalism, and to his efforts to secure diplomatic reciprocity by inducing the English government to treat Portugal as an equal ally and not as a subservient satellite. He had no intention of abandoning the Anglo-Portuguese alliance, or of siding with the 'Family Compact' formed between the Bourbon Crowns of France and Spain and directed against Great Britain. In an interview with Lord Kinnoull, the British envoy at Lisbon in October 1760, Pombal declared: 'that the King his master was bound in duty to consider the welfare and the interests of his own subjects in the first place and preferable to all others'. Since Portugal did not produce sufficient manufactured goods and foodstuffs, she must necessarily rely to a large extent on imports from abroad, Pombal admitted, adding: 'That upon consideration, he was always of the opinion that the King his master should prefer, in matters of commerce, the subjects of Great Britain to all other foreigners whatsoever, and consider them next to, though after, his own subjects.' Pombal told Lord Kinnoull pointedly that:

our trade to this country was in a most flourishing condition, and that we could not complain, since we engrossed the whole and no other foreign nation had any considerable share in it; that he hoped and believed that the subjects of the King his master in the Brazils would, by the expulsion of the Jesuits, become more civilised and more numerous, and their wants of course increase, by which the demand for British goods would be every year greater and greater. That he knew how advantageous the trade with Portugal was to Great Britain, and that it was the *only one* which supplied us with specie and enabled us to support such vast expenses.

Pombal reminded Kinnoull of the anti-English advice which the French envoys at Lisbon often pressed on the Portuguese government:

And he repeated what he has often said to me: 'We know as well as they do, the sums which Great Britain draws from this country; but we know, too, that our money must go out, to pay for what we want for ourselves and our colonies. The only question is, shall we send it to a friend who is willing and able to support us when we stand in need of assistance, or shall we send it to those who are at least indifferent to our welfare?'

That Pombal meant what he said was proved two years later when he persuaded King Joseph to reject a Franco-Spanish ultimatum to abandon the English alliance, and resisted the invasion which followed, despite the fact that Portugal was utterly unprepared for war. Fortunately, the invading Spanish army was hardly more efficient than the Portuguese; and although English auxiliary troops and a German commander-in-chief (Schaumburg-Lippe) were slow in arriving, the ensuing campaign was conducted so languidly on both sides that the war ended in a military stalemate.

Pombal's allusion to the Jesuits in the above-quoted interview with Lord Kinnoull affords a typical instance of what by then had become the dominating conviction of his life—that the backwardness and underdeveloped state (as we would say nowadays) of Portugal and her colonies were almost entirely due to the diabolical machinations of the Society of Jesus. The origin of Pombal's pathological hatred of the Jesuits is uncertain. There is no indication of it before 1750, and he owed his early advancement in part, at least, to them; but ten years later his phobia had become the maniacal obsession which it remained for the rest of his life. His step-brother, Francisco Xavier de Mendonça Furtado, who governed the State of Maranhão-Pará, sent him a constant stream of denunciations of the Jesuit missionaries in Amazonia, who were (so he said) continually flouting the authority of the Crown. These emphatically repeated assertions, whether true, false, or merely exaggerated, must have strengthened Pombal's anti-Jesuit feelings, if they did not originally inspire them. However that may have been, Pombal quickly became convinced that the Jesuits were deliberately fomenting opposition among the Amerindians to the drastic territorial adjustments in South America which had been agreed by the Treaty of Madrid in 1750. Although Pombal himself disliked this treaty (p. 176), the real or alleged reluctance of the Jesuits to implement its terms in their South American mission-territories infuriated him. Apart from difficulties in Amazonia, major campaigns had to be mounted by the combined Portuguese and Spanish colonial troops in order to suppress the Guaraní converts of the Jesuit Reductions in Paraguay.

Pombal thenceforth saw the hidden hand of the Society of Jesus in any difficulties or opposition that he encountered at any place or time, whether in Portugal or overseas. The only occasion on which he ever wavered in his loyalty to the English alliance was when some vague hints from the French Foreign Minister, Choiseul, convinced him temporarily (in June 1767) that the English were actively plotting the conquest of Brazil with the aid of a Jesuit fifth column! Last, not least, he was firmly persuaded—and in this conviction he was not alone—that the Jesuits were immensely wealthy and that their residences were full of hidden treasure, though no such treasures were found when all their properties throughout the Portuguese world were confiscated and searched by Pombal's orders in 1759–60. The Jesuits certainly had extensive landholdings, including sugar plantations in Bahia, cattle ranches in Marajó and Piauí, and agricultural estates worked by slaves in Angola and Zambesia; but it was not so much their sugar, cattle and slaves which Pombal was interested in as their reputed hoards of gold and silver, which they did not in fact possess.

To all appearances the Jesuits were nowhere more strongly established, or possessed more power and influence, than in Portugal and her overseas possessions at the time of the Lisbon earthquake. Yet within five years of this event the Society had been completely suppressed within the bounds of the Portuguese empire, and its members either imprisoned without trial or else deported under harrowing conditions to Italy. The Jesuits had never lacked powerful enemies in other Roman Catholic countries such as France, Spain and Venice, but they had never met with any comparable criticism in Portugal since they first achieved a commanding position there in the reign of King John III. Pombal's astonishing feat in crushing the Portuguese branch of the Society proved to be the prelude to the expulsion of the Jesuits from France and Spain (1764–7), and to the reluctant suppression of the whole Society by the Papacy in 1773. His initial success was largely achieved by convincing King Joseph that the Jesuits were deeply implicated in a plot to murder that monarch, which narrowly miscarried in September 1758. This plot was apparently the work of some members of the aristocratic Tavora family, who deeply resented the notorious liaison which the King was maintaining with the beautiful young marchioness who bore their name. The incriminating evidence against them was secured under torture and most of it is highly suspect; but Pombal used this opportunity to cow the high nobility by publicly executing the principal Tavoras in circumstances of the most revolting barbarity. He followed up this atrocity by garrotting and burning the mad old Jesuit Padre Malagrida, whose execution at Lisbon in 1761 was correctly described by Voltaire as 'a supreme combination of the ridiculous and the horrible'.

Pombal's campaign of defamation against the Jesuits was epitomised by the publication of a three-volume work entitled the *Deducção Chronologica* (*Chronological Deduction*) in 1767–8. By the use and still more by the abuse of the historical documents and State papers published in this work, Pombal purported to prove that all Portugal's economic, political, social and religious ills were directly or indirectly due to the nefarious actions of the Jesuits in Portugal, working in accordance with a secret master-plan which they had already drawn up in 1540. Though many of the documents which Pombal published in the *Deduction* were authentic, they seldom bear the forced interpretations which he put on them, and the book may fairly be compared with the spurious *Protocols of Zion*. It can also be regarded as an eighteenth-century equivalent of the *Thoughts of Mao Tse-tung*, as Pombal went to the most absurd lengths to ensure that it was widely read throughout the Portuguese empire. Copies were distributed to all administrative bodies, such as the town councils, whose members were enjoined to consult it frequently and to keep it under lock and key. The parish priests in the colonies were ordered to buy and carefully read this book and some of Pombal's other anti-Jesuit lucubrations, so that they could cure the 'sickly sheep' among their flocks (as Pombal instructed the Archbishop of Goa in 1774) with the 'salutary doctrines' enunciated therein. Before and after the publication of the *Deducção Chronologica*, Pombal inspired and organised a virulent anti-Jesuit propaganda campaign in the form of books and pamphlets, many of them published anonymously, and many of which were translated into French, Italian, English, etc. As with hate-propaganda in the printed word during our own day and generation, Pombal's anti-Jesuit works had a considerable cumulative effect, both then and later. Much of the dislike and suspicion with which the Society of Jesus has often been regarded in the last 200 years can be traced to these publications of Pombal.

One of the mainsprings of Pombal's anti-Jesuit obsession was clearly his own extreme form of regalism and his determination to subordinate the Church in virtually every sphere to the tight control of the Crown. He summarily removed, without reference to Rome, any prelate who ventured to incur his displeasure, such as the luckless Bishop of Coimbra in 1768. He styled the King in official decrees as Grand-Master of the Order of Christ (and of Aviz and Santiago), although by canon law the ruling monarch was only 'Governor and Perpetual Administrator'. He arrogated to the Crown, in the wording of a royal decree promulgated in April 1757, 'the power of founding in any of my Dominions, churches and monasteries for the Religious Orders which are recognised by the Apostolic See, without the permission of the Bishops, of the parish priests, of any other ecclesiastical personage whomsoever'. He stopped the Portuguese branch of the Inquisition from persecuting 'New-' Christians, but he used this tribunal as an instrument of vengeance against those whom he hated, like the wretched Padre Malagrida, making it function simply as a repressive organ of the Crown. He summarily expelled the Papal Nuncio (a cardinal) from Lisbon on a trivial pretext of protocol in June 1760, and he maintained a complete diplomatic breach with the Papacy for ten years. He only consented to the restoration of relations in January 1770, when Pope Clement XIV had yielded on all disputed points and addressed Pombal himself in the most abjectly fulsome terms. Small wonder that the English ambassador at Lisbon thought for a time that Pombal was trying to emulate Henry VIII and Thomas Cromwell in securing the complete national independence of the Portuguese Church; but Pombal always considered himself to be a good practising Roman Catholic and he certainly had no interest in Protestantism. It was regalism carried to the *n*th degree which really inspired him, as evidenced by his order to the Archbishop of Goa in 1774 that as soon as any royal decree or new law was promulgated 'the people must always refer to it in conversation by the epithets of *Holy* and *Most Holy*, and of *Sacred* and *Most Sacred*', since these measures originated from the Lord's Anointed.

The extent to which Pombal rode roughshod over the privileges of the Church in a nation of whom the great majority from King to commoner were more priest-ridden than in any other country in the world, with the possible exception of Tibet, reveals clearly how personal and how effective his dictatorship actually was. The prisons of Lisbon were crowded with unfortunate individuals of all ranks, who were confined in underground dungeons without any specific charge being brought against them and without their ever being brought to trial. Informers, spies, and tale-bearers naturally throve under such a dictatorship, which it is no mere cliché to style a reign of terror, between 1759 and 1777.

People felt they could not make critical remarks about Pombal even in private conversation among friends, and there was no outward or organised opposition whatsoever. The exact number of his victims will never be known, but some 800 individuals were released from the prisons of Lisbon and its immediate vicinity when King Joseph died and Pombal fell from power in February 1777. It has been calculated that in all probability double that number died during their confinement; and although some lucky individuals were released during those years, the total number of persons arrested and imprisoned for shorter or longer periods by order of Pombal may well have been around 4,000. This is a trifling number in comparison with the myriads who have perished in Nazi and in Communist concentration camps during the last thirty years, but it was something quite unprecedented in Portugal, even when due allowance is made for the terrors of the Inquisition. The Holy Office, after all, was regarded approvingly by many thousands of people, and *autos-da-fé* were popular with the Lisbon mob, which baited the wretched Jews who were slowly roasted to death at the stake. But in 1776 the Austrian envoy at Lisbon, who was personally on the best of terms with Pombal, accurately reported to his government:

> This nation, crushed by the weight of the despotic rule exercised by the Marquis of Pombal, the King's friend, favourite and Prime Minister, believes that only the death of the Monarch can deliver the people from a yoke which they regard as tyrannical and intolerable. The nation was never in a worse plight or in a more cruel subjection.

It is arguable how far King Joseph was a mere puppet in Pombal's hands, and how far the dictator enjoyed this monarch's active rather than his passive support. In either event the King did not fail to endorse all his minister's actions until his dying days, when he signed a declaration enjoining his daughter to release all the political prisoners and to pay all the debts incurred by the royal household. Queen Dona Maria I promptly released the prisoners and started to pay off the creditors, some of whose claims had been outstanding for many years. She also accepted Pombal's reluctantly proffered resignation a few days after she came to the throne. His enemies naturally clamoured for his trial and execution, but a lengthy judicial investigation showed that every responsible act of Pombal had been formally approved and signed by the late king. Out of respect to her father's memory the Queen contented herself with exiling the fallen dictator to his country house at Pombal, whither he had already retired after his fall from power, and where he died of a lingering and loathsome disease in May 1782.

As mentioned on page 178, controversy still rages in Portugal over Pombal's dictatorship, and a definitive assessment of his rule has still to be made. Perhaps the fairest summary to date was made by the learned Canon António Ribeiro dos Santos (1745–1818), whose opinion was echoed by several contemporaries who were in a good position to judge:

> This minister tried to follow an impossible policy; he wanted to civilise the nation and at the same time to enslave it; he wanted to spread the light of the philosophical sciences and at the same time to elevate the royal power to despotism; he greatly forwarded the study of the Law of Nature and of the Law of Nations, and of Universal International Law, founding chairs for these subjects in the University. But he did not realise that he was in this way enlightening the people to understand thereby that the sovereign power was solely established for the common weal of the nation and not for the benefit of the ruler, and that it had limits and boundaries in which it ought to be contained.

Other critics pointed out, when it was safe to do so after Pombal's fall, that many of his reforms were too hastily conceived, arbitrary, self-contradictory and enforced without regard to realities. Many decrees were cancelled by subsequent legislation, often within a few months, for although Pombal would not brook opposition he was usually ready to listen to constructive suggestions, and he was never afraid to change his mind, except in connection with his obsessive Jesuit-phobia. The piecemeal and unsystematic nature of his legislation, particularly the laws and edicts through which he strove to stimulate Portuguese industry from about 1765 onwards, was largely in response to the urgent need to take speedy and drastic measures in order to lessen Portugal's dependence on foreign imports during the worsening economic crisis of 1756–75.

If many of Pombal's reforms proved abortive, short-lived, or downright harmful, certain outstanding achievements survived his fall and the clerical reaction which followed. He abolished slavery in Portugal in 1761–73, although not so much from humanitarian motives as to prevent Negroes from being employed as household servants in Portugal instead of as field-hands and gold-miners in Brazil (pp. 265–6). Not only did he abolish the colour-bar in the Asian colonies by ordaining—and enforcing—the principle that 'His Majesty does not distinguish between his vassals by their colour but by their merits', but he went to absurd lengths in trying to encourage intermarriage between the white settlers in Brazil and the stone-age Amerindians. He drastically reformed the antiquated curriculum of the Coimbra University, modernising the teaching of law, mathematics and medicine. He tried to foster the growth of a better-educated middle class by such methods as the establishment of a Commercial College at Lisbon, and by the creation of government-subsidised schools in Portugal, Brazil, and Goa (pp. 362–4). He swept away the iniquitous legal and social distinction between the 'Old' Christians and the 'New', enacting the most stringent laws against anti-semitism, thus purging Portuguese society of an evil which had poisoned it for centuries (pp. 270–2).

Pombal's dictatorship also witnessed some profound developments for good and ill in Portugal's overseas possessions, which can only be briefly indicated here. The two monopolistic chartered companies which he founded for developing the trade and stimulating the economy of north-east Brazil and the State of Pará-Maranhão were largely successful in both respects, although both companies were abolished by the Crown soon after Pombal's resignation. After a difficult start, and against considerable local opposition from the small traders whose interests were adversely affected, Pombal's persistence in trying to channel the seaborne trade of those regions through the two companies began to pay off. Between 1757 and 1777 a total of 25,365 Negro slaves were imported into Pará and the Maranhão from West African ports, mainly from Cacheu and Bissau in Portuguese Guinea, which had hitherto been of relatively minor importance in the transatlantic slave trade. In order to help the settlers purchase these Negro slaves on long-term credit, the original rate of interest was cut from 5 per cent to 3 per cent, and finally abolished altogether, the slaves being sold for their cost price in West Africa plus a small charge for freight. Between 1755 and 1777 the export of cacao doubled in both quantity and sale price; and cotton, rice and hides all became important export crops, which they had never been before. The stagnant sugar trade of Pernambuco-Paraíba experienced a temporary revival, and the company of that name imported over 30,000 Negroes from West Africa to Brazil between 1760 and 1775.

The Maranhão, which in 1755 was one of the most backward, sluggish and underdeveloped regions of the Portuguese empire, twenty-one years later was one of the most dynamic and prosperous. This 'economic miracle' was given a great fillip by the War of American Independence, which forced Great Britain to turn to Portuguese America for the cotton she had previously obtained from her own American colonies. But the expansion was already well under way in the 1760s, and it admittedly owed much to Pombal's dictatorial methods, one instance of which will suffice. The planters were compelled under pain of severe penalties to cultivate a strain of the superior Carolina white rice instead of the local reddish variety, which they originally preferred, and its cultivation was soon extended to Rio de Janeiro. The result was that by 1781 the colony was producing enough rice to satisfy the entire demand of the mother country, and a substantial surplus was re-exported from Lisbon to London, Hamburg, Rotterdam, Genoa, Marseilles and elsewhere. The ethnic composition of the Maranhão was also entirely altered by the massive importation of Negro slaves into this region, whose sparse population had hitherto been chiefly a mixture of whites and Amerindians in varying degrees. 'White cotton turned the Maranhão black,' as Caio Prado, Jnr., has observed.

The material benefits which these two chartered companies brought to Brazil and the Maranhão-Pará did not prevent their liquidation in 1778–80 from being greeted with joy by many people on both sides of the Atlantic, some of the Lisbon traders celebrating a *Te Deum* in gratitude. This was rather short-sighted, but it is undeniable that the Portuguese traders who most obviously profited from the companies were certain wealthy merchants and entrepreneurs, including the Quintella, Cruz and Bandeira families, who had invested heavily in them and who were closely involved in some of Pombal's other monopolistic enterprises, such as the State tobacco monopoly and the Brazilian whaling contracts. The Quintella family fortune in 1817 allegedly amounted to over 18,000,000 *cruzados*.

Pombal's voluminous legislation concerning the gold and diamond mines of Brazil, and his reorganisation of the Crown finances in the centralised bureau of the *Real Erario* (Royal Fisc), did not obtain the hoped-for results; but this was mainly due to causes outside his control, such as the exhaustion of the most profitable mineral deposits, and to Portugal's involvement in the war of 1762–4. The consequences which flowed from his suppression of the Jesuits in the Portuguese empire are dealt with elsewhere (pp. 364–6), as are the effects of his legislation in the field of race relations (pp. 256–60). His transference of the colonial capital of Brazil from Salvador (Bahia) to Rio de Janeiro in 1763 was chiefly motivated by the war then being waged against the Spaniards. Thirteen years later Pombal's diplomatic miscalculations led to another war between the two nations in South America, which involved the final loss of Sacramento but ended with Brazil's main western boundaries of 1750 being confirmed by the terms of the Treaty of Santo Ildefonso in 1777.

Although Pombal understandably devoted more attention to the development of the Portuguese possessions in America than to the smaller and poorer colonies in Africa and Asia, he was by no means neglectful of these in his reforming zeal. Franciso Inocencio de Sousa Coutinho, who was governor of Angola from 1764 to 1772, made serious efforts not only to implement various administrative reforms decreed by Pombal but added others on his own initiative. He tried to make Angola and Benguela something more than mere slaving depots for Brazil, diversifying the economy by starting an iron foundry, leather and soap factories, a salt monopoly and various agricultural schemes, besides advocating white settlement of the healthy uplands in Huila. He founded an academy at Luanda for training military engineers, and a chamber of commerce for the traders. His efforts met with varying degrees of success, but most of his achievements did not outlast the term of his governorship owing to lack of continuity by his successors.

On the other side of Africa, Pombal detached the colony of

Moçambique from its administrative dependence on Goa; but its economic dependence on Portuguese India was not fundamentally affected by this measure, and there was no immediate improvement in the stagnant economy of Portuguese East Africa. The survival of Portuguese control in the Zambesi valley, and even a slight extension of their influence in this region during the second half of the eighteenth century, was entirely due to the action of the local *prazo*-holders with the local forces raised from among the Bantu on their lands. Pombal promulgated the most detailed and stringent instructions for the rebuilding and re-occupation of the old Portuguese city of Goa, which had been largely abandoned on account of its unhealthiness (p. 131), but here he was defeated by the endemic malaria and dysentery. He had to be content with abolishing the Goa branch of the Inquisition and the colour-bar against Indian Christians (p. 256).

Pombal's fall from power was greeted with unfeigned relief by the great majority of Portuguese, the chief exceptions being found among the monopolists, engrossers and entrepeneurs who had profited from his chartered companies and from some of the industrial enterprises which he had fomented. The clerical reaction which inevitably occurred with the accession of the ultra-pious Queen Dona Maria I to the throne did not, however, involve a complete reversal of all Pombal's policies by the new government, although contemporaries christened it the *Viradeira* or 'Turnabout'. Many of the fallen dictator's most trusted collaborators and henchmen were dismissed, but some of the most important were retained, including the Overseas Minister, Martinho de Mello e Castro. One of his leading officials, Inácio de Pina Manique, was appointed Intendant-General of Police. Pombal's eldest son, the Count of Oeiras, was continued in his influential post as president of the Lisbon municipal council.The Queen had promptly released all political prisoners in accordance with her father's last wishes, but she refused to readmit the Jesuits (though she gave some of them pensions). A judicial review of the sentences passed on those who were accused of plotting against the King in 1758–9 resulted in many of them being declared innocent, but others were pronounced to have been guilty. The Queen's conscience was so deeply affected by brooding over this case that it was undoubtedly the chief course of the recurring fits of melancholia and mental instability from which she subsequently suffered, and which developed into incurable madness by 1792.

The commercial revival which had begun in some sections of the Luso-Brazilian economy during the closing years of Pombal's dictatorship continued apace in the first years of the new reign, largely thanks to Portugal's neutrality in the war of 1776–83, in which Great Britain, the North American colonies, France, Spain and eventually the Netherlands were all involved. In pursuit of his policy of unbridled regalism, Pombal had induced King Joseph to sign a decree in July 1776, closing all Portuguese ports to North American ships and ordering them to be treated as pirates: 'Because such a pernicious example should induce the most uninterested rulers to deny all help and favour, directly or indirectly, to some vassals who have so publicly and formally rebelled against their natural sovereign.' The Queen's government was more sensible, and while rejecting Benjamin Franklin's letter of 16 July 1777, asking for the cancellation of this decree, it contrived to maintain a profitable neutrality in practice until according formal recognition to the U.S.A. in February 1783.

The Queen's government likewise continued Pombal's policy, which was the traditional colonial one for that matter, of trying to stimulate agricultural productivity and the export of sugar, rice, cotton and cacao from Brazil, while forbidding the development of any Brazilian manufactures, such as textiles, which might compete with the manufactured goods exported from Portugal, even though these were not necessarily of Portuguese origin. This was because the Crown derived a substantial part of its revenue from the duties levied on such goods. In 1756 the English Board of Trade calculated that on every £100 worth of British goods sent to Brazil, £68 was paid in taxes to the Portuguese government. Thus a royal decree of 1785 ordered the cessation of all textile manufacturing in the colony, except for the production of coarse cotton cloth used for clothing the slaves and for making sacks. On the other hand, the Crown fomented the growth of rice cultivation, for example by giving Customs exemption for Brazilian-grown rice between 1761 and 1804. On the initiative of the Viceroy, Marquis of Lavradio, the cultivation of indigo was successfully developed in the captaincy of Rio de Janeiro. By the end of the century there were 206 establishments processing the indigo produced on plantations in the region of Cape Frio, and the captaincy's total output had reached 5,000 *arrobas* in 1796. This apparently promising development was frustrated when the English East India Company, after the loss of the American colonies, invested large sums in rehabilitating the indigo industry in India. The Brazilian indigo, badly prepared and processed in comparison with its Indian competitor, was soon driven from the international market.

The backwardness of agricultural techniques in Brazil was the main reason why that country's most important export crops could not (as a rule) compete advantageously with those of its competitors, save when aided by fortuitous circumstances such as Portugal's neutrality during the War of American Independence, and the collapse of the French West Indian sugar colonies during the Revolutionary and Napoleonic Wars. Jamaica in 1788 exported more sugar, rum and molasses than did all the Brazilian captaincies put together. Caio Prado has pointed out that bagasse was first used as fuel for sugar-boiling on a Brazilian plantation in 1809, whereas it was in common use in the English, French and Dutch West Indies half a century earlier. Similarly, although Whitney had invented his saw gin in 1792, and its use had spread rapidly in the United States cotton regions, it was still unknown in Brazil twenty-five years later.

This indifference to modern techniques was mainly due to the inertia and conservatism of the Brazilian planters, for in Portugal itself the last quarter of the eighteenth century and the first years of the nineteenth witnessed a marked growth of intelligent interest in the economic, agrarian and social problems which faced the country. The Royal Academy of Sciences, founded at Lisbon in 1779, envisaged among other things 'the advancement of national education, the perfection of the sciences and the arts, and the increase of popular industry' in Portugal and its empire. A series of volumes published between 1790 and 1812 devoted special attention to agrarian and economic problems, but most of the contributors did not realise the full import of the industrial progress being made in Britain and France, concentrating rather on the deficiencies of agriculture as practised in Portugal and Brazil. Apart from the papers published by the Academy, the

Prince Regent (later King John VI) sponsored the publication in 1798–1806 of a ten-volume work by a Brazilian Franciscan friar, J. M. de Conceição Veloso, entitled *O Fazendeiro do Brazil* (*The Brazilian Landowner*), which can fairly be described as a manual of tropical agriculture, based largely on translations from the best English and French works available. Unfortunately, it would seem that these publications were virtually ignored in Brazil, for Fr. Veloso was advocating the use of bagasse as fuel in 1798.

The works of the French physiocrats and encyclopaedists, which provided the main inspiration for educated Portuguese who were anxious for administrative, agrarian and educational reforms, also inspired some educated Brazilians with political and social ideas which helped to set the colony on the road to independence. The writings of the *Philosophes* were banned in Portugal and her empire even after Pombal's educational reforms; but a fair number of wealthy Brazilians were now sending their sons to be educated in Europe, and not only at Coimbra University, but at Montpellier and elsewhere in France. These men brought back with them to Brazil the ideas which were circulating in Europe in the intellectual fermentation which accompanied the War of American Independence, the burgeoning of the Industrial Revolution, the spread of freemasonry and the prelude to the French Revolution. Their ideas could be propagated only among some of their better-educated compatriots, and they did not necessarily envisage a complete break with Portugal, although the independence of the United States certainly encouraged some Brazilians to contemplate this step. But there was an increasingly widespread discontent with Portuguese rule, although its incidence varied greatly in different areas, and the reasons for it were not everywhere the same.

There was general resentment at the oppressive weight of colonial taxation, particularly the royal fifth, the tithes, and the exactions of the contractors of Crown monopolies. These were all especially burdensome in Minas Gerais, where the Crown did not make adequate adjustments for the steep fall in gold production. The corruption and inefficiency of the ill-paid colonial bureaucracy was aggravated by the need to refer so many matters to distant Lisbon for a decision by ministers who were past-masters in the art of procrastination. The monarchs of the House

✠ IESVS. ✠

O PRIMEIRO CONCILIO
Prouinçial çelebrado em Goa,
no anno de 1567.

5. *Frontispiece of a book published at Goa, 1568*

6. *Map of Goa, 1596*
(from J. H. van Linschoten's Itinerario, *Amsterdam, 1596)*

7. *Goa. Tomb of St. Francis Xavier in the church of Bom Jesus*

8. *Diu. The west side of the city wall and the main gate (seventeenth century)*

9. *Diu. Jesuit church and convent (seventeenth century)*

10. *Fr. Antonio Ardizone Spinola celebrating communion with a multiracial congregation at Goa,* c. *1645. From his* Cordel Triplicado de Amor *(Lisboa, 1680)*

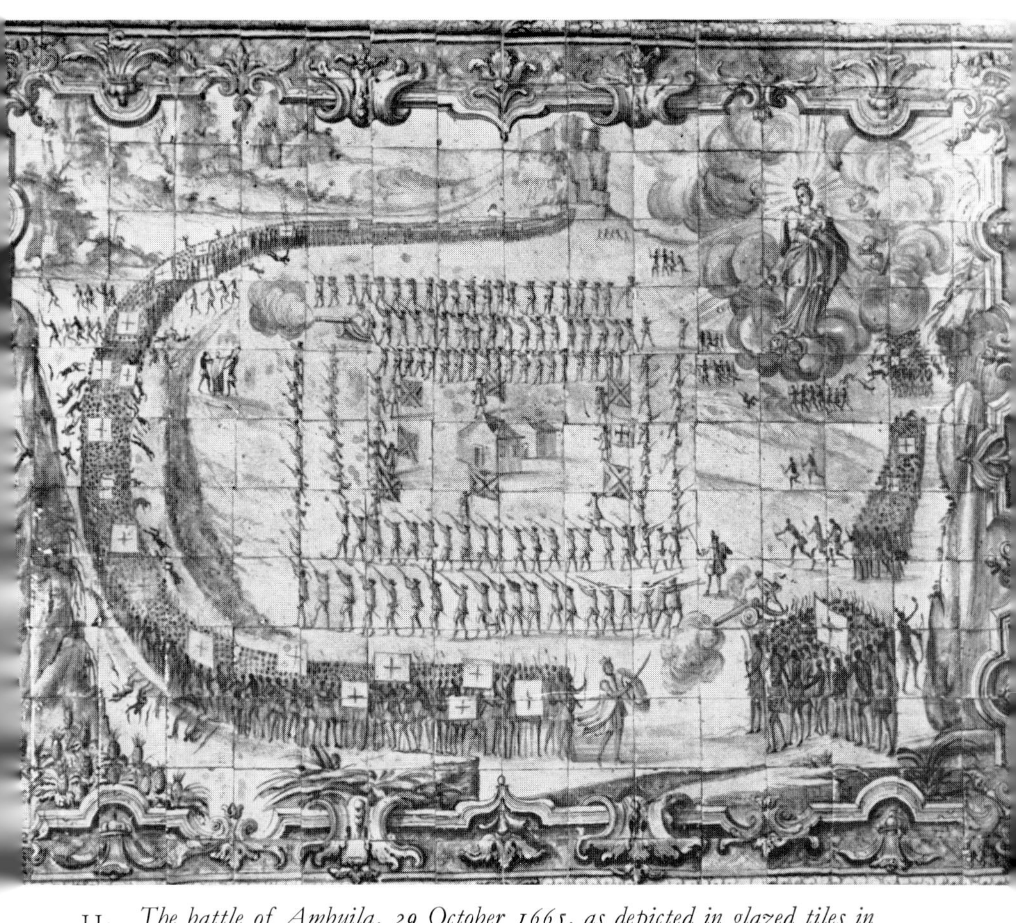

11. *The battle of Ambuila, 29 October 1665, as depicted in glazed tiles in the seventeenth-century hermitage of Nazaré, Luanda*

12. *Padre António Vieira, S. J., 1608–1697*
(engraving by Debrie, 1745, after a seventeenth-century portrait)

of Braganza regarded Brazil as their 'milch-cow', in the words of the first of this line, and there was growing resentment of this self-evident fact in many places. The population of continental Portugal at the end of the eighteenth century was probably nearly 3,000,000, and that of Brazil nearly 2,500,000. But about one-third of these latter were Negro slaves, and a large proportion of the remainder were what the colonial officials called an *infima plebe*, a 'lumpen proletariat' of unemployed vagrants or under-employed workers, mainly coffee-coloured but with a leavening of 'poor whites' and freed Negroes. There was increasing tension in many regions between the Brazilian-born, whether planters, priests, public officials or army officers, and the European-born merchants and traders who were often monopolists and engrossers in all branches of the colony's trade, or who were persons promoted to high office in Church and State over the heads of Brazilians. The tension between these two last categories should not, however, be exaggerated, as it often is. There was much intermarriage between them, and many *Reinóis*, as the European-born were called, participated in the abortive plots and revolts which preceded the attainment of Brazilian Independence, or joined it when it was attained.

The first and best publicised of these movements was the so-called *Inconfidência* of 1789 in Minas Gerais. This was an abortive and ill-organised scheme to free the country, or part of it, from Portuguese rule and to establish a republic. It had not got beyond the stage of general discussions and vague aspirations on the part of the conspirators when the movement was betrayed to the authorities. The ringleaders, who included both European- and colonial-born, were arrested and brought to trial. In the upshot, only one of the eleven men who were condemned to death was actually executed, the others being exiled to Africa or receiving terms of imprisonment. Incidentally, the clemency displayed by the Crown on this occasion contrasts strongly with the savage repression of a very similar movement in Goa two years previously. This was likewise an abortive plot to expel the Portuguese and declare Goa a republic, which had not got beyond the stage of discussion when it was betrayed to the authorities. The principal ringleaders were some Goan clergy who had been to France and returned with the ideas of the

'Enlightenment'. Fifteen of the civilian and military Goans involved were executed in circumstances of great barbarity, and although the guilty clergymen were saved by their cloth, several of them were allowed to die in prison at Lisbon without ever having been brought to trial. It is difficult to believe that this different treatment was due to anything else but colour prejudice, since those reprieved in the *Inconfidência Mineira* were all white and the Goan victims were all coloured.

A half-baked republican plot, obviously inspired by the success of the French Revolution, was uncovered at Bahia in 1798; but this movement was confined to low-class coloureds and Negro slaves, being suppressed with the execution of four ringleaders. Much more serious was a full-fledged Republican revolt which occurred at Recife in 1817. This rapidly spread to the neighbouring districts and found many supporters among the clergy, officials, soldiers and planters. It was crushed after a couple of months by Portuguese troops sent from Bahia, but the execution of eight ringleaders and the harsh imprisonment of many participants only increased the regional dislike of the European-born Portuguese, which was more deep-rooted here than in any other part of Brazil.

The French invasion of Portugal in 1807, when the Prince Regent, after much understandable hesitation, finally rejected Napoleon's demands that Portugal should join the continental blockade of Great Britain, led to the flight of the royal family to Brazil and the stay of the Portuguese Court at Rio de Janeiro until 1821. Immediately on his first arrival in Brazil, the Prince Regent had, under English pressure, promulgated a decree throwing open all Brazilian ports to the commerce of all friendly nations—which meant in effect to Great Britain alone until the end of the Napoleonic Wars. Brazil was elevated to the status of a kingdom in 1815, and in the following year Dom João became King of Portugal and Brazil on the death of the mad old Queen Mother. He showed no eagerness to return to Europe, although the Peninsula War was now over, but a constitutional revolution in Portugal which established a liberal representative government at Lisbon in 1820 reluctantly forced him to return to the Portuguese capital a year later. When King John VI finally left Rio he obviously had a foreboding that Brazil would not remain much longer united with Portugal. He told his eldest son, whom he left as Regent at Rio de Janeiro: 'Pedro, if Brazil goes its own way, let it be with you, who will still respect me, rather than with some of those adventurers.'

The actual break was precipitated by the folly of the members of the liberal Constitutional Cortes, who assembled at Lisbon in 1820–1. Instead of accepting the proposals of the Brazilian deputies that Portugal and Brazil should remain a United Kingdom on an equal footing, they insisted that full Portuguese military control should be re-established in Brazil, and that Dom Pedro should come to Europe to complete his education there. This tactless attitude naturally provoked violent irritation in Brazil, particularly in Rio, São Paulo, Minas Gerais and Pernambuco. Many prominent Brazilians, headed by José Bonifacio de Andrada e Silva, styled 'the Patriarch of Independence', urged Dom Pedro to stay where he was. The Portuguese garrison of Rio threatened to compel him to leave, but they were soon obliged to capitulate by the local levies. His hand having been forced, and probably recalling his father's advice, Dom Pedro decided to do what is nowadays termed: 'If you can't beat 'em, join 'em.' On 7 September 1822 he formally proclaimed in rather theatrical words: 'It is time! Independence or Death! We are separate from Portugal.' The declaration of independence was not received with equal enthusiasm in all parts of Brazil. The southern regions and Pernambuco adhered willingly on the whole, but Bahia was strongly garrisoned by Portuguese troops, and they were only expelled from the Maranhão and Pará by a scratch naval expedition led by the British adventurer, Lord Cochrane. By the end of 1823 the last Portuguese troops had left Brazilian soil and the authority of the Emperor Dom Pedro I was everywhere accepted. Partly as a result of British diplomatic intervention (or blackmail, as some termed it) the Portuguese government reluctantly recognised the independence of Brazil in 1825.

The loss of Brazil came at a singularly unfortunate time for Portugal, as the country had not yet recovered from the devastation caused by three successive French invasions during the Napoleonic Wars. The opening of Brazilian ports to direct English trade in 1808 had also been a body-blow to Portuguese commerce with Brazil; but the incipient Portuguese industries which appeared to be developing in a promising way at the end of the eighteenth century had already begun to collapse in the face of English industrial competition a few years later, for the reasons expressed by the contemporary economist José Acursio das Neves: 'The magical power of the steam-engine, which has revolutionised the mechanical arts within the last few years, has provided the English with the means to produce manufactured goods so cheaply that nobody else can compete with them.' Writing in 1810, Das Neves had gloomily prophesied that Portugal's few surviving industries would not be able to hold out any longer against the English textiles and other mass-produced manufactured goods, and ten years later he commented sadly:

> Having lost the exclusive market for our industrial products, which was chiefly in Brazil, and not being able to resist, even in Portugal, the competition of foreign manufactured goods, we see our own workshops virtually annihilated, after our agriculture has been ruined in the invaded regions, and without our having had a breathing space which might have enabled us to prepare for such great changes.

Portugal's inability either to cope with or to emulate the nations which were profiting from the Industrial Revolution was aggravated by such factors as the lack of any coal-fields, canals, good roads or adequate means of transportation, and by three decades of political turmoil and unrest, degenerating at times into civil war between liberals and absolutists, which plagued the country from 1820 onwards. The liberal reformers made insufficient allowance for the inherently conservative character of the priest-ridden and earth-bound peasants, living by subsistence farming, who formed the great majority of the Portuguese people. They proceeded too far and too fast in their efforts to dismantle the close connection between Church and State; and they concentrated on political, constitutional and administrative measures of reform at the expense of economic, social and technological realities.

Portugal's involvement in the Napoleonic Wars and the presence of the Court in Rio de Janeiro for so long, inevitably meant that the African and Asian colonies were left largely to their own devices by the authorities at Lisbon between 1805 and 1825. The independence of Brazil equally naturally turned some people's thoughts towards the possibility of developing Angola and Moçambique, in order to offset the loss of the American colony which had been Portugal's milch-cow for over a century and a half. But such ideas could not be implemented so long as the civil disorders distracted the government at home and the African slave trade absorbed the energies of Angola and Moçambique. Once the liberal monarchy had become firmly established and the slave trade effectively suppressed, the development of these two African colonies could be seriously taken in hand during the second half of the nineteenth century. But this is another story, which is admirably related by R. J. Hammond in his wise and witty *Portugal and Africa, 1815–1910: A study in uneconomic imperialism* (1966), to which the interested reader is referred.

PART II · CHARACTERISTICS OF EMPIRE

CHAPTER IX

The India fleets and the Brazil fleets

THE *Carreira da Índia*, or round voyage between Portugal and India in days of sail, was for long considered to be 'without any doubt the greatest and most arduous of any that are known in the world', as an Italian Jesuit wrote after experiencing its rigours in 1574. Over a century later another Italian, the globe-girdling Gemelli Careri, used almost exactly the same words to describe the annual voyage of the Manila galleon across the Pacific to Mexico, which he had just experienced to his intense discomfort in 1697–8. In point of fact, there was relatively little to choose between the dangers and difficulties attending these two major routes of oceanic trade which were developed by the Iberians in the sixteenth century. In both instances the seasonal winds of the tropics formed the chief determining factor, and the duration of the round voyage, including the ship's stay at Goa or at Manila, took about a year and a half under the most favourable conditions. But whereas the *carrera de Filipinas* lasted from 1565 to 1815, the *carreira da Índia*, inaugurated with Vasco da Gama's pioneer voyage, did not end until the coming of steam, although the glory had departed long since. Furthermore, whereas the voyage round the Cape of Good Hope in either direction normally took from six to eight months, as did the crossing of the Pacific from Manila to Acapulco, the outward-bound galleons from this Mexican port often reached the Philippines in less than three months, with the aid of a following wind and over a *Mar de Damas* or 'Ladies' Sea'.

The south-west monsoon, which normally begins on the west coast of India about the beginning of June, had the effect of virtually closing all harbours in this region from the end of May to early September. Outward-bound Indiamen therefore aimed at leaving Lisbon in time to round the Cape of Good Hope in July and to reach Goa in September or October. An experienced pilot of the *carreira da Índia*, when asked what was the best season for the departure of the annual Indiamen from Lisbon, is alleged to have replied: 'The last day of February is time enough, but the first day of March is late.' In practice, the ships often left in the second half of March, or in the first half of April, and belated departures in May were not unknown. In the latter eventuality the ships involved usually made *arribadas*, or abortive voyages, being compelled either to return to Lisbon or (more rarely) to winter in Brazil. Just as departures from Lisbon tended to take place later than was advisable, so did those from Goa. Instead of leaving at Christmastide, or at the New Year, returning Indiamen often left the river Mandovi in February or March, when the chance of weathering the stormy May and June 'winter' season in the latitude of the Cape of Good Hope was correspondingly reduced. In both cases these belated departures were usually due to the difficulty of securing an adequate supply of ready money to pay for the cargoes and the crews. The inevitable hardships of a six or seven months' voyage were often aggravated by the fact that the Portuguese Crown, for most of the sixteenth and seventeenth centuries, insisted that Indiamen should try to avoid calling at any port between Lisbon and Goa, whether homeward or outward bound. Only in cases of direst necessity were they authorised to touch at a few specific places, including Moçambique Island, the Azores and (less often) at St. Helena.

The most experienced pilots did not rely too heavily on the official *roteiros*, or sailing directions, being well aware of their inevitable deficiencies. Aleixo da Mota, writing with the authority of thirty-five years' experience in the *carreira da Índia*, gives the following warning in his rutter of *c.* 1625, which holds good for other seas and centuries besides those to which it refers:

Throughout this course and the region from the tip of the island of São Lourenço [Madagascar] to the Line, you must navigate with great care by day and night; remembering that the latitudes of the shoals and islands are not always accurately marked on the charts, and that there are others which are not marked at all. Therefore keep a man at the mast-head by day and watch for changes in the colour of the sea. And at night station a man on the bowsprit, keep casting the lead, and reduce sail; trusting only in God and in the good lookout you must keep.

The ships associated with the *carreira da Índia* for some three hundred years were first and foremost *Náos*, but the word *Náo* had a wide variety of meanings. Essentially it meant 'Great Ship', and as such it was applied to the carracks of the sixteenth and seventeenth centuries, and to the large frigate-type vessels which served in the *carreira* during the eighteenth century. Technically, there was a distinction between a carrack (*Náo*) and a galleon during the first two centuries, the former being broad, bluff and heavily built but lightly gunned merchant ships, with large and well-developed castles fore and aft, whereas galleons were built longer and narrower, with more moderate superstructures, and they were, as a rule, heavily gunned warships. In practice, the distinction was often blurred; and there are many instances of an Indiaman being termed indifferently a *Náo* and a *Galeão* (or a *Náo* and a *Fragata*) by the very seamen who sailed in her. Here again there is a parallel with Spanish maritime practice, as the Manila galleons were often called *Naos de China*, 'Great Ships from China', since their return cargoes consisted chiefly of silks and other Chinese goods.

For the first thirty years of the *carreira*'s existence most of the Portuguese Indiamen, whether carracks or galleons, were of about 400 tons burthen. The annual outward-bound fleets then averaged from seven to fourteen sail, but the homeward-bound fleets were often half that number, as many ships were retained for service in Asian seas. By the middle of the sixteenth century the size of most of the Indiamen had increased to between 600 and 1,000 tons, and the average number of ships in the yearly fleet had dropped to five. In 1570 the Crown strove to check this tendency to increase the tonnage of the Indiamen at the expense of their seaworthiness and manœuvrability by promulgating a decree that ships sailing in the *carreira* should range between 300 and 450 tons burthen. Little notice was taken of this decree, nor of its repetition in modified forms on later occasions, when the upper limit was raised to 600 tons. On the contrary, during the last quarter of the sixteenth century monsters of up to 2,000 tons were built at Goa, Lisbon and Oporto. The Spanish naval commander-in-chief, Don Alvaro de Bazán, writing in 1581, observed that the Portuguese Indiamen sailing that year were each of 600 Portuguese tons, 'which amount to over 1,200 Castilian'. Forty years later a patriotic Portuguese writer boasted that the cargo of a single Portuguese East Indiaman discharging at Lisbon was greater than that of four of the largest *Náos* in the Spanish transatlantic trade. Perhaps the best account of the impression which these huge carracks made on contemporaries is Richard Hakluyt's description of the *Madre de Deus*, captured by the English off the Azores and brought to Dartmouth, where she was the wonder of the West Country and was carefully surveyed by Captain Richard Adams and other naval experts in the year 1592.

The carrack being in burden by the estimation of the wise and experienced no less than 1,600 tons, had full 900 of these stowed with the gross bulk of merchandise, the rest of the tonnage being allowed, partly to the ordnance which were thirty-two pieces of brass of all sorts, partly to the passengers and the victuals, which could not be any small quantity, considering the number of persons betwixt 600 and 700, and the length of the navigation. . . . After an exquisite survey of the whole frame, he [Adams] found the length from the beakhead to the stern (whereupon was erected a lantern) to contain 165 foot. The breadth in the second close deck whereof she had three, this being the place where there was most extension of breadth, was 46 foot and 10 inches. She drew in water 31 foot at her departure from Cochin in India, but not above 26 at her arrival in Dartmouth, she being lightened in her voyage by diverse means, some 5 foot. She carried in height seven several stories, one main orlop, three close decks, one forecastle and a spar-deck of two floors apiece. The length of the keel was 100 foot, of the mainmast 121 foot, and the circuit about the partners 10 foot 7 inches; the mainyard was 106 foot long. By which perfect commensuration of the whole, far beyond the mould of the biggest shipping used among us either for war or receit [trade].

During the years 1570–1640 Portuguese Indiamen were, as a rule, notoriously ill-armed for ships of their size. The Crown promulgated an edict in 1604 to the effect that each carrack should mount at least twenty-eight guns, of which twenty were to be *peças grossas* or 'great guns'. The *Madre de Deus* in 1592 was one of the better-armed ships, since she mounted thirty-two bronze guns of all calibres; but most of the Portuguese Indiamen of the late sixteenth and early seventeenth centuries seldom carried more than twenty-two or twenty-five guns, and too high a proportion of these were only eight-pounders. From 1640 they were usually much better armed. In the eighteenth century we find at least two viceroys of India complaining (in 1703 and 1745) that the ships habitually used in the *carreira* were large frigates mounting from fifty to seventy guns, which were uneconomical for use in Asian seas, where ships mounting from thirty to forty guns would be preferable. Incidentally, the standing regulations for the armament of Portuguese Indiamen afford an interesting example of Lusitanian conservatism. They remained identical in successive editions from 1604 to 1756, although during this century and a half the types of ship varied widely from carracks through galleons to frigates.

The superiority of Indian teak over European pine and oak for shipbuilding purposes was early recognised by the authorities at Lisbon and Goa, but there was not such unanimity as to whether it was cheaper to build ships for the *carreira* in Portugal or in India. A royal order of 1585, repeated textually nine years later, emphasised the importance of building carracks for the *carreira* in India rather than in Europe, 'both because experience has shown that those which are built there last much longer than those built in this kingdom, as also because they are cheaper and stronger, and because suitable timber for these carracks is increasingly hard to get here'. Later experience showed that although India-built ships were certainly stronger, they were not always cheaper than those constructed in Europe. One reason for this was that the governors of Portuguese fortresses on the west coast of India, whose perquisites usually included the felling and sale of the local timber, habitually charged the Crown outrageous prices for the same. The captains of Baçaim and Damão, wrote the Viceroy of India in 1664, priced their timber at forty *xerafines* the *candil*, although it had only cost them five. European cordage was also more satisfactory than most of the Asian varieties. For these and other reasons the majority of Portuguese Indiamen during the seventeenth century continued to be built at Lisbon, where the *Ribeira das Náos*, or royal dockyard, employed 1,500 men in 1620.

Perhaps the most famous of the India-built carracks was the *Cinco Chagas*, constructed at Goa in 1559–60 under the personal supervision of the Viceroy, Dom Constantino de Bragança, 'who chose the timber piece by piece'. Nicknamed the *Constantia*, she served in the *carreira* for twenty-five years, making nine or ten round voyages apart from service elsewhere, and she was the flagship of five viceroys before ending her days as a hulk at Lisbon. When she was finally broken up, King Philip II (I of Portugal) had her keel sent to the Escurial as a trophy. Her long life was in marked contrast to that of the average ship in the *carreira*, which seldom made more than three or four round voyages or lasted for as long as a decade. For that matter, the English East India Company in the late eighteenth century did not normally allow any of its ships to make more than four round voyages to the East. The Spanish Manila galleons, though often built of hardwood in the Philippines which was even tougher than Indian teak, likewise rarely made more than a few trans-Pacific crossings.

During the eighteenth century many of the Portuguese East Indiamen were built in Brazil, for reasons explained by the Viceroy of India writing to the Crown in 1713, urging the extension of this practice:

> The ships which last longest in India are those built in Brazil, because the worm cannot penetrate them, as can be seen by the frigate *Nossa Senhora da Estrella*, and in that [*Nossa Senhora da Piedade*] which is now sailing for the kingdom; for although they have been in India for fifteen years, they are capable of service for as long again. It does not seem to me that there would be any difficulty in finding suitable ships at Oporto which could be used in the *carreira da Índia*, for most of them are built in Brazil.

Two of his successors, writing in 1719 and 1721 respectively, likewise recorded their preference for the use of Brazil-built ships as East Indiamen. One of the longest-lived Indiamen of the eighteenth century was the sixty-six-gun frigate *Nossa Senhora do*

Livramento, built at Bahia in 1724, which made several round voyages to India between 1725 and 1740.

The Portuguese Crown made considerable efforts to develop shipbuilding in Brazil during the late seventeenth and the eighteenth centuries, as some of the Brazilian hardwoods were superior to Indian teak, apart from their better worm-resisting qualities. But there was no vast reserve of cheap and skilled manual labour in Brazil, such as India, China and (to some extent) the Philippines possessed. The Brazilian sugar-planters objected to their slave labour and their stands of timber being utilised by the Crown without (so they claimed) adequate payment. Not only the master shipwrights but many of the carpenters and caulkers, etc., had to be sent from Portugal, and the prices of cordage and other naval stores in Portuguese America were apt to be much higher. A Jesuit padre, reporting in 1618 on the possibility of building galleons in Brazil, stated that it would cost at least twice as much to construct one there as it would in Europe. Arguments as to whether it was better and/or cheaper to build ocean-going shipping in Portugal, or in India, or in Brazil, continued until well into the eighteenth century. The Crown persisted in its efforts, and royal shipbuilding yards were successively established at Bahia, Rio de Janeiro and Belém do Pará. They turned out some excellent ships, like those above mentioned, as well as others whose faulty proportions were severely criticised. Of the Brazilian yards, that at Bahia, which functioned (somewhat intermittently at first) from 1655 onwards, was undoubtedly the most important, building ships for local merchants as well as warships and East Indiamen for the Crown. The shipwrights and dockyard workers were recruited from Negro slaves as well as from free white (and also convict) labourers.

The manning problem of the *carreira da Índia* was nearly always a difficult one, as already briefly indicated on pages 52, 114, above. Deep-sea sailors are not made in a day, and the wastage from death and disease in the India voyage was very high. As early as 1505, completely raw crews were being recruited for service in the *carreira*, as instanced by the chronicler Castanheda's anecdote of João Homem's rustic seamen. These yokels could not distinguish between port and starboard when his ship left the Tagus, until he tied a bundle of onions on one side of the ship and a bundle of garlic on the other. 'Now,' he said to the pilot, 'tell them to onion their helm, or to garlic their helm, and they will understand quick enough.' This may have been an extreme case, but throughout the three centuries of the *carreira*'s existence complaints abounded that tailors, cobblers, lackeys, ploughmen and *moços bizonhos* (raw youths) were entered as able seamen, despite repeated regulations which were framed to prevent this abuse. In 1524 an informant at Cochin reported to the Crown that there were only 300 Portuguese sailors in the whole of India, 'including the sick and the sound'. Diogo do Couto noted that in 1558 there were nearly 400 Portuguese sailors available for service at Goa, but this was quite an exceptional number. The shortage of European sailors was accentuated during the period of the union of the two Iberian Crowns from 1580 to 1640, when many Portuguese mariners preferred the Spanish sea service to their own, as the former was slightly better paid and the Castilian kings were inclined to encourage this trend. This was because the Spaniards were plagued for centuries by the same shortage of deep-sea sailors, despite their having in Biscay and Galicia many more than the Portuguese had. Captain Augustus Hervey, R.N., relates how when a Spanish fleet sailed from Cadiz to Leghorn in 1731 'the people were so ignorant what ropes they were to go to, having been put on board in such a hurry, that they put cards on all the different ropes, and so were ordered to "Pull away the Ace of Spades", "Make fast the King of Hearts", and so on'.

It has been claimed that the six months' voyage from Lisbon to Goa gave such improvised sailors as those of 1505 time enough to become 'perfect salts'. Certainly some of them did so, but many others did not, as Martim Affonso de Sousa, one of the most experienced sea commanders that Portugal ever had, complained from India to a minister of the Crown in 1538. A carrack in the *carreira* was supposed to be crewed by about 120 or 130 foremast hands, equally divided between able (and ordinary) seamen and *grumetes* (grummets). These latter were apprentice seamen, not necessarily boys, though most of them were usually in their teens. They did all the hardest work on board, and they slept on the deck at the waist between the mainmast and the foremast. Many of them had never been in a ship till they left Lisbon for Goa, and Martim Affonso de Sousa observed of this type:

Let nobody tell you that when they arrive here they are already sailors. This is the biggest lie in the world, for they are vagabonds who have never been to sea; and in order to become a sailor it is necessary to serve for many years as a grummet. And I assure you that these are the ones who desert to the Muslims here, . . . for they have no sense of duty, and as soon as they lack a farthing of their wages, off they go.

Perhaps the fairest summary of their problem, which was a perennial one in the Spanish *flotas* also, was given by the perspicacious Spanish Dominican, Fray Domingo Fernández de Navarrete, writing of his own experiences after having circumnavigated the globe over a century later: 'I've known men who even after sailing many seas have never learnt to read a compass, nor to distinguish the sheet or tack from the other ropes, while others, in less than a month, knew all the nautical terms so that you would think they'd been studying the art for years.'

One reason for the difficulty of securing an adequate number of sailors for service in the fleets of Spain and Portugal was, in all probability, the contempt and dislike with which the mariner's calling was for so long regarded in both those countries. This is all the more curious when we recall that these two Iberian kingdoms pioneered the overseas expansion of Europe, and that they owed their greatness and prestige in the sixteenth century mainly to their maritime discoveries and conquests. Nevertheless, Portuguese and Spaniards both rated the soldier far above the sailor in the social hierarchy. This fact was reflected not only in such matters as Court precedence, and in royal rewards and favours, but in both the official correspondence and the classical literature of Spain and Portugal. The Spanish humanist Luis Vives defined sailors as being *Fex Maris* ('Dregs of the Sea'); and the Portuguese chronicler Diogo do Couto—no land-lubber like Vives, but an experienced and intelligent voyager—alleged that the great majority of sailors were 'cruel and inhuman by nature'. A seventeenth-century Spanish Jesuit in the Philippines made the punning observation that sailors were aptly called *marineros* since they were connected with the sea (*mar*) and were as cruel and brutal as *Neros*. The outward-bound Viceroy of India, Marquis of Tavora, reporting to the Secretary of State at Lisbon on his voyage to Goa in 1750, affirmed that 'the callousness and lack of charity on the part of the seamen is unspeakable. I can assure you that, as a general rule, this sort of people feels more the death of one of their chickens than the loss of five or six of their fellow voyagers.'

Nothing could be easier than to find hundreds of similar derogatory remarks by other well-educated men who should have known better, but who shared that contemptuous dislike for sailors which was so common in the Iberian peninsula. Needless to add that this widespread and deeply rooted aversion to their calling could not have enhanced the Iberian mariners' self-respect, and the hard life which they led undoubtedly helped to brutalise them. Considering the harshness with which they were usually treated by those who regarded themselves as their social superiors, it is scarcely surprising that the Portuguese sailors in the *carreira* sometimes behaved in shipwrecks, or in similar crises, with an undisciplined arrogance towards people who had despised them. Sailors also found it difficult to get fair treatment from the Crown officials on shore who embezzled their wages or gave them short rations. Conrad Rott, one of the German entrepreneurs engaged in the pepper monopoly contracts, assured a senior Crown official in 1600 that by paying decent wages and by giving full rations he would be able to raise 3,000 Portuguese sailors at a time when the Lisbon officials could barely muster 300 'with blows and imprisonments'. The Crown was reliably informed in 1524 that one reason why it was so difficult to recruit experienced seamen for the *carreira* was the harshness with which they were treated by the *fidalgos* in India. A century later Admiral João Pereira Corte-Real averred that this branch of the sea service was so unpopular that some sailors had to be forcibly impressed and kept aboard in chains until the Indiamen left Lisbon.

Nor was it only the *carreira da Índia* which suffered from a perennial lack of qualified sailors. For most of the seventeenth and much of the eighteenth centuries the small, undermanned and ill-trained Portuguese Navy proved incapable of clearing the Barbary pirates away from its home waters for any length of time. In 1673, and again in 1676, the Crown tried to remedy the shortage of seamen by raising a body (*troço*) of 300 experienced mariners who would be available at Lisbon for service in an emergency. Sailors enlisting in this formation were given special privileges, such as exemption for themselves and their sons from military service; immunity of their homes from billeting troops; certain tax deductions; and permission to wear side-arms. The widows of those men killed in action would receive any arrears of pay due to their late husbands and a generous cash gratuity (but no pension). This modest scheme does not seem to have helped much. Foreign voyagers often commented that the crews of Portuguese warships, of Indiamen, and of Brazil ships comprised a remarkably wide range of nationalities, even more so than did the ships of other nations in an age when the seaman's calling was more of an international one than it is now. In particular, the homeward-bound Indiamen depended increasingly on Negro slaves to make up their crews, as explained by the Viceroy of India in 1738:

> All the seagoing personnel now in Goa, including officers, sailors, gunners, pages and grummets, scarcely amount (excluding the sick) to 120 men, which is just about the number required to man a single homeward-bound Indiaman; especially in this monsoon when no Kaffirs have come from Moçambique and there is a shortage of them here ashore, so that they will not be available to sail as deck-hands to do the hard work as they usually do.

The Viceroy was not exaggerating. He could have quoted the precedent of the Indiaman *Aguia* in 1559, which was only saved from foundering in the Moçambique Channel by the exertions of the Negroes on board, and the officials of the India House at Lisbon emphatically declared in 1712 that many of the homeward-bound Indiamen would not have reached Portugal 'but for the continual labour of the Negro slaves in them'.

The *Náos da Carreira da Índia* took out to Goa chiefly soldiers and silver specie (mainly in the form of Spanish, Mexican and Peruvian rials-of-eight), copper, lead and other metals together with a little coral, and some assorted European goods of no great value. They were not, as a rule, deeply laden, and the wine and water casks for the complement of 600 or 800 men served as part of the ballast. Their return lading, on the other hand, comprised bulky cargoes of pepper, spices, saltpetre, indigo, hardwoods, furniture, Chinese porcelain, silks and Indian cotton piece-goods. The holds were filled to capacity with the pepper, spices and saltpetre, while crates and packages of the other commodities were sometimes piled so high on the decks that a man could only make his way from the poop to the prow by clambering over mounds of merchandise. Boxes, bales and baskets of assorted goods were also lashed outboard to projecting planks and platforms, or were slung suspended over the ship's side. Such chronic overloading and irregular stowage was, of course, strictly forbidden by reiterated Crown *regimentos*, but these sensible regulations were often flagrantly ignored, particularly during the last half of the sixteenth and the first half of the seventeenth centuries. A very similar state of affairs prevailed in the trans-Pacific voyages of the Manila galleons. The outward-bound ships from Acapulco were mainly laden with soldiers and silver specie in the form of Mexican and Peruvian rials-of-eight. On the return voyage from Manila many of the *Naos de China* were dangerously overladen with cargoes of Chinese goods, despite much paper legislation framed against this inveterate abuse.

Most of the deck and cabin space above the hold was the perquisite of some officer or member of the crew, who could sell it, together with the accompanying privilege of stowing personal property there, to the highest bidder. This space allotment was called *gasalhado*. The officers and men were also allowed *caixas de liberdade* ('liberty chests') of a standard measurement, in which they were permitted to bring home certain Asian commodities wholly or partly duty-free. The regulations concerning this 'private trade', as the English East India Company's similar system was termed, varied from time to time, and there was a sliding scale according to rank. These privileges of private trade originated from the fact that the Crown was either unable or unwilling to pay adequate wages and consequently tried to recompense its servants in this way. The supporters of the system also argued that by giving the sailors a direct interest in a portion of the ship's lading they would fight better if the ship was attacked, since they would be defending their own property as well as that of the Crown. The system was inevitably grossly abused, as were the similar privileges concerning private trade in the Dutch, French and English East India Companies.

Though well aware of the widespread opposition which any thoroughgoing reform would arouse, the Crown made a determined effort to abolish the system of *liberdades* in 1647–8 and to replace it by an adequate wage-scale. This attempt was coupled with another innovation, viz. the replacement of *fidalgos* as captains of Indiamen by professional seamen whose nautical knowledge was not necessarily accompanied by noble blood. In March 1647 the *Conselho Ultramarino*, or Overseas Council, warned King John IV that this scheme was impracticable for many reasons, and advised that it should not be implemented. The King, however, insisted on trying it out, but the innovation met with such intense opposition from those concerned, whether officers or sailors, that the Crown was forced to restore the old system in 1649–52. As the Overseas Councillors had foreseen, the *fidalgos* flatly refused to serve under or to take orders from professional seamen, who they considered were not of their social standing. The captains of Portuguese Indiamen were usually gentlemen or noblemen who often had no experience whatsoever of the sea on their first appointment. This was the principal reason why the pilot, and not the captain, had the sole responsibility for the ship's course and the navigation. Only in the second half of the seventeenth century did it become fairly common to appoint professional seamen rather than landsmen to the command of Indiamen, and only during the eighteenth century did this become the rule rather than the exception.

The arrogant obstinacy of many Portuguese pilots in the *carreira* was proverbial, and it was the target of much bitter criticism by Diogo do Couto and other contemporaries. But the best of these pilots were as good as any in the world, and their devotion to duty was warmly commended by Sir Richard Hawkins in his *Observations* of 1622:

> In this point of steeridge, the Spaniards and Portuguese do exceed all that I have seen, I mean for their care, which is chiefest in navigation. And I wish in this, and in all their works of discipline and reformation, we should follow their examples. . . . In every ship of moment, upon the half-deck, or quarter-deck, they have a chair or seat out of which whilst they navigate, the Pilot, or his Adjutants (which are the same officers which in our ships we term, the Master and his Mates) never depart, day nor night, from the sight of the compass; and have another before them; whereby they see what they do, and are ever witnesses of the good or bad steeridge of all men that do take the helm.

Each Indiaman was supposed to carry a qualified physician and a surgeon, together with well-stocked medicine chests provided by the Crown. In practice, however, there was often only an ignorant barber-surgeon aboard, as in the fleet of 1633, which carried 3,000 men in four ships. The Crown was certainly generous with the provision of well-stocked medicine chests to each Indiaman, but only too often the contents were taken by unauthorised persons for their own use, or else they were sold on the ship's 'black market' instead of being freely distributed to the sick. It must be added that many of these medicines were noxious nostrums which had no therapeutic value, and that others if harmless were useless. Moreover, the Portuguese predilection for phlebotomy and purging often had fatal results when patients already weakened by disease and malnutrition were deprived of several pints of blood and subjected to violent purges. The spread of fecal-born and other infectious diseases among the overcrowded soldiers and *degredados*, packed together in most unsanitary conditions and often with no adequate shelter from tropical heat and freezing cold, inevitably resulted in heavy mortality from dysentery, typhus, gaol-fever and scurvy on many voyages.

Diogo do Couto tells us that in the fleet in which he returned to India in 1571 nearly 2,000 men died out of a total of 4,000 who left Lisbon. In the six-year period 1629–34, out of 5,228 soldiers who embarked at Lisbon for India, only 2,495 reached Goa alive. Fatalities on the return voyage were usually much less, as the ships were not nearly so crowded, and the great majority of people who embarked at Goa were already inured to the hardships of the voyage. Casualties on the voyage in either direction were almost invariably compounded if the Indiamen called, as they very often did, whether voluntarily or otherwise, at Moçambique Island. Between 1528 and 1558 over 30,000 men died there, mainly from malaria and bilious fevers, after having been landed from the Indiamen which called at this place in that thirty-year period.

The Italian Jesuit Alexander Valignano, who made the outward voyage himself in 1574, noted that:

> It is an astounding thing to see the facility and frequency with which the Portuguese embark for India. . . . Each year four or five carracks leave Lisbon full of them; and many embark as if they were going no further than a league from Lisbon, taking with them only a shirt and two loaves in the hand, and carrying a cheese and a jar of marmalade, without any other kind of provision.

Since it was nothing unusual for anything between a third and a half of these feckless individuals to die on the voyage, as did the *degredados* and convict-soldiers who succeeded them, it is not surprising that the *carreira da Índia* early achieved an unenviable reputation, which it retained down to the second half of the eighteenth century. In the nature of things it was these disastrous and deadly voyages, sometimes culminating in spectacular shipwrecks, which figure most prominently in contemporary accounts and reminiscences, but there were, of course, many exceptions. The chronicler Castanheda recalled the arrival of the four ships of the 1529 fleet at Goa 'at dawn on the morning of St. Bartholomew's Day [24th August]. And this fleet had made such a good voyage that the men thereof, who numbered five hundred, were so hale and hearty that it seemed as if they had only left Lisbon a fortnight earlier.' It is true that he added 'and I never saw the like happen again'.

The archives of the India House at Lisbon having perished in the great earthquake of 1755, we have no exact records of all sailings in the *carreira* before that date. But V. Magalhães Godinho, who has made the most thorough comparison of the available references, has calculated that in the years 1500–1635 some 912 ships sailed to the East, of which 768 reached their destination; the respective figures for the homeward voyage being some 550 sailings from the East, of which 470 reached Portugal.

We have seen (p. 206) that for the first century and a half of the *carreira da Índia* every effort was made by the Crown to prevent Indiamen calling at Brazilian ports on either the homeward or the outward voyage. The chief reasons for this prohibition were fear that the Indiamen might lose their voyage by so doing, and the high rate of desertion from such ships as did call there. During the second half of the seventeenth century it became increasingly common for homeward-bound Indiamen to touch at a Brazilian port, usually at Bahia, on the plea of stress of weather, or lack of provisions. After the discovery and exploitation of the rich goldfields of Minas Gerais in the 1690s this call became a settled habit. It was finally if reluctantly sanctioned by the Crown, but only for the purpose of refitting and provisioning homeward-bound Indiamen. These Indiamen often reached Bahia in a battered condition which justified a stay of some weeks, but their sojourn in the Bay of All Saints was invariably accompanied by the intensive and illegal exchange of Oriental goods for Brazilian gold and tobacco. All efforts to stop this flourishing contraband trade failed, because the military guards placed on board the visiting ships in order to prevent smuggling 'are those who most shamelessly and scandalously smuggle the goods ashore from the Indiamen and foreign ships', as the Viceroy at Bahia reported to the Crown in March 1718. Forty years later an official report stated that Chinese porcelain was the Asian commodity which was in most demand and fetched the best prices ashore, but large quantities of Indian piece-goods and even (on occasion) diamonds were likewise imported in this way. After refitting at Bahia the Indiamen then sailed for Lisbon in the convoy of the homeward-bound sugar-fleet, the organisation of which dated from the mid-seventeenth century.

The ships employed in the Brazil trade during the sixteenth century were mostly caravels and other vessels averaging less than about 100 or 150 tons burthen. Galleons and carracks were occasionally used, but these were almost invariably smaller than those engaged in the *carreira da Índia*. The caravels were very lightly gunned, when they carried any cannon at all, and their turn of speed does not seem to have saved many of them from the clutches of French, English, and Barbary rovers, as we have had occasion to observe (p. 105). The most obvious remedies for this state of affairs were that the ships should be either adequately armed or else convoyed by warships, as was the case with the Spanish *flotas* in the transatlantic trade. Two kinds of taxes, called respectively the *averia* and the *consulado*, were instituted to defray the costs of providing protection for the Brazil ships (and other colonial trades), but the administration of these taxes left a great deal to be desired, and no adequate protection was in fact provided. For this reason many Portuguese traders made use of neutral shipping whenever they could, chiefly Hansa and Dutch, the latter often masquerading as the former prior to 1624.

There were a number of reasons why the Portuguese Crown took so long to introduce an effective convoy system, despite the staggering losses which the Brazil ships often incurred, and despite the Spanish precedent which it was often urged to imitate.

Whereas the Spanish transatlantic trade was centralised at Seville and Cadiz on one side of the Atlantic and at Cartagena de Indias, Porto Belo and Vera Cruz on the other, the Portuguese ships trading with Brazil came from a number of small seaports in Portugal (Caminha, Viana, Aveiro, Peniche, Nazaré, Lagos, etc.), Madeira and the Azores, as well as from the large entrepôts of Lisbon and Oporto. On the other side of the Atlantic each of the fourteen Brazilian captaincies had its own port, although Recife, Bahia and Rio de Janeiro were far and away the most important. Many of the merchants and shipowners engaged in this trade were 'small men' who had not got the capital resources to build big ships, or to find the crews and cannon for them. Moreover, the annual sugar crop and its prospects fluctuated widely, and shipping capacity could seldom be calculated accurately in advance. In these circumstances small caravels ran less risk (than did large merchant ships) of being kept waiting for weeks, or even months, in Brazilian ports to complete their lading, and they had more chance of making two round voyages in a year. The Portuguese freighted at one time or another many foreign ships for use in the Brazil trade; and the owners and captains of these ships disliked being subjected to the restraints of a convoy. Last but not least, the unavoidable delay involved in unlading and lading a fleet sailing in convoy meant that the sugar might deteriorate in the interval. Both planters and merchants preferred to ship the sugar quickly to the European market, in the hope of obtaining higher prices, despite the risk inherent in shipping it in unarmed and unescorted caravels.

The crisis of the Dutch war eventually forced the King's hand in 1647–8. In those two years some 220 Portuguese Brazil traders were lost by enemy action, the vast majority being taken by Zeeland privateers operating in the South Atlantic. This figure represented a high proportion of all the shipping engaged in the Brazil trade, and although caravels were relatively cheap to build and relatively easy to man, it was obviously impossible to replace losses at this rate in a country that was chronically short of both shipping and seamen. Something drastic had to be done and something was. A royal decree was promulgated forbidding the construction (or the freighting) of ships of less than 350 tons and mounting less than sixteen guns, though the tonnage limit almost immediately had to be lowered to 250. A scale of armament was laid down for different kinds of shipping and bounties were offered for the building of well-gunned merchantmen.

King John IV's most influential adviser, Padre António Vieira, S.J., had long been urging upon him the formation of two chartered companies for the Brazil trade and the India trade respectively, on the lines of the Dutch and English ones. He suggested that the necessary capital would be subscribed mainly by the crypto-Jews (*Christãos-Novos*), whether at home or abroad, if they were given a guarantee that the money they invested in this way would not be confiscated by the Holy Office even if they themselves were arrested by it. Vieira's advocacy of the *Christãos-Novos* was regarded askance by some of his own colleagues, and his plan was strongly opposed by many influential people apart from the Inquisitors themselves. But his exceptional influence with the King and the desperate nature of the crisis eventually overcame that monarch's natural hesitancy, and the Brazil Company was formally incorporated on 8 March 1649.

Investors of all classes and nationalities were eligible to become shareholders with a minimum subscription of twenty *cruzados*. The Company promised to fit out and maintain a fleet of thirty-six warships, divided into two squadrons, to convoy all Portuguese shipping between Portugal and Brazil, with Oporto and Lisbon as the terminal ports on one side of the Atlantic and Recife (after its recapture in 1654), Bahia and Rio de Janeiro on the other. In return the Company was given the monopoly of supplying Brazil with the colony's four most essential imports other than slaves—wine, flour, olive oil and codfish—at rates to be fixed by itself. It was authorised to levy duties on all Brazilian exports, ranging from 100 *reis* for a hide to 3,400 *reis* for a chest of white sugar. It was given a wide range of fiscal immunities and Customs exemptions in Portugal, and it was provided by the Crown with land for its arsenal at Lisbon. Capital invested in the Company was exempted from confiscation by the Inquisition or by any other tribunal; even in the event of war between Portugal and the home country of a foreign investor the latter would not forfeit either his investment or his dividends. It is uncertain how many foreigners did subscribe, though its shares were touted at Amsterdam, Paris and Venice. The bulk of the capital which was raised (1,255,000 *cruzados*) came from the leading 'New'-Christian merchants of Lisbon, much of it apparently in the nature of more or less forced loans. The projected East India Company did not get past the paper stage, despite Vieira's urging then and later.

From the very beginning the Company encountered bitter criticism on both sides of the Atlantic, and not only from the rabid anti-Semites who abounded in all classes of Portuguese society. It could not raise sufficient capital to maintain its quota of thirty-six warships, and in some years it was unable to provide any convoy at all. The predominant part played by 'New' Christians on its formation and management rendered it suspect to the bigotedly Roman Catholic nation, and it was widely believed that King John IV died excommunicate for having overruled the Inquisition on this point. Although Lisbon and Oporto benefited from the concentration of the Company's shipping in those two ports, many of the smaller harbours from Caminha to Lagos were now deprived of a branch of maritime trade that had kept them going (however modestly) for generations. Small merchants and caravel skippers felt themselves squeezed out by the crypto-Jewish monopolists and engrossers of Lisbon. But the most valid and vocal criticism stemmed from the Company's inability to supply Brazil with the four basic imports of wine, flour, olive oil and codfish in sufficient quantities and at reasonable prices. As the Portuguese ambassador at Paris had written to King John IV when the formation of the Company was still under discussion: 'Monopolies of those articles which form the necessities of life always proved to be highly prejudicial to those monarchs who authorised them; for even though some benefit is derived by the royal exchequer therefrom, the harm suffered by the common people far outweighs that strictly limited advantage.'

The colonists' continual complaints on this score were warmly supported by most of the colonial governors and senior Crown officials. Vieira's influence at Court was drastically reduced by his absence as a missionary in the Maranhão and the death of King John IV in November 1656. A few months later the Company's exemption from interference by the Inquisition was removed, and in 1658 its monopoly of importing wine, flour, codfish and olive oil into Brazil was abolished. Further curtailment of its privileges was followed by its incorporation in the Crown in 1664, the shareholders being compensated by holdings in the royal tobacco monopoly. In this reorganised form it continued to function as a government organ under the title of *Companhia Geral do Comercio do Brasil*, for the purpose of providing convoys on a reduced scale for the Brazil fleets, until its extinction by a royal decree of 1 February 1720.

From the financial viewpoint Padre António Vieira's brainchild did not come up to expectation. Apart from the fact that the full amount of the capital originally envisaged was never subscribed, the exiled Portuguese Jews at Amsterdam and elsewhere did not invest in it to any considerable extent, and the Company only paid one dividend (of 15 per cent) before its reorganisation in 1662–4. On the other hand, the convoy system which it inaugurated in 1649 markedly reduced the number of losses at the hands of the Dutch and other corsairs. The recapture of Recife and the expulsion of the Dutch from their last toe-holds in north-east Brazil during January 1654 were also mainly due to the Company's fleet having temporary command of the sea at that time. The Company was likewise responsible for raising and maintaining a regiment of marines to serve in its convoy fleets, and this unit was continued under its successor, being popularly known as 'the regiment of the Junta' even after 1720.

Unfortunately we do not have lists of the annual Brazil fleets before the eighteenth century, although the names of virtually all the ships sailing in the *carreira da Índia* have been preserved in one form or another. But whereas the annual India fleets averaged only two, three, or four ships in the second half of the seventeenth century, the Brazil fleets of this period sometimes numbered over a hundred sail, thus making them much more impressive numerically than the contemporary Spanish *flotas*. They were for the most part a very heterogeneous lot, and despite the regulations of 1648–9 concerning their size and armament, some of them were pretty ill-found. The commander of four English warships who met the homeward-bound Brazil fleet of 107 sail off the Portuguese coast in July 1656 reported that 'they were the pitifullest vessels that ever I saw. I am confident that twelve or fourteen sail of good frigates would have taken and spoiled what they pleased.' Such a fate did, in fact, befall the homeward-bound

Brazil fleets which were intercepted by Blake and Popham in 1650, and by De Ruyter in 1657. Nevertheless, the institution of the convoy system gradually resulted in the building of bigger and better ships for the Brazil trade on both sides of the Atlantic, apart from the considerable numbers of foreign merchantmen which continued to be freighted.

The voyage from Lisbon to Bahia averaged about two and a half or three months, and slightly less to Recife and slightly more to Rio de Janeiro, under reasonably favourable conditions of wind and weather. It is obvious that a two or three months' passage in a Brazil ship was a very different affair from a six or eight months' passage to India in an overcrowded carrack with scurvy and dysentery rife among those on board. The weather conditions of the Brazil voyage were also much better as a general rule, although ships leaving at the wrong season ran the risk of being becalmed in the equatorial zone, or (on the return voyage) of encountering the late autumnal and early winter gales in the latitude of the Azores. 'July and August are the best ports of the Peninsula,' observed the great Spanish admiral Don Fadrique de Toledo. In 1690 a royal decree was promulgated that the annual Brazil fleets should leave Portuguese ports between 15 December and 20 January on the outward voyage, and sail from Brazilian ports between the end of May and 20 July on their return voyage. These timings were subsequently modified by successive royal decrees, but they were, in any event, seldom strictly adhered to. As the Viceroy Count of Sabugosa complained to the Crown in 1732, the masters of merchantmen and the captains of convoying frigates alike preferred to sail, not at the times ordered by the Crown, but at those which suited their private trade and personal convenience. At this period the Brazil fleets were organised in three distinct convoys, sailing from Lisbon to Rio de Janeiro, Bahia and Pernambuco respectively. All these fleets brought back cargoes of gold, sugar, tobacco, hides and timber, but the Rio fleet was usually the richest. The greater part of the gold mined in Minas Gerais, Goyaz, Cuiabá and Mato Grosso found its way to that port, as did quantities of Peruvian silver pieces-of-eight smuggled via Sacramento. Each fleet was convoyed by from one to four warships, and the gold, whether destined for the Crown or for private persons, was supposed to be carried only on board those warships. The system of sailing in fleets was abolished in 1765 and only briefly re-established from 1797 to 1801.

Since the conditions of the Brazil voyage were, as a rule, much easier than those prevailing in the India *carreira*, and since the duration of the former did not involve the sailors being away from their homes for so long, the manning problem was less acute in the Brazil ships than in the Indiamen. But the problem was there, and voyagers in the Brazil fleets, especially during the years 1660–1730, often commented on the high proportion of foreign sailors among the crews. One Italian Capuchin missionary friar observed (with evident exaggeration) that practically every race, creed and colour under the sun was represented in the ship in which he took passage for Lisbon from Bahia in 1703. The correspondence between the governors of Brazil and the Overseas Council at Lisbon during the eighteenth century contains repeated complaints concerning the 'inexplicable reluctance' of the inhabitants of Portuguese America to volunteer for either military or naval service. This was due, at least in part, to the Crown being regarded as a bad paymaster, even in the almost literally golden days of King John V (1706–50). Another reason was that the American-born did not take kindly to military and naval discipline, as evidenced by the very similar complaints of successive Spanish viceroys about the extreme reluctance of Mexicans and Peruvians to serve as soldiers. A shortage of experienced Portuguese sea officers persisted throughout the eighteenth century, which explains why so many Dutch, British, French, and even some Spanish officers were employed in the navy of His Most Faithful Majesty. On the other hand, there were a few outstandingly competent commanders, such as António de Brito Freire and Gonçalo de Barros Alvim, who served the Crown for thirty or forty years on practically continuous duty in the India and Brazil fleets.

The Bahiano chronicler Rocha Pitta, writing in 1724, boasted that 'our Portuguese America' sent about a hundred ships to Europe each year, laden on an average with a total of 24,000 chests of sugar, 18,000 rolls of tobacco, great quantities of leather and hides, 'many millions of gold in gold-dust, ingots and specie', besides shipbuilding timbers and other Brazilian products. He was writing at the most spectacularly prosperous period of the

Brazil trade, and the value of the colonial exports slumped for a time after 1760, owing to the fall in the production of gold and for other reasons indicated above (p. 181). This fall was offset to some extent by the great increase in the trade with Maranhão-Pará and Pernambuco-Paraíba with the impulse given by Pombal's monopolistic companies for those regions (p. 184 above). The former Company had a fleet of thirteen ships in 1759, twenty-six in 1768 and thirty-two in 1774, whilst the latter had a fleet of thirty-one ships in 1763, which had dropped to seventeen in 1776. The liquidation of these two companies between 1778 and 1788 was in its turn offset by an improvement in the seaborne trade of Rio de Janeiro and Bahia after 1780. By 1796 the City of the Saviour on the Bay of All Saints was once again the port with the greatest volume of trade in the Portuguese colonial world, a position which it retained until after the arrival of the Prince Regent and the refugee Court at Rio.

CHAPTER X

The Crown patronage and the Catholic missions

THE soldier-chronicler Diogo do Couto, who spent virtually all of his adult life in India, and who was certainly in a position to know what he was writing about, tells us in his sixth *Decada* (1612): 'The Kings of Portugal always aimed in this conquest of the East at so uniting the two powers, spiritual and temporal, that the one should never be exercised without the other.' The Franciscan chronicler Fr. Paulo da Trindade, writing his *Conquista Espiritual do Oriente* (*Spiritual Conquest of the East*) at Goa in 1638, observed: 'The two swords of the civil and the ecclesiastical power were always so close together in the conquest of the East that we seldom find one being used without the other; for the weapons only conquered through the right that the preaching of the Gospel gave them, and the preaching was only of some use when it was accompanied and protected by the weapons.' This indissoluble union of the Cross and the Crown was exemplified in the exercise of the *Padroado Real* or royal patronage of the Church overseas. It was one of the most jealously guarded and tenaciously maintained prerogatives of the Portuguese Crown, and during its long and stormy history in the struggle for souls it was often the cause of bitter disputes between Portuguese missionaries and those of other Roman Catholic powers.

The Portuguese *Padroado* can be loosely defined as a combination of the rights, privileges and duties granted by the Papacy to the Crown of Portugal as patron of the Roman Catholic missions and ecclesiastical establishments in vast regions of Africa, of Asia, and in Brazil. These rights and duties derived from a series of Papal Bulls and Briefs, beginning with the Bull *Inter caetera* of Calixtus III in 1456 and culminating in the Bull *Praecelsae devotionis* of 1514. In fact, the Portuguese *Padroado Real* in the non-European world was for long only limited by the similar rights and duties conferred on the *Patronato Real* of the Castilian Crown by a parallel series of Papal Bulls and Briefs promulgated in favour of 'the Catholic Kings' between 1493 and 1512. The Borgias and other Renaissance Popes, owing to their preoccupation with European politics, with the rising tide of Protestantism and with the Turkish threat in the Mediterranean, did not concern themselves very closely with the evangelisation of the new worlds opened by the Portuguese and Spanish discoveries. Successive Vicars of Christ saw no harm in letting the Iberian monarchs bear the expense of building chapels and churches, maintaining an ecclesiastical hierarchy, and sending missionaries to convert the heathen, in exchange for granting those rulers extensive privileges in the way of presenting bishops to vacant or (newly founded) colonial Sees, collecting tithes and administering some forms of ecclesiastical taxation.

In so far as Portugal was concerned, many of these ecclesiastical privileges had originally been granted to the Order of Christ, which (in 1455–6) had been given spiritual jurisdiction over the 'lands, islands, and places' hitherto discovered or yet to be discovered by the Portuguese. This military-religious Order was founded by King Dom Dinis in 1319 to replace the recently suppressed Order of the Knights Templar. Since the time of the Infante Dom Henrique, the headship of the Order (whether grand-master or governor and administrator) had been vested in a member of the royal family. It was formally incorporated in the Crown, together with the grand-mastership of the other two Portuguese military Orders, Santiago and Aviz, by the Papal Bull *Praeclara charissimi* of December 1551. In their dual capacity as kings of Portugal and as 'perpetual governors and administrators' of the Order of Christ, Dom Manuel and his successors had the right of patronage over all ecclesiastical posts, offices, benefices and livings in the overseas territories confided to the *Padroado* after the undiscovered worlds had been, in effect, divided between the Crowns of Portugal and Castile by the Treaty of Tordesillas in 1494. Within the sphere of the *Padroado*, which at its greatest extent in the mid-sixteenth century stretched from Brazil to Japan, no bishop could be appointed to an existing See, and no new See could be created without the permission of the Portuguese king—or so these kings claimed. They further claimed that no missionary could be sent to those regions without the permission of the Portuguese Crown, and then only if he sailed in a Portuguese ship.

Some adherents of the *Padroado* asserted that the King of Portugal was a kind of Papal Legate and that his ecclesiastical legislation had the force of canonical decrees. Pombal, in his ultra-regalism, told the newly appointed Archbishop of Goa in 1774 that the King of Portugal by virtue of his position as supreme head of the Order of Christ was a 'Spiritual Prelate' with jurisdiction and powers 'superior to all those of the diocesan prelates and to the Ordinaries of the said churches in the East'. Without always going quite as far as this, successive kings of Portugal certainly acted as if the overseas bishops and clergy were, in many ways, simple functionaries of state, like viceroys or governors. They gave them orders without reference to Rome, controlled their activities, and often legislated in matters ecclesiastical. They did the same with the provincials or acting heads of the religious Orders working in the territories of the *Padroado*, and even on occasion with individual missionaries and parish priests. They refused to recognise the validity of any Papal Briefs, Bulls or Provisions, relating to matters within the sphere of the *Padroado*, and which had not been approved by the Portuguese Crown and registered with the *Regium Placet* in the royal chancery. The tithes collected by the Crown were supposed to be used for supporting the missions and the Church establishments in the overseas possessions. They were often insufficient for this purpose and were then supplemented by grants, pensions, or other payments made from the general funds of the royal exchequer, though royal subsidies were apt to be paid 'ill, late, or never' (p. 77 above). On the other hand, the Crown sometimes used a substantial part of the money collected from tithes to help cover deficits in the general administration, as it did in the gold-mining districts of Minas Gerais during the eighteenth century.

The kings of Portugal, whether of the House of Aviz, the

Spanish Habsburgs (1580–1640), or the House of Braganza, while stubbornly defending their undeniably very extensive *Padroado* privileges, were also usually mindful of the duties and obligations entailed. Nor was there ever a lack of prelates and of missionaries who were prepared to remind the ruling monarch of his duty to the missions. The conviction that Portugal was the missionary nation above all others in the Western World—*Alferes da Fé*, 'standard-bearer of the Faith', as the poet-playwright Gil Vicente boasted—was widespread and deeply rooted among all classes. It was typically expressed by Padre António Vieira, S.J., in a letter written from the Maranhão mission-field to the young king Dom Affonso VI in April 1657:

> The other kingdoms of Christendom, Sire, have as their purpose the preservation of their vassals, so as to achieve temporal felicity in this life and eternal felicity in the next. And the kingdom of Portugal, besides this purpose which is common to all, has for its particular and special purpose the propagation and the extension of the Catholic faith in heathen lands, for which God raised and founded it. And the more that Portugal acts in keeping with this purpose, the more sure and certain is its preservation; and the more it diverges therefrom, the more doubtful and dangerous is its future.

This letter may not have made much of an impression on the fourteen-year-old illiterate spastic who had recently succeeded to the throne; but with the possible exception of that unfortunate monarch all the other rulers took their missionary responsibilities very seriously. They certainly would not have agreed with the Bishop of Cochin who observed of the Ceylon mission, *c.* 1606, 'that it is I, not the King, who is answerable for it at the hour of death and in the day of judgement'. Numberless royal dispatches addressed to viceroys, governors and bishops begin with the opening sentence: 'Forasmuch as the first and principal obligation of the Kings of Portugal is to forward the work of conversion by all means in their power . . .' or words to that effect. If this was sometimes merely conventional phraseology, much more often it was sincerely meant. Viceroys, governors and independent bodies such as the municipal council of Goa not seldom complained that the King was spending far too much from his limited local resources on the Church and on the missions, even in times of war or of acute economic crisis, as mentioned above (p. 77).

This said, it must be admitted that the monarchs of the House of Aviz were rather slow in organising an effective hierarchy in the Church overseas. The early Portuguese African and Asian discoveries came, as we have seen, under the ecclesiastical jurisdiction of the Order of Christ (with its seat at Tomar), until the erection of a bishopric at Funchal in Madeira in 1514. Despite the remoteness of this Atlantic island from the scene of Portuguese missionary activities in Asia, not until twenty years later was an independent diocese erected at Goa, with jurisdiction extending from the Cape of Good Hope to China. Only in 1557 did Goa become a metropolitan archbishopric with powers over two newly established Sees at Cochin and Malacca, followed (in 1575) by Macao. This long delay is in striking contrast to the rapid development of the *Patronato Real* in Spanish America, where a fully fledged ecclesiastical hierarchy was functioning in the Antilles before 1515, and where the archbishopric of Mexico dates from 1548. As indicated above (pp. 65–6), the really spectacular development of the Portuguese missions in Asia begins with the arrival of the Jesuits, who were also the most doughty exponents and defenders of the claims of the *Padroado* for the next two centuries.

The first challenge to the *Padroado* came from the Spanish missionary friars in the Philippines, where they had been established since 1565. Many of the friars regarded these islands as a stepping-stone to the more prestigious mission-fields of China and Japan, which had been a virtual monopoly of the Jesuits and the *Padroado* since 1549. Spanish missionaries of the Mendicant Orders first tried to breach this monopoly in the last quarter of the sixteenth century, but a good many years elapsed before they obtained the full consent of Madrid and Rome. King Philip II of Spain (I of Portugal) was mindful of the dubious loyalty of his newly won subjects, and by and large he accepted the contention of his Portuguese advisers that the two Far Eastern empires should be left to the Jesuit missionaries of the *Padroado*. His successor (or rather, the Duke of Lerma, who governed in his name) was not so concerned to pander to the Portuguese, and he was more responsive to the vociferous demands of his own compatriots. In 1608, with the concurrence of the Iberian Crown(s), Pope Paul V revoked the Portuguese monopoly of missionary enterprise in most of Asia, formally permitting the Spanish missionaries of the Mendicant Orders to go there in other than Portuguese ships. In 1633 this concession was extended to the other religious Orders, and in 1673 to the secular clergy. All of these measures merely sanctioned what had long been happening in practice.

One of the strongest arguments used by the spokesmen of the Spanish friars in their criticisms of the Portuguese and Jesuit monopoly of the mission-fields in the Far East was that neither the kingdom of Portugal nor the Society of Jesus, with the best will in the world, could possibly produce enough men to cope with the actual (let alone the potential) harvest of souls. Padre Nuno da Cunha, S.J., King John IV's unofficial envoy at Rome in 1648, reporting to his master a conversation which he had with Pope Innocent X about this problem, stated that His Holiness:

affirmed that the conquests of Portugal were greatly neglected, and that the Congolese alone were asking for sixty missionaries; and the demands from India and from the other conquests were so many and so great, that he was reliably informed that even if His Majesty would send out all the Religious that there were in Portugal, they would not supply a small fraction of the numbers actually required. He added that if I tried to deny this, I would be denying a self-evident truth, or else I would be showing that I was not concerned with the heart of the matter, which was that the conquests were only conceded [to the *Padroado*] for the sake of the salvation of souls.

Pope Innocent X therefore insisted, as had his three immediate predecessors, that the Portuguese missionary monopoly was ineffective and out of date and that missionaries from other European countries should be allowed to go to Africa and to Asia without any interference from the Portuguese.

The relative indifference of most of the Renaissance Popes to the overseas missions clearly was not shared by their seventeenth-century successors. Urban VIII (1623–44), in particular, was an enthusiastic patron of missionary endeavour. The Papacy was by now well aware that the extensive privileges which had been so freely bestowed on the Portuguese *Padroado* and on the Spanish *Patronato* were in many respects highly inconvenient and subversive of Papal authority. There was nothing that the Popes could do about the Spanish-American empire, where the Castilian kings maintained, and indeed increased, the scope of their *Patronato Real* down to the independence movements in the early nineteenth century—just as the kings of Portugal, whether Habsburgs or Braganzas, did in Brazil. But the Portuguese in Africa and Asia were in a much weaker position after their maritime monopoly had been broken by the Dutch and the English. The Papacy was therefore enabled to whittle down and pare away the claims of the *Padroado* in those two continents throughout the seventeenth and the eighteenth centuries. Urban VIII and his successors justified this action not only on the grounds of the manifest inability of Portugal to provide sufficient missionary personnel but with the more specious argument that the original concessions had been intended to apply only to those territories effectively controlled by the Portuguese and not to independent Asian and African kingdoms.

Portuguese pride and patriotism strongly resented this attitude of the Papacy, and the monarchs of the House of Braganza fought a tenacious rearguard action in defence of their cherished *Padroado* rights. King John IV emphasised, correctly enough, that the Portuguese Crown had never tried to stop foreign-born missionaries from going to the *Padroado* mission-fields, provided only that they did so with the permission of the Portuguese king, sailed in Portuguese ships and were directly subordinated to Portuguese government control through their provincials and superiors in the same way as the Portuguese missionaries were. This was perfectly true, and one has only to recall some of the most famous figures in Portuguese missionary history—Xavier, Valignano, Ricci and Schall in the East, Anchieta and Meade in Brazil—to see the justice of this argument. But the Portuguese monarchs insisted that the final choice of missionary personnel should rest with them and not with Rome. They claimed that they could reject men whom they considered unsuitable or potentially disloyal, such as Spaniards or, on occasion, Italians, Flemings and others who came from states or principalities controlled by the Spanish Crown during Portugal's War of Independence from 1640 to 1668. Equally understandably, the Papacy was no longer willing to accept the sweeping if legally well-founded claims of the *Padroado*, and it insisted on sending missionaries of its own choice to regions in Africa and Asia which were not subjected to Portuguese rule.

The increasing Papal control of the missions was exercised primarily through the Sacred College of the Propaganda Fide, founded at Rome in 1622, and secondarily through encouraging the establishment of various French and Italian missions in Africa and the East. The first secretary of this institution, the Italian prelate Francesco Ingoli, who held this key post for twenty-seven years, was very anti-Portuguese and very critical of the Jesuits. He took much time and trouble in compiling reports about conditions in the mission-fields of the *Padroado*, relying heavily on the information supplied by a Christian Goan *Brahmene*, Matheus de Castro, of whom more below (p. 255). Among the numerous sins of omission and commission with which Ingoli taxed the *Padroado* and its adherents were royal nomination of ecclesiastical functionaries; equating of royal ordinances with apostolic Briefs; supplying insufficient funds for the upkeep of churches; leaving bishoprics vacant; reluctance of the bishops to ordain Asians as priests, even when the latter possessed all the necessary qualifications, as did many of the Goan *Brahmenes*; baptism of pagans by force; refusal of the Jesuits to collaborate with the other religious Orders, and the pressures exercised by the Jesuits on their converts in the same sense. Several of the Sees in the *Padroado* were so vast in extent that the bishops could not carry out their spiritual duties properly, even if they tried to do so. Last not least, another common criticism of the Portuguese was that they were excessively devoted to the outward forms and ceremonies of the Church, but neglectful of the individual's spiritual development.

Some of these criticisms were exaggerated (Matheus de Castro was anything but an unbiased witness), others were unfair (the Papacy refused to recognise Portuguese independence and to consecrate any Portuguese bishops between 1640 and 1668), but several of them were perfectly true. Moreover they were reinforced by similar information from other sources, such as Antonio Albergati, the Papal Collector at Lisbon in 1623. He alleged that the cruelty and immorality of the Portuguese in Africa and Asia formed a great hindrance to the work of conversion. Their clergy, he asserted, both secular and regular, were mostly of a very low standard, though he excepted the Jesuits from this particular stricture, and many of them were more interested in mercantile than in missionary activities. He suggested that the only way of curbing this lamentable state of affairs would be to send out carefully selected missionaries of other than Portuguese nationality, and to send them overland by Syria and Persia. His suggestion was not immediately adopted, but during the second quarter of the seventeenth century Ingoli built up at Rome an influential body of opinion which was highly critical of the *Padroado*, especially of the *Padroado* in Asia, and which was not confined to the Cardinals of the Propaganda Fide. In 1658 the first Vicars-Apostolic, members of a new French missionary society, entitled the *Société des Missions Etrangères de Paris*, left for the East with the approval of the Propaganda Fide and the Papacy. They were followed by many others, mostly French and Italian, all of whom were directly responsible to the Holy See and completely independent of the *Padroado*. These pioneer Vicars-Apostolic were also titular bishops *in partibus infidelium*, and one of their chief tasks was to foster the formation of a native clergy in territories which were not effectively occupied by the Portuguese.

King John IV had been seated hardly a year on his still insecure throne when he sent orders to the Viceroy and Archbishop at Goa, forbidding them to receive missionaries sent out under the auspices of the Propaganda, unless they had come out to Asia via Lisbon and with the royal exequater. Any missionaries unprovided with the *Regium Placet* who ventured on to Portuguese territory were to be arrested and deported to Lisbon in the first returning Indiaman, being treated, however, with the respect due to their cloth. These orders were frequently reiterated during the next fifty years, but the degree of their enforcement varied. Padre António Vieira, S.J., noted approvingly that his friend the Count of São Vicente, who was Viceroy of India in 1666–8, 'shortly before his death wrote a letter to Cardinal Orsini at Rome, containing these formal words: that if Bishops came out to India who had not been presented by the King of Portugal, he would have them hanged publicly in Goa, even at the risk of the Congregation of the Propaganda declaring them to be martyrs.

And neither should His Eminence nor the Congregation think they could escape him anywhere, since he had plenty of soldiers and warships.' Two of these prelates had, in fact, been deported to Lisbon in 1652; but on the other hand the Portuguese gave sanctuary at Goa in 1664, and again in 1684, to some Vicars-Apostolic who were being threatened with persecution by Muslim or by Hindu rulers on the mainland.

Despite these and other sporadic instances of Christian charity which could be recorded, relations between the representatives of the *Padroado* and of the Propaganda remained very strained for centuries. Fr. Jacinto de Deus, a Macaonese Capuchin friar and chronicler of his Order at Goa, informed the Prince Regent, Dom Pedro, in 1671, that the Vicars-Apostolic had made no converts at all—'those that they claim in books published in Europe are sheer falsehoods. This harvest was sown and reaped by Portuguese, and Portuguese alone are fitted for it.' This ultra-nationalistic note was sounded in much of the correspondence of the time both by laymen and by the clergy. The Crown consequently had full backing for its policy of standing firm on its *Jus Patronatus*, which it always argued was a legal right, and one which, in the words of a Papal document of 1588, 'nobody could derogate, not even the Holy See in consistory, without the express consent of the King of Portugal'. A century later, times had changed for Rome if not for Lisbon. The Papacy now argued that the favours and privileges previously conceded to the Crown of Portugal could not be interpreted as a strictly bilateral contract, and that the *jus patronatum* was not in any way a total alienation of the Church's superior and essential right. The Holy See, under stress of circumstances, could modify, withdraw, or revoke the older *Padroado* privileges if higher interests and the greater good of souls postulated such an action. The ensuing struggle was consequently long and bitter, the final stages being enacted in our own day, and only a few of the major vicissitudes can be outlined here.

In Japan, which was the scene of the first conflicts, and where the rivalry between Jesuits and friars was at one time hardly less acute than war to the knife, the ruthless persecution of Christianity by the Tokugawa government from 1614 onwards had the effect of closing the missionary ranks. All the Orders were involved in the ensuing catastrophe, and their martyrs now vied with each other mainly in their steadfastness at the stake. In China the position was complicated by the problem of the 'Chinese Rites', which at times came near to tearing the missionary church asunder between 1650 and 1742. This problem had the most serious repercussions in Europe, where it became involved with the Jesuit-Jansenist controversy over grace and free-will, culminating in a veritable 'battle of the books', in which some of the most celebrated writers of that period took part, including Arnauld, Bayle, Leibnitz and Voltaire. Chinese society was based on the family system, with the veneration of ancestors and ritual sacrifice in their honour at its core. Parallel with these ancestral rites was the State cult of Confucius, which also involved ceremonies during which candles were lit and incense was burnt. Taken together, these rites formed a keystone of the system from which the Emperor and the governing class of China—the so-called literati or scholar-gentry—ultimately derived their authority. Neglect of these rites and rituals was regarded as something unpardonable, both socially and politically, whereas adherence to either or both of the 'popular' religions of Buddhism and Taoism was entirely optional.

Matteo Ricci, the famous founder of the Jesuit mission at Peking, was convinced after studying the Chinese classics that the Rites were 'certainly not idolatrous and perhaps not even superstitious'. He regarded them as essentially civic rites which could, in the fullness of time, be converted into Catholic practice. Not all of the Jesuit missionaries agreed with him, but the great majority did so, and his accommodating attitude to the Rites became and for long remained the official Jesuit standpoint. The Spanish missionary friars from the Philippines, Dominicans and Franciscans to begin with, followed in the 1680s by the Augustinians, mostly took the opposite line. They regarded the Rites as sheer idolatry and refused to allow their converts to participate in them, although some of the friars modified their attitude after years of experience. This controversy together with related problems, such as the correct Chinese term for God, were repeatedly referred to Rome for a final decision. After a good deal of vacillation and ambiguous, if not actually contradictory, declarations, the Papacy finally condemned the disputed ceremonies as idolatrous by the constitution *Ex illa die* published at Rome in 1715. The Jesuits, on one pretext and another, evaded compliance with this decree, so that a three-cornered struggle among the missionaries continued on roughly the following lines. The Portuguese Jesuits and their Italian colleagues supported both the claims of the *Padroado* and Ricci's interpretation of the Rites. The Jesuits of the French mission (patronised by Louis XIV), who had arrived in 1688, tolerated the Chinese Rites but opposed the Portuguese *Padroado*. The Spanish missionary friars, and the Vicars-Apostolic sent out by the Propaganda Fide, opposed both the Rites and the *Padroado*. The confusion over the Rites was only resolved by the promulgation of the Papal constitution *Ex quo singulari* of 1742, which compelled all present and future missionaries to take an oath that they would not tolerate the practice of the Rites in any shape or form upon any pretext whatsoever.

In 1717 Pope Clement XI formally recognised the three Chinese Sees, Peking, Nanking and Macao, as still being within the scope of the *Padroado*, and he gave a half-promise to create another three on the same terms. The official *Gazeta de Lisboa* jubilantly announced that King John V had been reinstated as 'the despotic director of the missions of the East', but this rejoicing proved premature. Vicars-Apostolic continued to be appointed to all the provinces in China without reference to Lisbon, and the Portuguese prelates in Asia gradually came into line with the Vatican's standpoint. When the Viceroy Count of Ericeira asked the Archbishop of Goa to publish a pastoral tolerating the Chinese Rites in 1719 the Primate retorted: 'Experience has shown that all previous disputes between kings and pontiffs had been amicably settled sooner or later, and that all those ecclesiastical prelates and dignitaries who directly or indirectly had ventured to oppose the decisions of Rome had been visited subsequently with the severe displeasure of the Vatican.' The Archbishop added that he had taken the oath to obey the constitution *Ex illa die* at the hands of the Nuncio at Lisbon, and he regarded the Papal instructions as more binding than the privileges of the Portuguese Crown. The Viceroy did not dissemble his indignation at what he termed the unpatriotic attitude of the Archbishop, and he wrote to the Portuguese Jesuits at Peking urging them to stand firm in defence of the *Padroado* and of the Chinese Rites. They did, in fact, continue to do so until they were compelled to take the oath denouncing the Chinese Rites in 1744, and they maintained their unqualified support of the *Padroado* until Pombal's abolition of the Society in the Portuguese empire in 1759–60.

By this act Pombal not only demolished the principal pillar of the *Padroado*, of which institution he was an even more ardent advocate than the Jesuits had ever been, but he dealt a nearly fatal blow to the Roman Catholic missions in Asia, most of which were already in a decline. Meanwhile the struggle over the Rites had led to the hitherto tolerant K'ang-hsi emperor threatening to ban the propagation of Christianity in China for the reasons which he noted in a marginal comment on a Chinese translation of the Constitution *Ex illa die*:

> After reading this decree I can only say that the Europeans are small-minded people. How can they talk of China's moral principles when they know nothing of Chinese customs, books, or language which might enable them to understand them? Much of what they say and discuss makes one laugh. Today I saw the Papal Legate [*Mezzabarba*] and the decree. He is really like an ignorant Buddhist or Taoist priest, while the superstitions mentioned are those of unimportant religions. This sort of wild talk could not be more extreme. Hereafter Europeans are not to preach in China. It must be prohibited in order to avoid trouble.

Although in the upshot the Emperor did not carry out his threat to banish all the missionaries from the provinces, they worked under increasing difficulties thenceforward. The Jesuits were allowed to remain unmolested at the Court of Peking, where use was made of their scientific and technical abilities, particularly in the bureau of mathematics and astronomy. Their colleagues who worked in the provinces were intermittently persecuted; but provided they behaved unobtrusively the provincial authorities usually left them and their converts alone. These latter were now drawn almost entirely from the poorest classes, since the final condemnation of the Rites in 1742 had made the conversion of any mandarins or officials all but impossible, although the Spanish Dominicans could claim a few in Fukien.

Another handicap to the Church in eighteenth-century China was that the Crown of Portugal was always badly in arrears in its payment of the bishops' stipends. The 'Magnanimous' King John V had ordered that the expenses of the bishops of the *Padroado* should be defrayed from the royal exchequer in Portuguese Asia. Owing to the continual warfare with the Omani Arabs, the Marathas and others, which prevailed for the whole of this period, there were never sufficient funds available at Goa and Macao to pay all the episcopal stipends in full, and some of the bishops received nothing at all from these sources for ten or twenty years on end. A mere fraction of the sums lavished by King John V on the palace convent at Mafra, or on the patriarchate at Lisbon, would have provided amply for all the bishops of the *Padroado*, but this monarch could never bring himself to economise on those particular *folies de grandeur*.

The exaggerated nationalism which led to so much bitter rivalry between the various European missionaries in China was not, of course, confined to the Portuguese, even if they had more than their share of it. The French Jesuits patronised by Louis XIV actively supported French temporal interests, and there was little love lost between them and their Lusitanian colleagues. Père Jean de Fontaney, on his way back to France to fetch more recruits for the mission, told a Spanish Augustinian at Canton in 1699 'that he would not rest until he had kicked out all the Portuguese Padres, and that he would bring back as many French Jesuits as he could, simply in order to achieve this aim'. The same Augustinian, Fr. Miguel Rubio, further stated that the thirty-four Spanish friars—Franciscans, Dominicans and Augustinians—who were then in China, would never submit 'to any bishop of another king'. He added that even if these friars were prepared to do so, their superiors at Manila would never allow them, nor would the King of Castile tolerate any such breach of his *Patronato*—'since we all came out to the Philippines at the expense of the royal exchequer, which likewise paid for our voyage hither and now pays for our maintenance here'.

The close connection between European spiritual and temporal power did not go unremarked at the Court of Peking. The position of Macao, as the headquarters of the Church Militant in East Asia, and as a Trojan Horse for the conversion of China, was a particularly invidious one. 'From this royal fortress', wrote an enthusiastic Portuguese Jesuit in 1650, 'sally forth nearly every year the gospel preachers to make war on all the surrounding heathendom, hoisting the royal standard of the holy cross over the highest and strongest bulwarks of idolatry, preaching Christ crucified, and subjugating to the sweet yoke of His most holy law the proudest and most isolationist kingdoms and empires.' Macao was heavily fortified in the European fashion after the unsuccessful Dutch attack in 1622, and many Chinese officials considered that it might become not merely a religious and commercial, but also a military and political, bridgehead of European expansion. All the tact and influence of the Peking Jesuits were needed to frustrate the periodic efforts made by xenophobic Confucian officials to induce the Emperor to ordain the destruction, or at least the evacuation, of the City of the Name of God in China.

The Yung-cheng emperor who ascended the Dragon Throne in 1723 was not nearly so well disposed towards the Jesuits as was his illustrious father, and he was even more conscious of the threat posed by Christianity as a religion at least potentially subversive of the established Confucian order. Discussing the matter one day with some of the Jesuits at Peking, he observed in a remarkably prescient forecast of the 'gunboat policy' which supported European missionary endeavours in the nineteenth century:

> You say that your law is not a false law. I believe you. If I thought it was false, what would prevent me from destroying your churches and driving you away from them? What would you say if I sent a troop of Bonzes and Lamas into your country to preach their doctrines? You want all Chinese to become Christians. Your law demands it, I know. But in that case what will become of us? Shall we become the subjects of your King? The converts you make will recognise only you in time of trouble. They will listen to no other voice but yours. I know that at the present time there is nothing to fear, but when your ships come by thousands then there will probably be great disorder. . . . The [K'ang-hsi] emperor, my father, lost a great deal of his reputation among scholars by the condescension with which he let you establish yourselves here. The laws of our ancient sages will permit no change, and I will not allow my reign to be laid open to such a charge.

When there were so many obstacles to the propagation of Christianity in China, not the least of which were some of the

Europeans' own making, it is surprising that the missionaries achieved as much success as they did. Reliable figures for the numbers of converts are lacking, and those claimed by the sowers of the gospel seed were usually inflated, but the total number can hardly have been more than about 300,000 when the *Padroado* was at its peak in the beginning of the eighteenth century. This is a remarkable figure having regard to the relatively small number (about 120) of missionaries in China; but it is very modest in relation to the total population of the empire, which was then about 100,000,000. The number of converts declined rapidly in the second half of the eighteenth century, particularly after the expulsion of the Jesuits, and it may be doubted whether there were as many as 50,000 Roman Catholics by the year 1800.

In Indochina and Siam the missionaries of the *Padroado* likewise fought a stubborn but losing battle against the encroachments of the Vicars-Apostolic and the missionaries sent by the 'Sun King' of France, who regarded themselves as much better trained and educated than those of the 'Grocer King' of Portugal. Continual quarrels over ecclesiastical jurisdiction between the two parties were settled in favour of the newcomers by a Brief of Clement X in 1673, directed to the Archbishop of Goa, and which in practice removed from the jurisdiction of the *Padroado* all territories not actually governed by the Portuguese Crown—*extra dominium temporale regni Portugalliae*. The Portuguese missionaries from Macao who had built up flourishing missions in Tongking and Cochinchina (North and South Vietnam) did not yield finally until 1696. They were later joined by Spaniards (from Manila) and Italians, the French having previously got a footing with Father Alexandre de Rhodes, S.J., who played in Vietnam a role in adapting Christianity to the regional culture and society, somewhat like that of Matteo Ricci in China. In the course of two centuries the missionaries succeeded in forming in Vietnam a native clergy and a Christian community which was in some ways the strongest and most deeply rooted in mainland Asia, with long-term results that are painfully evident in our own day and generation.

With the expulsion of the Portuguese power and Portuguese priests from Ceylon in 1656–8, the Roman Catholic converts in that island were subjected to active persecution by the Dutch in the maritime and lowland provinces which came under their control. The Catholic communities were saved from the extinction which threatened them by the labours of the Venerable Fr. José Vaz, a Goan missionary of the Oratory, who arrived in Ceylon in 1687 and died there in 1711. Establishing his headquarters in the Buddhist kingdom of Kandy in the mountainous interior, he and his successors gave the Catholics in the lowlands the moral and material leadership necessary for their survival under a persecuting Calvinist regime. Indian *Brahmenes* by origin, they could circulate in disguise with relative ease, and they re-established the connections between the Ceylon Catholics and their co-religionists on the mainland. A Buddhist revivalist movement at Kandy in the second half of the eighteenth century caused the local rulers to be less tolerant of these Catholic missionaries in their midst; but by then the Goan Oratorians were sufficiently well established in the maritime regions to dispense with the use of Kandy as a base. The Calvinist church in Ceylon had also ceased to be a proselytising church (in so far as it ever was one), and the anti-Catholic laws on the statute book were no longer rigidly enforced by the local Dutch officials. When the English replaced the Dutch in Ceylon at the end of the eighteenth century they found an active and virile Catholic community. Though not so large as it had been at the height of the Portuguese power, when there were some 75,000 Christians in the Hindu Tamil kingdom of Jaffna alone, it comprised a hard core of believers scattered all over the island who had been fortified in their faith by the self-sacrificing labours of the Goan Oratorians. As the Overseas Councillors at Lisbon had testified to the Crown in 1717: 'These missionaries proceed in such an exemplary way that only they and the Fathers of the Company are the real missionaries and the fittest to convert the souls of the natives of Asia.'

The ecclesiastical authority of the *Padroado* over the diocese of Meliapor (Mailapur), which was created in 1606 and embraced the east coastal region of India, Bengal and Pegu, was respected, more or less, down to 1776. In that year the French government of Pondicherry abolished the jurisdiction of the *Padroado* in the French territories in India, and the Papacy accepted the *fait accompli*; but Calcutta and Madras were not separated from the

Padroado until 1834. The Madura region on the extreme south-east coast was evangelised in part by Jesuit missionaries inspired by the Italian Roberto de Nobili (d. 1656), who made considerable concessions to the Hindu caste-system in his endeavours to attract high-caste converts. The 'Malabar Rites', as they came to be called, inevitably came under the same suspicion of unorthodoxy as did the Chinese Rites, and they were finally condemned after a violent controversy (which likewise had literary repercussions in Europe) by Pope Benedict XIV in 1744.

On the other side of India the *Padroado* ran into serious trouble after the English occupation of Bombay, where the priests of the *Padroado* were suspected of forming a Portuguese fifth column. The East India Company expelled these Portuguese priests from Bombay in May 1720, replacing them by Italian Carmelites from the Vicariate-Apostolic at Delhi, whose prior agreement had been secretly obtained. The Portuguese authorities at Lisbon and Goa continually and energetically protested against this breach of the *Padroado*. Nearly seventy years later the East India Company decided to give way, since there was no longer any possibility of Portugal recapturing the lost 'Province of the North' from the Marathas. In May 1789 Bombay was returned to the jurisdiction of the Archbishop of Goa, but many of the local Catholics now took the side of the dispossessed Italian Carmelites, and their appeals, followed by counter-appeals by the supporters of the *Padroado*, succeeded each other rapidly at Lisbon, London and Rome. After much hesitation and shilly-shallying the East India Company finally solved the problem—at any rate temporarily—by a preliminary Solomonic judgement, awarding two of the four disputed parishes to the *Padroado* and two to the Vicar-Apostolic.

During the seventeenth and eighteenth centuries the East African missions remained unchallenged within the sphere of the *Padroado*, with the exception of Abyssinia, whence the Jesuits were violently expelled (or martyred) in 1632–8, that country remaining thenceforward impervious to European penetration in much the same way as did Tokugawa Japan. On the other side of Africa the Christianised kings of the old kingdom of Congo, originally the showpiece of Portuguese missionary enterprise, tried hard to induce the Papacy to transfer the ecclesiastical jurisdiction of their realm from the *Padroado* to the direct control of Rome in the seventeenth century. They were not successful, but the remote control exercised by the Bishop of Luanda (to which place the See of São Salvador do Congo had been officially transferred in 1676) broke down completely with the relapse of the Bantu kingdom into anarchy about the same time. The Italian Capuchins sent out by the Propaganda Fide to work in the Congo and Angola took the oath of obedience to the *Padroado* from 1649 onwards. They were by general consent for over a century by far the most effective missionaries in the interior. But their death-rate from tropical fevers was always appallingly high. By the year 1800 there were only two of them left, and their once flourishing mission was virtually extinct. The good they did lived after them, and mid-nineteenth-century travellers bore witness to the 'love and veneration in which their memory is held amongst all classes of Blacks'. Spanish and Italian Capuchins were also sent out by the Propaganda Fide to establish missions at Benin, Warri, and elsewhere in Lower Guinea (actual Nigeria) between 1648 and 1730, at first in deliberate disregard of the claims of the *Padroado*, but later with the permission and co-operation of the Portuguese Crown. They had no lasting success, partly owing to heavy mortality among the missionaries and partly owing to their inability or unwillingness to make a deep study of the religious beliefs of those whom they were trying to convert.

The ecclesiastical jurisdiction of the *Padroado* was never effectively challenged in Portuguese (Upper) Guinea or in the Cape Verde Islands, and still less in Portuguese America, as we have seen (p. 234 above). The extent to which King John V, usually regarded as the monarch most subservient to the Holy See, was prepared to push his rights as *Padroeiro* in Brazil was exemplified by his adamant refusal to allow any of the religious Orders to establish themselves in Minas Gerais. This policy was originally adopted on the grounds that renegade friars were smuggling gold from the mining areas. Its continuance was probably due to the Crown's determination to avoid the expense of maintaining converts and monasteries for the regular clergy in a region from which it was equally resolved to extract the last ounce of gold in tithes. There were continual complaints throughout the eighteenth century of the mediocre quality of many of the secular clergy in Minas Gerais. To a great extent this was the fault of

the Crown, which did not provide adequate maintenance for the ordinary parish priests out of the tithes which it collected, thus forcing them to demand more money from their own parishioners (p. 230 above).

Any study in depth of the history of the *Padroado* during the seventeenth and eighteenth centuries must show that it was far more often the subject of criticism than of enthusiastic praise by outsiders, whether these latter were Roman Catholic French, Spaniards and Italians, or Protestant English and Dutch. It will be clear from the foregoing sketch that frequently these criticisms were justified, but it is equally clear that even when the *Padroado* had become a liability rather than an asset to the Church as a whole, there were some very creditable exceptions, such as the missions served by the Goan Oratorians in Ceylon and by the Italian Capuchins in Angola. This peculiar institution was, moreover, capable of inspiring a devoted loyalty in some of the native clergy who served it, even in its darkest days. Among them is the rather pathetic figure of the Vietnamese priest Filipe Binh, alias Filipe do Rosario. Born and bred in the Jesuits' Tongking mission, he arrived at Lisbon with three companions in 1796, as an envoy from his people to ask for some Portuguese missionaries under the auspices of the *Padroado*. The times of the French Revolutionary and Napoleonic Wars were singularly unpropitious for any such project, and he died in 1833 without seeing his native land again. He was the last defender of the *Padroado* in Indochina, and he left twenty-three volumes of manuscript works in Vietnamese, Portuguese and Latin as proof of his attachment to this lost cause.

The year of Binh's death at Lisbon was also the year in which the anti-clerical and liberal monarchy of Dom Pedro IV came to power in Portugal. The nation was bankrupt after a civil war which had lasted three years, and Dom Pedro with several of his leading supporters was convinced that the monastic orders possessed enormous wealth. The belief was unfounded, but it was largely responsible for the government's decision to suppress all the religious Orders and to confiscate all their property, as was done by a decree dated 28 May 1834. Relations with the Vatican had been severed in the previous year and they were not restored until 1841, but these and subsequent developments lie outside the scope of the present work. The point I wish to make here is that both the liberal monarchy and the anti-clerical republic which succeeded it in 1910, while either hostile or indifferent to the Church at home, did their best to maintain the historic claims of the *Padroado*, particularly in the East. The same applies to the pro-clerical Salazar dictatorship, although the sphere of the *Padroado* which was once co-extensive with Asia is now reduced to Macao, Portuguese Timor and the modest Roman Catholic communities of Malacca and Singapore.

CHAPTER XI

'Purity of blood' and 'contaminated races'

THERE is no lack of distinguished contemporary authorities who assure us that the Portuguese never had any racial prejudice worth mentioning. What these authorities do not explain is why, in that case, the Portuguese for centuries laid such emphasis on the concept of *limpeza* or *pureza de sangue* (purity of blood), not just from a class but from a racial standpoint, and why terms such as *raças infectas* ('contaminated races') are so frequently encountered in official documents and private correspondence until the last quarter of the eighteenth century. An indication, albeit unconscious, of the real state of affairs, is implicit in the late Professor Edgar Prestage's assertion in 1923: 'It is to the credit of Portugal that, slaves and Jews apart, she made no distinction of race and colour and that all her subjects, once they had become Catholics, were eligible for official posts.' Since Negro slaves and persons of Jewish origin both formed, in their different ways, very important segments of society in the Portuguese empire, this admission goes a long way to undermine the simultaneous claim about the absence of race and colour prejudice. In point of easily ascertainable historical fact, Crypto-Jews and Negro slaves were not the only people discriminated against; and by no means all Roman Catholics were eligible for official posts. The real position was more complex, and varying attitudes and policies were uppermost at different times and places, theory being one thing and practice another. In view of the predominant role played by the Roman Catholic Church in Portuguese society at home and overseas, we may begin with a consideration of the problem of the native clergy in Portuguese India.

We have seen (p. 99) that a Lisbon-educated Congolese was ordained as titular Bishop of Utica in 1518. This particular precedent of a Negro bishop was not followed for several centuries, but a Papal Brief of the same year authorised the royal chaplain at Lisbon to ordain 'Ethiopians, Indians and Africans' who might reach the moral and educational standards required for the priesthood. This was the first step towards the formation of an indigenous Indian clergy, although it was not until 1541 that a serious effort was made to implement any such project. In that year the Vicar-General of Goa, Miguel Vaz, persuaded the local civil and ecclesiastical authorities to sponsor the foundation of a seminary of the Holy Faith (*Santa Fé*) for the religious education and training of Asian and East African youths, neither Europeans nor Eurasians being admitted.

This institution was taken over by the Jesuits soon after their arrival at Goa, and attached to their College of St. Paul. They allowed the admission of a few European and Eurasian youths, but basically this establishment continued to be a seminary for the training of Asian catechists and secular priests, who were destined to work in the mission-fields between the Cape of Good Hope and Japan. In 1556 there were 110 pupils in this seminary, composed of the following nationalities: 19 European-born Portuguese (*reinões*); 10 *Castiços*, or boys born of white Portuguese parents in Asia; 15 *Mestiços* or Eurasians; 13 'Malabares', who were probably St. Thomas Christians; 21 Canarins, or Marathi-Konkani inhabitants of Goa; 5 Chinese; 5 Bengalis; 2 Peguans; 3 'Kaffirs' or Bantu from East Africa; 1 Gujarati; 1 Armenian; 5 'Moors' or ex-Muslims; 6 Abyssinians, and 5 boys from the Deccan Sultanates. The age of admission was fixed at not less than thirteen or more than fifteen years. The curriculum was closely modelled on that of the Jesuit colleges in Europe, with Latin and theological studies predominating. But the students had to practise their own vernaculars in their respective national groupings twice daily, so that they would remain fluent in their native tongues. Those who graduated were eligible to be ordained as secular (but not as regular) priests, though not before attaining the age of twenty-five if they were non-Europeans.

The Seminary of the Holy Faith was, therefore, a multi-racial institution in the strictest sense of the term and, as such, it was unique. Inevitably, there were sharp differences of opinion among the Portuguese in India over the characters and potentialities of these indigenous students in the early years. Some of the Jesuit missionaries themselves were very sceptical about the whole experiment. These critics shared the widely held view which was later epitomised in the aphorism ascribed to Hilaire Belloc: 'The Faith is Europe, and Europe is the Faith.' One of the early rectors, Fr. António Gomes, asserted: 'The people of this land are for the most part poor-spirited, and without Portuguese priests we will achieve nothing. For the Portuguese laymen here will not go to confession with an Indian or with a Eurasian priest, but only with a pure-bred Portuguese.' St. Francis Xavier, who warmly supported and reorganised the seminary and the contiguous Jesuit College of St. Paul, did not advocate that Indian aspirants should be admitted to the Society of Jesus itself. He and his successors envisaged that the Indian trainees would become good catechists, auxiliaries and assistants to the parish priests who were then mostly drawn from the European regular clergy. Some of the few pioneer Indian secular priests who had been ordained by the Franciscans before the arrival of the Jesuits did not turn out well. Some of the pupils in the College of St. Paul could not last the exacting course, where the medium of instruction for higher studies was in Latin. These disappointments, inevitable though they were in first- and second-generation Christians, together with the contemptuous dislike expressed by Portuguese laymen for Indian and Eurasian priests, led to a hardening of the attitude of all the religious Orders working in the sphere of the Oriental *Padroado*. A Jesuit Visitor at Goa wrote to the General of the Society at Rome in December 1568:

Experience has taught us that it is not now convenient for us to admit the natives of the land into the Society, not even if they are *mestiços*. The Superiors of the other Religious Orders have likewise come round strongly to this way of thinking. Withal, I personally feel that if they are well trained and indoctrinated, some of them may be able to help the Ordinary; and in course of time we may even be able to admit a very few of them ourselves, so as not to close the door altogether against any nation, since Christ our Lord died for us all.

Despite the Visitor's suggestion, only one Indian was ordained as a priest in the Society of Jesus before its suppression in 1773. This man was a Christian Brahmin (*Brahmene*) named Pero Luís, who was admitted in 1575. Although he proved to be an excellent priest, who warmly pleaded for the admission of a few of his countrymen before his death in 1596, the fourth Jesuit General, Everard Mercurian, firmly closed the door against the admission of Asians and Eurasians in 1579. At the recommendation of Alexandre Valignano, the great reorganiser of the Jesuit missions in Asia between 1574 and 1606, an exception was soon made in favour of admitting Japanese to the priesthood, and this favour was later extended to Chinese, Indochinese and Koreans. But Valignano remained strongly opposed to the admission of Indians to the Society, and was almost equally uncomplimentary about the Eurasians:

> both because all these dusky races are very stupid and vicious, and of the basest spirits, and likewise because the Portuguese treat them with the greatest contempt, and even among the inhabitants of the country they are little esteemed in comparison with the Portuguese. As for the *mestiços* and *castiços*, we should receive either very few or none at all; especially with regard to the *mestiços*, since the more native blood they have, the more they resemble the Indians and the less they are esteemed by the Portuguese.

The same arguments were advanced nearly a century later by another Jesuit, Padre Nuno da Cunha, at Rome. He declared that the experience of 160 years' evangelisation in the East had shown that the Indian clergy were not fitted for anything better than being ordinary parish priests. Neither Hindus nor Muslims respected them, as they did the European missionaries; and the Indian secular clergy thus lacked the status and prestige required of those who spread the Faith. Even when the Goan Fathers of the Oratory had proved that the indigenous clergy could attain the highest standards (p. 244), the Jesuits still declined to admit such Goans into their own Society, while warmly praising the virtues of Fr. José Vaz and his companions.

Sooner or later all the other religious Orders working in the sphere of the Asian *Padroado* adopted the precedent set by the Jesuits. The Franciscans, who in 1589 were still admitting *mestiços* as novices at Goa (though they had been ordered not to do so by their superiors in Portugal), fifty years later were priding themselves on the fact that they had a rigidly exclusive colour-bar. In the 1630s a determined attempt was made by the European-born Franciscan friars at Goa to prevent any Creole (born of white parents in the East) from holding high office in the Asian branches of the Order. This attempt was only defeated by the Creoles sending to Rome one of their number, Fr. Miguel da Purificação, who had been born near Bombay. He took with him an Indian syndic in order to show His Holiness the Pope the difference between a Creole and an Indian. Fr. Miguel eventually carried his point and obtained a Papal Brief to the effect that friars born of pure white parents in Asia were eligible to hold a fair share of offices in the Order. But he only achieved this result in the teeth of bitter opposition from the Portuguese-born Franciscans. The European friars alleged that their Creole colleagues, even if born of pure white parents, had been suckled by Indian ayahs in their infancy and thus had their blood contaminated for life. Fr. Miguel rejected this argument and retorted that many dark-complexioned Portuguese who came out to India were in reality Mulattos and Quadroons, contaminated by Negro blood, 'although they allege that they got sunburnt during the voyage'.

As for the Dominicans, although they admitted to their Order a brother of the Paramount Chief or 'Emperor' of the Monomotapa tribal confederacy in Zambesia, this was one of the few exceptions which merely verified the general rule. Fr. Antonio Ardizone Spinola, an aristocratic Italian Theatine who knew this Bantu Dominican friar personally at Goa, later recalled: 'Although he is a model priest leading a very exemplary life, saying Mass daily, yet not even the habit which he wears secures him any consideration there, just because he has a black face. If I had not seen it I would not have believed it.' Fr. Ardizone Spinola was a highly vocal critic of the Portuguese maintenance of a rigid colour-bar in Church and State, as he showed in a series of sermons preached during his stay at Goa (1639–48), and which he had printed at his own expense in book form in 1680 after his return to Europe. He accused the Portuguese in India of regarding all coloured races (but especially Indians and Africans) as intrinsically inferior to the white. He alleged that Portuguese priests and prelates often refused to allow low-class coloured converts and Negro slaves to receive communion, although no such discrimination was exercised against them in Portugal itself.

> A slave-owner will ask indignantly: 'Should my Kaffirs receive communion? God forbid that I should ever allow them!' His wife says the same: 'Should my Negress receive the Lord? God save me!' And if you ask them why not, the former will reply: 'They are not fit for it, they are great rascals', and the latter will answer: 'She is a vixen and full of vices.'

By the time that the Portuguese had decided to foster the growth of an Indian secular (as distinct from a regular) clergy, they had also come to realise that they could not demolish the age-old Hindu caste-system by a frontal attack, and that they would have to compromise with it. Without entering into the intricate ramifications of this system, with its closed, hereditary and self-perpetuating groups, each with its own characteristics, we may recall the four traditional main divisions. The *Brahmins*, or the priestly class; the *Kshatriyas*, or the military class; the *Vaysias*, composed of merchants and peasants; and the *Sudras*, or the menials and servants, with the 'untouchables' at the bottom of the social pyramid. The Indian secular clergy were recruited almost entirely from the Brahmins, or *Brahmenes*, as the Portuguese called them, after these had been converted in large numbers by the carrot-and-stick methods applied from 1540 onwards (pp. 66–72 above), though candidates of *Kshatriya* origin were occasionally ordained. The converted *Brahmenes* retained their pride of caste and race, and they very seldom intermarried with the Portuguese and never with their Indian social inferiors. Similarly, the lower castes who became Christians did not lose their ingrained respect for the *Brahmenes*, and they continued to venerate the latter as if they were still their 'twice-born' and natural superiors. At one time the *Brahmenes* tried to exclude the Christian *Sudras* from their churches, and although they did not succeed in this the *Sudras* still have to take their places at the back of the church, as far away as possible from the high altar.

Increasing numbers of *Brahmenes* had been ordained as secular priests from 1558 onwards, and after two or three generations they naturally came to resent their systematic exclusion from the ranks of the religious Orders and from high ecclesiastical office. The reasons for this discrimination against the Indian secular clergy were threefold. In the first place, the Portuguese did not fully trust them, and therefore they kept the frontier parishes of Bardez and Salcete in charge of the Franciscans and of the Jesuits respectively. In the second place, as we have seen, the great majority of the Portuguese had an overwhelming contempt for the *Canarins*, as they called the sons of the soil, whom they despised as a base, cowardly, weak and effeminate race—an attitude still reflected, incidentally, in the writings of the great nineteenth-century Portuguese novelist Eça de Queiroz. The term *Canarim* did not originally have an offensive connotation, but it had acquired one by the middle of the seventeenth century, and it has retained this pejorative sense down to the present day. In the third place, the European and the Creole regular clergy, or many of them, were anxious to keep the most lucrative benefices and the most profitable positions for themselves.

The *Brahmene* secular clergy eventually found an outstanding champion in one of their number, Matheus de Castro. Having been refused ordination by the Archbishop of Goa after graduating from the Franciscan College of Reis Magos, he made his way to Rome, where he was patronised by Francesco Ingoli (p. 235). Consecrated Bishop of Chrysopolis, *in partibus infidelium*, in 1637, he thenceforward devoted his considerable polemical talents to forwarding the cause of the *Brahmene* clergy in his successive roles as Vicar-Apostolic in the Bijapur kingdom of the Adil Shah, and as confidential adviser to the Cardinals of the Propaganda Fide at Rome, where he died at an advanced age in 1677. Matheus de Castro's violent denunciations of the Portuguese colonial authorities for their racial prejudice and discrimination, although obviously exaggerated at times, certainly helped to stiffen the conviction of the Propaganda Fide and the Holy See that the formation of a native clergy was essential for the sound development of Christianity in Asia. Pope Innocent XI told Mgr. Pallu, Bishop of Heliopolis and Vicar-Apostolic of Tongking, on the eve of his departure for the Far East in 1671: 'We would rather learn that you have ordained one native priest than that you have baptised half a million pagans. The Jesuits have baptised many such, but subsequently their work has vanished in smoke because they did not ordain native priests.' This was a palpable (and presumably a deliberate) exaggeration; but it does reflect the increasing awareness at Rome that the prelates of the *Padroado* and the *Patronato* were unduly hesitant about encouraging the formation of a native clergy—as indeed they were, even more in Spanish Manila than in Portuguese Goa.

Despite the Vatican's declared enthusiasm for the native clergy in 1671, nearly a century elapsed before anything effective was done to improve their subordinate position in Portuguese India. Partly as a result of the growing scarcity of missionary vocations in Europe, the Theatines at Goa accepted Indian aspirants to their Order in 1750; but it was the Marquis of Pombal who did more to break down the ecclesiastical colour-bar against Indians than did the Papacy and the Propaganda Fide combined. His first move was the promulgation of the celebrated decree of 2 April 1761. This edict informed the Viceroy of India and the Governor-General of Moçambique that henceforth the Asian and East African subjects of the Portuguese Crown who were baptised Christians must be given the same legal and social status as white persons who were born in Portugal, since 'His Majesty does not distinguish between his vassals by their colour but by their merits'. Moreover, and this was something unprecedented, it was made a criminal offence for white Portuguese to call their coloured fellow-subjects 'Niggers, *Mestiços* and other insulting and opprobious names' as they were in the habit of doing. This decree was repeated in even more categorical terms two years later, but the authorities at Goa took no steps to implement it. More than ten years passed before anything effective was done, and then only because the Indian secular clergy at Goa sent a petition to Pombal, complaining that they were still kept in a strictly subordinate position by the Archbishop, with no prospects of promotion. They alleged that there were then over 10,000 native priests in Portuguese India—surely a great exaggeration—many of whom were fully qualified to fill vacant posts in the cathedral chapter and other benefices. Yet the Archbishop obstinately refused to appoint any of them, filling all vacancies with hurriedly ordained and semi-literate low-class Europeans, or even with 'illegitimate Chinese' from Macao.

This representation produced a spirited reaction from Pombal, who on this occasion appears as a veritably enlightened despot. A new viceroy and a new archbishop were sent to Goa in 1774, with strict instructions not only to enforce the anti-racialist legislation which had been quietly shelved by their predecessors, but to favour the Indian secular clergy over and above the European regular clergy in cases where the claims of both to ecclesiastical preferment were roughly equal. Pombal explicitly cited the classical Roman methods of colonisation as the ideal to be aimed at in Portuguese overseas territory, where the conferment of Portuguese citizenship on the Christianised natives (there was no question of giving Hindus, Muslims or Buddhists, etc., the same equal status) would henceforth equal them in every respect with the white inhabitants of Portugal. The sentiments of the Enlightenment can be clearly discerned in Pombal's instructions to the new viceroy in 1774:

> Your Excellency must arrange matters in such a way that the ownership of the cultivated lands, the sacred ministries of the parishes and the missions, the exercise of public offices, and even the military posts, should be confided for the most part to the natives, or to their sons and grandsons, irrespective of whether they be lighter or darker in the colour of their skins. For apart from the fact that they are all equally the vassals of His Majesty, it is likewise conformable with Divine, Natural, and Human Laws, which under no circumstances allow that outsiders should exclude the natives from the fruits of the soil where they were born, and from the offices and Benefices thereof. And the contrary procedure gives rise to an implacable hatred and injustice, which cry out to Heaven for condign satisfaction.

Pombal's anti-racialist policy was continued after his fall from power by the government of Queen Dona Maria I. The new Secretary of State, writing to the Bishop of Cochin in March 1779, stressed the continuing need to give benefices to those of the Indian clergy who were qualified for them.

> In this point [added Martinho de Mello e Castro] it is necessary to warn Your Excellency that the repression and contempt with which the said natives have been treated up to now in that State is the prime cause of the inertia and incapacity which are attributed to them. And this is the reason why Her Majesty has in the provinces of Goa, Salcete, and Bardez, over 200,000 persons of both sexes who are absolutely useless for the service of the Church, of the Crown, and of the State.

In justice to the Portuguese Crown and its advisers it must be said that the abortive independence plot of 1787, which was organised by some of the native clergy and which was repressed with such cruel severity by the local authorities (p. 200), did not affect the continuance of Pombal's anti-racialist policy. The older Mendicant Orders had gradually followed the example of the Theatines in admitting Indian novices, a process speeded up by the decline of missionary vocations in Europe after the fall of the Jesuits. By the time of the suppression of all the religious Orders throughout the Portuguese empire in 1834–5, out of some 300 regular clergy in Goa only sixteen were Europeans, all the others being Indians. Moreover, in 1835 a Goan priest became administrator of the vacant archbishopric for two years, although not until the twentieth century did a priest of Goan origin become a cardinal. But if the Portuguese Indian clergy had a long and difficult struggle to shed the stigma of belonging to an inferior race, and if centuries elapsed before they achieved full equality with priests of European origin, the same applied in the rest of the colonial world. In fact, thanks mainly to that erratically enlightened despot, Pombal, they achieved a relatively high degree of recognition much earlier than did their colleagues in the Philippines and elsewhere.

The strength of colour prejudice in the Portuguese empire, more especially where Negroes were concerned, is further shown by Pombal's failure to achieve the formation of an indigenous clergy in East Africa. A royal decree dated 29 May 1761, which was inspired by him, ordered the erection of a seminary on the island of Moçambique, wherein not only whites but also Mulattos and free Negroes would be trained for the secular priesthood. This decree explicitly quoted the precedents of 'the kingdom of Angola and the islands of São Tomé and Príncipe, where the parish priests, canons and other dignitaries are usually drawn from the black clergy who are natives of those regions'. Despite the peremptory wording of this edict, nothing whatever was done to implement it. A contemporary ecclesiastical historian of Portuguese East Africa, Canon Alcantara Guerreiro, observed sadly in 1954: 'Although nearly two centuries have passed since the promulgation of this decree, the first native priest has yet to be ordained in Moçambique.' It is true that a few Bantu from

East Africa were ordained as priests at Goa during the seventeenth and eighteenth centuries, as instanced by the exemplary Dominican friar mentioned by Padre Ardizone Spinola (p. 253). But these Negro priests remained in Portuguese India and they never returned to the land of their birth. Whether this was done as a matter of deliberate policy, I cannot say. The fact remains that the coloured clergy of Moçambique, who were the target of much criticism by governors and Crown officials during the eighteenth century, were invariably Goans and Indo-Portuguese.

In West Africa, by contrast, a much more liberal attitude prevailed, some Lisbon-educated Congolese having been ordained as early as the reign of King Dom Manuel (p. 99). This precedent was successively followed in the Cape Verde Islands, São Tomé, and, after considerable hesitation, in Angola, with varying results. Padre António Vieira, S.J., who spent Christmas week at the Cape Verde island of Santiago in 1652, was greatly impressed by some of the indigenous clergy. 'There are here', he wrote, 'clergy and canons as black as jet, but so well-bred, so authoritative, so learned, such great musicians, so discreet and so accomplished that they may well be envied by those in our own cathedrals at home.' Vieira's enthusiasm for the West African coloured clergy was not shared by most of his compatriots. A Bishop of São Tomé had alleged in 1595 that unconverted Negroes would only accept baptism from white priests, as they despised the black. Nearly two centuries later the Governor of Angola criticised the coloured clergy on the grounds that 'whiteness of skin and purity of soul' were usually interdependent. The Italian Capuchin missionaries were likewise very critical of the low standards and morals of the coloured clergy, stigmatising them as concupiscent, simoniacal and actively engaged in the slave trade. But the extremely high death rate among white men in West Africa, combined with the extreme reluctance of the Portuguese clergy to serve there, ensured that a Mulatto—and to a much lesser extent a Negro—clergy continued to function if not exactly to flourish. In the island of São Tomé the Mulatto canons of the cathedral chapter petitioned the Crown in 1707 that no more Negroes should be appointed to this sacerdotal dignity, thus provoking the latter to retaliate in kind.

In Brazil there was never any question of ordaining full-blooded Amerindians, for obvious reasons. The Pombaline decrees of 1755–8, which placed the Christianised aborigines on exactly the same level as the white *moradores* in theory and in law, made no practical difference in this respect. The synodal constitutions of the archbishopric of Bahia, which were drawn up in 1707 and printed in 1719–20, were based on those obtaining in Portugal and they reflect a long-standing situation. They laid down that candidates for ordination must be, among other things, free from any racial stain of 'Jew, Moor, Morisco, Mulatto, heretic or any other race disallowed as contaminated' (*outra alguma infecta nação reprovada*). The candidate's purity of blood had to be proved by a judicial enquiry, in which seven or eight 'Old' Christians testified on oath from personal knowledge that his parents and grandparents on both sides were free from any such racial and religious taints. In cases where some ancestral 'defective blood' was proved to exist, a dispensation might be obtained from the local bishop or from the Crown, as it could be for other judicial impediments, such as illegitimate birth and physical deformity. In practice, this was quite often done; but there could be no prior certainty of obtaining a dispensation and the judicial enquiry was seldom a mere farce. Moreover, it was always easier to secure a dispensation if the candidate had some remote Amerindian or white European Protestant forbear than if he had some Negro or Jewish blood in his veins. All of the religious Orders which were established in Brazil maintained a rigid colour-bar against the admittance of Mulattos.

Just as had happened in Portuguese India, considerable rivalry developed in Brazil between the Creole friars and their European-born colleagues of the regular clergy. The incidence of this rivalry between 'the sons of the soil' and 'the sons of the kingdom' varied with the different Orders and at different times. By 1720 it was so acute in the Franciscan province of Rio de Janeiro as to provoke a Papal Brief enjoining that all offices should be held alternately by Creoles and by European-born. This *Lei da Alternativa*, as it was called, remained in force until the year 1828, but it does not seem to have quieted the feuding factions for any considerable length of time in that period. The Order with the most rigid racial requirement was the branch of the Teresian barefooted Carmelites established at Olinda in 1686. For the next

195 years these friars steadfastly refused to admit any aspirants of Brazilian birth, however 'pure' their blood, but recruited their numbers exclusively from European-born and -bred Portuguese, mainly from the region of Oporto.

The Benedictine monks at Rio de Janeiro were apparently more broadminded at the time of Lord Macartney's visit to that city in 1792. They educated some of the Mulatto offspring of slave mothers; and 'these friars mentioned, with some degree of triumph, that a person of mixed breed had been lately promoted to a learned professorship at Lisbon'. But the Benedictines did not, of course, admit Mulattos to the ranks of their own Order. Similarly, most, though not all, of the *Irmandades* or lay-brotherhoods in colonial Brazil likewise maintained a class-cum-colour-bar, as we shall see in the next chapter.

If racial prejudice was omnipresent in a Church which ostensibly preached the brotherhood of all true Christian (i.e. Roman Catholic) believers, it was inevitably even more obvious in other walks of life. We find it in the armed services (pp. 312–13), in the municipal administration (pp. 280–1) and in the working-class guilds (pp. 281–2). Its development can also be traced in the rules and regulations governing admission to the three Military Orders of Christ, Aviz and Santiago, to one or another of which all noblemen, most gentlemen and many commoners might aspire to belong. The statutes of the Order of Santiago, for instance, had originally envisaged that a small number of persons of Jewish descent might be received as knights, if the Order was likely to benefit from their talents and services. But in the course of the sixteenth century this concession was revoked, and it was stipulated that under no circumstances whatever were any such individuals to be admitted. All entrants must be 'Old' Christians of gentle blood and legitimate birth, 'without any racial admixture, however remote, of Moor, Jew or "New" Christian'. They had further to prove that their parents and grandparents on both sides 'were never at any time heathen, tenants, money-changers, merchants, usurers nor employees of the same, nor did they ever hold such offices, or live off them, nor had they at any time exercised any art, craft or occupation unworthy of our knightly Order, and still less should any entrant ever have earned his living by the work of his hands'. From 1572 onwards the statutes of all three Orders contained such stringent racial and class requirements. A royal edict of 28 February 1604 announced that henceforward no dispensation whatever would be granted for lack of purity of blood, and no requests for such dispensations would be entertained either by the Crown or by the Board of Conscience and Military Orders.

Admittedly the Crown's bark was worse than its bite, and dispensations were far from uncommon. João Baptista Lavanha, 'chief mathematician and cosmographer-royal' of Portugal in 1591, was granted a knighthood in the Order of Christ although he was of full Jewish descent on both sides. A full-blooded Amerindian, Dom Felipe Camarão, and a full-blooded Negro, Henrique Dias, were both given knighthoods in the same Order for their outstanding services in fighting the Dutch in Brazil, 1630–54 (p. 119). Several Goan *Brahmenes* were admitted to the Order of Santiago in the eighteenth century; though when the Crown bestowed a knighthood in the Order of Christ on a Goan in 1736, this allegedly 'unprecedented favour' evoked such a strong protest from the Viceroy that King John V promptly transferred the recipient to the less coveted Order of Santiago. There were also instances when individuals of plebeian origin, such as pilots and gun-founders, were given a knighthood (usually that of Santiago); but such awards were relatively rare and they had to be earned by many years of continuous service. The racial disqualifications had originally been limited to persons of Jewish, Moorish (that is, Muslim) and heretic descent, being as much religious as racial; but by the early seventeenth century Negroes and Mulattos were being legally and specifically discriminated against, on account of the close association between chattel slavery and Negro blood. This was confirmed and renewed by a law promulgated in August 1671, which recalled that nobody with any Jewish, 'Moorish' or Mulatto blood, or who was married to such a woman, was allowed to take any official post or public office, and ordered that the existing procedures designed to prevent this should be tightened up. By and large, Negroes and crypto-Jews bore the brunt of racial prejudice and persecution in the Portuguese world. Free Negroes were often classed together with slaves in administrative regulations, and they were usually awarded severer punishments than white persons who were found guilty of identical breaches of the laws.

Although there were always a few individuals who had their doubts about the validity of the Negro slave trade, they were voices crying in the wilderness for the best part of three centuries. The vast majority of Europeans, if they thought about the matter at all, saw nothing incongruous in simultaneously baptising and enslaving Negroes; the former procedure often being advanced as an excuse for the latter, from the time of the Infante Dom Henrique onwards. Aristotle's theory of the natural inferiority of some races, with its corollary that they could be lawfully enslaved, was grafted on to the Old Testament story of Noah's curse of perpetual servitude on the offspring of Canaan, the son of Ham (Genesis ix, 25), from whom Negroes were supposed to be descended. Other authorities claimed that they were descended from Cain, 'who had been cursed by God Himself'. Theologians and laymen alike were convinced that Negro slavery was authorised by Holy Writ, though some of them deprecated on humanitarian grounds the cruel mistreatment of slaves. Apart from this scriptural justification of Negro slavery, modern Portuguese and Brazilian writers who claim that their ancestors never had any feeling of colour prejudice or discrimination against the African Negro unaccountably ignore the obvious fact that one race cannot systematically enslave members of another on a large scale for over 300 years without acquiring in the process a conscious or an unconscious feeling of racial superiority. The general attitude was reflected by Francisco Rodrigues Lobo in his *Corte na Aldeia* of 1619. He emphasised that the Portuguese took their slaves 'from among the most barbarous peoples in the world, like those of all Ethiopia [Africa] and some slaves in Asia, who are drawn from the lowest people in those regions; both categories being subjected to rigorous servitude by the Portuguese in those parts'.

One of the few critics of the slave trade in Portugal (or in Europe, for that matter) was Padre Fernando Oliveira, a singularly outspoken cleric who was at one time in the service of Henry VIII of England and who was later imprisoned by the Inquisition at Lisbon for his unorthodox views. Author of the first printed Portuguese grammar (1536) and of a pioneer manual on naval warfare (*Arte da guerra do mar*, 1555), he devoted an entire chapter in this last work to a violent denunciation of the slave trade. He stated flatly that there was no such thing as a 'just war' against Muslims, Jews or heathens who had never been Christians and who were quite prepared to trade peacefully with the Portuguese. To attack their lands and enslave them was a 'manifest tyranny', and it was no excuse to say that they indulged in the slave trade with each other. A man who buys something which is wrongfully sold is guilty of sin, and if there were no European buyers there would be no African sellers. 'We were the inventors of such a vile trade, never previously used or heard of among human beings', wrote the indignant padre in a passage which does more credit to his heart than to his head. He scornfully dismissed those merchants who alleged that in buying slaves they were saving souls, retorting that the slave-traders were in the business merely for monetary profit. Not only were the slaves bought, herded and treated like cattle, but their children were born and brought up in servitude even when the parents were baptised Christians, something for which there was no moral justification.

Two centuries elapsed before another systematic criticism of the slave trade was published in a Portuguese book, the title of which may be rendered in English: *The Ethiopian ransomed, indentured, sustained, corrected, instructed, and liberated* (*Ethiope Resgatado*, etc., Lisbon, 1758). The author, Manuel Ribeiro Rocha, was a Lisbon-born priest, long domiciled at Bahia. He did not go as far as his sixteenth-century precursor in advocating the total abolition of the slave trade, but he suggested several ways of seriously limiting its abuses, and he vehemently denounced the sadistic corporal punishments which were frequently inflicted on slaves by their owners in Brazil. *Ethiope Resgatado* amounts to a plea for the substitution of Negro slavery by a system of indentured labour, under which the slaves brought from Africa would automatically be freed after working for their masters satisfactorily during an agreed period. The book seems to have made no impression on the Brazilian planters and slave-owners to whom it was specifically addressed; and Santos Vilhena's detailed description of slavery at Bahia forty years later shows that the old abuses and cruelties still persisted there. On the other hand, Lord Macartney, who visited Rio de Janeiro in 1792 on his way to China, observed that 'whatever may be the sufferings of slaves, under taskmasters upon plantations, those residing in the town wore no appearance of wretchedness'. He found that they were easily reconciled to their situation, seldom sought distraction in drunkenness, had many opportunities of exercising their natural musical talents and enjoyed fully 'whatever share of pleasure happened to come within their reach'. As an ex-governor of Grenada, one of the British West Indian sugar islands, his lordship was in a position to distinguish between the rigours of plantation and household slavery; and Santos Vilhena likewise testified that slaves were usually worse treated in the rural regions than in the towns. The conscience of the Crown was occasionally pricked by accounts of the horrors of the Atlantic slave trade, and royal edicts were promulgated in 1664 and again in 1684, 1697 and 1719, to prevent overcrowding and inadequate provisioning in the slave-ships. The Crown and the colonial bishops likewise sometimes denounced the wanton ill-treatment of slaves by their masters, as exemplified by the printed proceedings of the Goa Ecclesiastical Councils in 1568 and 1649, and by the synodal constitutions of Bahia in 1719–20. But these sporadic exhortations and denunciations had no lasting effect, as the more humanitarian governors and prelates complained. It is perhaps needless to add that the Portuguese were not the only nation to behave in this way; or to remind the reader that from the reign of King Charles II until well into that of George III the British government was the greatest promoter of the slave trade in the world.

Even the socially enlightened legislation inspired by Pombal continued to reflect the age-old prejudice against Negro blood for some time. An *alvará* of 19 September 1761 declared that all Negro slaves landed in Portuguese ports after the space of six months from the date of publication in Brazil and Africa (after a year in Asia) would automatically become free persons. The wording of the decree makes it clear that this decision was taken for utilitarian and economic reasons and not on humanitarian grounds. The main object was to prevent slaves being taken from the gold-mines and sugar plantations of Brazil to serve as superfluous lackeys and footmen in Portugal. Negro slaves already living in Portugal were specifically excluded from emancipation by the terms of this *alvará*, but twelve years later they were all unconditionally emancipated by another royal decree. This final and complete emancipation of 1773 was upheld by the Crown, despite protests by some landowners in the Alentejo. They complained that they had been deprived of an essential labour supply, since the freed Negroes flatly refused to work for them as hired hands. Neither Pombal nor his successors had any intention of abolishing slavery in the overseas possessions, where both the laws and social custom continued to discriminate against persons of Negro blood, whether bond or free. An Amerindian chief who married a Negress was officially degraded in 1771 for having 'stained his blood by contracting this alliance'. This attitude persisted for long after Brazil achieved her independence. The sugar-planters who endorsed the break with Portugal in 1822–5 naturally showed no more interest in abolishing slavery than had the Virginian planters who accepted the Declaration of Independence and its affirmation that all men were created equal with an unalienable right to personal liberty.

If Negroes, Mulattos and all individuals with an admixture of African blood were for centuries regarded as *pessoas de sangue infecta* in the Portuguese empire, the same applied to the descendants of the Jews (including many thousands of refugees from Spain) who had been forcibly converted to Roman Catholicism in 1497. Thenceforward Portuguese society was divided into two categories, 'Old' Christians and 'New' Christians, and so it remained for nearly three centuries. King Manuel had ordered these forced conversions, solely in order to obtain a bigoted Castilian princess as his bride. No sooner were they effected than he promulgated an edict forbidding any inquiry being made into the genuineness of the 'New' Christians' new faith for a period of twenty years (later extended by another sixteen). In 1507 and 1524 other royal decrees prohibited all forms of discrimination against them. 'New' and 'Old' Christians mated and married with each other in all classes of society, but the mixture was particularly heavy in the mercantile and professional middle classes, and among the urban artisans. By the end of the sixteenth century between a third and a half of the total population was alleged to be 'infected' in varying degrees with a strain (and a stain) of Hebrew blood. There were no rabbis functioning in Portugal, no Hebrew books or manuscripts were allowed to circulate, and within two or three generations the great majority of so-called 'New' Christians were probably genuinely, as well as outwardly, practising Roman Catholics. The small minority who secretly adhered to what they believed to be the Law of Moses knew little more than a few ritualistic observances, such as changing into clean linen on Saturdays, avoiding pork, shell-fish, etc., in their food, and keeping the Jewish Passover instead of Easter. Nevertheless, the rapidly increasing rate of racial assimilation was accompanied by an intensification of anti-semitic feeling, directed against the 'New' Christians or persons who were reputed to be such. This feeling was fostered mainly by fanatical friars and clergy, but it found enthusiastic adherents among 'Old' Christians of all classes, and it was given expression in the Cortes of 1525 and 1535. It was largely based on the erroneous conviction that the 'New' Christians were actively if surreptitiously propagating the full range of their ancestral Jewish beliefs, and not merely trying to retain some rapidly dwindling traces.

Unfortunately for the 'New' Christians, after about 1530 they could no longer rely on the protection of the Crown, which thenceforth usually sided with their persecutors. King John III had become convinced of the reality of the crypto-Jewish threat, and at his insistence the Holy Office of the Inquisition was introduced into Portugal, after much hesitation on the part of the Holy See and some singularly sordid backstairs intrigues at Rome. Within two decades the Portuguese branch of the Holy Office had literally become a law unto itself, being exempted from all episcopal interference and having secured overriding authority above the civil and the ecclesiastical courts. Its principal tribunals were at Lisbon, Evora and Coimbra. It took cognisance of Protestant and other heresies, witchcraft, sorcery, bigamy, sodomy and so on, and it exercised a rigorous censorship over the printed word. But from 1536 to 1773 its principal energies were concentrated on ferreting out and exposing all traces of Judaism. As an engine of persecution, the Portuguese Inquisition was regarded as being more efficient and more cruel than the notorious Spanish Inquisition by those of its victims who had experienced the rigours of both these infamous institutions. People brought before these tribunals were never told the names of their accusers, nor were they given adequate information about the charges secretly laid against them. Blandishments, threats and torture were alike freely used in order to extort confessions of their real or alleged guilt and, above all, to induce them to incriminate others, beginning with their own families.

A good part of the records of the Portuguese Inquisition perished with its final suppression in 1820, but there still remain over 36,000 documented cases covering the years 1540–1765 in the archives at Lisbon. From the incomplete records which survive it has been calculated that some 1,500 persons were sentenced to death by garrotting and/or burning at the stake after having been 'relaxed' to the secular arm (in the euphemistic and hypocritical terminology of the Inquisitors). As indicated above, this is a very modest number when compared with the millions who perished in the holocaust of Hitler's 'final solution'; but the damage done by the Inquisition and its judicial procedures cannot be judged merely by the statistics of the death-sentences. Thousands died in their prison cells, or were driven mad, without ever having been sentenced. Anyone who spent any length of time in the prisons of the Inquisition, and who was not subsequently completely exonerated (which happened very rarely), was *ipso facto* regarded as contaminated by Hebrew blood—a contamination which was automatically extended to all the members of that person's family. The families of those arrested on suspicion were mostly turned out into the street forthwith and left to fend for themselves. The methods adopted by the Inquisition for collecting evidence placed a premium on the activities of informers, tale-bearers and slanderers. Private grudges could be paid off merely by denouncing a man for changing his shirt, or a woman her shift, on a Saturday. Nobody save the titled nobility, the clergy and the veriest country bumpkins could feel safe from anonymous denunciations. Consequently mutual mistrust and suspicion permeated much of Portuguese society for over two centuries. Last not least, the spectacle of 'New' Christians being slowly roasted to death in the *autos-da-fé* gave most onlookers much the same sadistic satisfaction as did the public executions at 'Tyburn Tree' in contemporary England.

From 1588 onwards all persons of 'New' Christian origin (to

the fourth degree in some instances, to the seventh degree in others) were officially and legally excluded from all ecclesiastical, military and administrative posts, in so far as they had not been already, as they were in the Military Orders, the municipal councils and the *Misericórdias*, etc. After 1623 the ban was extended to include all university and college teaching posts, while 'New' Christian lawyers and physicians were also systematically discriminated against. These restrictions were not always enforced with equal efficiency everywhere and at all times. 'New' Christians did succeed in infiltrating into such forbidden posts or occupations, particularly in the remoter parts of the overseas empire, such as São Paulo in Brazil and Macao in China. But they could never feel entirely secure, and when such exceptions came to public notice it only served to increase the existing prejudice against them. For most of this period the emigration of 'New' Christians and the transference of their capital to foreign countries (at times even to parts of the Portuguese empire) were strictly forbidden. Occasionally these bans were lifted in return for colossal bribes, or subsidies paid to the Crown, mainly by the 'New' Christian mercantile community of Lisbon, such as that given to King Sebastian when preparing his expedition to Morocco. But the Crown invariably reneged on its part of the bargain when it had got all or part of the money it demanded, so these respites were never of long duration. Despite the difficulties placed in their way, many of the most enterprising 'New' Christion entrepreneurs and merchants sooner or later escaped abroad, together with all or part of their wealth. In this manner Portugal was deprived of some of her most useful citizens, whose energy, enterprise and capital helped to enrich the commercial rivals of Lisbon, including Antwerp, Amsterdam and London.

The legal and social discriminations against 'New' Christians, and the insistence on *limpeza de sangue* as an essential qualification for Crown employment and administrative posts, were likewise characteristics of the overseas empire in varying degrees. A tribunal of the Holy Office, with jurisdiction over Portuguese Asia, was established at Goa in 1560, but this was the only fixed establishment in the colonies. Elsewhere the metropolitan Inquisition contented itself with the periodic dispatch of visiting commissioners, as it did in Brazil from 1591 onwards. Persons arrested by order of the Inquisition in Brazil were sent to Lisbon for trial, and no *auto-da-fé* was ever celebrated in Portuguese America. The latest and best historian of the Jews in Brazil has calculated that between 1591 and 1763 a total of some 400 real or alleged Judaisers were shipped to Portugal in this way. Most of them were there sentenced to terms of imprisonment and eighteen were condemned to death. Only one of these, Isaac de Castro, was actually burnt alive (15 December 1647), the others being garrotted. The action of the Holy Office was therefore relatively mild in Brazil, which undoubtedly provided a haven for thousands of 'New' Christians during the period 1580–1640. Some of those established in Pernambuco openly professed and practised Judaism during the Dutch occupation of Recife (1630–54), but they emigrated when the Dutch left: the Jewish community in New York originating in this way. The Goa Inquisition was much more severe, but it is not possible to give an accurate estimate of those who died while awaiting trial and who perished in the *autos-da-fé*, since the surviving records are so incomplete. It is clear, however, that during the seventeenth and eighteenth centuries the great majority of those imprisoned by it were not real or alleged Judaisers but crypto-Hindus. Fear of the Inquisition was responsible for the emigration of many Indian weavers and artisans from Portuguese territory to Bombay after the English occupation of that island, as several viceroys attested.

The emancipation of the 'New' Christians and the drastic curtailment of the powers of the Portuguese Inquisition were directly due to Pombal, who could stomach no tyranny but his own, which he exercised in the name of the Crown. In 1773 he induced King Joseph to promulgate two decrees, abolishing the requirement of 'purity of blood' as a condition for office-holding, and sweeping away all forms of discrimination between 'Old' and 'New' Christians. Severe penalties were imposed—and enforced—for the use of the latter term or for any of its synonyms. All previous legislation discriminating against the 'New' Christians was declared null and void, while the royal decrees of 1507 and 1524, which had forbidden any such invidious distinctions, were rehabilitated. The Portuguese Inquisition was reduced to the status of a subsidiary Crown tribunal, and its procedures were brought into line with those of the civil courts. Public *autos-da-fé* had already been forbidden in 1771, and no capital sentences had been inflicted since Malagrida's judicial murder ten years earlier. The Goa branch of the Holy Office was abolished, and though it was restored in the *viradeira* of the next reign, it was only in an emasculated form. No more death sentences were inflicted before its final abolition in 1820.

Pombal's measures were completely successful, and the 'New' Christians vanished almost overnight as if they had never been. Once the opprobrious term had been removed, there was nothing to distinguish the average 'Old' Christian from the 'New' in so far as physical appearance went—though some of the obscurantist friars and clergy at Macao in 1790 were still propagating the cretinous belief that crypto-Jews were born with the stump of a tail and that their men menstruated like women. If we except such unimportant survivals as the village in Tras-os-Montes where the inhabitants preserved the Hebrew name of God (*Adonai*) down to 1910, all traces of pure Judaic beliefs had long since disappeared in Portugal and her empire, where the 'New' Christians were practising Roman Catholics just as much (or as little) as the 'Old'. The instantaneous implementation of the decrees of 1773 proved that the Jewish bogy was largely the creation of the repressive action of the Inquisition coupled with the discriminatory laws against the 'New' Christians. No sooner were these counter-productive agencies removed than the crypto-Jews ceased to exist. As one of the more cynical seventeenth-century Inquisitors observed, the Inquisition fabricated Jews like the mint coined money.

It only remains to add that the repressive action of the Portuguese Inquisition and the enforcement of the anti-semitic legislation were counter-productive in another and most mortifying way. They convinced foreigners that Portugal was a nation of crypto-Jews, as exemplified by the coarse Castilian proverb: 'A Portuguese was born of a Jew's fart.' The tragically farcical nature of the forced mass conversions in 1497 was not soon forgotten. Writing to a friend in 1530, Erasmus petulantly dismissed the Portuguese as 'a race of Jews' (*illud genus judaicum*). All educated Portuguese who travelled or resided in other European countries noticed this widespread conviction, as Gaspar de Freitas de Abreu lamented in 1674: 'It is only we Portuguese who are stigmatised with the name of Jews or Marranos among all nations, which is a great shame.' The name of 'Portuguese' was synonymous with that of 'Jew' in foreign countries, observed Dom Luís da Cunha in 1736, towards the close of his long and distinguished diplomatic career. Spanish Jesuits in seventeenth-century Paraguay stigmatised the inhabitants of São Paulo as 'Jewish bandits', and many foreign visitors to Pernambuco, Bahia, Rio de Janeiro and other Portuguese colonies were almost equally uncomplimentary. Pombal, after his years as envoy at London and Vienna, was certainly in a position to realise this. There is a well-known story that on one occasion King Joseph was considering a proposal by the Inquisition that all the 'New' Christians in his realms should be compelled to wear white hats as a sign of their Jewish blood. Next day Pombal appeared in the royal cabinet with three white hats, explaining that he had brought one for the King, one for the Grand Inquisitor, and one for himself. *Se non è vero, è ben trovato.*

CHAPTER XII

Town councillors and brothers of charity

AMONG the institutions which were characteristic of the Portuguese seaborne empire, and which helped to weld its disparate settlements together, were the town or municipal council (*Senado da Camara*) and the charitable brotherhoods and lay confraternities, the most important of which was the Holy House of Mercy (*Santa Casa da Misericórdia*). The *camara* and the *misericórdia* can be described, with only mild exaggeration, as the twin pillars of Portuguese colonial society from the Maranhão to Macao. They afforded a continuity which transient governors, bishops and magistrates could not supply. Their members were drawn from identical or comparable social strata, and they formed to some extent colonial élites. A comparative survey of their development and functions will show how the Portuguese reacted to the different social conditions which they encountered in Africa, Asia and America, and how far they succeeded in transplanting and adapting these metropolitan institutions to exotic environments. We can also thereby test the validity of some widely accepted generalisations, such as Gilberto Freyre's assertion that the Portuguese and Brazilians always tended, in so far as possible, to favour the social ascent of the Negro.

By the early sixteenth century the system of municipal government in Portugal had set in the following pattern, which was laid down in a *Regimento* of 1504, and which was not drastically reformed until 1822. The core of the town council comprised from two to six *vereadores* (councillors or aldermen), depending on the size and importance of the place, two *juizes ordinarios* (magistrates or justices of the peace with no legal training), and the *procurador*, or municipal attorney. They all had voting rights at council meetings and were collectively known as the *oficiais da Camara*. The *escrivão* (secretary or clerk), though he originally had no voting rights, was often included in the *oficiais*. The same applied to the *Tesoureiro*, or Treasurer, when his job was not, as it often was, taken in rotation by the councillors. The subordinate officers of the municipality had no voting rights, and their number varied from town to town. But they usually included the *almotacéis*, or market-inspectors; the *juiz dos orfãos*, who looked after the interests of orphans and widows; the *alferes*, ensign or standard-bearer, whose post was sometimes combined with that of the *escrivão*; the *porteiro*, doorkeeper or porter, who often acted as archivist; the *carceiro* or gaoler; and in large towns the *veador de obras* or foreman of public works. The *vereadores* and *juizes ordinarios* were not originally salaried personnel, but they enjoyed considerable perquisites during their terms of office.

The *oficiais da Camara* were elected through a complicated system of annual balloting from voters' lists which were drawn up every three years under the superintendence of a Crown judge. The annual ballot was usually held on New Year's Day, or on New Year's Eve, a small boy being selected at random from passers-by in the street to draw the names out of a bag or ballot-box. The triennial voting lists were compiled confidentially by six representatives elected for that purpose by a meeting of all the substantial and respectable heads of households who were entitled to vote. These individuals of recognised social standing were collectively known as the *homens bons* (good or worthy men), or, more loosely, as the *povo*. The Crown judge scrutinised the voting lists to ensure that none of the persons nominated for office in any given year were closely related to each other by ties of blood or of interest.

Some, but not all, of the *camaras* had a form of working-class representation which was based on the guild system. The leading trades and handicrafts (goldsmiths, armourers, masons, coopers, tailors, cobblers, etc.) elected annually from their guild-members twelve representatives (known as the *doze do povo*) in the case of most towns, and twenty-four in the case of Lisbon, Oporto and a few others, where they formed the *Casa dos Vinte e Quatro*. These men in their turn nominated four from among their number, called the *procuradores dos mesteres*, to represent their interests on the municipal council. These four representatives had the right to attend all council meetings and to vote in all matters which affected the workers' guilds and corporations, and the economic life of the town or city. They advised the *camara* as to what prices artisans and journeymen should charge for their respective services, and they also laid down the conditions for apprenticeship, guild membership, and so forth. The guilds were organised in *bandeiras*, so called from the large square or oblong banners which they carried in religious processions and on festive occasions. These banners were usually made of crimson damask or brocade, bordered with gold or silver tinsel, and bore the device of the patron saint or of the craft which they represented. A *bandeira* might consist of the practitioners of one craft only, or it might comprise several crafts, one of which was recognised as the *cabeça* or head. The senior of the *doze do povo* (or of the *Casa dos Vinte e Quatro*) came to be entitled the *juiz do povo*, or people's tribune. As such he had the right and duty to represent the interests of the working class to the *Senado da Camara*, and in the case of Lisbon, direct to the Crown.

Meetings of most municipal councils were usually held twice weekly, on Wednesdays and Saturdays, though more often when required. The *camara* of Lisbon, having far more business to cope with than any of the others, was meeting regularly on six or seven days a week by the end of the sixteenth century. The presidency of the *camara* originally devolved upon each of the *vereadores* alternately, the one who took the chair being termed the *vereador do meio* from his seat in the middle. From about 1550 the *juiz de fora*, in towns or cities where this Crown (district) magistrate functioned, seems to have assumed the presidency in most of the *camaras*, thus giving the Crown an important (though not necessarily a controlling) voice at council meetings. Councillors who failed to attend meetings were fined, unless they could give a valid excuse, such as illness. Decisions were taken by a majority vote, after the matter had been freely debated at the council table. The decisions of the *camara* in municipal matters could not be revoked nor set aside by superior authority, save only if they involved unauthorised innovations which might adversely affect the royal exchequer. The *camara* acted as a court of first instance in summary cases, subject to appeal to the nearest *Ouvidor* (Crown Judge) or *Relação* (High Court). The *camara* was theoretically liable to periodic inspections (*correições*) by the *corregidor de comarca* or district judge; but this seems to have been an empty formality on many occasions, and some *camaras*, including those of Lisbon and Goa, were exempted altogether from this procedure. Similarly, the treasurer's accounts were often not submitted for audit to any superior authority, even when this was supposed to be done.

The *camara* supervised the distribution and the leasing of municipal and common lands; assessed and collected municipal taxes; fixed the sale price of a wide range of commodities and provisions; licensed street-vendors, hawkers, etc., and checked the quality of their wares; issued building licences; maintained roads, bridges, fountains, gaols and other public works; regulated public holidays and processions, and was responsible for the policing of the town and for public health and sanitation. The *camara*'s income was derived chiefly from the rents of municipal property, including houses which were leased as shops, and from the taxes it levied on a wide range of foodstuffs offered for sale, though the basic provisions such as bread, salt and wine were originally exempted. Another source of income was derived from the fines levied by the *almotacéis* and other officials on those who transgressed the municipal statutes and regulations (*posturas*), such as vendors who were unlicensed or who gave short weight. Municipal taxes, like those levied by the Crown, were often farmed out to the highest bidder. In times of emergency the *camara* could impose a capital levy on the citizens, scaled in accordance with their real or assumed ability to pay.

The *oficiais da Camara* were privileged individuals who could not be arrested arbitrarily, nor subjected to judicial torture, nor imprisoned in chains, save only in cases (such as high treason) which involved the death penalty and from which *fidalgos* were likewise not exempted. They were also absolved from military service, save only when their town was directly attacked. They were exempted from having government officials and soldiers billeted on them, and from having their horses, carts, etc., confiscated for use in the service of the Crown. The *Senado da Camara* had the privilege of corresponding direct with the reigning monarch, and the senators during their terms of office enjoyed various judicial immunities in addition to those enumerated above. They received *propinas* (perquisites) when they attended the statutory religious processions, the chief of which was the feast of Corpus Christi, and the next that of their town's patron saint. When walking in these processions, or when engaged on official duties, the municipal magistrates carried a red-coloured wand or staff with the royal arms (*quinas*) at one end, as the badge of their office, that of the *juiz de fora* being white.

During the second half of the sixteenth century the Crown directly concerned itself with the election of the *vereadores*, at least in the case of the more important provincial towns. The triennial *pautas*, or voting lists, were sent to Lisbon, originally for scrutiny, but later for the Crown to designate the *vereadores* for the incoming year by making its own choice from the names submitted therein. The list of *vereadores* thus selected was sent in a sealed letter to the *camara* concerned and opened with due formality on 1 January. In the course of the eighteenth century many of the provincial *camaras* tended to become self-perpetuating oligarchies, re-electing the same *oficiais*, or rotating the municipal offices among themselves and their relatives, contrary to the *regimento* of 1504. The *juiz do povo* and the *procuradores dos mesteres* were also dropped from many *camaras* at this period, thus depriving the working classes of direct representation and strengthening the oligarchic nature of these institutions. There was increasing laxity in attendance at council meetings, and in some instances the *Senado da Camara* only met at long and irregular intervals instead of twice weekly. In other instances the statutory requirements of *limpeza de sangue* were more or less tacitly ignored. The *juiz de fora* of Odemira in the Alentejo, reporting on the leading householders who were listed in the *pautas* as eligible for municipal office in 1755, stated that four out of a total of eighteen were in fact 'contaminated' by their ancestry. One of them, who had already served as *vereador* like his father before him, 'had both Negro and Jewish blood; his father had been a servant in the house of a *lavrador* and his grandmother was a black slave'. Some of the provincial *camaras* no longer bothered to send their *pautas* to Lisbon for scrutiny or for nomination by the Crown, which seems to have acquiesced in this state of affairs for much of the time.

These changing attitudes and circumstances did not necessarily mean that the *camaras* became less important and influential locally, nor that the Crown necessarily exercised a very tight control over them through the *juiz de fora*. Internal communications were so bad for centuries that many provincial towns and districts were left almost entirely to their own devices. The best (or least bad) road connection was that from Lisbon to Braga via Coimbra, Aveiro and Oporto; and a regular posting service was only established between Lisbon and Oporto in 1797. The physical and other obstacles in the way of efficient communication inevitably left the *camaras* with a large measure of autonomy, and they continued to administer local taxation down to 1822. The Lisbon municipal council, which was largely staffed by qualified Crown lawyers (*desembargadores*) and presided over by a nobleman or *fidalgo* from 1572 onwards, also retained its working-class representatives and the *juiz do povo* with the *Casa dos Vinte e Quatro* until 1834. Presumably because Lisbon was much more populous and had a much higher proportion of artisans than any other Portuguese city, these working-class representatives were always more important and influential here than elsewhere. The corresponding *Casa dos Vinte e Quatro* in Oporto had a rather chequered existence, being abolished between 1661 and 1668, and again between 1757 and 1795, owing to the involvement of its members in riotous assemblies.

The colonial municipal councils were closely patterned on those of the mother country, but there were naturally marked differences as well as close resemblances in the ways in which they subsequently developed. Sometimes they dated from the first occupation or foundation of the town or city concerned, as was the case, for instance, with Goa (1510), Bahia (1549), Luanda (1575) and sometimes after a long period of growth (Cachoeira, 1698), or even after the lapse of centuries (Moçambique, 1763). Some municipalities were originally founded with the permission of the Crown on a specific metropolitan model, and those that were not sooner or later sought the confirmation of their privileges and charter in a form identical with those of a specific

Portuguese municipality. In this way Goa received the privileges of Lisbon; Macao those of Evora; Bahia, Rio de Janeiro, Luanda and many others those of Oporto. It is not clear why the privileges of Oporto were the most sought after, since reference to the printed edition of the *Privilegios dos Cidadaõs da Cidade do Porto* (1611) shows that they were identical with and textually copied from those of Lisbon. Working-class representation also differed from place to place. Goa, which was closely modelled on Lisbon, had strong working-class representation down to the second half of the eighteenth century, with the *procuradores dos mesteres* having full voting rights at council meetings where they were accorded the status of 'temporary gentlemen'; Macao, modelled on Evora, never had any working-class representation at all; Bahia had a *juiz do povo* and *procuradores dos mesteres* on the council only from 1641 to 1713.

The composition of the council as regards the number of aldermen, absence or presence of a presiding Crown judge, etc., also varied in accordance with the relative size and importance of the municipality concerned. Generally speaking, the metropolitan model was retained in so far as was possible, as exemplified by the *Senado da Camara* of Malacca, which, on the occasion of the capture of this stronghold by the Dutch in 1641 after 130 years of Portuguese rule, was constituted as follows: Three aldermen, two magistrates, a procurator and a secretary, 'all respectable white citizens', the presidency devolving monthly on each of the aldermen in turn. Another acted as treasurer and received all incoming funds, which included a third of all duties and the excise on arrack, and which were expended on the upkeep of the fortifications and other public works. The council priced all provisions, verified weights and measures, and was responsible for public health and sanitation. The treasurer received a yearly salary of 500 *cruzados* from the municipal funds, but the other aldermen were unpaid, though receiving emoluments of fifty *cruzados* 'to buy a fine suit of clothes' at Christmas, Easter, and Corpus Christi. They acted as a court of first instance, with the right of appeal to the local *Ouvidor* (Crown judge). The procurator was likewise an elected official, but he received a yearly salary of 500 *cruzados*, as did the secretary, who served a triennial term. The subordinate officials included two *almotacéis* (market-inspectors), elected monthly from the most respectable citizens, and who served unpaid, besides a *juiz dos orfãos* who served for three years (unpaid). This set-up corresponded very closely to those of many Portuguese towns of comparable size.

As regards the class and racial composition of the colonial *camaras*, it is obvious that the requirements concerning 'purity of blood' could not have been strictly observed in places like São Tomé and Benguela, where white women were conspicuous by their absence for several hundred years. Nor could the stipulation that the *oficiais da camara* should not be closely related to each other by blood or by business ties be enforced in places like São Paulo and Macao, with an exiguous white population engaged in identical activities. Thus we find that in 1528 the governor of São Tomé was reprimanded by the Crown for opposing the election of Mulattos to the town council. He was informed that so long as they were married men of substance they were perfectly eligible for municipal office. The same was probably true of most of the West African *camaras*, with the exception of Luanda down to the eighteenth century at least. White men seldom lived long in West Africa, and the overwhelming majority of both sexes had more than a 'touch of the tar brush' after a few generations, as all contemporary accounts make abundantly clear. For most of the seventeenth and eighteenth centuries São Tomé was in a condition of chronic anarchy, with its ingrown and quarrelling society tending to become Africanised rather than Europeanised.

Elsewhere, however, the tendency was to keep the white (European) element dominant for as long as possible. This was certainly done in places like Bahia and Rio de Janeiro, where there was a constant infusion of white blood from Portugal every year, and where a local aristocracy of sugar-planters was firmly established. The same was true of Goa and Macao for 200 or 300 years, even though far fewer white women went out to Asia than to Brazil. In both these places, and doubtless in most other Asian and African settlements as well, male emigrants from Portugal (*reinóis*) married local women, who almost invariably had a mixture of coloured blood. These *moradores* then married their daughters by preference to a *reinol*, even though the man might be, as he often was, of lowly birth. This pattern was repeated with successive generations, thereby ensuring Portuguese predominance in the local élite, particularly where the *reinól* father could get his *reinól* son-in-law on to the voting lists for the *camara* and the *misericórdia*. Gregorio de Matos Guerra, the satirical Bahian-born (but Coimbra-educated) poet, has some famous verses which allege that this procedure was standard form in the City of the Saviour at the end of the seventeenth century. In this he would seem to have been exaggerating, or perhaps anticipating. Recent research into the social structure of the *camara* and *misericórdia* at Bahia shows that the local *poderosos* or 'great ones' were still drawn overwhelmingly from the established sugar-planting families of the *Recôncavo* at that period, the merchant class (in which the European-born predominated) only achieving social parity with the planters in 1740. In Rio de Janeiro, during the second half of the seventeenth and the first half of the eighteenth centuries, the *camara* on various occasions tried to limit its membership to Brazilian-born individuals, deliberately excluding the Portuguese-born merchants, even when these latter were married to Brazilian girls of good social standing. The *filhos do reino* as often protested to the Crown against this discrimination, and royal decrees of 1709, 1711 and 1746 took their side in this dispute, stressing that emigrants from Portugal who had established themselves in Rio 'with opulence, intelligence and good behaviour' were to be placed on the voting lists on an equal footing with the locally born who were qualified to hold office. It must, however, be emphasised that the social ascent of the Negro, which Gilberto Freyre claims was fostered in Brazil, was, on the contrary, deliberately retarded in that colony by the maintenance of a rigid colour-bar on full-blooded Negroes during the whole of the colonial period, in so far as municipal office-holding was concerned. Light-skinned Mulattos had a chance of social advancement in some regions, such as Minas Gerais, but it is very doubtful if any of them ever became *vereadores* in Bahia or in Rio de Janeiro.

The prejudice against 'New' Christians also had a long life in the municipal administration. King Manuel, as we have seen, despite his forcible conversion of the Jews in 1497, subsequently did his best to integrate these wretched converts into Portuguese society by forbidding all discrimination against them. In 1512, for example, he decreed that one of the four *procuradores dos mesteres* on the Lisbon municipal council should be a 'New' Christian and the other three 'Old' Christians. A partial ban was placed on 'New' Christians holding municipal office at Goa in 1519, but it was stated that they might do so in exceptional circumstances. In 1561 the Goa *camara* petitioned the Queen Regent to promulgate a decree strictly forbidding 'New' Christians from serving on the *camara* in any capacity. In her reply (14 March 1562) Queen Catherine declined to make such a public proclamation 'owing to the scandal which this would cause'; but she added that the *camara* and the Viceroy should act in collusion to ensure that no such undesirable individuals were elected. As late as 1572 the Lisbon goldsmiths' guild was still electing its representatives on a fifty-fifty basis as between 'Old' and 'New' Christians. After the accession of the Spanish Habsburgs in 1580 the ban on municipal (and any other) office-holding by 'New' Christians was made more rigid and absolute; but breaches inevitably occurred in distant colonial settlements, whither many Marranos had fled to avoid the Inquisition. In 1656 the *vereadores* of Luanda reminded the Crown that 'New' Christians had been forbidden by law to serve in the municipal council or on the magistracy 'since the time of King Philip of Castile'. They alleged that some crypto-Jews had nevertheless wormed their way into such positions after the recapture of the colony from the Dutch in 1648, and they requested that the anti-semitic regulations should be 'observed inviolably'. We have seen (p. 272) that hostile Spanish Jesuits had alleged that the Paulistas of Brazil were strongly contaminated with Jewish blood, but this was an obvious exaggeration. In Brazil as a whole the ban on office-holding by 'New' Christians was rigidly enforced after about 1633, and though a few individuals of Marrano origin may have served in some Brazilian municipal councils since that date, I cannot recall a specific example for about another century, whereas there are certainly some in Goa and Macao.

Among the characteristics which the colonial *camaras* shared with those of the mother country was the tendency to lavish money on the celebration of the statutory religious festivals and patron saints' days, which often left them with insufficient funds for the upkeep of roads, bridges and other public works. The Lisbon municipality was virtually bankrupted by the fantastically lavish way in which it celebrated the Feast of Corpus Christi in the year 1719, at the direct insistence of King John V. The Goa *camara* was reluctantly compelled to curtail the number and scope of these religious processions in 1618 as the *mesteres* could no longer afford to stage their costly displays, since the economic decline of the city after the Dutch and English had damaged the Portuguese trade in Asia so severely. The finances of the councils were further crippled by the long-term contributions with which they were saddled by the Crown. These included the dowry of Catherine of Braganza on the occasion of her marriage to Charles II, which was combined with the indemnity paid to secure peace with the United Provinces. This dual levy, entitled the *Dote de Inglaterra e paz de Holanda*, was apportioned on a pro-rata basis between the home and the colonial *camaras*, the share of Bahia alone amounting to 90,000 *cruzados* yearly in 1688. Hardly had the final instalments been paid off in 1723 than another similar levy, euphemistically entitled *donativo* or 'free gift', was imposed to help finance the royal marriages between the Portuguese and Spanish ruling houses in 1729. Payments for this purpose were spread over a period of twenty-five years, and no sooner had the final instalments been paid than another and even larger contribution was demanded from the Brazilian *camaras* in aid of the rebuilding of Lisbon after the earthquake of 1755. Annual payments were still being made on this account when Brazil achieved its independence seventy years later.

These financial burdens were aggravated in the case of the chief colonial *camaras* (Goa, Bahia, Rio de Janeiro, among others) by the Crown or its representatives raising loans from or through the municipalities in order to pay for naval and military operations. These loans were seldom repaid in full, and sometimes not even token repayments were made. The classic instance is, of course, the loan which Dom João de Castro raised from the city of Goa for the relief of Diu in 1547, on the security of a hair from his beard, but this loan was repaid in full. The *camara* of Goa provided the bulk of the money for the expeditionary force which sacked Johore Lama in 1587, for the armada which relieved Malacca from its siege by the Dutch in 1606, and for the armada which relieved Malacca when besieged by the Achinese in 1629. On the other side of the world the municipality of Rio de Janeiro raised 80,000 *cruzados* as an 'outright gift' for the fleet with which Salvador Correia de Sá e Benavides retook Luanda from the Dutch in 1648, whereas the government at Lisbon had supplied 300,000 *cruzados* for this purpose but as a loan secured on the Customs. Both Rio de Janeiro and Bahia later contributed generously and often with loans and donations in money, men and supplies for expeditions sent to relieve Sacramento in the Rio de la Plata estuary from siege or harassment by the Spaniards between 1680 and 1770. In 1699–1700 the municipality of Bahia even contributed a newly built warship and 300 men for the relief of Mombasa, then besieged by the Omani, although operations in East Africa were of no conceivable benefit to Brazil, unlike those in Angola, to which both Bahia and Rio frequently contributed.

The colonial *camaras* were likewise made responsible in whole or in part for the upkeep, feeding and clothing of their garrisons, and for the building and maintenance of their fortifications, as well as for equipping coastguard flotillas against pirates, etc. When these and other compulsory but extraordinary charges on their resources are considered, it is not surprising to learn that they were seldom able to make two ends meet, and were generally deeply indebted. Since religious festivals and naval and military expenditure took precedence over everything else, the upkeep of roads, bridges and drains was often sadly neglected. Here again the neglect of public works was often aggravated by the fact that the *poderosos*, in other words the *fidalgos* and the clergy, often refused to pay their share of such municipal imposts, pleading aristocratic privilege or ecclesiastical exemption; or else these privileged classes simply ignored the demands, the threats, and the pleas of the municipality. This is a constant complaint in the correspondence of nearly all the *camaras*, including that of Lisbon, where the Crown occasionally intervened to support the council's demands for the enforcement of the municipal sanitary regulations, but with no lasting results. Only when a really serious epidemic occurred, such as the yellow fever visitation at Bahia in 1686–7, did the *poderosos* take any notice of the *camara*'s admonitions; and no sooner was the emergency over than they relapsed into their obstructive and non-cooperative ways.

It must, however, be acknowledged that although the colonial councils were usually composed of conscientious individuals who took their duties seriously—as a careful reading of their records shows—there were inevitably instances of nepotism, corruption and embezzlement of municipal funds. As happened in Portugal, attendance at the council meetings tended to become slacker and the meetings themselves less frequent and more perfunctory in the course of the eighteenth century, though this tendency certainly did not apply to all the *camaras*. Where it existed it was probably, as in Portugal, a reflection of the councillors becoming more of a self-perpetuating oligarchy, rotating office among themselves and their relations. This never happened, incidentally, to the same extent as it did in contemporary Spanish America. The more important municipal councils made full use of their right to correspond direct with the Crown, and on many occasions they were able to influence Crown policy and to obtain the revocation or the modification of unpopular royal decrees. This correspondence also provided the Crown with a useful check on the reports of viceroys, governors and archbishops. Successive monarchs of the dynasties of Aviz, Habsburg and Braganza thanked the *camara* of Goa for the objective information which it supplied. On the other hand, the Crown sometimes thought that the *camaras* went too far in protesting against unpopular decrees or government decisions. The municipal councillors of Bahia were severely reprimanded in 1678 for acting as if they shared with the Prince Regent, Dom Pedro, the responsibility of ruling the Portuguese empire. In any event, the Crown and its advisers nearly always gave careful consideration to the requests and demands submitted by the leading colonial *camaras*, even when the final decision was unfavourable.

Contrary to what is sometimes asserted, the colonial *camaras* seldom became mere rubber stamps and uncritical 'yes-men' to the senior government officials, whether these were viceroys or high-court judges. With all their faults, and even where the councillors had become something like a self-perpetuating oligarchic coterie, they usually continued to represent the local interests of other classes besides their own, at any rate to some extent. Their power, influence and prestige were considerable during the whole of the colonial period, though naturally more so at some times and places than at others. The most consistently important was the municipal council of Macao, which had the chief share in governing that peculiar settlement for some two hundred and fifty years. The Chinese authorities would only deal with the council, which was represented by its *procurador*, and not with the governor, whose authority was limited to the command of the forts and of the exiguous garrison. The *camara* of Macao was also exceptional in that it retained its extensive powers virtually unimpaired down to 1833, whereas the other Portuguese metropolitan and colonial councils were shorn of all save their purely administrative municipal functions by the decree of 1822. The Brazilian *camaras* suffered the same fate about the same time since their powers were drastically curtailed by the new imperial government's reforms of the provincial administration in 1828–34.

Quem não está na Camara está na Misericórdia, 'Whoever is not in the *camara* is in the *misericórdia*' ran the Alentejan proverb, and this was equally true of both those institutions overseas. The equivalent saying in 'Golden' Goa, even after its glory had long since departed, was that whoever wanted to live high, wide and handsomely should try to become an alderman on the municipal council or else a brother of the *misericórdia*—or preferably both. The colonial branches of the *Santa Casa da Misericórdia* (Holy House of Mercy) were usually founded about the same time as the local *Senado da Camara* was instituted. In some settlements, Macao and Moçambique for example, the *misericórdia* was the older of the two. As with the *camaras*, the colonial *misericórdias* were closely patterned on those of Portugal, more specifically on the mother house of Lisbon which had been founded under royal patronage in 1498. This charitable brotherhood in the larger towns retained the medieval organisation of dividing its members into gentry and plebeians until the early nineteenth (or, in some cases, twentieth) century. The former were termed 'brothers of higher standing' (*irmãos de maior condição*). The rules of the Lisbon *misericórdia* provided for a total of 600 members, of whom half were gentry (*nobres*) and half plebeians or *mecânicos*, the last-named being artisans and tradesmen like those of the guilds represented in the *Casa dos Vinte e Quatro*. In some of the colonial *misericórdias*, such as that of Macao, all the brothers were of *maior condição*, since none of the exiguous white population would admit to being of working-class origin and to gaining their livelihood by the work of their hands and the sweat of their brows. At Goa and Bahia, on the other hand, the division into brothers of higher and lower standing was retained. The total of the brothers varied widely. Goa began with 100, rising through 400 in 1595 to 600 in 1609, but thereafter numbers fell off rapidly with the economic decline of the city.

The *compromissos* or statutes of the *misericórdia* varied slightly according to place and time, but they only differed from those of Lisbon in relatively minor details. The revised Lisbon *compromisso* of 1618, which was accepted by most of the colonial brotherhoods with few modifications, enjoined that all members must be 'men of good conscience and repute, walking in the fear of God, modest, charitable and humble'. In addition, they were supposed to be endowed with the following qualifications, in default of any of which they were liable to instant expulsion on detection.

1. Purity of blood, without any taint of Moorish or Jewish origin, both as regards the brother and his wife, if he was a married man.
2. Freedom from ill-repute in word, deed and law.
3. Of a suitably adult age, not less than twenty-five full years in the case of an unmarried man.
4. Not suspect of serving the *misericórdia* for pay.
5. If an artisan or shopkeeper, he should be the foreman or owner, supervising the work of others rather than using his own hands.
6. That he should be intelligent and able to read and write.
7. In sufficiently comfortable circumstances to obviate any temptation to embezzle the funds of the *misericórdia*, and to serve it without financial embarrassment to himself.

It would be expecting too much of human nature to assume that these high standards were invariably maintained, particularly in a colonial society in which every man who rounded the Cape of Good Hope, or who sought his fortune in Brazil, was as proud as Lucifer and tried to pass himself off as a *fidalgo* whenever he had the chance, according to a great cloud of witnesses, Portuguese and foreign. Abuses and malversations certainly occurred, particularly in the eighteenth century, but on the whole the *misericórdias* maintained surprisingly high standards of honesty and efficiency for centuries. This much was admitted by many foreigners who were otherwise severely critical of the Portuguese, including the French physician Charles Dellon after his experiences in Portuguese India in 1673–6. 'Charity is the whole foundation of this noble and most glorious society,' he wrote, 'and there is scarce a city, no not a borough of note, under the jurisdiction of the Portuguese but what has a church dedicated to the same use, with some revenues to be applied to the same purpose with this society, though for the rest they have no dependence on one another.' They all, however, acknowledged the mother house of Lisbon as their *fons et origo*, and corresponded with that institution direct.

The duties of the brotherhood of the *misericórdia* were defined as being seven spiritual and seven corporal works, the latter comprising:

1. Giving food to the hungry.
2. Giving drink to the thirsty.
3. Clothing the naked.
4. Visiting the sick and the prisoners.
5. Giving shelter to the weary.
6. Ransoming captives.
7. Burying the dead.

In many places the *misericórdia* maintained a hospital of its own, and in some settlements it also managed the local branch of the royal hospital for the reception of sick and wounded soldiers, where this existed. The statutes of the Macao *misericórdia* show that it was originally instituted in 1569 for the exercise of charity to all in need, regardless of race or colour, while specifying that charity began at home with Christians as its principal beneficiaries. Here, as elsewhere, population growth subsequently made it quite impracticable to give indiscriminate charity to all of the pullulating proletarians who might apply for it. In most settlements, therefore, the beneficent action of the *misericórdia* was limited to the local Christian community; though this was already much, especially when the slaves were likewise included, as often happened. The regulations for the *misericórdia* hospital at Macao, as revised in 1627, stipulated that the staff of Timorese and Negro slaves should be given as much rice and fish as they could eat, 'so as to ensure that they should be kept well fed and contented'. This was a singularly intelligent and humane stipulation, since legislation to ensure the adequate feeding of slave personnel was very seldom, if ever, enacted by any of the other colonial powers.

The *provedor*, or president of the board of guardians, was the most important of the elected officials who served in the *misericórdia*, his qualifications being described in the Lisbon *compromisso* of 1618 as follows:

The *provedor* must always be a *fidalgo* of authority, prudence, virtue, reputation and age, in such wise that the other brothers can all recognise him as their head, and obey him with greater ease; and even if he should have all the above qualities he cannot be elected until he is at least forty years old. He must be very patient, owing to the discordant characters of many of the persons with whom he has to deal. He must also be a gentleman of leisure, so that he has the time to attend carefully to his frequent and manifold duties. And in order to ensure that he has some experience of these, no brother will be elected a *provedor* during the first year in which he has been received into the brotherhood.

One qualification that was almost universally disregarded was that the *provedor*, who was elected for a yearly term of office, should be a 'gentleman of leisure'. A survey of the list of *provedores* in the *misericórdia* of Goa between 1552 and 1910 shows that this post was filled by fourteen viceroys, eleven archbishops, two inquisitors and a great number of active governors, captains, secretaries of state, comptrollers of the exchequer, high-court judges and Crown functionaries with full-time jobs, as well as by others who had retired from active service. Inevitably some of these exalted dignitaries did not take their duties very seriously, and the routine work of the board (*mesa*) then devolved mainly on the *escrivão*, or secretary, in the absence of the *provedor*. Others, however, found the time to attend and perform their duties conscientiously, and these seem to have been in the great majority. The post of *provedor* was highly valued on account of its exalted social status, although it involved a conscientious man in heavy expenditure, as Dellon noted in 1676:

Formerly none but noblemen were chosen to that dignity, but of late the rich merchants are chosen as well as the noblemen. All the contributions here are made for the advantage of the poor, and there is scarce a *provedor* who at the year's end does not contribute 20,000 *livres* of his own. . . . The chief citizens of Goa, and persons of the best quality, not excepting the Viceroy himself, are ambitious of being members of this fraternity. . . . They choose every year new officers, by which means every one of the members is in a probability of bearing his share, and though all these offices are chargeable, there's very few but what are very eager after them.

In Bahia the *mesa* was dominated for centuries by the local landed aristocracy of the sugar-planters, thus forming much more of a self-perpetuating oligarchy than did the board of guardians at Goa, where transient high officials frequently served as brothers. Russell-Wood has shown that all but half a dozen of the *provedores* of the *misericórdia* at Bahia between 1663 and 1750 were related in some degree. Merchants first appeared as such in the admissions registers of this confraternity about 1700; and from 1730 onwards there was a marked increase in the numbers who were accepted as brothers. This development reflected the gradual redistribution of wealth at Bahia, as riches derived from the possession of real estate and the growing of sugar or raising of cattle were replaced by wealth gained by financial speculation and entrepreneurship. In the 1740s several businessmen were elected *provedores* of the Bahia *misericórdia*, thus breaching the monopoly of the landed aristocracy.

The funds of the *misericórdia* were derived almost entirely from private charity and legacies, although the Holy House of Mercy at Luanda got its share of the export trade in Negro slaves. Testators with guilty or tender consciences often bequeathed large sums to the *misericórdia* on their death-beds, thus hoping to abbreviate their stay in purgatory. A Dominican friar at Goa wrote to the King in 1557 that high officials who had embezzled Crown funds took care to make their confessions with 'lazy, stupid and ignorant priests, who then said to them: "Sir, what you have stolen from the King, you can make restitution in pious works; have you stolen 5,000 *pardaos* from the Crown? Then give 1,000 to the *misericórdia* and that will be enough." ' Nearly two centuries later Dom Luís da Cunha, who was himself an (absentee) brother of the *misericórdia* in Portugal and rightly appreciative of its charitable work, deplored the widespread belief 'that people can atone for what they steal from Peter or from Paul by leaving their property to the *misericórdia*, or to some other pious or religious corporation'. Still, this procedure did ensure that a percentage of ill-gotten gains was returned in due course to the poor and needy from whom it had (perhaps) been squeezed in the first place.

Moreover, there were many legacies and endowments made from purely philanthropic motives. The princely sums bequeathed to the *misericórdia* at Bahia by João de Mattos de Aguiar at the end of the seventeenth century and by Martha Merop to the *misericórdia* at Macao over a hundred years later are two among many instances which could be cited. Both of these benefactors had progressed in their different ways from rags to riches; and the *misericórdia* at Bahia benefited to the tune of over a million *cruzados* from the former's legacy. This capital certainly had more respectable origins than the comparable fortune left to the Lisbon *misericórdia* by Dom Francisco de Lima on his death at San Lucar in 1678. The foundations of this fortune had been laid by his exactions during his governorship of Moçambique in 1654–7; and at the time of his death he was a fugitive from justice on account of his real or alleged complicity in the murder of the Marquis de Sande (1667), who had negotiated the marriage of Charles II with Catherine of Braganza six years previously. Last not least, slaves often benefited from the charity of testators who left some or all of their bondservants to the local *misericórdia*, on the condition that they would be emancipated if they worked satisfactorily for a given term.

The golden age of the Asian *misericórdias* covered most of the sixteenth and the early seventeenth centuries. That of Bahia coincided roughly with the second half of the seventeenth century, whereas those of Minas Gerais presumably benefited from the economic boom which accompanied the exploitation of the gold and diamond mines in the reign of King John V. The *misericórdias*, like other pious foundations (*obras pias*) in the Iberian world, also acted as bankers and brokers on occasion. Their reliability in this respect was convincingly attested by the Italian traveller Cesare Fedrici, writing in 1583 of his eighteen years' travels in Asia. He stated that any merchant of any nationality dying in Portuguese Asia, who had bequeathed his estate to heirs in Europe through the intermediary of the *misericórdia* could unfailingly rely on payment (via Goa and Lisbon) being punctually made 'into what part of Christendom soever it be'. The Jesuit Fr. Fernão de Queiroz, writing at Goa a century later, relates the classic case of a 'Granadine Moor' dying at Macao, who bequeathed his estate to Muslim heirs at Constantinople. On the realisation of his assets the *misericórdia* at Goa sent to inform the heirs, who duly received the full amount at the Portuguese factory at Kung in the Persian Gulf, thus avoiding the additional expense and delay involved if the money had been sent around the Cape and via Lisbon. The financial rectitude of the *misericórdia*, and the prestige which it deservedly enjoyed for so long, not only encouraged testators to leave their money to the *Santa Casa* in the knowledge that it would be well spent, but it also tempted viceroys and governors to raid its coffers in emergencies, though this practice was strictly forbidden by the Crown. The *misericórdia* of Goa was the worst sufferer in this respect, thus helping to accentuate its decline in the eighteenth century.

It is undeniable that the general relaxation of standards which affected the *camaras* in the eighteenth century was equally evident in the *misericórdia*, since the *Vereadores* of the former and *Irmãos de maior condição* of the latter were both drawn from the same social classes. They were, indeed, often the same people. Originally, persons elected to office in the one institution were not supposed to act as office-holders in the other at the same time, but this stipulation was increasingly disregarded, especially in the smaller settlements with dwindling populations and a resultant dearth of qualified men. The brothers on the *mesa* became inclined to avoid doing the most unpleasant of their monthly chores, such as visiting the prisoners in their noisome gaols. The Viceroy Count of Ericeira, who had served as *provedor* of the Goa *misericórdia* in 1718, was informed two years later that none of the newly elected guardians would volunteer to serve as prison visitors, excusing themselves for one reason or another. He promptly offered his own services in this humble capacity, which implied rebuke shamed the laggards into doing their duty. The *misericórdias* of Bahia, Luanda and Macao all endured financial crises of various magnitudes during this period, but they all survived to continue their charitable work in one form or another down to the present day.

Whereas the *misericórdia* concerned itself with charity to a wide range of the poor and needy, the other lay-brotherhoods or confraternities of the various religious Orders mostly restricted their charitable activities to their own members and their respective families. The social status of these *Irmandades* (Tertiaries, or Third Orders, as they were also called) varied from those whose membership was limited to 'pure' whites of good families to those composed mainly of Negro slaves. The more exclusive white brotherhoods built gorgeous churches, and board-rooms whose garish opulence with portraits of the periwigged members induced a modern French visitor to wonder if he was not 'in a sort of religious Jockey Club'. That, indeed, is what some of them closely resembled in the careful social screening which they gave to entrants. The statutes of the Third Order of St. Francis at Mariana in Minas Gerais stipulated (in 1763) that any applicant for admission must be 'of legitimate white birth, without any rumours or insinuation of Jewish, Moorish or Mulatto blood, or of Carijó or any other contaminated race, and the same will apply to his wife, if he is a married man'. Nor was this a mere formality. The testing of a candidate's antecedents often took several years, and involved writing to the *camaras* or to the *misericórdias* of remote provincial towns in Portugal to check on the information supplied. Members who subsequently married a coloured girl, or one with 'New' Christian blood, were summarily expelled without further ado. The composition of most of these *Irmandades* was on racial lines, whites, Negroes and Mulattos each having their own brotherhood. A few made no distinctions of class or colour, or between bond and free; but the brotherhoods of Negro slaves, or of free Negroes, usually had a white man for their treasurer, as specified in their statutes. Even so, these religious brotherhoods for Negroes and coloureds certainly afforded the depressed and despised classes a source of mutual aid and comfort which was entirely lacking in the French, Dutch and English colonies. In eighteenth-century Salvador (Bahia) there were eleven brotherhoods for coloured people dedicated to the Virgin Mary alone.

The *misericórdias*, like the exclusive white religious *Irmandades*, were usually, though not invariably, staunch defenders of white ethnic superiority and of class distinctions, as were the *camaras* with which they were so closely connected. Given the perennial shortage of white women in all of the Portuguese settlements, particularly in the Asian and African *conquistas*, it was inevitable that *mestiços* should sooner or later be accepted, as Mulattos had been in the island of São Tomé from the early sixteenth century. But the inclusion of full-blooded Christian natives was quite another matter, and this was a very late development where it occurred at all. In Malacca, membership of the *camara* and of the *misericórdia* was still restricted to 'white' Portuguese in 1641, though these gentlemen certainly included some Eurasians. King John IV ordered the *misericórdia* of Macao to admit some of the local Chinese Christians as *Irmãos*, and over 100 years later a Pombaline decree of 1774 enjoined the senate to include six leading natives among the *almotacéis* in the municipal councils, but both decrees remained a dead letter. Even illiterate or semi-literate European-born Portuguese were admitted as aldermen during the eighteenth century in preference to well-educated *mestiços* at Macao. In Goa the first *Canarim*, or full-blooded Christian Indian, was admitted as an *Irmão* of the *misericórdia* in 1720, but it is rather significant that this innovation was not formally approved by the Crown until 1743. Despite Pombal's strongly worded anti-racialist legislation of 1774, there is no reason to suppose that any *Canarim* was elected to the municipal council at Goa until well into the nineteenth century. An official representation by that *camara* in 1812 stated that at this period the *Vereadores* were nearly always professional military officers (*militares graduados*), and that the *naturaes*, or Goans with little or no mixture of European blood, were mostly priests and lawyers. At Bahia, white supremacy in both the *camara* and the *misericórdia* seems to have lasted for the whole of the colonial period, though there is some evidence that the prejudice against the admission of persons of 'New' Christian origin had weakened considerably between 1730 and 1774.

The *misericórdia* was an essentially Portuguese institution, the finest (some people may think) that 'Fair Lusitania' ever produced, but it inspired at least two establishments of this name outside the bounds of the empire. There was a flourishing branch at Manila, founded in 1606 on the pattern of the mother house at Lisbon. There was another at Nagasaki, which was famed

13. *Brazilian costume in the eighteenth century: a lady of quality in her sedan chair (from a coloured drawing by Carlos Julião,* c. *1785)*

14. *Brazilian costume in the eighteenth century (from a coloured drawing by Carlos Julião, c. 1785)*

throughout Japan for its charitable works before it was extinguished during the persecution that began in 1614. In their different ways the *camara* and the *misericórdia* provided a form of representation and a house of refuge for all classes of Portuguese society. A study of these two institutions shows that the good which they did more than outweighed their members' occasional human shortcomings. The way in which the municipal council and the Holy House of Mercy adapted themselves to such varied and exotic surroundings from Brazil to Japan, while retaining such close ties with their European medieval origins, well exemplifies the conservatism, the resilience and the tenacity of the Portuguese in *Ultramar*.

CHAPTER XIII

Soldiers, settlers, and vagabonds

ONE of the outstanding differences between the Eastern empire of Portugal and the Western empire of Spain was that the former had a conspicuous military element, whereas the latter, after the conquest of Mexico and Peru, was essentially a civilian empire. To a much lesser extent there was a similar difference between the Portuguese and Spanish empires in America; but it was in 'Golden' Goa that the peculiar Portuguese social system of *soldados* and *casados*, bachelor soldiers and married settlers, was carried to its greatest extreme and lasted longest. Virtually all of the male Portuguese who sailed from Lisbon for Goa during three centuries went out to the East in the service of the Crown—the missionaries as soldiers of the Cross under the *Padroado*, and the great majority of laymen as soldiers of the King. *Fidalgos* and soldiers who married after their arrival in India were usually allowed to leave the royal service if they so wished and to settle down as citizens or traders, being then termed *casados* or married men. The remainder were classified as *soldados* and were liable for military service until they died, married, deserted, or were incapacitated by wounds or disease.

'This is a frontier land of conquest', wrote a Franciscan missionary friar when Goa was at the height of its precarious splendour in 1587, and this, as we have seen (pp. 132–3), is a theme repeated yearly in official and unofficial correspondence from the days of Afonso de Albuquerque onwards. Many experienced soldiers besides the anonymous author of a sixteenth-century treatise on the *Excellency and honourableness of a military life in India* agreed that virtually all Asians were openly or secretly enemies of the Portuguese. 'Nor is this to be wondered at, since we are the sworn foes of all unbelievers, so it is hardly surprising if they pay us back in the same coin. . . . We cannot live in these regions without weapons in our hands, nor trade with the natives except in the same manner, standing always upon our guard.' Considering the stress that so many people who were well qualified to judge laid on 'Portuguese Asia' being a military enterprise, it is rather curious that the Crown was so slow in organising a proper military system to maintain it. For over 150 years after Albuquerque's capture of Goa the Portuguese soldiery in the East (and in Africa for that matter) were not organised in the form of a standing army, but in companies and small units (variously called *estancias*, *bandeiras*, *companhias*) which were raised and disbanded as occasion offered. All the men were registered, or were supposed to be, in muster-books (*matricolas*), of which a central register was kept at Goa, and their pay was calculated in accordance with a complicated threefold system. *Soldo*, the basic pay of a man's rank, depended partly on his birth, previous experience, etc., and when paid quarterly it was termed *quartel*; *mantimento*, or subsistence-allowance, paid in money or in kind, or in a combination of both; *ordenado*, or the pay of an appointment, such as the governorship of a fortress or the captaincy of a ship. A man who received *ordenado* was not entitled to draw the first two, but a man who received *soldo* (or *quartel*) generally got *mantimento*. Originally, men were paid from the date of embarkation at (or of sailing from) Lisbon, but after about 1540 men were sent out with no *soldo*, which was due to be paid to them within six months, or in some cases within a year of their arrival. The Crown provided basic ship-board rations for these men, but often in uncooked form, so that the recipients had to make their own arrangements about using the ship's galley.

From early times the Crown was almost always in arrears with its payments ('ill, late, or never', see p. 77), and there were no barracks for the reception of the men on their arrival. Inevitably, the newly arrived *reinóis*, as these greenhorns were called, had little or no chance of earning an honest living while waiting to be called up for service in some expedition, garrison, or campaign.

They either starved in the streets or begged for relief at convent and church doors, or took service with some wealthy *fidalgo* who could maintain them, or hired themselves out as bravoes and bully-boys, or else they found some complaisant woman (married or otherwise) who would keep them. After the men had managed to get some pay, and if they did not lose it at once in gambling (as often happened), they might mess together in small groups, perhaps taking turns to parade in the streets in the one fine suit of clothes which they possessed between them. During the rainy season from May to September the men were necessarily idle in these demoralising circumstances at Goa, or else they were vegetating in one of the coastal garrisons. During the remainder of the year they were liable for service in any of the coastguard fleets and convoys, or in punitive and raiding expeditions against the Malabar corsairs and other enemies, or in garrison service in the numerous Portuguese forts scattered from Sofala to the Moluccas. If they lived for more than about eight or ten years, they then might try to return to Portugal with their carefully kept certificates of military service, in order to claim some reward from the Crown. Relatively few of them could do this, since the Viceroy's leave had to be obtained before anyone could embark on a homeward-bound Indiaman, and then the man had to pay for his own passage. The majority therefore stayed in Asia, where they became *casados* and submitted their petitions for pensions and rewards through the viceregal government at Goa—a lengthy procedure at the best of times.

When the Crown decided that the petitioner was worthy of some reward, this usually took the form of the reversion of an office. These offices ranged from the captaincy of a highly profitable (thanks to perquisites and pickings) fortress such as Ormuz, or the grant of a trading voyage (that to Japan being the most lucrative between *c.* 1550 and 1640), down to a factor's or clerk's post in some obscure *feitoria*. Most of these grants were triennial and they were given very lavishly. Diogo do Couto instanced a recent arrival from Lisbon who had one for the captaincy of Mombasa, of which he could not avail himself until over thirty other grantees had preceded him for their triennial terms. When Couto pointed out that he would have to wait for about a century before taking office, he replied that meanwhile he could make a good marriage with some half-caste girl, since wealthy Eurasian parents were very anxious to marry their daughters to white men. Subject to certain conditions, most of these grants could be bequeathed to others, or even bought and sold, for the sale of office was a world-wide commonplace for centuries, literally from China to Peru. Offices were also given by the Crown as a form of dowry for the orphan girls sent out from Lisbon (p. 129), or to other deserving females, so that their future husbands could enjoy them. As the European death rate in the East was very high, some grantees at least did not have to wait long before they could step into their predecessors' shoes. The worst feature of the system was that it inevitably led to the beneficiaries trying to fill their pockets during their trienniel term of office. Only thus could they reimburse themselves for the expenses which they had incurred either in waiting for their turn or in the actual purchase of their grant.

The notorious indiscipline of the Portuguese soldiery in Asia, and their favourite tactic of the headlong charge, were often criticised by friend and foe alike (p. 117). Diogo do Couto, commenting on a disastrous reverse suffered at the hands of the Moplah corsair, Kunhali, in 1599, observed that just as the Portuguese exceeded all other nations in the impetuosity of their attacks, so they also surpassed them in the speed of their retreats. His contemporary, Francisco Rodrigues da Silveira, who had likewise participated in both triumphs and disasters, explains that the latter nearly always came about in the same way. The Portuguese, disembarking from their boats on a hostile shore, seldom waited to form up properly on the beach and then advance in close formation, but each individual soldier rushed impetuously forward as if he was racing against his comrades. If the enemy, who were usually drawn up some distance away, did not flee at this onset, then the first soldiers to reach them arrived panting and exhausted, in no condition to fight, and unsupported by their slower-footed comrades trailing along behind. The front runners then had no resource but to turn tail and retreat as fast as they could, often flinging away their weapons while doing so. The enemy, being lightly equipped and fleeter of foot, easily caught up with the unarmed fugitives and decapitated them. On other occasions, as happened at the storming of Calicut in 1509, the

Portuguese would successfully assault a seaside city, but the soldiers would then disperse through the streets and houses in search of plunder, discarding their own weapons to pick up heavy or bulky goods. This gave the enemy the opportunity to rally and return in force, cutting down the plunderers who were staggering about under the weight of their booty.

The tactic of the offensive *à outrance* was advocated by most *fidalgos* and soldiers on the ground that as the Portuguese were nearly always markedly inferior in numbers to their opponents, any hesitation would be fatal. A headlong charge, they claimed, usually unnerved the enemy, who broke and fled at the sight of cold steel; whereas if the Portuguese advanced in close formation they would present a sitting target to the Indian archers, who could not fail of their mark. Rodrigues da Silveira rebutted these arguments by pointing out that the Portuguese firearms had a greater range than bows and arrows, and that a determined attack in regular formation by well-drilled and well-trained men would be much more effective as well as much safer. Fortunately for the Portuguese, most of the people with whom they had to contend on the battlefield likewise fought as armed mobs rather than highly trained and disciplined units, although Turks, Persians and Mughals were usually as well equipped as they were. In these circumstances the quality of the leadership was even more vital than usual, and the Portuguese produced many outstanding leaders who fought like medieval champions at the head of their men. *Conquistadores* of the calibre of Afonso de Albuquerque, Dom João de Castro, Dom Luís de Ataide and André Furtado de Mendonça—this last the acknowledged hero of the ultra-critical Rodrigues da Silveira—could and did impose some sort of order and discipline, even if only temporarily. Under such commanders, who could restrain as well as inspire their men, the Portuguese won many resounding and spectacular victories; just as on other occasions, when led by inept and over-confident *fidalgos*, they suffered severe and humiliating reverses. An early example of the former was Duarte Pacheco's brilliant defence of Cochin against tremendous odds in 1504; and an early example of the latter was the death of the first viceroy, Francisco de Almeida, with over sixty of his companions in a squalid skirmish with the Hottentots near the Cape of Good Hope in March 1510.

Sporadic efforts were made to remedy this lack of military discipline and training, but they achieved no lasting result before the last quarter of the seventeenth century. Afonso de Albuquerque had asked for (and had received) some officers who had been trained in the Swiss military service, which was the finest in contemporary Europe, but their influence did not outlast his life. The Viceroy Dom Luís de Ataide (1568–71) attempted an equally short-lived reformation, and the efforts of the Spanish Habsburgs between 1580 and 1640 were no more successful. Neither Dom Antonio de Leiva, a veteran of Lepanto, who was sent out in the 1590s, nor (thirty years later) Dom Francisco de Moura, who had served in Flanders, was able to reorganise the Portuguese soldiery at Goa on the model of the Spanish infantry *tercios*, owing to the stubborn opposition of the *fidalgos*. Even the defeats suffered by the Portuguese at the hands of the Dutch in Ceylon did not make the former change their anachronistic military system or, rather, lack of system. The first *terço*, or regular infantry regiment, which lasted more than a few months, was organised at Goa in 1671, and this regiment was supposed to be kept up to strength by yearly drafts of recruits from Portugal; but the wastage from sickness and desertion was so high that half-castes and coloured soldiers always formed a proportion of the rank and file. The Portuguese also raised some auxiliary Indian troops, termed *lascarins*, in the sixteenth and seventeenth centuries, and *sipais* (sepoys) in the eighteenth. The unwarlike *Canarins* or Marathi-Konkani inhabitants of Goa did not make good cannon fodder. This helps to explain why the Portuguese never made as much use of their sepoy troops as did the French and the British from the days of Dupleix and Clive onwards.

On the other hand, the Portuguese relied much more on the fighting qualities of their African slaves than did any of the other European colonising nations. Writing in 1539, João de Barros extolled the courage and loyalty of the Negro slaves from Guinea, urging his countrymen to employ them on the scale that the Moors of Barbary did, since their military potential was superior to that of the famous Swiss mercenaries. 'And they are so brave that with them we have conquered the other regions which we hold and which do not produce the like.' Nearly a century later Edward Monnox, after witnessing the repulse of a Persian assault on the breach of Ormuz Castle during the siege of 1622, noted in his journal of the defenders' tactics: 'The most that was done was done by the Negroes, whom the Portugals did beat forwards to throw powder-pots, with which many of the Persians were pitifully scalded and burnt.' On the other side of Asia the disastrous failure of the Dutch attack on Macao on midsummer's day of the same year was ascribed by the Dutch leaders to the prowess of the defenders' Negro slaves.

> Many Portuguese slaves, Kaffirs and the like, having been made drunk, charged so fearlessly against our muskets, that it was a wondrous thing to see. . . . The Portuguese beat us off from Macao with their slaves. It was not done with any soldiers, for there are none in Macao, and only about three companies of 180 men in Malacca. See how the enemy thus holds his possessions so cheaply while we squander ourselves.

The Portuguese accounts of this remarkable victory, while naturally claiming a greater share in it for the white and Eurasian defenders than the Dutch were willing to allow, also stressed the loyalty and courage of the Negro slaves, many of whom were freed after the battle by their grateful masters. These accounts make special mention of a Negress who wielded a halberd with such deadly effect that she was admiringly compared to a medieval Portuguese heroine, the legendary baker's wench of Aljubarrota, who slew seven Spaniards with a shovel. Negro slaves were frequently used as auxiliary troops in the fighting in Ceylon, and the Sinhalese epic poem *Parangi Hatane* enumerates the 'Kaffirs, like mountain cats, fattened on beef and steeped in drink' as among their most redoubtable opponents.

The Governor of Macao, writing to the Viceroy of Goa concerning reinforcements for the scanty garrison in 1651, asked him to send *Reinóis* (European-born Portuguese) and Negro slaves, who were tough and bellicose, unlike the 'puny Eurasians' (*mestiçinhos*) from India who were useless as soldiers. Modern panegyrists of Afonso de Albuquerque's policy of founding a mixed but legitimate and Christian Indo-Portuguese race, through the intermarriage of European men with selected Indian women of Aryan origin, often overlook how much opposition this scheme encountered in Albuquerque's day and generation, and for long afterwards. In 1545 the Crown categorically forbade 'the sons of

Portuguese born in those parts' from being enlisted as soldiers, a prohibition which was renewed in 1561. The town council of Chaul protested against this discrimination in 1546, and fifteen years later the Viceroy of Goa suggested that the King should allow the enlistment of some deserving Eurasians. In point of fact, this prohibition could not have been enforced for very long, since it was quite impracticable to exclude *mestiços* from serving when there was such a colossal annual wastage among the European-born. But most viceroys were very critical of the quality of the *mestiços*, whom they regarded as too soft and effeminate for military and naval active service. A relatively high proportion of European blood was required of those enlisting in 1634. They had to bring a certificate from their parish priest attesting that they were either the sons or grandsons of European-born Portuguese. It is interesting to note that the only exception made by Pombal in his policy of enforcing racial equality between European and Asian-born Christians was the artillery regiment raised for service at Goa in 1773, which was exclusively recruited from European-born Portuguese. A royal decree of 28 April 1792 abolished this regulation, and with it the last vestige of official (as distinct from unofficial) racial discrimination in the armed services of Portuguese India.

Unofficial prejudices, as nearly always, ran much deeper and lasted much longer than the changing official attitudes concerning race relations. The correspondence of successive viceroys of Goa from the sixteenth to the nineteenth centuries abounds with complaints of the real or alleged physical and moral inferiority of *mestiços* and *Canarins* as compared with European-born and -bred Portuguese. Whenever possible, the viceroys and governors placed white Portuguese in the chief military and administrative posts, just as archbishops and bishops did when selecting the occupants for high ecclesiastical offices. The town councillors of Goa, most of whom were married with Eurasian women, complained to the Crown in 1607 that when military commands or government posts fell vacant they were given to striplings newly arrived from Portugal who had never seen any fighting. There were some exceptions, of course, such as Gaspar Figueira de Serpa in Ceylon. This *fidalgo* was the son of a Portuguese father and a Sinhalese mother. His outstanding military prowess led to his eventually being given the chief command in the field against the Dutch and Sinhalese in 1655–8. There were also instances of *Brahmenes*, with no trace of European blood, being awarded the status of squires and knights in the royal household (*escudeiro logo acrescentado a cavalleiro*, in 1646, for example). But such instances remained exceptions. Many European-born *fidalgos* who had married Eurasian women and made their homes in the East complained that not only their sons but they themselves were passed over for promotion in favour of raw youths who had just arrived from Portugal and had every intention of returning thither. Portuguese contempt for the *Canarim* was still more outspoken and longer-lasting. From early times they were stigmatised as base, cowardly and unreliable. Frederico Diniz d'Ayalla, scion of a Goan military family, portrays this racial tension between Europeans, *mestiços* and *Canarins* in his *Goa Antiga e Moderna* (Lisbon 1888). He stresses the constant contempt with which the Portuguese always treated the local Indians—'a contempt so profound and so natural that any single Portuguese considered himself capable of storming a whole township of them'.

Although colonial society in Portuguese India retained such a marked military stamp for centuries, it also had equally marked mercantile and maritime characteristics for nearly as long, since almost everyone, from the viceroy to the cabin-boy, was trading openly or on the side. The *casados*, or married citizens, earned their living in whole or in great part by participating in the interport trade of Asia, and to a lesser extent by the Cape route to Lisbon. The lengthy Dutch war (1600–63) ruined many of these families, and the Portuguese share of the Asian interport trade was thenceforward a very modest one in comparison with that of the Dutch and the English. Such wealth as the *casados* of Goa now enjoyed was chiefly derived from the income they received from their lands in the fertile 'Province of the North', until these were lost to the Marathas in the war of 1737–40. Thenceforward, virtually their sole economic resource was service in the officer corps of the Indo-Portuguese army, where Pombal's egalitarian policies gave them better chances of promotion than they had previously enjoyed. Although some of the military and naval officers who came each year from Europe during the eighteenth century, and likewise some of the civil government officials who were posted to Goa, Damão and Diu, married into local Eurasian families and remained there, the resultant class of *Descendentes*, as the *mestiços* were now called, never became numerous. There were still 2,240 of them at Goa in 1866, but the disbandment of the Indo-Portuguese standing army six years later deprived most of the menfolk of their livelihood. Many families were reduced to indigence, and some of them were forced to merge with the *Canarins* whom they had so long despised. By 1956 there were only a little over 1,000 *Descendentes* in a population totalling about half a million, and their numbers must have been further reduced by emigration after the Indian occupation of Goa six years later. Nothing is more erroneous than the common conception that all Goans have a considerable dose of Portuguese blood in their veins. The great majority are ethnically Indians, though their centuries-old adoption of the Roman Catholic religion, and of the Portuguese language and mores, together with their assumption of Portuguese names, have firmly integrated them in the Portuguese cultural orbit.

The sexual licence which is inevitably a feature of any society based on slave labour was a constant theme of denunciation by clerical critics of the soldiers and settlers in Portuguese Asia. An Italian Jesuit missionary writing from India to St. Ignatius Loyola at Rome in 1550 commented:

> Your Reverence must know that the sin of licentiousness is so widespread in these regions that no check is placed upon it, which leads to great inconveniences, and to great disrespect of the sacraments. I say this of the Portuguese, who have adopted the vices and customs of the land without reserve, including this evil custom of buying droves of slaves, male and female, just as if they were sheep, large and small. There are countless men who buy droves of girls and sleep with all of them, and subsequently sell them. There are innumerable married settlers who have four, eight, or ten female slaves and sleep with all of them, as is common knowledge. This is carried to such excess that there was one man in Malacca who had twenty-four women of various races, all of whom were his slaves, and all of whom he enjoyed. I quote this city because it is a thing that everyone knows. Most men, as soon as they can afford to buy a female slave, almost invariably use her as a girl-friend (*amiga*), besides many other dishonesties, in my poor understanding.

Writing a century and a half later, the Luso-Brazilian Jesuit Padre Francisco de Sousa, made almost identical complaints about the prevalence of female slave prostitution in Portuguese Asia and the sexual excesses of the Portuguese soldiery with native women, 'an irremediable abuse among us'. An ordinary European or Eurasian artisan would have fifteen or twenty female slaves; and one seventeenth-century Mulatto blacksmith at Goa was alleged to own twenty-six women and girls, exclusive of the male slaves in his household. Well-to-do citizens and officials often owned between fifty and a hundred household slaves, and rich ladies sometimes had over 300. These unnecessarily large slave households were maintained to give social status and prestige to their owners, and they were a feature of Portuguese colonial life in Africa and South America as well as in Asia.

Quite apart from the attractions of female slaves of various colours, such as the dusky 'Barbara Escrava' to whom Camões addressed one of his most charming poems, Indian nautch-girls and temple-prostitutes exercised a fatal fascination over many *fidalgos*, as testified by a continual stream of official denunciations and legislation against these 'harpies', promulgated by successive viceroys and archbishops between 1598 and 1734. A generation titillated by the amorous exploits of James Bond and his kind is unlikely to react to the excesses of the Lusitanian libido in sixteenth- and seventeenth-century Asia with the horrified fascination evinced by Jan Huigen van Linschoten, Pyrard de Laval, Nicolao Manucci and other foreign observers, to say nothing of the scandalised disgust displayed by Jesuit missionaries and prelates of the Church. It is, however, obvious that the children of this sexual promiscuity with slave mothers seldom had the chance of an adequate upbringing or education, while those who were born in lawful wedlock were only too likely to be early corrupted by their surroundings. Moreover, the sexual licence accorded to men, whether *soldados* or *casados*, was not extended to their womenfolk in this (or in any other) colonial society. Cuckolded husbands were never blamed for killing their erring spouses out of hand, and men who slew their innocent wives on mere suspicion were seldom punished for it.

Obviously there must have been more happily married couples and more respectable households in the society of 'Golden' Goa than the lurid accounts of foreign visitors or the stern denunciations of clerical moralists would imply. Nicolao Manucci, one of the severest critics of the Portuguese in India, who described Goa (in 1666) as a 'place where treachery is great and prevalent, where there is little fear of God and no concern for foreigners', admitted that 'there are among them men of sincerity, as there are in other nations'. We have seen (p. 288) that the most hostile witnesses bore testimony to the good work done by the brotherhood of the *misericórdia* in all the principal Portuguese settlements, and the officiating brothers were, like the conscientious aldermen of the municipal councils, recruited largely from the local *casados*. If lechery, thieving and treachery were often to be met with in the Portuguese settlements from Moçambique to Macao, piety, charity and hospitality were likewise often to be found. The Cornish traveller Peter Mundy has left us a charming glimpse of the wealthy family with whom he stayed at Macao in 1637. His Portuguese host had several beautiful little Eurasian daughters 'that, except in England, I think not in the world to be overmatched for their pretty features and complexion; their habit or dressing becoming them as well, adorned with precious jewels and costly apparels, their uppermost garments being little *kimonos* or Japan coats, which graced them also'. Dinner was a lavish affair of many courses served on silver plates, which were changed with every new dish. 'Almost the same decorum in our drink, every man having his silver goblet by his trencher, which were no sooner empty but there stood those ready that filled them again with excellent good Portugual wine. There was also indifferent good music of the voice, harp and guitar.' Whether due to economic or to other causes, complaints of the luxury, immorality and insecurity of life in Portuguese Asia—particularly in Goa—during the sixteenth and seventeenth centuries, are replaced in the eighteenth by lamentations over its poverty and dullness.

If colonial society in Portuguese Asia was essentially a military and commercial one for several centuries, society in Portuguese America developed very differently in some ways. Both societies relied heavily upon slave labour, but the plantation slavery which was so characteristic of the latter was entirely absent in the former, unless we include some of the Zambesian *prazos* which produced a small surplus of export crops. After the pioneer days of 'New Lusitania' were over, the brazilwood-loggers and traders were replaced by the sugar-planters and (in due course) by the tobacco-growers in the settled regions of the coastal belt, where sugar was the king of the economy for the rest of the colonial period. A sugar plantation was a self-contained entity with its cane-fields, grinding-mill, coppers, vats and stills, its ox-carts and its boats and barges. All of these were operated by Negro slaves under the direction of the mill-owner, through his overseers, factors and foremen, many of whom by the eighteenth century were Mulattos. The leading sugar-planters, or *senhores de engenho* ('lords of the mill'), quickly became and long remained a patriarchal rural aristocracy, whose authority on their own lands was virtually absolute, and who exercised great influence on civic affairs through their membership of the municipal councils. As Antonil noted of this class at the dawn of the eighteenth century:

> To be a lord of the mill is an honour to which many aspire; because this title brings with it the services, the obedience, and the respect of many people. And if he should be, as he ought to be, a man of wealth and of administrative ability, the prestige accorded a lord of the mill in Brazil can be compared to the honour in which titled noblemen are held among the *fidalgos* of Portugal.

A century later Santos Vilhena observed that the *senhores de engenho* were 'usually haughty and so puffed up with vainglory that they think nobody can compare with them'. Proud and haughty as a class, they were also, as a general rule, famed for their lavish hospitality. The copyholders, or *lavradores de canas*, who were obliged to send their cane to the plantation-owner's mill for processing, and the tobacco-growers and rum-distillers who sometimes made sizeable fortunes, seldom achieved the prestige and respect accorded to a *senhor de engenho*, who was more or less monarch of all he surveyed.

Two other social categories developed a comparable importance, at any rate at some times and in some regions, during the late seventeenth and early eighteenth centuries. These were the cattle-barons who owned vast tracts of land and vast herds of scrawny kine in the scrub and grazing lands of the interior (*sertão*), and the adventurers who struck it rich in the gold-diggings of Minas Gerais. The concentration on the cultivation of sugar and tobacco in the coastal region indirectly fostered the gradual opening-up of the *sertão*. Cattle ranchers and drovers, the great majority of the latter being of mixed blood—white, Negro and Amerindian—penetrated ever farther into the backlands in search of new pastures, by the São Francisco river valley and other natural routes. This movement became particularly noticeable after about 1650, and many place-names in the interior (Campo Grande, Campinas, Curral d'El-Rei, Campos, Vacaria, etc.) show that modern towns had their origin in the westward expansion of cattle-ranching and stock-raising. These different occupations were not necessarily mutually exclusive, and some of the most enterprising individuals combined several of them. João Peixoto Viegas, whose graphic pen gives us such colourful glimpses of late seventeenth-century Bahia, was a successful sugar-planter, tobacco-grower and cattle-rancher, as well as a leading member of the town council and the *misericórdia*. Manuel Nunes Viana, a Minhoto emigrant of humble origin, became one of the leading ranchers in the sparsely populated São Francisco river valley before he made another fortune in the gold-fields of Minas Gerais, where he was the leader of the intruding *Emboabas* against the Paulista pioneers in the broils of 1708–9. As had happened with the sugar-planters, the cattle-barons and territorial magnates of the backlands (*poderosos do sertão*, as they were termed) were apt to become very much of a law unto themselves. The Crown's efforts to limit by legislation the extent of their latifundia seldom met with any lasting success. During the eighteenth century wholesale and retail traders in the principal towns, and the contractors of the numerous Crown monopolies, became of increasing importance in urban centres such as Salvador, Recife, Rio de Janeiro and Ouro Preto. But the patriarchal aristocracy of colonial Brazil was always personified chiefly by the *senhores de engenho*, and it was still from this class that many of the leading statesmen and politicians were drawn in the nineteenth-century empire.

The sugar-planters early secured the passage of a law forbidding the distraint for debt of their plantations, mills and appurtenances, creditors not being allowed to foreclose on more than a single season's crop. Division of the patrimony was also forbidden, and the first-born succeeded to the whole succession. Despite the relatively humble origin of many of the leading sugar-planting families, the position of this patriarchal rural aristocracy was in some ways stronger than that of the landed aristocracy in Portugal, which the English envoy at Lisbon succinctly described in 1719 as follows: 'The constitution of this kingdom is such that the nobility must submit in everything to the King's pleasure. Their titles are only for life, and their estates are chiefly Crown lands granted to them for life; and though they are both commonly regranted to their heirs, yet it depends upon the King's favour and therefore binds them to their good behaviour.' Endogamy, with cousins marrying cousins, and uncles marrying nieces, was frequently practised in both Portugal and Brazil among the upper classes. This custom greatly contributed to the formation of a closely inter-married Brazilian landed aristocracy. Their vast and often neglected estates in the interior were virtually immune from interference by the colonial officials, even though these lands had originally been granted in *sesmarias* of limited extent by the Crown, and were theoretically liable to expropriation by the reigning monarch if they were not being adequately cultivated or otherwise developed.

If the military side of colonial life was not so evident in Portuguese America as it was in Portuguese Asia, there was one aspect of it which became a characteristic of eighteenth-century Brazil. The big landowners, whether sugar-planters, cattle-ranchers, or gold-miners, showed themselves increasingly avid for military titles, honours and ranks, for reasons both of power and prestige. Colonial governors were well aware of this fact, and they often reminded the Crown that the judicious distribution of military ranks and titles was the best and cheapest way of securing what would otherwise be the doubtful loyalty of the *poderosos do sertão*. The process began in Minas Gerais with the lavish bestowal of the ranks of brigadier, colonel and so forth in the *ordenança* or militia regiments after the 'War of the Emboabas' in 1709. The sugar-planters of the *Recôncavo* of Bahia and the *Várzea* of Pernambuco, the cattle-barons of the São Francisco region and of Piauí, were equally desirous of these distinctions. The Crown sometimes demurred at the readiness with which colonial governors distributed honorific and militia commands, as when King John V declined to approve the creation of a new militia post in 1717, 'because I have been informed that such appointments are sought more for the title and honour than for the execution of the duties involved'. Such militia commands also carried with them certain tax exemptions and other privileges, which the Crown was reluctant to bestow on too many people, but the practice continued to flourish none the less. The 'colonel' who never saw active service became a familiar figure in the Brazilian countryside, and the landowners who officered the regional militia were thereby enabled to increase their own political power and social prestige. On the other side of the empire, honorific military ranks were freely conferred on the *prazo*-holders of Zambesia, and on the tribal chiefs and *datus* (headmen) of Portuguese Timor, in which island the custom has survived to the present day.

In sharp contradistinction to the eagerness with which the members of the Brazilian upper classes sought senior commands in the militia was the extreme reluctance of Brazilians of all classes to enlist in the regular army, or in the navy, as we have already had occasion to notice (p. 226). The three interim governors of Brazil in 1761, one of whom was the garrison commander at Bahia, reported to the home government that the Bahianos had such a horror of military service 'that none of them will persuade his son to enlist and, what is more, even the serving regular officers, who have a prodigious quantity of male offspring, will not try to induce one of them to enlist'. The rank and file of the regular units at Bahia were therefore recruited mainly from 'itinerant vagrants and locally born Mulattos'. Similar tales of woe came from Paraíba, Pernambuco, Rio de Janeiro and Sacramento at frequent intervals throughout the eighteenth century. Desertion was rife in all these places, since access to the wide spaces of the *sertão* was so easy.

As had happened in Portuguese Asia and Africa, regular military units were only tardily introduced into Brazil and the Maranhão. The first standing infantry regiment (*terço*) arrived at Bahia in 1625, with the expedition which retook the city of Salvador from the Dutch. It was later supplemented by another one, and in due course by an artillery regiment. Other regular units subsequently were raised for service in Rio de Janeiro,

Sacramento and elsewhere, besides the famous dragoons of Minas Gerais, who were recruited exclusively in the north of Portugal from 1719 onwards. After the transference of the colonial capital from Bahia to Rio de Janeiro in 1763, several infantry regiments (Moura, Beja and Estremoz) were sent out from Portugal to reinforce the southern garrisons. All these regular units were supposed to be kept up to strength by drafts periodically dispatched from Portugal, but in most instances their ranks had to be supplemented by local recruitment, difficult and unsatisfactory as this proved to be.

White and coloured soldiers served alongside each other in the regular infantry regiments, and in 1699 the Crown reprimanded the Governor of Sacramento for rejecting some recuits on the grounds that they were Mulattos. The militia units, however, were usually organised on a colour basis, each company being commanded by officers of the same hue as their men. Despite the reluctance of the local whites to serve under or alongside men of colour in the Bahia militia, the Crown ordered that they should do so in 1731. The Viceroy reported that the white Bahianos flatly refused to be integrated with Mulattos or with free Negroes in the same companies, and the Crown reluctantly had to sanction the reversion of these regiments to a differential colour basis in 1736. It may be added that even in the regular army units, where whites and coloured served alongside each other, preference in pay and promotion was systematically accorded to the former, as a point of official policy. Thus a Mulatto soldier of the Bahia garrison petitioned the Crown for permission to retire after eighteen years' service, 'since he is a coloured man [*pardo*] and will not be given, neither can he expect, any promotion'. The problem was further complicated by the fact that military service in Portugal itself was very unpopular, partly because the Crown was a notoriously bad paymaster and the troops, when paid at all, often received only half-pay, even in wartime. The long-standing popular aversion to military service is reflected in many Portuguese folk-songs besides the following one from the Douro valley:

Rapariga, tola, tola,
Olha o que tu vais fazer!
Vais casar com um soldado
Melhor te fora morrer!

('You foolish girl, take care what you are going to do! You want to marry a soldier, you would be better dead!')

In these circumstances recourse was increasingly had to the forcible recruitment of 'sturdy beggars', vagrants, and gaol-birds, who were forcibly enlisted for military service overseas for terms varying from a few years to a lifetime. There were *degredados*, or exiled criminals, in the pioneer fleets of Vasco da Gama (1497) and of Pedro Álvares Cabral (1500); but the proportion of those who were deported from their country for their country's good was much greater in the seventeenth and eighteenth centuries than in the sixteenth, when the spicy 'fumes of India' still attracted many volunteers. Similar methods of forcible recruitment for the armed forces were, of course, employed in many other countries. It is only necessary to recall that the English Navy depended heavily on the press-gang for centuries, and that men regarded as potential or actual criminals were often given the choice between enlistment or imprisonment until well into the nineteenth century. In Portugal the magistrates and justices were sometimes criticised for sentencing men who were guilty of capital offences to banishment overseas instead of to the gallows; and the Crown itself often commuted a death sentence to deportation 'for the term of his natural life'. The savage jurisprudence of the old regime, in Portugal as in Great Britain, sentenced multitudes of petty thieves and minor offenders to lengthy terms of imprisonment, or to exile, for offences which nowadays would be dismissed with a caution or a small fine. Every fleet, indeed almost every ship, that left Lisbon for India, Africa or Brazil in the seventeenth and eighteenth centuries took its quota of *degredados*; and some notoriously unhealthy or ill-famed regions, such as Benguela and São Tomé, hardly received anyone else save these exiles and government officials after the mid-seventeenth century.

In the year 1667 alone, for example, we find the Crown promulgated a series of edicts concerning the expediting of gaol deliveries, which there is no reason to suppose were in any way exceptional. Justices and magistrates were ordered to sentence summarily persons still awaiting trial; those guilty of relatively minor crimes, such as vagrancy, being sentenced to deportation to Mazagão (the last remaining Portuguese stronghold in Morocco). Those guilty of more serious offences were to be deported to the Maranhão, to Brazil and to Cacheu (in Portuguese Guinea). This last place being then short of blacksmiths and stone-masons, the magistrates were to deport thither any such artificers who might be found among the gaolbirds. The *Lisbon Gazette* of 15 March 1723 recorded the departure of two ships for Goa on the previous day carrying many officers and soldiers who had volunteered to serve there. 'There are also on board many vagabond and dissolute persons from whom His Majesty's great clemency has been pleased to deliver these two cities' of East and West Lisbon. At this period it was customary that some weeks before the departure of the annual Indiamen, official circular letters were sent to all the district judges (*Corregidores da Comarca*), reminding them to round up and arrest potential and actual criminals, preparatory to sentencing them to deportation to India. 'Your Worship will not only arrest such persons as live to the prejudice and scandal of the common weal by committing crimes, but also those who live in idleness', all who were young and fit being sentenced to serve as soldiers. Among those who were victimised in this way were entire communities of gypsies, against whom King John V seems to have conceived an obsessive hatred, for no reason that I can discover. These unfortunates of all ages and both sexes were shipped off in successive levies to Brazil and Angola, without any specific charge being made against them, in a (largely futile) attempt to banish the Romany race from Portugal altogether.

The frequent arrival of so many dissolute *degredados*, rogues, vagabonds and sturdy beggars, exiled from Portugal to colonial ports like Recife, Bahia, Luanda, Moçambique and Goa, inevitably aggravated an already difficult social situation. The prevalance of slave-prostitution and of other obstacles in the way of a sound family life, such as the double standard of chastity as between husbands and wives, all made for a great deal of casual miscegenation between white men and coloured women. As the soldier-chronicler António de Oliveira de Cadornega observed at Luanda in 1682: 'There is a high birth-rate caused by the infantry soldiers and other individuals among the black ladies, for want of white ladies, which produces many Mulattos and coloureds.' The children of these (for the most part) irregular and shifting unions, if they lived to grow up, usually became rogues, prostitutes and vagrants, living on their wits and on the margins of society. Many of the *degredados* promptly deserted on arrival at their place of deportation, and those who did not helped to swell the pullulating proletariat or *ínfima plebe*, as the colonial officials contemptuously termed these social outcasts and misfits. The task of keeping law and order with a large and shifting criminal element in the urban population was not an easy one, as is amply proved by contemporary official correspondence and by travellers' accounts. Murder and mayhem were of daily, or rather nightly, occurrence.

In August 1671 the Governor of Pernambuco sent to Lisbon a list of 197 persons of both sexes who had recently met with violent deaths in the town of Olinda, apart from others who had been lucky to escape with wounds. They ranged from white captains killed with sword-thrusts to Negro slaves who had been flogged to death, the majority being of lowly social origins. An Italian artist who stayed for some weeks at Bahia in 1699 wrote that anyone who went out in the streets of Salvador after nightfall did so at considerable risk. Every morning the corpses of twenty-five or thirty newly murdered people were found in the streets, despite the vigilance of the soldiers who patrolled them at night. For that matter, Lisbon itself had an unenviable reputation for being exceedingly unsafe after dark, as were many other European cities before the introduction of street lighting and an adequate police force. The agents of these crimes in Brazil were usually 'peons, mamelucos and persons of this kind', as an early eighteenth-century governor of Pernambuco reported, but they were often paid to do the dirty work by their social superiors. Like his predecessor in 1671, he asked the Crown for authority to sentence to death 'Indians, Bastards, Carijós, Mulattos and Negroes found guilty of atrocious crimes', as the governors of Bahia, Rio de Janeiro, São Paulo and Minas Gerais were already empowered to do; but the authorities of Pernambuco only received the required permission in 1735–7.

The ideals—or the ideas—which animated the Portuguese who voluntarily left their country as discoverers, mariners, soldiers, settlers, merchants and missionaries between 1415 and 1825 naturally ran the gamut from high-minded and self-sacrificing idealism to the most sordid lust for material gain. The majority, like most emigrants before and since, probably left simply in the hopes of bettering themselves socially and economically, being faced with destitution if they remained where they were. But the crusading spirit lingered on in the Iberian peninsula longer than elsewhere in Europe, and many of those who went to Africa and the East in the fifteenth and sixteenth centuries were certainly animated by the desire to be dubbed knights on the battlefield against the Infidel. This chivalrous ideal is well reflected in the speech made by King Affonso V to his son and heir, 'the Perfect Prince', when knighting him in the blood-stained mosque of Arzila on the day that this Moorish stronghold was stormed after fierce hand-to-hand fighting (24 August 1471):

> . . . And before I, your king and your father, dub you a knight with my own hand, you should know that knighthood is a combination of virtue and honourable power, very fit of itself to impose peace on the land when covetousness or tyranny, with the desire of dominating, disturbs kingdoms, commonwealths, or ordinary persons. By its rule and institution it obliges knights to depose from their estates the kings and princes who do not administer justice, and to put in their places others of the same rank who will do it well and truly. Knights are also obliged to serve loyally their kings, lords and captains, and to give them good service; for the knight who professes the true faith and does not conform thereto, is like a man who declines to use the reason which God gave him. Knights must be generous, and in time of war share their goods with each other, save only their weapons and chargers, which they must keep as a means to gain honour. Moreover, knights are obliged to sacrifice their lives for their religion, for their country, and for the protection of the helpless. For just as the sacerdotal estate was ordained by God for His one and only divine cult, so knighthood was instituted by Him in order to do justice, to defend His Faith, and to succour the widows, orphans, poor and forsaken. And those who do not do this cannot rightly be termed knights.

There were doubtless some *fidalgos* and soldiers who lived up to this chivalric ideal which, of course, likewise implied taking a good and hearty bash at the Infidel whenever opportunity offered. But there must have been many more emigrants like Fernão Mendes Pinto, who told the Jesuits at Goa in 1554, when (temporarily) repenting of his misspent life: 'I thought that so long as a man did not steal the chalice or treasure of a church or become a Muslim, there was no reason to fear Hell; and that it was enough to be a Christian, for God's mercy was great.' Or, as a Paulista slave-raider retorted to a Spanish Jesuit missionary, who threatened him with God's vengeance for killing one of his Christianised Amerindians in 1629: 'I shall be saved in spite of God, for I am a baptised Christian and believe in Christ, even though I have done no good deeds.' An attitude shared by many Europeans other than Portuguese, including the piratical Captain Kidd's English crew, who said: 'they looked on it as little or no sin to take what they could from such heathens as the Moors and Indians were'.

CHAPTER XIV

Merchants, monopolists, and smugglers

NOTHING is more characteristic of the old Portuguese seaborne empire than the constant complaints of its inhabitants about the pernicious activities of monopolists and engrossers. These complaints range in time from the age of Prince Henry the Navigator to that of King John VI, and in space from the Moluccas to the Mato Grosso. Equally characteristic is the reverse side of this medal—the constant complaints by the monopolists and engrossers (of whom the 'Grocer King' of Portugal was a leading exemplar) about the pernicious activities of smugglers and contraband-traders. Likewise characteristic, if more paradoxical, was the fact that a society which laid such stress on military, ecclesiastical and seigneurial status was largely dependent on trade and commerce for its development and survival.

To take the last point first, disdain for the trader and his calling was deeply rooted in Portuguese society, as it was, for that matter, in many others. This disdain had its roots in the Christian medieval hierarchy which rated the merchant lower in the social scale than the practitioners of the seven 'mechanical arts': peasant, hunter, soldier, sailor, surgeon, weaver, blacksmith. In the course of time some distinctions were made between the various 'mechanical arts', whether traditional or otherwise. Thus an applicant for a lawyer's degree in the eighteenth century could claim that although his great-grandfather was a gunfounder, and therefore of 'mechanical' (artisan) status, this calling was 'not so base as that of cobbler, carpenter and others like those'. It need, perhaps, hardly be added that such prejudices were not confined to Christendom or to the Middle Ages. In Catholic Portugal, as in Confucian and in Communist China and in Marxist Russia, the merchant was regarded as a parasitic and profiteering middleman, resolved to enrich himself at the expense of his fellow-men. Despite periodical legislation by the Portuguese Crown to encourage overseas trade in one way and another, beginning with the laws stimulating national shipping and maritime insurance is the reign of Dom Fernando (1377–80), this prejudice persisted for centuries during the reigns of the monarchs of Aviz and Bragança, who styled themselves, among other things, 'lords of the commerce' of India, Ethiopia, Arabia, Persia, etc. This long-standing prejudice was criticised by the mercers of Lisbon in a remonstrance to the Crown, drawn up in 1689:

> Without trade, there is not a kingdom which is not poor, nor a republic which is not famished. Yet in this capital city of your Majesty, the merchants are so little favoured, and commerce is despised to such a degree, that not only are men discouraged from becoming traders, but all those of spirit decline to have anything to do with it, since they see with their own eyes that in the conceit of the Portuguese a merchant is no better than a fish-porter. This is the reason why there are so few Portuguese merchants in this kingdom, and why so many foreigners of all nations swarm here, who are the bloodsuckers of all your Majesty's money

and the monopolists and engrossers of the national wealth. Similar complaints occur with monotonous regularity for centuries, and they were often voiced by the representatives of the third estate in the Cortes, though seldom with any lasting effect.

The abiding nature of this anti-mercantile prejudice was evinced overseas even in places like Macao, whose citizens confessedly depended entirely on commerce for their own existence, let alone for their prosperity, as the Senate repeatedly reminded the Crown. Since it was the prevailing practice for several centuries that virtually all Portuguese laymen who went out to the East did so either as soldiers or as government officials (pp. 296–7 above), many of those who turned traders and left the service of the Crown continued to call themselves captains, or by other military ranks, even when they were no longer entitled to do so. Similarly, in the Atlantic regions of the Portuguese empire, many of the slave-traders of Angola, and of the sugar-planters, the tobacco-growers and the gold-miners of Brazil, likewise sought to enhance their social status by securing honorific military ranks and titles in the regional militia or in some other way (p. 310). Thus among the sugar-planters of Bahia who petitioned the Crown in 1662 there were many who styled themselves '*fidalgos* and knight-commanders of the Military Orders, colonels of infantry and other military officers', even though their military qualifications were, in some instances, virtually nil.

The mercantile aspects of Portuguese colonial society are readily apparent if we consider briefly four or five main categories which reveal those characteristics. The Crown and its representatives, whether civil or military officials; the Church and the religious Orders; the contractors and farmers of the numerous Crown monopolies; the private traders and merchants, who were for centuries, whether rightly or wrongly, largely identified with the hated and despised 'New' Christians. After surveying each of these in turn we will conclude this chapter with a few words on the smugglers and contraband-traders who personified the inevitable reaction to the monopolists and engrossers.

The reader who has persevered thus far will hardly need reminding that the Portuguese Crown and the royal family were deeply engaged in the commercial exploitation of the Portuguese discoveries along the West African coast. In order to help finance the cost of the initial voyages, the Infante Dom Henrique had received from the Crown a wide variety of commercial monopolies, including not only those connected with the trade of West Africa and the Atlantic islands, but tunny-fishing rights off the Algarve, the importation of dyes and sugar, and the control of the soap industry in Portugal. His activities as a monopolist and engrosser provoked reiterated protests from various sectors of Portuguese society, including forcible (but futile) representations by several of the municipal councils, and by the third estate (*povo*) in the Cortes. King John II, it will be recalled, reorganised and strengthened the Crown's monopolistic hold of the most profitable items of the West African trade, gold and slaves. With both the Portuguese and the Spanish *conquistadores*, trading in precious metals or in slaves did not affect their knightly status in any way, perhaps as a hangover from the Crusades and the selling or ransoming of Saracen prisoners. On the other hand, King Manuel was, of course, the 'Grocer King' or the 'Pepper Potentate' personified. But it was not only luxury or high-priced goods which were Crown monopolies in Portugal and its 'conquests'. Among the more mundane sources of income for the Crown was the salt-gabelle of Setubal, which was operated in various ways, ranging from a tight Crown monopoly to a limited share for the reigning monarchs, between 1576 and 1852. The manufacture and sale of soap was also monopolised in whole or in part by the Crown for centuries, and regional or district monopolies were granted to favoured individuals and courtiers. In 1660, for instance, the white soap monopoly of Lisbon was granted to a Carmelite nun, the Countess of Calheta, on condition she gave a share of the profits to two distinguished general officers, Dom Luís de Menezes and Gil Vaz Lobo.

One of the most lucrative Crown monopolies during the eighteenth century was undoubtedly the royal *estanco* of tobacco in Portugal and its empire. Then as now, few people could be induced to give up the tobacco habit once they had acquired it, whether in the form of snuff-taking or leaf-smoking, however highly tobacco was taxed, and however low the grade and state of the government-sponsored product. As with the other monopolies, this one was farmed out; and the British envoy at Lisbon in 1733 observed that frequent foreign protests against the rigorous enforcement of the tobacco monopoly got nowhere.

Great trouble has been given to ships in former times for tobacco found on board them, even in the smallest quantities, and many representatations have been made to the Court of Portugal by the Ministers my predecessors on this head, [but] as this branch of the King of Portugal's revenue is farmed out, and is a very favourite point with His Majesty, as it is a very beneficial one, and as the King has always seemed resolved to give the farmers of this branch all the power and support they can desire, no satisfactory answer has ever yet been obtained to any representation in this respect.

A modern French historian has calculated that between 1676 and 1716 the Crown tobacco farm in Portugal yielded on the average more than forty times per head the amount derived from the corresponding royal monopoly in France, and more than two and a half times that of the Spanish farm.

It would take too long to enumerate here all the overseas sources of wealth which were exploited by the Crown at one time or another, whether in the form of a (theoretically) rigorous monopoly, or a percentage of the profits, or in the way of Customs duties and export and import dues. They included several items which have been mentioned previously, such as the Asian spice monopolies; duties on slaves, sugar and salt; the royal fifths on the production of gold; the Brazilian diamond-mining monopoly; the collection of ecclesiastical tithes in Minas Gerais; the whaling contracts at Bahia and Rio de Janeiro; the logging of dye-woods and shipbuilding timbers; the sale of certain offices and commands, such as commercial voyages to Japan and Pegu, captaincies of fortresses, and minor legal and administrative posts such as that of notary-public in the Brazilian Backlands. Even such trivia as river ferry-crossings and the dues from washermen, limeburners and fishermen were often rented out by the Crown or by its representatives. Perhaps more than in any other country, it was a long-established practice in Portugal for the Crown (and its successor republic) to farm out the smallest public offices which might be expected to produce any revenue; and the same procedure was followed in Portuguese India, Ceylon, Africa and Brazil.

Despite the wide-ranging nature of the Crown's fiscal arm, successive Portuguese rulers were never able to enjoy an excess of income over expenditure for any length of time, even during the traditional 'golden ages' of King Manuel and King John V. In both reigns the Crown's income was greatly increased, through the Asian spice trade in the first instance and through Brazilian gold and diamonds in the second; but in both reigns the Crown's expenditure increased much more. The illusion of great wealth was given to many contemporaries by the prodigal expenditure of both those monarchs, but with both of them all that glittered was not gold. For most of the sixteenth century the Crown operated to a large extent with money borrowed on onerous terms from merchant bankers against the security of future pepper imports; and King John V's spectacular extravagances were achieved at the cost of letting his army, navy and many other essential services decline in penurious neglect—a decline which was only partially checked by fleeting remedial measures, such as those taken during the scare of a war with Spain in 1735–7. As was the case with other and richer empires under the old regime, the Portuguese Crown was never able to pay adequate salaries to a wide range of its officials and servants, with results that have been mentioned above (pp. 216, 297) and will be further considered here.

Since the Crown was unable to pay adequate wages, its officials overseas were sometimes expressly and sometimes tacitly permitted to trade for their own accounts. This concession was usually made on the understanding that the Crown's monopolistic or preferential commercial rights were not seriously infringed thereby, and that this 'private trade' did not take precedence over the official trade, which was channelled through the Crown's Factors and the Customs established in all the principal ports of the Portuguese empire. At some times and places the captains or governors were actually authorised to engross all the trade to themselves, having contracted with the Crown to do so in return for a substantial down (or annual) payment during their triennial term of office. Thus the captain of Moçambique told a visiting Dutch skipper and his officers in 1677: 'That we as private individuals could not sell any of our merchandise save only to him. That he was also a merchant, and he would buy our goods for gold or ivory, so we should give him a list of those which we had to sell.' In either of its forms, whether outright monopoly or limited private trade, this system was inevitably and almost invariably abused in practice. Colonial governors and high officials often became silent partners in mercantile enterprises, or money-lenders on a considerable scale. Complaints of the rapacity and venality of government officials in general, and of the captains of the Asian and African fortresses in particular, are a constant theme of official and unofficial correspondence for over three centuries. When all allowances for the traditional Portuguese failing of *murmuração* (backbiting) have been made, there is more than abundant proof from official and archival sources of the allegations made by caustic—but well-informed—critics, such as Diogo do Couto and Francisco Rodrigues da Silveira, not to mention St. Francis Xavier, and Padre António Vieira, S.J.

Not all colonial governors were as corrupt or as cynical as was Dom Álvaro de Noronha, the Captain of Ormuz in 1551. He boasted that since his predecessor, a scion of the Lima family, had made a profit of 140,000 *pardaus* out of the place, he would certainly, as a Noronha, surpass him by making much more. But many governors were hardly less greedy, and the rigidly honest ones were few and far between. The 'spoils' system put a premium on dishonest and arbitrary government, particularly in the remoter regions where the authority of the Crown or of the viceroy reached only tardily and ineffectively. As Captain João Ribeiro, a veteran of nineteen years' service in Ceylon and India, observed in 1685: 'I do not doubt that among those who went out to govern those fortresses there were some who behaved kindly, but they could not set matters right. For the wrongs done by one bad man remain deeper impressed in the memory than the kindnesses done by a hundred good men.' When Pedro de Mello left the captaincy of Rio de Janeiro at the end of his triennial term in 1666, the Overseas Councillors at Lisbon notified the Crown that in their collective experience he was the only colonial governor against whom no complaints of misconduct had been made. Two years later the same councillors sadly advised the Crown: 'The robberies and excesses of many governors are such that their perpetrators should not only be brought to trial but beheaded out of hand'—a suggestion that was not implemented any more than Gaspar Correia's similar proposal a century earlier (p. 144). When King John IV asked Padre António Vieira whether the unwieldy colony of Maranhão-Para ought not to be subdivided into two governorships, the outspoken Jesuit advised him to leave things as they were, 'since one thief in a public office was a lesser evil than two'.

A determined attempt to abolish the trading privileges of all government officials, from the ranks of viceroy and governor down to army captains and their civilian equivalents, was made by King John V in 1720. A royal decree published in September of that year strictly forbade all such officials to engage in any form of trade, under any pretext whatsoever, either directly or indirectly. A general (if rather modest) increase in the salary-scales of all those categories affected by this reform was authorised in order to compensate them for the loss of their commercial privileges. It need hardly be said that this law was totally ineffective in the long term, and even the immediate results were rather counter-productive. As the clear-sighted Duke of Cadaval pointed out when this reform was still under discussion by the King and his advisers at Lisbon, if colonial governors and high officials were not allowed to make an honest profit in some form of commerce, it would be very difficult to find suitable candidates for such posts, since there would be no inducement for them to serve in unhealthy climates and dangerous regions. The complete failure of this well-intentioned reform is belatedly reflected in the indignant wording of another *alvará* or royal decree, promulgated in April 1785, and addressed to the senior government officials of Moçambique. They were reproached, among other malpractices, for trading with their own capital 'and even with that of My Royal Treasury', through third parties and under assumed names. At the same time that they stressed in their official reports the underdeveloped state of the colony and the abject poverty of its inhabitants, they themselves were amassing considerable fortunes, which they either remitted abroad or else invested as silent partners in retail merchandising. The severe penalties threatened transgressors of the *alvarás* of 1720 and 1785 had no more lasting effect than had similar enactments since the days of Afonso de Albuquerque, who never tired of telling King Manuel that the worst enemies which that 'Fortunate Prince' had in India were some of his own officials.

Apart from denouncing their dishonesty, Albuquerque was highly critical of the competence of the Crown Factors in India, alleging that a clerk trained in the counting-house of Bartolomeo Marchione, the famous Florentine merchant-banker and entrepreneur at Lisbon, would be worth more than all of them put together. In this he was exaggerating. Some at least of the factors had gained commercial expertise in the Guinea or in the Moroccan trades; and there was a well-established organisation of Crown Factors in the ports of southern Spain, maintained for the purchase of provisions and supplies for the Portuguese strongholds in Morocco. In any event, the Portuguese in the East soon familiarised themselves with the ramifications and variations of the interport trade in Monsoon Asia. Their share in this seaborne commerce was carried on largely by the *casados*, and it was usually the work of individuals trading on a relatively small scale. But the seventeenth-century merchants of the powerful Dutch and English East India Companies often wrote resentfully, enviously, or (on occasion) admiringly of the commercial acumen of their Portuguese competitors.

The government officials and the clergy who engaged in this maritime trade usually commanded greater capital resources than the average *casado*, and hence the latter sometimes complained of unfair competition by the former. Often enough they co-operated, and both categories likewise traded in conjunction or partnership with Asian merchants and potentates. An outstanding exemplar of this type was Francisco Vieira de Figueiredo, who from his base at Macassar between 1642 and 1665 drove a brisk trade to Timor, Macao, Manila, Batavia, Bantam, Meliapor, Madras and Goa, among many other places. Unfortunately it is impossible to calculate the volume and importance of the trade driven by government officials and by private individuals in the Portuguese empire, since so much of it was contraband and since so few of the relevant account books and records have survived. One of the rare exceptions is the commercial ledger or *Livro de Rezão* of António Coelho Guerreiro, who served successively as a soldier and government official in Brazil, Angola, India and Timor, between 1678 and 1705, trading actively in all these places, where his business associates included four governors, an Inquisitor and a Jesuit, besides three women and two silversmiths. Most of the fortunes made in this way by the lucky ones who returned to Portugal were not invested in further commercial undertakings, but were employed in the purchase of houses, land and the formation of entailed estates (*morgados*), while charitable foundations, such as the *misericórdia* and the religious brotherhoods, also benefited from them, as we have seen.

If many colonial governors and high officials made fortunes in trade (legitimately or otherwise) and by judicious money-lending, the Crown also expected that such individuals should come to its aid in financial emergencies, as in fact they often did. Diogo do Couto instances, as typical of these public-spirited *fidalgos*, the ex-Governor-General of India, Francisco Barreto, who had made a fortune during his tenure of the captaincy of Baçaim (1549–52), but spent it freely in the service of the Crown. Writing in his old age, Couto averred that this generosity was no longer the fashion in 1611; but in reality there are many later instances of it in Asia, Africa and Brazil. There are also many instances when officials

15. *Brazilian costume in the eighteenth century: a couple engaged in duck-shooting (from a coloured drawing by Carlos Julião, c. 1785)*

MAPPA

Do cabedal que trouſe a Frota da Bahia de todos os Santos, que neſte Porto de Lisboa entrou em 25. *de Março de* 1758. *com* 95. *dias de viage, de que he Capitania a Nào Noſſa Senhora das Brotas, Commandada pelo Capitam de màr, e guerra Antonio de Brito Freire.*

PARA SUA MAGESTADE

Ouro em pò, e Barra	9:064U180.
Em moeda	48:355U727.
Hum por cento cobrado	827U473.
Soma	58:247U380.

PARA PARTES

Ouro em pò, e Barra	15:745U189.
Em moeda	686:462U613.
Manifeſtado nos Navios	25:817U701.
Soma	728:025U503
Prata em marcos 260. marcos 2. onç. 4. oit. a 6900.	1:796U155
Prata em pezos 5088. pezos a 800.	4:070U400.
Soma ao todo	792:139U438.

Carga dos Navios Mercantes.

10U016	Caixar de aſſucar
1U217	Fechos dito
1U251	Caras dito
14U558	Rolos de Tabaco
U143	Fardos dito
U070	Barricas dito
U010	Caixotes dito
84U641	Meyos de ſola
5U489	Couros em cabello
3U968	Atanados
3U304	Milheiros de coquilho
U006	Barris de cebo e rama
U483	Barris de mel
U540	Barris de ſeco
3U655	Varas de parreiras
U171	Braços, e curvos
8U048	Coſſoeiras
U031	Frexais
U311	Vigas
U030	Pàos de varaes
U008	Amarras de piaſſá
3U180	Toros de pau
103U000	Achas de lenha
1U160	Taboas de tapinhuan
U053	Taboas de coſtado
U034	Pranchoens
U003	Eixos de moinho
U697	Aduelas
U078	Eixos da artilharia
U030	Pipois de azeite de peixe
U016	Barricas de ſementilhas.
U036	Eſcravos

16. *Printed cargo manifest of the Bahia fleet which reached Lisbon, 25 March 1758*

claimed thumping rewards or repayments by the Crown, for expenditure allegedly incurred in the royal service, but which, if made at all, had certainly not come out of the claimants' own pockets. 'Cooking the books' is not a modern invention, and there was plenty of scope for it in the Portuguese and in other colonial bureaucracies. Galliots trading between Macao and Goa in the 1620s, for example, carried two sets of cargo-lists. One set for presentation to the Customs, wherein all items were grossly undervalued, and the other (confidential) set for owners or shippers of the goods.

The Crown found it much harder to extract contributions from the Church and from the religious Orders, which were always intensely jealous of preserving their ecclesiastical immunities and tax-free privileges. We have seen (pp. 77–8) that members of the clergy, both as individuals and in their corporate capacity, were often deeply involved in mercantile transactions, and that some of the Jesuit missions in the East could only be maintained in this way. Those in Brazil and Angola were also partly financed from the sale of sugar, slaves and livestock originating in Jesuit-owned plantations, ranches and estates. The Jesuit College of Santo Antão in Lisbon derived a good income from the Bahian plantation of Sergipe do Conde, and an experienced administrator advised in 1635: 'When the price of sugar is low in Brazil, it is better not to sell it there, but ship it to the kingdom, where it is always in great demand and gives a profit of over a hundred per cent. And it is of more benefit to us than to the merchants, since we pay no duties on our sugar.' This mixture of God and Mammon periodically provoked a good deal of grumbling among the laity, though they realised that it was unavoidable in some instances, as the Jesuit Visitor of the Far Eastern missions reported in 1664: 'The merchandise of Macao depends on the sea, and the whole city lives by this means, there being nothing of value other than what is brought by the wind and the tides. If these fail then everything else fails, nor is it possible for this Province with its missions to maintain itself in any other way.' He added that since long experience had taught the citizens the truth of this fact, they no longer grumbled so much about the Jesuits' commercial activities as they had done in the palmy days of the Japan trade.

More serious, perhaps, were the equally numerous complaints that the religious Orders were wealthier than the laity, and that they owned a disproportionate amount of landed property, despite much legislation enacted to prevent this development. The Viceroy of India told the Crown in 1666 that many of the religious were rich, and those of them who were poor were sustained by the alms of laymen who were even more impoverished. 'It is very noteworthy,' he added, 'that Goa and its jurisdiction do not contain more than some 320 Portuguese householders, whereas the friars number over 700. There are five monasteries in Chaul, which place has only twenty-one householders; and Thana, which is a still smaller place, has four monasteries.' The Augustinian nuns of Santa Monica at Goa, and the Poor Clares of the Franciscan convent at Macao, were both accused of trading in competition with the local Portuguese merchants, and of lending money on *respondencia* (bottomry) to foreign traders. The constant refusal of the religious Orders to pay tithes and other imposts to the Crown tax-farmers is another perennial complaint which bulks large in the official correspondence from all quarters of the Portuguese seaborne empire. To give one out of many such instances, in 1656 the Crown gave categorical orders that the regular and secular clergy should not be exempted from paying their share of the taxes imposed in Brazil for the payment of the garrisons and for defence against the heretic Dutch, but the town council of Salvador complained in the following year: 'The religious Orders, which in this captaincy possess much property and many sugar-mills, estates, farms, houses, cattle and slaves, refuse to contribute anything at all to the cost of the war, so that the rest of the people are heavily burdened, and the poor suffer continual oppression.' In June 1661 the Governor-General of Brazil, Francisco Barreto, complained to the Crown that the religious Orders, and particularly the Jesuits, still refused to pay tithes on the plantations and estates which they possessed, although these lands were both extensive and profitable.

It was urged in defence of the religious Orders, whether in Asia, Africa or Brazil, that the Crown's original grants of land and endowments of their establishments overseas were usually inadequate to maintain them properly by the seventeenth century.

Hence they relied to a much greater extent on the proceeds from land, housing properties, livestock and other benefactions which pious testators bequeathed them, as well as utilising the capital accumulated by their trading and money-lending activities. Since testators' wills were usually prepared with the assistance of some religious, the Crown decreed that no testator could bequeath anything to the Order to which that particular priest or friar belonged. This law was easily and frequently evaded, as the Viceroy of India reported in 1666, and it is undeniable that in one way and another the religious Orders accumulated both urban and rural properties on an impressive scale. They were also, of course, large slave-holders in Brazil and Angola. The Jesuits at the time of their suppression in the Portuguese empire (1759–60) were undoubtedly the wealthiest of them all, even though the vast treasures of gold and silver which they were widely believed to possess in subterranean vaults and in iron coffers existed only in the imaginations of Pombal and their persecutors. At the time of their sequestration in Portuguese America, their extensive and varied properties included seventeen sugar plantations, seven ranches with more than 100,000 head of cattle on the Amazonian island of Marajó, and 186 buildings in the city of Salvador. But the income from these and many other rural and urban estates did not leave them a large financial surplus after paying for the upkeep of their nineteen colleges, five seminaries, several hospitals, over fifty mission villages (*aldeias*) and many smaller establishments, staffed by a total of over 400 Jesuits (exclusive of novices) between the Upper Amazon and Santa Catarina.

We are less well informed about the extent of the Jesuits' properties in India and the income which they derived from them. But it is certain that they possessed—as did the Mendicant Orders—*palmares*, rice-fields and other agricultural estates, particularly in the 'Province of the North' between *c.* 1550 and 1737, from which they derived funds to finance their missionary work. All the Orders likewise received some wealth from interest-bearing capital which they loaned to laymen, but no documented study has been made of this aspect of their economic activities. Four points may be made in conclusion. Firstly, the same laymen who penned long denunciations of the preponderant economic wealth of the Church often did their damnedest to get at least one of their sons into a religious Order and their daughters into a nunnery. Secondly, the ecclesiastically owned agricultural estates were, in all probability, usually better managed and more productive than those owned by their vociferous lay critics. Certainly many of the Jesuits' well-cultivated rural properties reverted to waste land and jungle after the suppression of the Society in the Portuguese dominions, 1759–60. Thirdly, even though the religious were often tax-dodgers, or evaded paying their fair share of fiscal burdens whenever they could, yet the Crown itself sometimes abused its *Padroado* right of ecclesiastical taxation, as it did in eighteenth-century Minas Gerais (p. 230). Last but not least, the religious Orders almost invariably dispensed free food and drink to the destitute of all ages and both sexes daily at their convent doors; whereas the only form of poor-relief practised by the Crown was to round up beggars and vagrants and pack them off to the colonies as *degredados*.

Disputes between the religious Orders and the tax-farmers of the Crown's ecclesiastical tithes formed only one aspect of the fluctuating relationship between successive Portuguese monarchs and their financiers. We have indicated above (pp. 321–2) the exceptional degree to which the Portuguese Crown farmed out all possible sources of revenue, even in an age when the Holy Roman Emperor exercised a copper-mining monopoly, the Most Christian King of France and the Catholic King of Spain tobacco monopolies, and the Duke of Bavaria one in beer—not forgetting the fact that from the reign of Charles II to that of George III the British government through the *Asiento* was the greatest promoter of the Negro slave trade in the world. In Portugal and its empire the Crown contractors were usually exempted from paying the normal taxes, such as *dizima* and *siza*, for the period of their respective contracts; and they were also exempted from military service, as were their representatives and employees. Crown contracts usually ran for a triennial period, and they might be operated by an individual or by a syndicate. Sub-contracting was common, especially in the larger and more complicated trades, such as the West African slave trade to Brazil. Contractors usually had to pay *propinas*, or rake-offs, to some of the Crown officials connected with the administration of their contracts. Some contractors made fortunes, others were bankrupted, and others oscillated between poverty and affluence. We have space only for one example of each of these categories.

One of the most successful businessmen of the sixteenth century was Lucas Giraldi, member of an Italian merchant family established at Lisbon. He contracted to buy all the sugar of the Crown tithes at Madeira in 1529, and from 1533 until his death in 1565 he was one of the leading contractors for the purchase of pepper and other spices in India and their sale at Lisbon and Antwerp. His other activities included the export of Negro slaves to the West Indies, a concession for the colonisation of Ilhéus in Brazil, and a partnership with the Cavalcanti Bank at Rome, through which he lent money to Portuguese diplomats and Italian ecclesiastics. He was a personal friend and the executor of the will of the famous Viceroy of Portuguese India, Dom João de Castro, a shipowner in the *carreira da Índia* and one of the principal buyers of jewels and precious stones at Goa through his resident agent there. Like many of the successful Italian merchants at Lisbon, he became a naturalised Portuguese, and his descendants intermarried with the Portuguese aristocracy and were absorbed by them. The same thing happened with some of his partners, the Affaitati from Cremona, who had become the Portuguese family of Lafetá by the end of the century.

Although Italian, German, Flemish and Spanish merchant-bankers played an important part as Crown financiers and contractors during the reigns of Dom Manuel and Dom João III, they did not always dominate the Portuguese economy as is sometimes assumed. During the second half of the century they were gradually replaced by their Portuguese partners and competitors, who were almost invariably 'New' Christians. In particular, these latter obtained a virtual monopoly of the contracts for the export of slaves from West Africa to Brazil and Spanish America, which they retained for a hundred years or more. Prominent among them was António Fernandes de Elvas, who operated the Angola and Cape Verde contracts in 1615–23. He died deeply indebted to the Crown, the deficit for the year 1619 alone amounting to 16,750,000 *reis*, which the Crown was still vainly trying to collect from his widow and heirs in 1635.

Dona Virginia Rau has traced for us the biography of one of the leading contractors and entrepreneurs in the Brazil trade during the eighteenth century. Manuel de Basto Viana, son of a modest Minhoto innkeeper, made his first fortune in Brazil by trading between Rio de Janeiro and Minas Gerais in the boom decade of the 1720s. Returning to Portugal in 1730, he married a girl from Braga and settled his business at Lisbon. In 1738 he contracted for the whole of the Brazilian salt-gabelle for a term of six years, with annual payments of 91,000 *cruzados* to the Crown. Accused of defaulting on his obligations to the amount of 33,300,000 *reis*, his large Lisbon house and all his goods and chattels were distrained for debt in 1744. Six years later he had made a second fortune, when he put in a bid (unsuccessful) of 140,000 *cruzados* for the tobacco monopoly at Rio de Janeiro. He died in May 1760, without having made a will, but leaving a substantial fortune to his family and reputed as one of the wealthiest and most active businessmen of Lisbon. As was usual in such cases, his eldest son and heir forsook a business career to become a lawyer and a Crown judge with the social status of a gentleman.

The social ascension of successful merchants, contractors and entrepreneurs was given a great impulse during the Pombaline dictatorship of 1750–77 through the privileged trading companies established by the omnipotent minister in his efforts to foster the development of a wealthy commercial class, as briefly indicated above (p. 192). Shareholders with more than ten shares in these two chartered companies were automatically given the status of gentlefolk (*nobreza*). One of the most successful of these new men was Pombal's friend and adviser, Inácio Pedro Quintela. Principal contractor of the immensely profitable Crown tobacco monopoly, he was a director both of the Pernambuco-Paraíba and the Pará-Maranhão companies; contractor, treasurer and administrator of the Brazilian whaling monopoly; monopolist of the Brazilian salt-gabelle and contractor of various other Brazilian tax-farms, and connected with a firm exporting tobacco to Spain. He held several other commercial and administrative posts of great importance, and was closely associated by marriage and business ties with others of Pombal's protégés, the wealthy entrepreneur family of Da Cruz. Their contemporary, Jacome Ratton, tells us in his *Memoirs* that these families introduced among the commercial classes 'a certain sociability and politeness' which had been lacking hitherto in the Portuguese bourgeoisie. 'In other words, they introduced the custom of giving parties, which was gradually extended to all the commercial class, and in imitation of them to other classes, which has greatly contributed to extinguishing what remained of the Moorish customs, and has brought the nation to the same level as the most polished countries in Europe.'

Oddly enough, Ratton, a French merchant and nationalised Portuguese who had lived in Lisbon since 1747, does not mention Pombal's decree of 1773, which abolished the invidious distinction between 'Old' and 'New' Christians. Yet this emancipatory measure must have done more to enhance the self-respect of the Lisbon commercial bourgeoisie than the soirées and receptions given by the Quintela and Da Cruz merchant-princes. We have seen above that by the early seventeenth century the terms 'New' Christian, 'merchant' and 'businessman' (*homem de negócio*) were virtually interchangeable, both in popular parlance and in official documents. In the course of the eighteenth century a distinction developed between the *homems de negócio*, who were essentially financiers and money-lenders, and the ordinary merchants and traders who usually lived over their shops. The distinction was not always a hard and fast one, it being sometimes sufficient for a prosperous trader to live 'nobly' in a house of his own at some distance from his shop, to qualify for the superior social status of the *homem de negócio*. In such cases they qualified as 'businessmen and wealthy merchants (*homems de negócio e mercadores de sobrado*), who did not weigh, measure, sell or pack goods with their own hands, but employed assistants specifically for such purposes'. Those traders who were genuine 'Old' Christians, such as Manuel de Basto Viana, strove to publicise the purity of their blood by becoming members of one of the lay brotherhoods (pp. 293–4), or, better still, as he did, a Familiar of the Inquisition. Of course, it does not follow that all merchants who were alleged to be 'New' Christians were in reality of Jewish origin, as this was an aspersion which jealous rivals or competitors could easily fasten on anyone they disliked. Nevertheless, it is clear from the Inquisition and other contemporary records that a high proportion of the wealthier traders and businessmen belonged to this unpopular category until well into the eighteenth century. The

British envoys at Lisbon during the first three decades of that century repeatedly stressed in their dispatches (to quote one of 1720) that 'the only rich merchants here are suspected or liable to suspicion of Judaism'. Most of them tried 'to keep their effects either in other countries, or so secretly lodged here that the Inquisition cannot reach them'. Numbers of them were, nevertheless, taken up by the Holy Office during this period; and some of the lucky ones managed to escape, with or without their capital, in English ships, despite reiterated orders that refugees from the Inquisition were not to be received on board them. But, as Lord Tyrawly notified his government in 1732, the English captains invariably ignored this order 'whenever a purse of gold shall be offered them, which has always been and will continue to be the motive for these practices'.

This continual emigration of 'New' Christian' commercial and financial talent from the reign of King John III to that of King John V was advantageous for the prosperity of Amsterdam, London, Rouen and Leghorn, but obviously disadvantageous for the Portuguese economy. It was clearly one of the reasons, perhaps the principal reason, why the foreign trading communities at Lisbon and Oporto, and above all the English 'factories' at those places, secured such a preponderant share of the export trade of Portugal, including that with Brazil.

Lord Tyrawly claimed in 1732 that 'the greatest dealers to Portugal in our woollen goods are the Jews of London', many of whom were refugees from the Portuguese Inquisition, but who continued trading with Lisbon under assumed names. They naturally preferred to deal with the English merchants at Lisbon rather than with Portuguese traders, since their goods and capital in the hands of the former were less liable to confiscation by the Holy Office. Ratton alleged that in 1755 there were only three Portuguese firms at Lisbon which practised double-entry bookkeeping, and whose directors were thoroughly familiar with foreign currencies, weights and measures, and with the trade movements and exchange rates at London, Amsterdam and Paris. Moreover, these three firms (Bandeira, Ferreira and Brito) all had foreign partners, and the foreign merchants at Lisbon all sent their sons abroad to be educated in commercial techniques, as Ratton did with his own, in France and Germany. He claimed that the *Aula do Commercio* (Commercial High School) established by Pombal had done excellent work in producing properly trained graduates by the end of the century. The reports of the French consuls at Lisbon between 1760 and 1790 also make it clear that during this period the Portuguese merchants trading to Brazil became increasingly active on their own account and were not, as many of them had been hitherto, simply agents for foreign (chiefly English) business firms established in the capital. But the further development of a strong and well-qualified commercial class was greatly hindered by Portugal's involvement in the Revolutionary and Napoleonic Wars and the subsequent civil strife and turmoil at home.

Portuguese complaints that foreign, and particularly English, merchants were monopolising and engrossing the export trade of Portugal, while often exaggerated, demonstrably had some basis of fact in the century *c.* 1654–1764. The privileged position of the English merchants, which dated back to medieval times, was enlarged and cemented by Cromwell's treaty imposed on the helpless King John IV in 1654—a *diktat* if ever there was one. Not unfairly described by the Marquis d'Abrantes in 1726 as 'the most pernicious that ever had been made with a crowned head', the treaty of 1654 gave the English a wide range of tax-exemptions, immunity from interference by the Inquisition, and a large measure of extraterritoriality. Most of these privileges were subsequently extended to other foreign traders in Portugal, beginning with the Dutch in 1662. Continual complaints by the English that their privileges were being constantly infringed, whittled away, or downright disregarded, are largely offset by the undeniable fact that their trade greatly expanded in volume and value during the same period. The Portuguese, on their side, complained with equal monotony and vehemence that the English and (to a lesser extent) other foreigners were driving an active contraband trade with Brazil, and were smuggling gold from Lisbon on a colossal scale, as we have seen that indeed they were (pp. 165–6).

Such practices were inevitable in a day and age when all governments strove to enforce monopolies of one kind and another, and when they often levied high duties on commodities that were in great demand. We have only to recall the avid desire for smuggled brandy and tobacco in eighteenth-century England, and the even greater demand for contraband tea before the passage of Pitt's Commutation Act in 1784. The *psychose de fraude*, which Huguette and Pierre Chaunu have documented so impressively in the Spanish-American transatlantic trade, was present in a greater or lesser degree in the seaborne trade of all the maritime and colonial powers. The Portuguese were no exception to this general rule, as we have already seen, and only a few further typical instances need be adduced here.

Afonso de Albuquerque, summing up in his inimitable way the tendency of the ill-paid colonial officials and others to embezzle, smuggle and defraud the Crown of its dues whenever they could, told King Manuel in 1510: 'The people in India have rather elastic consciences, and they think they are going on a pilgrimage to Jerusalem when they steal.' For most of the period between the reigns of King Manuel and King Joseph, it was the 'New' Christians who bore the brunt of the allegations, whether true or false, that they were not only monopolists and engrossers, but inveterate smugglers and contraband-traders. During the 'Sixty Years Captivity' of 1580–1640 Spanish memorialists deluged the Crown of Castile with complaints that Portuguese Marranos were monopolising the trade of the viceroyalties of Mexico and Peru 'from the vilest African Negro to the most precious pearl'. Such complaints were doubtless often exaggerated; but it is an easily ascertainable fact that such Portuguese traders were active and influential in places as far apart as Cartagena de las Indias, Mexico City, Lima, Potosí and Buenos Aires.

Typical of these Spanish complaints was a letter written by Gregorio Palma Hurtado from Cartagena de las Indias to the Crown in June 1610. He alleged that a Portuguese merchant at this port, Jorge Fernandes Gramaxo, was the centre of a commercial network whose agents were defrauding the Treasury of its dues by shipping 'vast quantities of contraband merchandise via Brazil', as well as in the licensed Portuguese slave-ships from Cape Verde and elsewhere. Fernandes Gramaxo kept his correspondents in Lisbon advised (by means of returning slave-ships and advice-boats sailing without convoy) of the state of the markets in Spanish America, so that they were able to supply goods in accordance with the varying regional demand for them before the Spanish merchants in the annual *flotas* could do so. Hurtado urged the Crown to deport all the Portuguese living in Spanish America, in order to deprive the monopolists and engrossers of Lisbon of their trusty agents there, since nothing would induce them to rely on Castilians. Cartagena de las Indias was the principal depot for the Portuguese slave-traders, and the 'New' Christians who monopolised these slave-import contracts —forerunners of the *Asientos* which the English enjoyed in the eighteenth century—had their agents and correspondents in all the principal European ports as well as in Brazil. The efforts of the Iberian governments and the Inquisition to break up this network by persecuting the principals in Spain and Portugal and confiscating their capital merely helped to divert most of their trade into the hands of the English merchants at Lisbon who were legally and largely immune from the attentions of the Inquisition. The place of the crypto-Jewish merchants and financiers could seldom or never be taken by 'Old' Christians, since these did not have the long-standing commercial connections in the principal European ports where the refugee Marrano communities were settled, and which their foreign competitors possessed.

We have seen that it was the smuggling of Brazilian gold which gave the Portuguese Crown its greatest fiscal headaches during the eighteenth century, and that this branch of contraband was one in which the English were very deeply involved. Royal Navy warships and the regular Falmouth–Lisbon packet-boats formed the favourite means of remittance for gold coin and bullion, since they were exempted from search by the Portuguese authorities. Their boats' crews also went armed, despite repeated efforts by the Portuguese government to stop this practice, and the mutual ill-will caused by the numerous waterfront affrays which resulted from it. Gold-smuggling was rife at all stages from the production of alluvial gold by the Negro slaves in Minas Gerais to its clandestine shipment from Lisbon by the English, as explained by Lord Tyrawly in 1732:

> The penalty of running gold is very great, no less than confiscation with banishment or the galleys, and the temptation to it is also very considerable. The King's *quinto* or fifth, and duty of coinage before the last year was 26¾ per cent, but by a new law it is reduced to about

20 per cent. The traders to the Mines, finding this duty too heavy upon them, have chose for several years to run the risk, which they have hitherto done with great success, and the gold they brought in this clandestine way, whether in dust or in bar, has been bought chiefly by our English factors, from whence our own mint in the Tower has been from time to time so well supplied.

Two years later Tyrawly told the Duke of Newcastle:

Your Grace perhaps does not know that there is not an English man-of-war homeward-bound from almost any point of the compass that does not take Lisbon in their way home, and more especially if it be at a time that the Portuguese Rio de Janeiro and Bahia fleets are expected. The reason of this is in hopes that when the effects of these fleets are given out, that they may pick up some freight by carrying part of it to England. This I know, my Lord, puts the King of Portugal out of all patience, because it is breaking in so plain and bare-faced a manner upon the prohibition of carrying money and gold dust out of the country.

Seven years later, on the eve of his departure from Lisbon, the irascible envoy confided to Newcastle: 'I would rather see Pandora's box with all the evils the poets feign it with come into this river than one of our men-of-war, whose sole view is in search of profit for themselves by carrying home merchants' money.' Tyrawly considered that gold-smuggling should be left to the masters and crews of the Falmouth packet-boats, who were much more tactful and less brazen about it.

Although periodic seizures of gold were made by the Lisbon Customs House officers when searching merchant-ships, these ill-paid officials were often easily bribed and induced to return the money. The contraband gold trade thus continued with only minor interruptions, as did the smuggling of all kinds of commodities, both in and out of Brazilian ports, in order to evade the prevailing high duties. The Crown naturally offered rewards to informers, but these gentry were evidently not very numerous in Brazil, since both rich and poor colonists benefited from participating in this contraband trade. 'To be an informer is the worst dishonour that can befall a man here,' wrote an eighteenth-century governor of Bahia. The numerous and repeated edicts threatening dire penalties against smugglers and contraband-traders, which were promulgated throughout the Portuguese colonial empire for over three centuries, clearly reflect the inefficacy of most of these enactments and the frequency with which they were evaded or ignored. The 'psychosis of fraud' to which we alluded above became an ingrained habit among mariners of all nations, as Lord Macartney noted on the occasion of his embassy to China in 1793–4:

> So strong is the passion for smuggling, and the habit of it so indefeasible to persons accustomed to it, that W. N. Hamilton, the second mate of the *Hindostan*, although all that ship's goods were exempted from duties, could not help smuggling, or bringing up under his coat a parcel of some watches, which coming in that manner were seized by the Emperor's officers, and confiscated, but afterwards restored on representation. And yet we complain of extortion and injustice in these people against whom we are constantly practising fraud and deception ourselves, and that too, as in this instance, without interest or provocation. If N.H. did it [concluded his lordship] what must others do who have stronger motives?

What indeed? The fascinating history of the contraband trade in Brazilian gold, when it comes to be written, will supply the answer.

CHAPTER XV

The 'Kaffirs of Europe', the Renaissance, and the Enlightenment

THE great Jesuit Padre António Vieira (1608–1697), though a patriotic Portuguese if ever there was one (*'et Dieu sait si l'on est patriote au Portugal!'* as a Belgian writer on Vieira observed recently), in moments of exasperation termed his compatriots *os Cafres da Europa*, 'the Kaffirs of Europe'. José Bonifácio de Andrada, the 'patriarch' of Brazilian independence, stigmatised his Luso-Brazilian countrymen in very similar terms while the Court of Dom João VI was still at Rio de Janeiro. Such sweeping condemnations of the Portuguese lack of intellectual curiosity need not be taken too seriously; but they reflect a charge which was levelled against Portuguese society in general for some three centuries, both by Portuguese intellectuals (as they would be called nowadays) and by foreign visitors and residents. Leading humanists of the Portuguese Renaissance, such as João de Barros, Sá de Miranda and Luís de Camões, all asserted in virtually identical terms that gentle blood and material wealth (*o sangue e os bens*) counted for more than learning and literature with their compatriots at home and overseas.

In 1603 Diogo do Couto, writing of some of the underground passages which he mistakenly believed to exist between Salsete and Cambay, alleged that the failure to explore them was

> due to the meanness and lack of curiosity of this our Portuguese nation; for until nowadays there has not been a viceroy, nor a captain of Baçaim, nor anyone else who has tried to reveal and probe these secrets, which it is highly desirable to know. This would not be so

with foreigners, who are much more politic and intelligent than we are, not only in important things like this, but in far more trivial matters, which they do not fail to probe and investigate until they understand them thoroughly.

Some two centuries later Brigadier Cunha Matos, after a lifetime spent in Portuguese West Africa and Brazil, lamented:

In point of fact, the Portuguese cannot nowadays evade the reproach of being ill-informed. I do not know whether this is due to self-centredness, or to laziness, or to dislike of being considered as mere writers. Perhaps also the high cost of publication, and the necessity of submitting unpublished works to the government censors, tend to prevent the Portuguese from publishing their literary works when these impinge on anything which comes under the heading of 'Reason of State'. . . Things will indeed go ill for Portugal if the governors of the colonies do not try to advance the geographical and political knowledge of the countries which are confided to them. For my part, I have done what I could, and I would have done more if I had been better supported.

Foreign criticisms of Portuguese ignorance or indifference were often either malicious or superficial; but many sensible foreigners who knew the country and the people well voiced similar sentiments. Francis Parry, the English envoy at Lisbon in 1670, observed that 'the people are so little curious that no man knows more than what is merely necessary for him'. Over a century later Jacome Ratton complained that:

Geography, so well treated by Camoens in his epic poem, was so little regarded in my day that when I tried to buy some maps from booksellers and print-dealers, they all replied that they had none, since this line sold very slowly in this country, and they ordered them piecemeal in small quantities owing to the length of time they remained unsold in their shops.

Adolfo Coelho (1847–1919), Portugal's pioneer philologist in modern times, stated that intellectual and scientific pursuits, or even simple curiosity about them, developed only tardily and incompletely among all classes in Portugal as compared with other countries. It would not be difficult to assemble much more evidence in support of Mary Brearley's assertion that 'the bulk of the people were disinclined to independence of thought and, in all but a few instances, too much averse from intellectual activity to question what they had learned'.

Some of the foreign criticisms could have been applied, at least in part, to the compatriots of those individuals who made them. The average well-born—though not necessarily well-bred—English country gentleman in the seventeenth century was far more interested in horses and hounds (and in the bottle) than in books and manuscripts. He would undoubtedly have considered himself to be vastly superior to an Oxford don, let alone a country parson, unless these were from families of the same social status as his own. Similarly the vast majority of European laymen who emigrated overseas to the forts, the factories and the settlements of their respective nations, went with the idea of bettering themselves materially, and not with the intention of writing books which would advance the horizons of knowledge. Nevertheless, when due allowance is made for the human tendency to see the beam in our neighbour's eye while ignoring the mote in our own, the conviction that Portugal was a backward country (even more so than Spain) persisted among many people for centuries. This was just as true of Roman Catholic French and Italians as of Protestant English and Dutch; although Giacome Leopardi (1795–1837) was evidently exaggerating somewhat when he wrote that nobody would think of including Spaniards and Portuguese among the civilised peoples of the world. Such scathing indictments may well have been fostered by the Jesuit-phobia of Pombal. In his efforts to discredit the Society of Jesus the Portuguese dictator stressed time and again in his propaganda that the machinations of the Fathers had reduced the Portuguese to the intellectual level of 'the Malabars, the Chinese, the Japanese, the Negroes of Africa and the Indians of America'.

Criticisms of the intellectual backwardness of the inhabitants of the home country were inevitably extended to include those of the colonies, and it is worth considering how far they were justified. Any such consideration must begin by emphasising the preponderant role played by the Church in Portugal and its overseas possessions, to which frequent allusions have already been made. The traditional and deeply rooted Portuguese veneration for the clergy was typically expressed by the Luso-Brazilian writer Nuno Marques Pereira, whose *Compendio Narrativo do*

Peregrino da America went through five editions between 1728 and 1765. Explaining why the sacerdotal calling is superior to all others, he wrote:

> If the Angels were capable of feeling envy, it seems that they would be envious only of the priests. And consider why. With five words they can bring God himself down into their hands; and with another five they can open the gates of Heaven to a sinner and close those of Hell: the first five words being those of consecration, and the second five those of absolution. How could there be any greater power or empire in any living creature? Many authors affirm that if they saw an angel and a priest together they would first respectfully greet the priest by virtue of his authority.

One is reminded of James Joyce's similar emphasis: 'No king or emperor on this earth has the power of the priest of God . . . the power, the authority, to make the great God of Heaven come down upon the altar and take the form of bread and wine.'

This stress on the sacerdotal and sacro-magical aspects of religion naturally implied that the ordained priest had a singularly privileged position in Portuguese society, as exemplified in the popular proverb: 'The worst priest is better than the best layman.' The fact that higher education was concentrated almost entirely in the hands of the Church further strengthened the social position of the clergy. Moreover, the Church was the best and easiest way of ascension in the social hierarchy for the able and ambitious son of a poor family—always provided that he could establish that he was of unblemished 'Old' Christian stock from about 1550 onwards. At the top of the social ladder, high positions in the Church were secured from a complacent Papacy by successive monarchs for their sons or nephews—irrespective of whether they were legitimate or illegitimate. The second sons of the higher nobility likewise were often destined for the Church, as they were in other countries. Even the deeply devout King John III, while warmly pressing the Papacy at Rome to mend its ways and abolish nepotism, continued to secure bishoprics and abbeys for scions of the aristocracy who were often unfitted for them.

Although the clergy were, generally speaking, better educated than the laity, there were many exceptions, particularly in the remoter parts of the countryside, where there was no great competition for livings. The Archbishop of Braga, after visiting the rural districts of his diocese, lamented in 1553 'the harm caused by the ignorance of the greater part of the clergy'. Seven years later his successor, the saintly Fr. Bartholomeu dos Martires, complained that 'after visiting personally a great part of our archbishopric, we found, apart from what we had been told previously, that there was a great want of qualified persons to preach the word of God and the catechism, both among the clergy and the laity', especially in mountainous Tras-os-Montes. A contemporary Jesuit alleged that the country people of Beira needed elementary religious instruction almost as much as did the newly arrived Negro slaves from Guinea. The foundation of seminaries, as enjoined by the Council of Trent, and still more the action of the Jesuits by precept and example, did something to remedy this state of affairs. But the low intellectual level of many of the Portuguese clergy at home and overseas continued to arouse unfavourable comment for centuries. In 1736 Dom Luís da Cunha went so far as to deplore that there was no native Protestant community in Portugal, since it was the challenge posed by the Huguenots which had kept the French Roman Catholic clergy up to the mark and prevented them from sinking to the 'sordid' level of their Portuguese counterparts.

Conditions in Portugal were inevitably reflected in the Church overseas. We have seen that it was the Jesuits who, by and large, maintained higher standards in the mission-fields than did their colleagues of the Mendicant Orders and the secular clergy. Conscious of their moral and their intellectual superiority, and proud of their tightly knit *esprit de corps*, the Jesuits were apt to give offence by their contemptuous impatience of lesser men. In 1639 a lay-brother who had been expelled from the Society could publicly boast that a cook in a Jesuit House was a better theologian than any erudite Franciscan friar. In 1605 two adventurous Spanish Dominican friars from the Philippines, who had stayed for some time at Goa on their way back to Europe, reported that although the Jesuits were using some very questionable missionary methods, nobody dared to criticise them openly, as their power and influence with the home government were believed to be dangerously great. 'A Viceroy thinks that if he has them for his friends he has no need of any other agents for his affairs at

His Majesty's Court, and that if they are his enemies then he will have the whole world against him.' Dominican criticisms of the Jesuits must often be taken with more than a pinch of salt, but similar complaints were made at this period by the municipal councillors and by Franciscan friars at Goa. 'The nib of a Jesuit's pen is more to be feared than the point of an Arab's sword' was a proverb in Portuguese India at the end of the seventeenth century. Jesuits were often confessors to governors and other high officials, who frequently sought their advice on mundane matters as well. Their influence was undeniably great in every sphere of life and work in the Portuguese world.

Nowhere was it greater than in that of education. They had secured control of the College of Arts, which formed the preparatory college for the University of Coimbra, in 1555, with the exclusive right of publicly teaching Latin and philosophy. It was thus the gateway to the university proper, with its four faculties of theology, canon law, civil law and medicine. A few years later their college at Evora was raised to a university with the same status and privileges as those of Coimbra, save only that Evora did not have a faculty of civil law nor one of medicine. Coimbra and Evora remained the only two universities in the Portuguese world until Pombal suppressed the latter in 1759–60, and drastically reorganised the former in 1772. Coimbra then reverted to its original status as the sole Portuguese university until the liberal republican government created those of Lisbon and Oporto in 1911. Both the Jesuits and the citizens of Bahia several times petitioned the Crown to raise the local Jesuit College to the status of a university, but without success, partly because of the opposition of the university and the Jesuits at Coimbra. This niggardly attitude to colonial education contrasts unfavourably with that of the Spanish monarchs, who encouraged the foundation of universities in the New World in the sixteenth century (Santo Domingo 1511, Mexico City 1533, Lima 1571).

Apart from their privileged positions at Coimbra and Evora, the Jesuits had a virtual monopoly of higher education through the network of colleges which they established in Portugal and her empire, literally from the Maranhão to Macao. These colleges were attended by the sons of the local aristocracy and gentry, as well as by those of the middle class, or even working class on occasion, who were anxious for their boys to have the best available education. In all of these colleges the instruction was based on the Jesuit pedagogical manual *Ratio Studiorum*, which received its definitive form in 1599 and remained essentially unaltered until the nineteenth century. The education given by the Jesuits, though originally the best of its day and generation, as Francis Bacon testified, did not keep pace with the expansion of knowledge and the ferment of ideas in the seventeenth century. With some relatively minor exceptions it became formalistic, pedantic and conservative, with Latin as the medium of instruction for most subjects. Particular attention was paid to the teaching of grammar, dialectic (=logic) and rhetoric. The main objectives were to develop and polish the pupils' use of Latin, both oral and written; to foster their capacity for scholastic argument within the limits of the strictest Roman Catholic orthodoxy; and to indulge in literary conceits and exhibitionism, through debates, recitations and competitions, theatrical representations, etc.

Both teachers and pupils were usually discouraged from doing anything which might lead them to develop an independent critical judgement, or to advance propositions which were not supported by chapter and verse from the established and recognised authorities, or which might cast any doubt on the philosophical principles and the authority of Aristotle and St. Thomas Aquinas. Macaulay was not far wrong when he qualified his observation that no religious community could produce a list of men so distinguished for learning as the Jesuits, with the rider that 'the Jesuits appear to have discovered the precise point to which intellectual culture can be carried without the risk of intellectual emancipation'. The conferment of degrees in civil law and in medicine remained the exclusive privilege of the University of Coimbra, but some instruction in history, geography and mathematics was given in the Jesuit colleges when there was a demand for them.

Emphasis on classical studies was one aspect of humanism which the Jesuits adopted; but their enthusiastic cultivation of Latin (they were far less concerned with Greek and Hebrew) did not lead them to accept any Greek or Roman philosophical ideas which might run counter to orthodox Roman Catholic Christianity as defined at the Council of Trent. As the young King

Sebastian's Jesuit tutor Martim Gonsalves da Camara observed, it was better to educate students to be 'good Christians and Catholics rather than good latinists' (*mais cristãos e catolicos, ainda que menos latinos*). This attitude was the prevailing one for centuries, but at any rate the Jesuits did turn out many educated men who possessed both qualifications. Their college libraries at Goa, Macao and Bahia were as well stocked with standard editions of Cicero, Sallust, Virgil, Terence, Horace, etc., as were those of Coimbra, Lisbon and Portalegre. The Mendicant Orders likewise maintained some colleges and schools where similar instruction was given, but these institutions were, as a general rule, neither so numerous nor so efficiently managed as were those of the Jesuits. Their libraries were also generally less impressive, though foreign visitors to the Augustinian monastery at Goa noted that it had a magnificent library which rivalled that of the Jesuit College of St. Paul.

The success of the ecclesiastical and civil authorities in ensuring (from about 1555 onwards) that all education should be given within the limits of the strictest Roman Catholic orthodoxy, was largely attained through the organisation of a vigilant literary censorship. The Portuguese branch of the Inquisition promulgated its first list of prohibited books in 1547. This list was successively augmented in later editions, culminating in a very comprehensive one of 1624. The prohibited books included not only those by heretic or free-thinking authors, but even some works by such devoutly Catholic writers as Gil Vicente, João de Barros and Fray Luis de Granada, O.P. From *c.* 1550 onwards, no book could be published in Portugal without running the gauntlet of a triple censorship: that of the civil *Desembargo do Paço*, or High Court of Justice; that of the ecclesiastical authority in the bishopric concerned; and that of the Holy Office of the Inquisition. The importation of books from abroad was carefully controlled by inspectors deputed by the Holy Office to meet all incoming shipping and by the periodic inspection of bookshops and libraries. This triple censorship functioned both vigilantly and effectively for the best part of three centuries, although it began to slacken its efforts in the reign of King John V (1706–50). This form of 'thought control' was a much greater deterrent than it was in some other countries, such as England and France, where government censorship existed but was not so rigorous, or in the northern Netherlands where it operated on a provincial basis and was often a mere farce.

In so far as the overseas empire was concerned, virtually all potential authors had to send their manuscript works to Portugal for censorship and publication, and this procedure naturally involved vexatious delays apart from anything else. An enterprising Lisbon publisher established a press at Goa in 1560, but this was soon taken over by the Jesuits, who also maintained mission presses at various times and places, including Japan, Peking, Macao and Malabar. These presses naturally concentrated on the publication of works which were strictly relevant to their missionary and their teaching methods. A tentative check-list of books published at Goa in the sixteenth and seventeenth centuries shows that only two out of some forty extant titles were written by laymen. One of these two was the famous *Coloquios dos simples e drogas da India* (*Colloquies of the simples and drugs of India*) by the crypto-Jewish physician Garcia d'Orta, which came off the press in 1563; but it had a far wider circulation abroad in the numerous translations and adaptations made by Carolus Clusius (1526–1609) than it ever obtained in the Portuguese world, where it lay neglected for centuries.

The Jesuit mission presses in Asia published a variety of grammars and guides to vernacular languages, including Tamil, Japanese and Marathi-Konkani, for which the missionaries deserve great credit. But the rigours of the Portuguese government and ecclesiastical censorship form another unfavourable contrast with the relatively more liberal attitude of the Castilian kings. The Spanish monarchs allowed printing-presses to function in their American possessions (under local censorship, of course) from relatively early dates—Mexico in 1539, Peru in 1584, the Philippines in 1593. In 1706, and again in 1747, the Portuguese government swiftly suppressed a couple of attempts to start printing and publishing in Brazil. The Portuguese missionaries in Brazil and Angola had to send their grammars, catechisms and dictionaries of native languages to Portugal for censorship, printing and publication. Their Spanish colleagues could and did see theirs through the presses at Mexico City, Lima and Manila. It is typical of the 'enlightened despot' Pombal that when he was asked to consider the re-establishment of a press at Goa he brusquely rejected the suggestion.

The imposition of such rigid and effective controls on the publication and circulation of books, the abiding strength of Portuguese religious orthodoxy (Portugal was the only nation to accept at once and unhesitatingly all the final decisions of the Council of Trent), and the naturally conservative temper of the great majority of the people—all these factors help to explain why the Renaissance had such a relatively brief flowering in Portugal. During the last years of the fifteenth century and the first half of the sixteenth, many Portuguese had gone abroad to study at the universities of Spain, France, Belgium, Italy and (in a very few instances) England; some at their own expense and others subsidised by the Crown. King John III was a particularly generous patron of learning in this respect, maintaining a large number of Portuguese students at the University of Paris (*bolseiros del Rei*) and inviting several distinguished foreign humanists (including the Fleming Nicholas Cleynaerts and the Scot George Buchanan) to work and teach in Portugal. But the rising tide of heresy in northern Europe on the one hand and the growing strength of the Counter-Reformation on the other inclined him more to the latter camp during the last years of his life as it had done with the Emperor Charles V a few years earlier. After his death, and with the increasing power of the Jesuits and of the Inquisition, the triumph of religious orthodoxy became complete. No more Portuguese scholars were sent to study abroad with the idea that they would make suitable professors at Coimbra on their return. The Erasmian ideals which had flourished in a modest way at the Courts of Manuel I and John III were no longer openly professed by 1580, though they were still to be found in a vestigial form in Portuguese literature as late as the early seventeenth century.

No national culture can have a healthy and continuous growth without being periodically fertilised by fresh inspiration and new ideas from abroad. This was almost impossible in Portugal between about 1560 and 1715, owing to the factors mentioned above, the strongest of which was the fear of foreign heresy. This danger did not yet exist in 1483, when King John II, 'the perfect prince', authorised two French booksellers to import tax-free as many books as they chose 'because it is good for the common weal to have many books circulating in our kingdom'. A century later this enlightened attitude had been completely reversed. Thenceforward the one idea of Church and State was to exclude all foreign books, save only those on canon law, hagiography, and such innocuous topics. The censorship was not, of course, equally efficient and equally ruthless everywhere and always. The Portuguese Jesuits, or some of them, seem to have accepted and even taught Harvey's theory of the circulation of blood at Coimbra and Bahia. But when the scientific discoveries and the philosophical ideas of Galileo, Bacon, Descartes, Newton, Huyghens, Hobbes, Leibnitz and others were being more or less freely discussed in northern Europe and in Italy, the Jesuits of Portugal (like those of Spain) declined to publicise them in their teachings and expressly banned their discussion as late as 1746.

The Portuguese did not make adequate use of the scientific discoveries to which their fifteenth- and sixteenth-century navigators (Duarte Pacheco, Dom João de Castro), mathematicians (Pedro Nunes), physicians (Garcia d'Orta) and others had made such striking contributions. It was left to a Dutchman, Linschoten, to popularise the Portuguese *roteiros* or sailing directions, in the same way as Clusius had popularised the botanical works of Garcia d'Orta and Christovão da Costa. From being leaders in the van of navigational theory and practice, the Portuguese dropped to being stragglers in the rear. By the end of the seventeenth century several of their pilots in the *carreira da India* were foreigners, and they were using foreign nautical charts in preference to their own. The Jesuits did maintain an *aula da esfera*, which included a course of mathematics and theoretical navigation at their Lisbon College of Santo Antão, but its great days were over by the end of the sixteenth century.

To their credit the Jesuits did not confine themselves to collegiate and university education, but they maintained the equivalents of kindergartens and primary schools in connection with some of their colleges, both at home and overseas. Peter Mundy gives us a charming glimpse of a play acted by over a hundred children which he saw at the Jesuit College of Macao in December 1637:

It was part of the life of this much renowned Saint Francis Xavier, in the which were divers pretty passages, viz.–A China dance by children in China habit; a battle between the Portugals and the Dutch in a dance, where the Dutch were overcome, but without any reproachful speech or disgraceful action to that nation. Another dance of broad crabs, commonly called stool crabs, being so many boys very prettily and wittily disguised into the said form, who all sang and played on instruments as though they had been so many crabs. Another dance of children so small that it almost seemed impossible it could have been performed by them (for it might be doubted whether some of them were able to go or no), chosen of purpose to breed admiration. Last of all an Antic, wherein one of them (the same that represented Francis Xavier) showed such dexterity on a drum, tossing it aloft, turning and whirling it about with such exceeding quickness, withal keeping touch and stroke with the music, that it was admirable to the beholders. The children were very many, very pretty, and very richly adorned both in apparel and precious jewels; it being the parents' care to set them forth for their own content and credit, as it was the Jesuits to instruct them, who not only in this, but in all other manner of education are the tutors and have the care of the bringing up the youth and young children of this town, especially those of quality. The theatre was in the church and the whole action was performed punctually. Not so much as one among so many (although children and the play long) was much out of his part. For indeed there was a Jesuit on the stage that was their director as occasion offered.

Mutatis mutandis, similarly elaborate theatrical spectacles were frequently staged at Jesuit colleges throughout the Portuguese world, even in such unlikely places as the slave-trading centre of São Paulo de Luanda. The plays staged by the older pupils were for the most part written and performed in Latin. In this neo-Latin theatre the Portuguese certainly showed themselves to be good Catholics and good Latinists.

Despite this idyllic glimpse of Portuguese colonial life from Peter Mundy's journal, the Jesuits often found it hard to educate their pupils in the way they should go in the tropical world with its enervating climate and demoralising slave households. A Jesuit who attended a Latin play by the pupils of the college at Goa, performed before the Viceroy and a large audience in October 1855, commented:

By the goodness of God, everything went off very well and smoothly, and everyone agreed that it was a very necessary and edifying thing. For in this way the students are encouraged to persevere in their studies, and the parents are induced to send their children to school. But education is very difficult in this region, as it is very hot and enervating; and also because the people who live here commonly give themselves no sort of trouble about any kind of work.

Some twenty years later the Jesuit Visitor, Valignano, remarked despondently that Portuguese India was a frontier land of war and trade, rather than one of learning and study. Similar complaints came from Brazil, where the saintly Anchieta wrote at Bahia in 1586: 'The students in this country, as well as being few, likewise know but little, owing to lack of ability and want of application. Nor does the nature of the country help of itself, for it is relaxing, slothful and melancholic, so that all the time is spent in *festas*, in singing, and in making merry.' The Jesuits persisted, and they must be given full credit for the remarkable, if intellectually rigidly circumscribed, educational work which they performed in the tropical world until the catastrophe of 1759–60.

Since ecclesiastical influence was so strong in all spheres of education from the village priest's school (or the Jesuit kindergarten) to the university, it is not surprising that painting, handicrafts, architecture and music were all indelibly marked with this stamp. Portuguese painting was for centuries almost entirely devoted to representing religious themes, lay portraits being very rare, and landscapes almost unknown. The chief patrons of art were the heads of the churches, the monasteries and the convents. They naturally ordered only religious paintings for their interior decoration, whether in Portugal, in Brazil, or in Asia and Africa. The Portuguese kings, nobles and prelates likewise seem to have preferred religious subjects for such pictures as they had in their own palaces and houses. Moreover, they usually collected Flemish and Italian paintings in preference to Portuguese. The low social status accorded to professional painters, who were contemptuously classified as mere *mecânicos*, did not help to forward the progress of their art. Francisco de Holanda, Michelangelo's Portuguese friend and admirer, complained bitterly of the lack of aristocratic patronage in his day, as did other Portuguese artists down to the reign of King John V. Due to their modest social condition, many of them did not sign their works, and this in turn makes their identification difficult.

The religious Orders often provided their own artists and craftsmen from among their lay-brothers, and they likewise trained some of their indigenous converts to become painters, sculptors and craftsmen of various kinds. These men, whether Europeans, Asians, Africans or Amerindians, were also regarded as being relatively obscure in the scheme of things, and few of their names have survived. On the other hand, some of their surviving works reveal admirable technical and artistic ability, whether Indo-Portuguese ivory carvings, church furniture from Brazil, Africa and Asia, or the Japanese lacquer-work and gilded screens which were influenced by European art motifs.

Architects were also to be found in the ranks of the religious Orders, on whom the Bolognese architect, Filippo Terzi, exercised a great attraction between about 1590 and 1720, when Italianate influence was at its height. An interesting synthesis of Eastern and Western artistic influences and techniques was provided by the Jesuit Collegiate church at Macao. Designed by an Italian Jesuit, Carlo Spinola, later martyred in Japan (1622), and decorated by Chinese and Japanese craftsmen under Jesuit supervision, it aroused the admiration of Peter Mundy in 1637:

> The roof of the church appertaining to the college (called St. Paul) is of the fairest arch that yet I ever saw to my remembrance, of excellent workmanship, done by the Chinese, carved in wood, curiously gilt and painted with exquisite colours, as vermilion, azure, etc., divided into squares; and at the joining of each square, great roses of many folds or leaves, one under another, lessening until all end in a knob; near a yard diameter the broadest, and a yard perpendicular to the knob standing from the roof downwards. Above there is a new fair frontispiece to the said church with a spacious ascent to it by many steps. The last two things mentioned are of hewn stone.

Unfortunately this superb building was destroyed by fire in 1835, with the exception of the stone façade, which still stands with its curious mixture of Occidental and Oriental art motifs.

The richly decorated church of Bom Jesus at Old Goa, which was built about the same time, is one of the best surviving examples of Jesuit church architecture and decoration overseas, but many of the more modest chapels and hermitages were equally remarkable in their way. As a Portuguese missionary in Asia commented in 1691: 'The churches are beautifully clean, even the smallest hermitages. If God still preserves us in India, it is because of the grandeur, magnificence and ostentation with which the churches are maintained and the divine worship celebrated. The smallest village church here can put to shame those of the best towns in Portugal.' That true-blue Protestant, Mrs. Nathaniel Kindersley, who found plenty to criticise during her stay at Bahia in 1764, was constrained to admit of the churches which she visited:

Some of them are large and superb, and by being unencumbered with pews, the double rows of pillars have a very fine effect, and give the whole choir an open airy appearance which our churches can never have. They are kept in the greatest order, and adorned, particularly the altars, with carving, paintings, and gilding; with candlesticks and ornaments of gold and silver to a vast expense.

If the Renaissance, Mannerist and Baroque churches, monasteries, chapels and hermitages which the Portuguese scattered throughout the length and breadth of their overseas empire, still form their most impressive historical monuments, almost equally so is the chain of coastal forts and castles which ran from Morocco to the Moluccas (and to the Rio de la Plata). In most instances the military architects and engineers were Portuguese, but between about 1550 and 1630 some of the best were Italian, as the Italians were then the acknowledged masters of the art of fortification. The castle of Diu off the Kathiawar peninsula in north-west India is, perhaps, the most impressive of the surviving strongholds, its cyclopean walls and bulwarks recalling those of Malta and Rhodes. But Ceuta, Tangier, Mazagão, Ormuz, Muscat, Malacca and Macao were all famous in their day and generation, as were Moçambique and Mombasa on the East African coast, both of which are now carefully restored and maintained.

Even in the remote island of Solor in the Lesser Sunda group the Portuguese built a castle whose strength surprised its Dutch besiegers in 1613. There was another in the even obscurer Indonesian island of Endeh, which has a romantic legend still attached to it. The ubiquity of these coastal fortifications in Asia helps to explain why almost any old stone ruin is ascribed to the Portuguese by the local inhabitants in the same way as English yokels ascribe relatively recent stone ruins to 'the old monks' or 'to the Romans'. These forts were built by local labour, but under the direction of Portuguese master-masons. In the instance of Moçambique (and probably of Mombasa and some other forts as well), Gujarati stone-masons were hired as contract-labour from Diu. With the exception of the two castles in Guinea at Mina and Axim, the Portuguese settlements in West Africa and Brazil had no adequate fortifications before the Dutch war of 1600–63. Those which form the tourist attractions of today date from the late seventeenth and from the eighteenth century.

Portuguese private housing, naturally enough, did not partake of the monumental character of so much of the religious and military architecture. The poor lived in ground-floor hovels, or in tightly packed tenements, as they did elsewhere. The town houses of the nobility and gentry, and those of the wealthy merchants, were often large and spacious, but the rooms were apt to be badly arranged and sparsely furnished, according to the nearly unanimous testimony of foreign visitors to Lisbon, Bahia and Goa. One of the few exceptions is Peter Mundy, who commended the 'very fair houses', richly furnished with Chinese and Japanese art-objects, which he visited at Macao in 1637. Another exception is formed by the delightful Portuguese *quintas* and *solares* (country-houses and manors), built or reconstructed with the gold from Brazil in the eighteenth century, and which still await their art-historian.

The seventeenth century in Portugal was characterised by the development of a strongly ingrowing nationalism, taking such forms as Sebastianism and Messianism, which are discussed in the next chapter. The exhausting wars with the Dutch and the Spaniards, and the severe economic depression which followed them, were not particularly conducive to a renewal of intellectual contacts with the rest of Europe, although the close political relationship between the Courts of Portugal and France facilitated the infiltration of French cultural influences at the expense of those of Spain. Portugal's unhappy involvement in the War of the Spanish Succession was a further setback to normal progress, but the years of peace inaugurated by the Treaty of Utrecht coincided with the exploitation of the gold and diamond mines of Brazil. These developments gave not merely King John V but the country at large a feeling of security and self-confidence. This in turn created more favourable conditions for the reception of foreign ideas and influences. In the 'Golden Age' of King John V we find, if on a modest scale, a thirst after knowledge and an interest in the cultured world beyond the Pyrenees among some of the aristocracy and the higher bourgeoisie.

These men, who were designated by the rather derogatory term of *estrangeirados* ('foreignised', 'denaturalised'), included *fidalgos* such as the ambassador Dom Luís da Cunha (1662–1740), the fourth (1673–1743) and fifth (1689–1742) Counts of Ericeira and the third Count of Assumar (1688–1756). Either through residence abroad or through the study of foreign (mainly French) books and ideas, they became dissatisfied with Portugal's cultural isolation, and they wished to raise their country to the level of the more advanced nations. Most of the *estrangeirados*, whether of aristocratic or of bourgeois origins, would have subscribed to many of the ideas advocated by Dom Luís da Cunha, who was in some ways their oracle. He set down his ideas and his criticisms of the existing regime on paper towards the end of his long life, and they circulated confidentially among his friends and sympathisers, although they were not printed until the nineteenth century.

Dom Luís criticised the despotic attitude of King John V, who seldom consulted his advisory council of state. He was critical of the aristocratic 'Old' Christians, who called themselves *Puritanos* (Puritans) and refused to intermarry with any family that had a drop of 'New' Christian blood. He was critical of the cruel procedures of the Holy Office, and contemptuous of those *fidalgos* who eagerly competed for the honour of becoming Familiars of the Inquisition. He criticised what he termed the 'unbridled ambition' of the Jesuits and their pliable theology, which he alleged made them complacent confessors to kings and princes, but strict with the common people. He denounced the multiplication of the religious Orders, who then (so he said) owned nearly a third of the land in Portugal, and he criticised the ignorance of both the friars and the secular clergy. He deplored the government's failure to foment agriculture and industry, thus reducing Portugal to the role of 'the best and most profitable colony of England'.

The *estrangeirados* wished to introduce the scientific and philosophical works of Bacon, Galileo, Newton, Gassendi and others into Portugal, and to reform higher education by separating philosophy from theology and by introducing new subjects into the curriculum. Naturally they differed among themselves in some matters, and several of them advocated going considerably farther and faster than did others. Martinho de Mendonça (1693–1743), who based his own *Apontamentos para a educação dum menino nobre* (1734, reprinted 1761) mainly on John Locke's *Some thoughts concerning education*, which he had studied in a French version, was a self-conscious 'Old' Christian who was proud of being a Familiar of the Inquisition. On the other hand, Alexandre de Gusmão (1695–1753), who was of 'New' Christian origin, was much more critical of clerical obscurantism. The same was true of Dr. António Ribeiro Sanches (1699–1782), who invented the term *parvoice de frades* ('friars' folly'), which was used as a battle-cry by nineteenth-century liberals, and whose religious beliefs by the end of his life amounted to a form of Deism. The two Ericeiras, father and son, were sincerely devout Roman Catholics; but they shared the view of the majority of the *estrangeirados* that many heretic authors could safely be followed and trusted in anything which did not directly impugn the basic tenets of the faith.

The attitude of King John V to the *estrangeirados* was ambivalent, reflecting the dichotomy of his own character. His personality was split between what Lord Tyrawly termed his naturally quick and lively intelligence and his almost cretinous form of Catholicism, which was the result of his education by priests and women. He was determined to be an absolute monarch after the style of Louis XIV, and for this reason he mistrusted the higher nobility as a general rule. He took his confidential advisers from all sorts and conditions of men, including a *valet de chambre*, his private secretary, Alexandre de Gusmão, the Italian Jesuit Carbone, and Cardinal da Mota. At one time he banished nearly all of the higher nobility from the Court, and he barely concealed his personal dislike of the two 'enlightened' Counts of Ericeira. Yet he sometimes asked for their advice, though he did not always take it. He promised the elder Ericeira that he would pay the expense of translating and publishing all of Francis Bacon's works in Portuguese—a promise which he did not fulfil.

He was anti-semitic in a crudely reactionary way, and an assiduous attender at *autos da fé*; yet he patronised (at a distance and for a time) the exiled Jewish Dr. Jacob de Castro Sarmento in England. He lavishly endowed the library of the Oratorian Fathers at Lisbon, and he implicitly approved of the new methods which they introduced into their teaching; but in other respects he continued to favour the Jesuits. He accepted the proposals of the Chief Engineer, Azevedo Fortes (1660–1749), for a complete renovation in the teaching of mathematics, military engineering and astronomy, spending large sums on the purchase of maps, charts and scientific instruments from abroad, but he did not finance all of these projects through to the end. He made an excellent start with the mapping of the interior regions and the frontiers of Brazil, dispatching a team of experts to make surveys for this purpose; but he failed to implement his promise to Azevedo Fortes that he would finance a triangulation and topographical survey of Portugal itself, despite constant reminders from the disgruntled Chief Engineer. He founded a royal academy of history at Lisbon in 1720, whose fifty members were exempted from all forms of outside censorship, including that of the Inquisition. This academy was to compile a gigantic history of Portugal and its overseas possessions, primarily ecclesiastical and political, but one which would also include relevant geographical, ethnographical and natural history materials as well. Unfortunately, many of the nobles and priests whom he nominated as academicians had no proper qualifications for this task; and he allowed their meetings to degenerate, for the most part, into fulsome panegyrics of the royal family and mutual eulogies of each other.

King John V sent Luís António Verney (1713–1792) to Rome with the intention that the latter should, in due course, produce a plan for the complete reform of the Portuguese educational system. This Verney did in his *Verdadeiro Methodo de estudar* (*True Method of studying*), but King John V failed to support the publication of this work, which had to be issued anonymously and clandestinely in three editions, 1746–51. In this famous book Verney violently criticised the Jesuits' pedagogical methods and the textbooks used in their curriculum. He advocated that the subjects taught in schools and universities should be primarily selected for their practical utility and relevance to daily life. He stressed the importance of teaching the vernacular and of modern foreign languages, specially French and Italian. He urged the substitution of the Jesuits' singularly complicated Latin grammar, with its 247 rules in Latin verses for the syntax of nouns alone. He argued that the study of philosophy should be completely separated from that of theology, and he suggested the inclusion of history and geography in the curriculum. Like Martinho de Mendonça, whose pioneer work of 1734 he does not mention, he was greatly influenced by John Locke's *Thoughts on education*, and he adopted or adapted many of the Englishman's ideas. In some respects he went a good deal further. He advocated the establishment of primary schools in every main street, or at least in every municipal ward. Most revolutionary of all, he stated that women should be educated to a standard comparable with that of men. When this seminal and highly controversial work first appeared, King John was already suffering from the illness which killed him four years later; and this may account, at least in part, for his failure to support Verney's sweeping proposals.

King John was more successful and more prodigal in his patronage of music, for which, like nearly all the monarchs of the House of Bragança, he had a true and discriminating passion. He made the Lisbon opera the best in Europe outside Italy, a position which it consolidated in the early years of his son and successor, who was an even more ardent devotee. The high standard of church music in this reign can be gathered from an entry in the journal of the purser of H.M.S. *Winchester* in 1719:

> I was at this [cathedral] church upon a high festival when the King, the Queen, all the royal family, and a great many of the Court and nobility were there. The King's eunuchs with a great number of fine musicians performed to admiration, in so much that although I stood upwards of five hours, it was impossible to be weary; and had not the priests' bowing, crossing, and other gestures of adoration appeared to me to be ridiculous idolatry, as being paid to painted and gilded posts and stones, I should have esteemed it as the finest musical entertainment I had ever heard in my life.

The Portuguese kings' passion for music (for several of the House of Aviz had this trait) was shared by many of their subjects. They took the folk-music and the folk-dances of Portugal to Asia, to Africa and to Brazil. Some of it survives to the present day in the Indonesian islands of Tidore, Amboina and Flores, while Brazil is perhaps the only country where thousands of wandering guitar-players can earn a full-time living in the countryside, at any rate in the north-east. There was a flourishing school of Mulatto composers and musicians of sacred music in late eighteenth-century Minas Gerais; but there was apparently no equal development in any of the other Brazilian captaincies, although some of these men likewise worked in Rio de Janeiro.

The action of the *estrangeirados* in Portugal was not without its influence overseas, though naturally in somewhat tardy and attenuated forms. Literary academies were founded in Brazil in imitation of those which abounded in eighteenth-century Portugal; but their existence was equally ephemeral, and their poetic effusions were equally boring. The royal academy of history nominated correspondents in Brazil and in Portuguese India, and in 1742 this body sent two representatives, a Jesuit priest and a Franciscan friar, to make copious transcripts from the documents in the archives of Macao. The Academy sent comprehensive questionnaires to colonial governors, bishops and town councils, asking them to supply information about the records in their charge, and about monuments of historical or archaeological interest. Not all of the recipients bothered to reply, and others quietly shelved the questionnaires after politely acknowledging them. But some individuals were more co-operative, though most of the information which they sent to Lisbon is still lying unused in the archives there. The Portuguese padres at Peking corresponded with the fifth Count of Ericeira during his first vice-royalty of India (1717–20), sending him information about China in return for French and other books for their library. They also corresponded with Dr. Ribeiro Sanches, when the latter was physician at the Russian Court, and they received through him the publications of the Imperial Academy at St. Petersburg.

The Peking padres made the most of their freedom from the Portuguese censorship, amassing a library which aroused the competitive envy of their French colleagues. One of these, Antoine Gaubil, wrote to the Jesuit procurator at Paris:

The Portuguese Fathers have a very old library, well furnished as regards history, scripture, commentaries, theology, mathematics, etc. They have excellent books on medicine and surgery, and Latin and French books on natural history, physics, astronomy and geometry. They have decided to have a complete library for this country, and they spend lavishly to get books from Italy, Holland, France and England. . . . I know from good sources that the Portuguese have resolved to surpass us in everything.

Among the books so ardently collected and which have survived in Peking to this day (unless destroyed by the Red Guards recently) are Verney's *Verdadeiro Methodo*, several of Isaac Newton's works and a Latin edition of John Locke's *Essay on Human Understanding*.

Despite these and other manifestations of intellectual curiosity and activity in the Portuguese world, it must be admitted that the reign of King John V was one of seed-time rather than of harvest. The principal reasons for this were lack of continuity, the ambivalent attitude of the King, and the fact that the *estrangeirados* comprised a small group of people at the top (or with access to the top) of society, whose influence had not time to percolate very far downwards. Typical of the lack of continuity was the scientific academy founded with a great flourish by an Englishman named Lewis Baden at Lisbon in 1725. He advertised an ambitious curriculum of 'experimental philosophy' for the nobility and gentry, including courses in physics, optics, chemistry and mechanics, but Baden's academy only functioned for a few weeks. In an age of absolutism, too much reliance had perforce to be placed on royal support and patronage. King John V, as we have seen, became more bigotedly devout in the last years of his life, and less concerned with the progress of the arts and sciences, save only for his beloved church music, which he patronised to the end. Several of the leading *estrangeirados*, Castro Sarmento, Verney and Ribeiro Sanches, never returned to Portugal from their self-imposed exile. Others, including the Ericeiras, died about the same time as the King.

The seed, nevertheless, was sown, and when Verney's polemical *Verdadeiro Methodo de estudar* appeared in 1746 it achieved an instant success and a wide circulation, despite the violent criticism which it likewise aroused, and despite the confiscation of the first edition by the Lisbon Inquisition. Indeed, one of the Inquisitors was responsible for printing a clandestine edition on the printing press of the monastery of St. Eloi! In the same year of 1746 the Jesuit Rector of the College of Arts at Coimbra had published a sharp warning against the teaching or the discussion of any new or subversive ideas, 'such as those of Descartes, Gassendi, Newton and others, . . . or of any deductions whatsoever that are opposed to the system of Aristotle, which must be followed in these schools, as has been repeatedly affirmed in the statutes of this College of Arts'. The wording of this reprimand shows that the basis of scholasticism was already being undermined in its stronghold at Coimbra. Doubtless this was mainly due to the dissemination of the ideas propagated by the *estrangeirados* during the previous three decades.

The surviving *estrangeirados* were mostly delighted by Pombal's expulsion of the Jesuits, and by the dictator's adoption of some (though by no means all) of their ideas, as evidenced by the educational reforms which he undertook between 1759 and 1772. The official educational system was now completely laicised, although Pombal was unable to find occupants for many of the autonomous chairs of Latin, Greek, Rhetoric and Philosophy, which were founded (on paper) in Portugal. He even had difficulty in finding 500 teachers to give instruction in the new elementary schools. The confiscated Jesuit libraries were mostly left to rot, or were sold locally for trifling sums, instead of being embodied in those of other institutions. In 1761 Pombal founded the College of Nobles (*Colégio dos Nobres*), more on the lines indicated by Ribeiro Sanches than on those advocated by Martinho de Mendonça. Whereas the latter, following John Locke, had chiefly in view the education of a country gentleman, the former visualised the training of an élite to serve as army officers and as diplomatists. It may be recalled here that Ribeiro Sanches was an influential adviser in the reorganisation of the Russian Imperial cadet corps in 1766. The curriculum at the College of Nobles included modern foreign languages, mathematics, experimental science and physical training; but the College languished after the year 1772, since most of the teaching staff was transferred to the reorganised university at Coimbra, although it was not finally abolished until 1838.

Pombal was more successful in his reform of the university system. The Jesuit one at Evora was abolished altogether, and Coimbra was drastically reformed in 1772. Faculties of mathematics and philosophy were created, and the existing faculties of theology, law and medicine were modernised. A botanical garden, a museum of natural history, a physics laboratory, an observatory and an anatomical theatre were successively installed, as well as a teaching hospital. Once more staffing difficulties prevented the full implementation of Pombal's reforms in this as in other fields, but at last a clean break was made with scholasticism. Yet in blindly condemning anything and everything which the Jesuits had done, Pombal in his reforming zeal frequently threw the baby out with the bath-water. Moreover, many of his reforms reflected his authoritarian temper and his ultra-regalistic convictions.

He abolished the Inquisitorial censorship, but the Board of Censorship (*Mesa Censória*), which he established in its place, continued to ban the works of Bayle, Hobbes, Espinoza, Voltaire, Rousseau and other controversial writers. The Board also banned long-forgotten works, such as the Italian Theatine, Fr. Ardizone Spinola's *Cordel Triplicado de Amor* (Lisbon, 1680)—presumably because this particular book (which had been cleared and commended by the censorship on its first publication) severely criticised the Portuguese authorities in India for the maintenance of a strict colour-bar in Church and State, an accusation which Fr. Ardizone most convincingly documented. Pombal's censorship also closed down the *Gazeta Literaria*, a periodical edited and published by an Oratorian canon at Oporto in 1761–2. The *Gazeta Literaria* had an admirably wide range, and was in fact the Portuguese equivalent of the *Journal des Sçavants* and the *Philosophical Transactions*, on both of which it drew heavily, besides keeping abreast of books and periodicals in the Netherlands, Denmark, Germany and Italy.

If the results of Pombal's expulsion of the Jesuits and of his subsequent educational reforms were somewhat mixed in Portugal itself, they were nothing short of disastrous in the Portuguese empire, at any rate for several decades. There was nobody to replace the Jesuits, particularly in Brazil, save some members of the other religious Orders, most of which were at this time in an advanced state of decay, and the chaplains of the sugar-planters and wealthy families. A Pombaline decree of 1772 established the *Subsídio Literario* ('Literary Subsidy'), which, as its name implies, was a tax levied to subsidise primary and secondary schooling, both in Portugal and overseas. The results were meagre in the extreme, since the money came slowly and irregularly, and qualified teachers were still far to seek. The first major step forward was taken in 1798, with the founding of the Seminary at Olinda by Bishop Azeredo Coutinho. This institution was not confined to students for the priesthood, and the subjects taught (and taught on surprisingly modern lines) included Greek, French, history, physics, geometry, drawing and natural history, besides the traditional grammar, Latin, rhetoric and philosophy. Olinda Seminary quickly became a seed-bed of liberal ideas, more so than the founder, who was inspired by Pombaline precedents, had intended. Many of its graduates played leading parts in the events which culminated in the independence of Brazil.

As mentioned in the previous chapter, increasing numbers of Brazilian youths went to Europe to take their degrees in theology, law, or medicine. Most of them went to Coimbra, but a fair number to French and Italian universities, more especially to the medical school at Montpellier, and one or two as far afield as Edinburgh. From about 1770 those who did so were increasingly exposed to the ideas of the *philosophes* and the freemasons. Equally naturally, they brought back to Brazil some of these ideas, and even the books which expressed them, as the Brazilian censorship was not particularly efficient at this period. But these men were, of course, a small intellectual élite, in a colony consisting largely of illiterates; and those of their compatriots who had received their whole education in Brazil received it in the traditional forms. Essentially, colonial education in Brazil, whether the teachers were the Jesuits or their successors, was characterised from beginning to end by an exclusively literary approach. It was based upon the study of grammar, rhetoric and Latin, with the intention of forming priests, lawyers and bureaucrats. There was, inevitably, no place in this system either for natural science or for modern languages. Nor was there any demand for these subjects among the great majority of the office-holders, the sugar-planters, the *latifundia* landowners and the rich merchants of the coastal towns, who, together with the clergy, constituted the colonial élite.

Still less was there any thought of educating the mass of the people, the poor whites, the coloured proletariat and the Negroes, bond and free. The *estrangeirados* were the product of an autocratic age, and most of them shared some of its concepts. Dr. Ribeiro Sanches argued that there was no need to found primary schools in the remoter country districts, as this would result in a shortage of rural labourers, such as journeymen, fishermen and shepherds. Similar sentiments were voiced by the Lisbon municipal councillors in 1815, this time with respect to urban workers, nor are other such instances difficult to find.

Ribeiro Sanches also adhered to the view that colonies should be regarded primarily, if not exclusively, as colonies of exploitation. He criticised his countrymen for trying to make each colony 'a little Portugal'. He urged that the only branches of agriculture and industry allowed in the overseas territories should be such as did not compete with those of the mother country. In every way, including the sphere of education, 'a colony should be considered politically as a village in comparison with the capital city', in order to prevent the settlers from becoming anything more than peasants, merchants and minor officials. More perceptive in this respect was the Overseas Councillor, António Rodrigues da Costa, who had prophesied in 1715 that Brazil, which was already larger and richer than Portugal, would not be content indefinitely with an inferior status.

If the Brazilian aristocracy of planters, priests and landowners was in some respects ill-prepared to guide the destinies of their country when the break with Portugal came in 1822–5, there were enough able and well-educated individuals among them to save the new empire from fragmentation and collapse. There might well have been many more equally talented men if Pombal's violent methods of breaking the Jesuits' virtual monopoly of higher education had not wrecked the existing structure before it could be adequately replaced. 'You know', wrote Fr. Antoine Gaubil, S.J., from his vantage-point at Peking to a French colleague at Macao, 'that the Portuguese as a rule are intelligent, but the majority need a little prodding in order to keep them up to the mark.' It was not in Pombal's character to tolerate opposition; but if he had employed constant prodding instead of the mailed fist, perhaps the transition from the old to the new would have been more effective and less painful for all concerned.

CHAPTER XVI

Sebastianism, Messianism, and nationalism

'WHAT can be expected of a nation, one half of which is looking out for the Messiah and the other half for Dom Sebastian who has been dead for nearly two centuries?' This quip, variously ascribed to a British and to a French envoy in eighteenth-century Lisbon, was evidently a common jest among foreigners living in Portugal, reflecting the belief that most Portuguese were either crypto-Jews or else Sebastianists. The former allegation has been dealt with in Chapter XI, and we may here briefly consider the origin and evolution of the latter.

Sebastian had received the appelation of *o desejado* ('the desired', or 'the wanted') when still in his mother's womb. His father had died a few days before his birth, and all of King John III's other nine sons were dead without leaving legitimate heirs. The only other surviving son of King Manuel I, Dom Henrique, was an elderly cardinal, so a male child was the only hope of saving Portugal from an eventual Castilian succession. Hence, as Diogo do Couto, then a page in the royal palace, recalled when writing at Goa some seventeen years later, Sebastian was a king 'who had been begged from God with so many tears, pilgrimages, processions and alms', his birth being signalised by great popular rejoicings. His mother left for Spain soon after his birth and she never returned. He was educated mainly by the Jesuits, but his studies ended when he took over the government from his uncle on his fourteenth birthday (20 January 1568).

The young monarch had a fiery and exalted temperament, which was greatly excited when reading about Portuguese exploits overseas, and he was correspondingly upset when he read about the evacuation of the Moroccan coastal strongholds by order of his grandfather in 1549–50. While still a child he contemplated the conquest of Morocco, writing on the flyleaf of a missal which his Jesuit tutors gave him: 'Fathers, pray to God that He will make me very chaste, and very zealous to expand the Faith to all parts of the world.' His great desire was to be 'a captain of Christ', and a crusading *conquistador* spirit permeates the instructions which he gave to the Viceroy and the Archbishop at Goa. From the age of two he suffered from some physical ailment which afflicted him periodically until his death, but which has not been diagnosed with any certainty. Whatever it was, it affected his sexual organs, made him dislike women, and raised grave doubts about his ability to have children. Various projects for his marriage to a Spanish or to a French princess came to nothing, any more than did a proposal for a match with Mary Queen of Scots—this being the only one in which he showed any interest, as it appealed to his knight-errant temperament. This was only a passing phase, and the Spanish ambassador at Lisbon reported that 'speaking to him about marriage was like speaking to him about death'. His continual evasion of all serious marriage negotiations aroused the increasing disquiet of his subjects.

His physical disability did not prevent him from developing a craze for physical fitness, which he achieved by taking violent exercise in all weathers and for long hours—hunting, hawking, jousting, bull-fighting, etc., and riding out storms in a small boat at sea. As he grew older he increasingly rejected the advice of his grandmother, his uncle, or of anyone more experienced than himself, talking only with young nobles of his own age who flattered him to the top of his bent. He seldom visited Lisbon, which city he heartily disliked, spending most of his time riding around the Alentejo and the Algarve, indulging in physical training and field sports, often going without sleep for two or three nights on end. This peculiar behaviour did nothing to endear him to the mass of his subjects, and the more serious courtiers were alarmed by his growing obsession with the conquest of Morocco. This craze culminated in his defeat and death at the battle of El-Ksar el-Kebir (4 August 1578), after one of the worst mismanaged campaigns in recorded history. His badly wounded and naked corpse was found on the battlefield next day; but the identification was done rather perfunctorily, his rich armour and weapons were never found, and none of the survivors would admit to having seen him killed.

Rumours that he was not really dead began to circulate with the arrival of a few fugitives at the town of Arzila in the dead of the night after the battle. These rumours quickly found credence and spread rapidly throughout Portugal, despite all the efforts of the government to discount or deny them. The expedition itself had been highly unpopular with the overwhelming majority of the people, and the most ruthless means had been used to recruit the ramshackle army which sailed from Lisbon in June and July 1578. The humiliating defeat and disastrous annihilation of the expedition did not, however, result in the people blaming the King for his headstrong folly and military ineptitude, still less did it lead them to execrate his memory. On the contrary, he was now widely regarded as a tragic hero of epic proportions, whose disappearance was only temporary, and who would one day return and redeem the disaster of El-Ksar el-Kebir by leading the nation to new heights of conquest and glory.

With surprising swiftness this belief became fused with the Arthurian legend cycle and with various Messianic beliefs and prophecies which were current in Portugal. The resulting versions assumed different forms, such as that Sebastian was biding his time in a cave, or on a mist-covered island in mid-Atlantic. Other stories credited him with doing penance disguised as a wandering pilgrim until such time as he had expiated his responsibility for El-Ksar el-Kebir. Alternatively, it was rumoured that he was really a prisoner of the Moors, or even of the Spaniards, who were keeping him loaded with chains in an underground dungeon. There were other versions of his survival which need not be mentioned here, but one or another gave pretexts and opportunities for several Perkin Warbeck-type adventurers, who tried to pass themselves off as Dom Sebastian between 1584 and 1603, and who all attracted a following of some sort before they were rounded up and sent to the gallows or to the galleys.

The burgeoning Sebastianist legend became identified in the minds of many people with the prophetic *trovas*, or doggerel verses, of the cobbler-rhymster of Trancoso, Gonçalo Anes (*c.* 1500–1556), generally known as *o Bandarra* 'the Doodler'. These verses were compounded largely of a belief in the coming of a Messiah-king, deriving from the Old Testament, together with remnants of the Arthurian legend-cycle which survived in popular memory. They also reveal traces of the apocalyptic belief in a coming spiritual 'Golden-Age', originally propagated by the Cistercian Abbot, Joachim of Fiore (d. 1202), and which had been popularised by the Spiritual Franciscans and which greatly influenced Columbus. The *Trovas* of Bandarra, like the pronouncements of the Delphic Oracle, were very vaguely and cryptically worded. Hence anyone could read into them almost anything that he wished, but they were implicitly critical of the existing state of affairs. They also foretold the coming (or the return) of a future redeemer-king, who would establish a world empire of right and justice—the fifth world-monarchy prophesied in the Book of Daniel, which would be accompanied by the reappearance of the lost tribes of Israel and the conversion of all unbelievers to Christianity.

In most versions of the *Trovas* the redeemer-king was styled the *Encuberto* ('hidden', 'secret', 'disguised'), possibly deriving from the leader of a revolt in Valencia who took this sobriquet in 1532. The *Trovas* had a wide and continuing circulation in manuscript copies, although they were banned by the Inquisition, which tribunal likewise compelled Bandarra formally to abjure them in 1541. Their circulation was not confined to the lower classes or to the 'New' Christians, but they found avid readers among all sorts and conditions of men. Very soon after El-Ksar el-Kebir, Sebastian became identified with the *Encuberto* of the *Trovas*, which gave an additional impetus to their popularity. This popularity steadily increased during the 'Spanish Captivity' of 1580–1640, when they gave many people the hope that this was the darkest hour before the dawn.

Some modern Portuguese writers have argued that the Arthurian and Messianic influences in the *Trovas* appealed respectively to the Celtic and to the Jewish strains in the national character, which helps to explain their abiding popularity.

António Sergio and other scholars have denied this, pointing out that similar legends were current in other countries, although these latter do not seem to have had such a widespread reception and such a long life. However that may be, people can always believe what they want to believe, or what it suits them to believe, as instanced by the millions who believe in a life after death without thinking much about it. The religious attitudes prevailing in Portugal between 1580 and 1640 undoubtedly predisposed many people to hope for a Messianic deliverer in some shape or form. Direct divine intervention in daily life was considered as something normal, and miraculous occurrences could be expected almost any day.

With the Portuguese restoration of December 1640 and the accession of King John IV, it was suggested that he was the promised redeemer-king rather than a returning Sebastian. The great exponent of this interpretation of the *Trovas* was Padre António Vieira, S.J., who proclaimed as much in a sermon preached before the King and his Court in the royal chapel at Lisbon on New Year's Day, 1642. Vieira insisted that the prophecies, whether Biblical or Bandarran, applied to King John IV and not to King Sebastian. He based his arguments not only on the Book of Daniel and on the *Trovas*, but on rather shadowy Dark Age and medieval prophecies, such as those ascribed to Fray Gil and Saint Isidore of Seville. Vieira and the dyed-in-the-wool Sebastianists whom he was trying to confute and convert differed as to their interpretation of the *Trovas*; but they agreed that the cobbler of Trancoso was a true prophet, fully entitled to as much credit as those of the Old Testament.

Like many people in seventeenth-century Europe, whether Catholic or Protestant, Vieira firmly believed that the prophetical books of the Old Testament could be interpreted largely in terms of the actual present and the immediate future. He had no inclination towards abstract thought, but a veritable passion for Messianic lore and Biblical commentary. As the English envoy at Lisbon noted in 1668, Vieira 'besides his natural eloquence has the art of making the scriptures say what he pleases'. Like many of his English Puritan contemporaries, he concentrated on the Old Testament rather than on the New. His God was in many respects the God of battles, as was perhaps inevitable in an age of violent theological and confessional conflict. For instance, he concluded his New Year sermon of 1642 with the hope that the fratricidal struggle with Catholic Castile would soon cease, thus enabling the victorious Portuguese to bathe their swords 'in the blood of heretics in Europe, in the blood of Muslims in Africa, in the blood of heathen in Asia and in America, conquering and subjugating all the regions of the earth under one sole empire, so that they may all, under the aegis of one crown, be placed gloriously beneath the feet of the successor of St. Peter'. We may smile at such extravagances today, but Vieira was one of many Christian preachers who were careless of the incongruities into which their addiction to the Old Testament landed them. We need only recall the Calvinist ministers of the Scots army at Dunbar with their battle-cry of 'Jesus and no quarter' and Major-General Thomas Harrison and his Fifth Monarchy men who believed that England was destined to play the part which Vieira assigned to Portugal.

Vieira's belief in Portugal as the fifth universal monarchy was greatly strengthened by his own experience as a missionary in the wilds of South America. He remarked on the exiguous number of missionaries who, even in the most favourable circumstances, would be available for evangelising the teeming millions of three continents; and he stressed the virtual impossibility of catechising cannibals armed with poisoned arrows who would let nobody approach them in the depths of the Amazonian jungle. From these premises he argued that the conversion of the world to Christianity could not possibly be expected to result from the labours of a few thousand European missionaries, however devoted. This consummation, so devoutly to be wished, must await the direct intervention of God, working through His chosen kingdom of Portugal, as prophesied in the Old Testament, in the miraculous appearance of Christ to Dom Afonso Henriques at Ourique, and in the *Trovas* of Bandarra.

The death of King John IV in November 1656 did nothing to shake Vieira's conviction that he was the promised Messiah-king who would one day lead Portugal against the Ottoman Turks for the recapture of Constantinople and Jerusalem, and thus inaugurate the fifth universal monarchy. On the contrary, it served to strengthen his conviction, since he now decided that the *Trovas* of Bandarra were more applicable to a king who would be raised from the dead, and there were plenty of biblical precedents for miracles of this kind. Most of the Sebastianists did not follow him in this respect, but they retained (or reverted to) their original belief, since the notoriously pacific King John IV was hardly likely to prove a conquering redeemer-king. They maintained that Sebastian was not dead but would come from his enchanted hiding-place in mid-Atlantic to fulfil the apocalyptic visions of the scriptures and the *Trovas*.

I have cited Vieira at some length because he was the most famous and the most influential of those people who believed that a glorious destiny awaited Portugal in the very near future, either through the return of Dom Sebastian or through the resurrection of John IV, or with the advent of some other (as yet unidentified) Messianic figure who would fulfil the Biblical and the Bandarran prophecies. As mentioned above, these messianic beliefs, or variants of them, were widely shared in all classes of society, and they were accepted and propagated by many influential Portuguese Jesuits, aside from Vieira. Among them were Fr. Domingos Coelho, the Jesuit Provincial of Brazil, who was captured by the Dutch at Bahia in 1624; Fr. João de Vasconcelos, the (highly unreliable) chronicler of the Jesuits in Brazil (1668); Fr. Nuno da Cunha, the previously mentioned representative of the Portuguese Jesuits at Rome (p. 233); and Fr. Fernão de Queiroz, writing at Goa on the loss of Ceylon and on the apocalyptic visions of a local lay-brother, Pedro de Basto (1689).

Since these Messianic beliefs in Portugal's glorious future were propagated by so many of the Lusitanian empire's foremost educators, it is not surprising to find that these convictions were even more prevalent among the laity, literally from the Maranhão to Macao. Foreign visitors to the Portuguese colonies and trading settlements often commented on the prevalence of Sebastianist beliefs there, even if only to ridicule them. The regions where these Messianic beliefs lingered longest, and where they have in fact survived to the present day, albeit in modified forms, are in the *sertões* or backlands of Brazil, more particularly in the São Francisco river valley and in the arid wastelands of the north-east. One of the classics of Brazilian literature, *Os Sertões* of

Euclides da Cunha, translated into English by Samuel Putnam under the title of *Revolt in the Backlands*, narrates the campaigns which the Republican government of 1896–7 was forced to mount against the followers of António Conselheiro, a religious fanatic of this Messianic type, who fought literally to the last man. These self-styled prophets or redeemers still reappear at intervals in the Brazilian backlands.

In Portugal and in its Eastern empire the Sebastianist-Messianic beliefs gradually weakened during the eighteenth century, but only very gradually. In 1725 we find the Archbishop of Goa, Dom Fr. Ignacio de Santa Teresa, a singularly pugnacious prelate who quarrelled fiercely with viceroys and Jesuits, firmly convinced that the inauguration of Portugal's universal monarchy was only a few years away.

> And the reason is because God has deliberately chosen the Portuguese out of all other nations for the rule and reform of the whole world, with command, dominion, and Empire, both pure and mixed, over all of its four parts, and with infallible promises for the subjugation of the whole globe, which will be united and reduced to one sole empire, of which Portugal will be the head.

Explaining why Vieira had miscalculated on one occasion that this monarchy would begin in the year 1666, the Archbishop rearranged the figures to prove to his own satisfaction that the time for the fulfilment of the Biblical and Bandarran prophecies would come in the decade 1730–40. Unfortunately for Fr. Ignacio de Santa Teresa, who was transferred from Goa to the See of the Algarve in 1740, this was just the period when the rising Maratha power swept the Portuguese out of the 'Province of the North', and Goa was only saved by the payment of a heavy indemnity (p. 136). Whether the sanguine prelate rearranged his calculations after his arrival in the Algarve, I cannot say. But it is very likely that he did so, since the Sebastianists and their ilk were never put out for long by arithmetical miscalculations any more than the British Israelites are nowadays with their varying computations of the Great Pyramid.

It was typical of Pombal that in his reforming zeal to discredit and extirpate the Sebastianist (and allied) beliefs he accused the Jesuits and Vieira of forging the *Trovas* of Bandarra, although it was an easily ascertainable fact that these verses were already circulating widely before 1540 when the Society was born. The French invasion of 1808 gave Sebastianism a new lease of life, just as the traumatic events of 1580 and 1640 had done; but thereafter the cult was limited to uneducated people. Its romantic appeal is reflected in the work of some of the most famous Portuguese poets, including Guerra Junqueiro (1850–1923) and Fernando Pessoa (1888–1935). The *Trovas* of Bandarra, which were first printed (as distinct from circulating in manuscript) in France in 1603, were reprinted in Portugal at intervals throughout the nineteenth century and down to 1911 at least. These versions were not published as works of erudition or texts for the use of scholars, but for their popularity with the lower classes.

The persistence and strength of Sebastianist and Messianic beliefs in Portugal and its overseas empire naturally reinforced the fervid patriotism for which the Portuguese have long been noted. It was during the sixty years' 'Spanish captivity' that the *Lusíadas* of Luís de Camões attained the status of a national epic in the eleven editions which were published between 1581 and 1640. These years also saw the rise of a school of monkish historians at Alcobaça, whose influence was great and lasting both on contemporaries and on posterity. These chroniclers varied a good deal in their historical sense and professional integrity, but they all accepted and propagated the story of the miraculous appearance of Christ to Dom Afonso Henriques at Ourique. Thanks to them, the legend of Ourique was elevated to the position of an unquestioned national dogma, and the role of the Portuguese as the chosen people of God was asserted with a wealth of biblical and historical (or pseudo-historical) citations.

The descent of the Portuguese kings was traced back in an unbroken line to Tubal, grandson of Noah. Greek mythological figures such as Bacchus, Hercules and Atlante were also invoked as ancestors of the Portuguese nation. The claims of Braga over Toledo as the primary See of the Iberian peninsula were examined and exalted. Above all, emphasis was placed on the inherent autonomy and on the grandiose future of Portugal as promised by Christ to Dom Afonso Henriques in the vision at Ourique: 'that He would never remove the eyes of His mercy from him and his peoples, for He had chosen them as His workers and harvesters, who would reap for Him a great harvest in different regions'. Exactly the same conviction animated Fr. Ignacio de Santa Teresa when he wrote at Goa a century later: 'God had called Portugal His chosen kingdom to found His firm and eternal empire and to make known His name to these barbarous and outlandish nations . . . for the Portuguese always and everywhere have introduced and will introduce the light of the Faith and of the Gospel by means of their weapons throughout the whole wide world.'

The work of the historical school of Alcobaça during the years 1580–1640 clearly implied that Portugal would one day shake itself free from the Castilian connection; but this did not prevent these writers from dedicating their works to the Castilian kings nor these monarchs from accepting them. Perhaps the most curious example of this dichotomy is afforded by the *Flores de España, Excelencias de Portugal*, written by a young Crown lawyer, Dr. António de Sousa de Macedo, and published at Lisbon with a dedication to the reigning King Philip in 1631. The author sets out to prove, with a mass of citations, that the Spaniards (more specifically the Castilians) were superior to all the other peoples of Europe save only the Portuguese, who in their turn surpassed their neighbours in every respect. I doubt whether a more hysterically nationalistic work has ever been published, although the twentieth century can supply some formidable competitors. Sousa de Macedo maintains that instead of calling Camões 'a second Homer or a second Virgil' it would be more accurate to term the Greek and Roman poets as the first Camões. He claims that the Portuguese were the first and the most steadfast converts to Christianity, and that they were and are the propagators, crusaders and defenders of the Faith *par excellence*. Their orthodoxy left nothing to be desired, since they were always great persecutors of unbelievers, beginning with Luso, or Lusio, a captain of Trajan, who distinguished himself by the number of Jews which he personally killed in the capture of Jerusalem. The geographical situation and the natural resources of Portugal are compared with those of Spain and found to be vastly superior. Portuguese monarchs, poets, *conquistadores*, and women, were all and each of them superior to their Spanish counterparts.

This ultra-patriotic panegyric concludes by emphasising the divine origin and inspiration of the national escutcheon of the *Quinas*.

Dr. António de Sousa de Macedo was not an irresponsible literary hack, but a man who played a role in formulating government policy during the reigns of the first two Bragança kings, and who had travelled to France, England and the Netherlands. The ultra-nationalistic and imperialist sentiments which he expressed as a young man in 1631 remained with him for the rest of his life, and they are likewise to be found in the state-papers from his hand. Neither he nor Padre António Vieira, S.J., nor Fr. Ignacio de Santa Teresa, can be dismissed as ranting but uninfluential jingoists, in view of the prestige and authority which they all enjoyed in their respective lifetimes. There is no doubt but that the majority of their compatriots were fervently nationalistic and few of them questioned the validity of the legend of Ourique. One of these few was the *estrangeirado*, Luís António Verney, who dismissed it as a fable fit for children in his *Verdadeiro Methodo de estudar* (1746). But Verney was more than half French; and he was patriotic enough to be delighted at the news of the Marquis of Alorna's victories in India, which he celebrated in Latin epigrams at Rome.

It is a fairly accurate generalisation that the mass of the people in most countries consider themselves to be inherently superior to those of any other. 'No nation thinks that it is inferior to another in courage', as Captain João Ribeiro observed when writing his history of the wars between the Portuguese and the Dutch in Ceylon, 1640–58. The Portuguese who pioneered the expansion of Europe and their successors during three centuries certainly possessed this conviction in full measure—and perhaps to a greater degree than did any other nation, in the opinion of some foreign observers. The certainty that God was on their side, and that He would and did intervene directly on their behalf, was undoubtedly an important factor in the capture and retention of Ceuta, as well as in the voyages of discovery and conquest which followed. When the belief that they were God's chosen people for the expansion of the Faith was reinforced by the popularisation of the legend of Ourique, and by the Sebastianist and Messianic currents outlined above, the result was a nationalism of exceptional durability and toughness. This exalted nationalism helps to explain why the Portuguese held on to so much of their precarious seaborne empire for so long, and why they are so reluctant to relinquish any part of it nowadays, whether economically viable (Angola, Moçambique) or otherwise (Goa, Guinea).

Appendix I: Outward-bound Portuguese East Indiamen 1501–1800

Year period	*Departures*	*Year period*	*Departures*
1500–1509	138	1656–1660	14
1510–1519	96	1661–1666	9
1520–1529	76	1667–1670	12
1530–1539	80	1671–1675	12
1540–1549	61	1676–1680	13
1550–1559	51	1686–1690	5
1560–1569	49	1691–1695	10
1570–1579	54	1696–1700	13
1580–1589	56	1701–1705	13
1590–1599	44	1706–1710	9
1600–1609	68	1711–1715	11
1610–1619	56	1716–1720	9
1620–1629	67	1721–1725	10
1630–1635	16	1726–1730	9
1636–1640	14	1731–1735	11
1641–1645	18	1736–1740	13
1646–1650	26	1741–1745	11
1651–1655	18	1746–1750	16

Year period	*Departures*	*Comments*
1751–1755	7	No figure available for 1753
1756–1760	10	
1761–1765	9	
1766–1770	7	
1771–1775	7 or 8	
1776–1780	5	
1781–1785	7	No figure available for 1784
1786–1790	8	
1791–1795	4	No figures for 1793 and 1795
1796–1800	5	No figure for 1796

Based on the tables given in Godinho, *Os Descobrimentos e a Economia Mundial*, Vol. II (Lisboa, 1968), pp. 77–9, and C. R. Boxer, *The prin-*

cipal ports of call in the Carreira da India (in the press) and the sources there quoted. Though tentative in some instances, these figures are very close approximations and more reliable than any other estimates to date. Figures for the return voyages are sparser and more tentative, but fairly reliable estimates of them are given by V. Magalhães Godinho and C. R. Boxer, *opera et loc. cit.* Before 1510 the majority of Indiamen called first at Cochin, but after 1510 the overwhelming majority were bound for Goa, although the above totals include a few stray ships for Malacca and elsewhere.

Appendix II: Monarchs of Portugal 1385-1826

Dynasty of Aviz

Dom João I (6 April 1385–14 August 1433)
Dom Duarte (1433–9 September 1438)
Dom Affonso V (1438–28 August 1481)
Dom João II (1481–25 October 1495)
Dom Manuel I (1495–13 December 1521)
Dom João III (1521–11 June 1557)
Dom Sebastião (1557–4 August 1578)
Dom Henrique (1578–31 January 1580)

Dynasty of Spanish Habsburgs

Felipe II (I of Portugal, 1580–13 September 1598)
Felipe III (II of Portugal, 1598–31 March 1621)
Felipe IV (III of Portugal, 1621–1 December 1640)

Dynasty of Bragança

Dom João IV (1640–6 November 1656)
Dom Affonso VI (1656–deposed 22 November 1667; died 12 September 1683)
Dom Pedro II (Prince Regent, November 1667–1683; King, 1683–9 December 1706)
Dom João V (1706–31 July 1750)
Dom José (1750–24 February 1777)
Dona Maria I (1777—declared insane in 1792; died 20 March 1816)
Dom João VI (Prince Regent, 1792–1816; King, 1816–10 March 1826)

Dom João VI left Brazil for Portugal on 22 April 1821, leaving his eldest son Dom Pedro as Regent. The latter proclaimed the independence of Brazil on 7 September 1822, which was recognised by Portugal on 29 October 1825.

Appendix III: Imports of Brazilian gold and diamonds and of English goods into Portugal 1711-50 (in thousands of pounds sterling)

Five-year period	*Brazilian gold and diamonds*	*English goods*
1711–1715	728,000	638
1716–1720	315,168	695
1721–1725	1,715,201	811
1726–1730	693,465	914
1731–1735	1,113,980	1,024
1736–1740	1,311,175	1,164
1741–1745	1,371,680	1,115
1746–1750	?	1,114

This table is taken from Jorge Borges de Macedo, *Problemas de História da Indústria Portuguesa no século XVIII* (Lisbon, 1963), p. 56, and the sources there quoted. Owing to the amount of contraband trade involved, all such calculations must be regarded as tentative, and they all differ from each other, as can be seen by comparing those in Visconde de Carnaxide, *O Brasil na administração pombalina* (São Paulo, 1940), pp. 241–52 (for the yield of the *quinto*, etc.); V. Magalhães Godinho, 'Le Portugal, les flottes du sucre et les flottes de l'or' (in *Annales E.S.C.*, April–June 1950, pp. 184–97; C. R. Boxer, *The Golden Age of Brazil 1695–1750* (California University Press, 1962), pp. 333–40; F. Mauro's article in the *Dicionário de História de Portugal*, Vol. I, pp. 626–7 (1963). Diamonds were only officially discovered in 1729, but some were certainly shipped to Lisbon before that date.

Appendix IV: Ships trading between Bahia and West Africa 1681-1710

Five-year period	*Mina Coast*	*Angola*
1681–1685	11	5
1686–1690	32	3
1691–1696	49	6
1697–1700	60	2
1701–1705	102	1
1706–1710	114	0

From Pierre Verger, *Bahia and the West Coast Trade, 1549–1851* (Ibadan University Press, 1964), p. 11, and sources there quoted. These figures are likewise subject to caution and are more indicative of a trend than anything else, since the correspondence of the Municipal Council at Luanda for this period indicates that many more ships were engaged in the trade with Bahia than the few listed above (Cf. C. R. Boxer, *Portuguese Society in the Tropics. The Municipal Councils of Goa, Macao, Bahia and Luanda, 1510–1800* (Wisconsin University Press, 1965), pp. 130–1, 193–5.

Appendix V: Slave exports from Angola and Benguela 1710–48

1710	3,549	1729–30	?
1711	4,158	1731	5,808
1712	4,188	1732–3	?
1713	5,617	1734	9,962
1714	5,581	1735	9,257
1715–17	?	1736	12,250
1718	6,747	1737	9,900 (?)
1719	6,886	1738	8,809
1720	7,213	1739	?
1721	5,378	1740	8,484
1722	5,062	1741	8,693
1723	6,744	1742	10,130
1724	6,108	1743	?
1725	6,726	1744	8,849
1726	8,440	1745–6	?
1727	?	1747	10,112
1728	8,542	1748	11,592

Taken from David Birmingham, *Trade and Conflict in Angola, 1483–1790* (Oxford, 1966), pp. 137–41.

These figures, like those in the previous tables, should not be taken too seriously, and they are more indicative of trends than firm statistics. Birmingham points out that they do not include the 'unknown numbers who were illegally exported from both Benguela and Luanda'. Moreover, he does not state—and perhaps his sources do not specify—whether the individual numbers were reckoned *per capita* or in *peças de Indias*, in which last case they might include anything from one to three slaves according to age, sex, and physical condition. Ralph Delgado, *Historia de Angola*, Vol. IV (Lobito, 1955), p. 437, states that between 1 January and 20 July 1733 (one of the missing years in Birmingham's statistics) eleven slave-ships left Angola (including Benguela?) for Brazil, with a total of 3,446 *head* of slaves and 514 infants (*crias*); but on many other occasions the numbers were reckoned in *peças de Indias*.

Appendix VI: Value of Portuguese manufactures exported to the colonies in 1795–1820

Year	*Value in thousands of cruzados*
1796	6,106
1797	7,160
1798	10,329
1799	14,080
1800	9,606
1801	10,030
1802	8,676
1803	6,936
1804	8,449
1805	6,311
1806	4,799
1807	2,936
1808	568
1809	1,129
1810	1,079
1811	974
1812	995
1813	1,388
1814	1,855
1815	2,348
1816	2,895
1817	2,829
1818	3,350
1819	3,106
1820	2,589

Based on the tables in Adrien Balbi, *Variétés politico—statistiques de la monarchie portugaise* (Paris, 1822), p. 49, and Jorge Borges de Macedo, *Problemas de História da Indústria Portuguesa* (Lisbon, 1963), pp. 237–8.

Glossary

Most of these words are explained on their first appearance in the text, but are collected here for the convenience of the reader. Some of the judicial and legal terms have no exact equivalents in English and must be regarded as rough approximations.

Aldeia: Village, mission-village
Alferes: Ensign; standard-bearer
Almotace (l): Market inspector; inspector of weights and measures
Almotacel de limpeza: Sanitary inspector
Alvará: Royal decree
Armada: Fleet; *armada de alto-bordo*, high-seas fleet; *armada de remo*, fleet of oared vessels
Arribada: Abortive voyage
Arroba: The Portuguese quarter of 32 lb. avoirdupois, there being four *arrobas* to the *quintal*
Auto da fé: Act of the Faith. Burning or other public condemnation of crypto-Jews, heretics, etc.
Averia: Convoy-tax

Bahar: An Indian weight which varied widely in different regions and according to the different commodities for which it was used. In the Far East the Portuguese usually reckoned the *bahar* as equal to three *piculs*, or 400 lb. avoirdupois
Bandeira: (1) Flag or banner; (2) working-class guild or corporation with its banner; (3) military company with its flag
Bandeirante: Pioneer, explorer, or raider in search of Amerindians to enslave; usually but not invariably of Paulista (São Paulo) stock
Brahmene(s): Christian convert(s) from the Hindu Brahmin caste and their descendants

Caboclo: (1) Cross-breed of white and Amerindian parentage; (2) derogatory term for a low-class person, or for a domesticated Amerindian in Brazil
Cafila: Convoy (by sea) or caravan (by land) of merchants
Caixa de liberdade: Seaman's liberty chest or bounty chest
Camara (Senado da Camara): Municipal or town council

Canarim: Term applied by the Portuguese to the people of Goa and its neighbourhood who, geographically, are Konkani-Marathi; ethnically are Indo-Aryan and glotologically are Indo-European. By the mid-seventeenth century the word had come to have a pejorative connotation, which it has retained to the present day

Candil: An Indo-Portuguese weight, usually corresponding to about 500 *arrateis* or Portuguese pounds, but sometimes equated with the *bahar* of 400 lb.

Capitania: (1) Territorial area of a captaincy; (2) flagship

Carijó: Amerindian tribe in Brazil, whose name was often extended to cover all Brazilian Amerindians indiscriminately during the eighteenth century

Carreira da Índia: Round voyage between Lisbon and Goa.

Cartaz: Ship's licence or passport; navicert

Casa da India: India House at Lisbon

Casa dos Vinte e Quatro: Representatives of the guilds at Lisbon who, in their turn, elected four representatives to the municipal council

Casado: Married man, usually a householder

Castiço: Person born of white parents in a tropical colony

Cavaleiro: Knight; by extension, a gentleman

Christão-Novo: 'New' Christian; converted or crypto-Jew

Christão-Velho: 'Old' Christian; free of Jewish, heretic, Muslim or heathen ancestry

Compromisso: Statutes of a brotherhood

Conquistador: Conqueror

Conquistas: The term most commonly used by the Portuguese for their overseas possessions, whether these had been acquired by force of arms or peacefully

Consulado: Convoy-tax

Cortes: Portuguese parliament, or assembly of the three estates of nobility, clergy and people

Cruzado: Portuguese coin, originally of gold, whose value was fixed at 400 *reis* in 1517; later also of silver with the same nominal value, but of greatly differing intrinsic worth. During the seventeenth century the *cruzado* was roughly valued at four shillings (English), but in 1710 the English envoy at Lisbon equated it at 'about half a crown'

Degredados: Exiled criminals or convicts; banished men

Descendentes: Polite term in Portuguese India for Eurasians (*mestiços*)

Desembargador: High Court judge; senior Crown magistrate

Dizima: Tithe; tenth

Dizimo: Church tithe

Dobra: Gold coin of varying value. Applied in Brazil to the 12,800 *reis* gold coin struck between 1727 and 1734, inclusive

Donatário: Lord-proprietor; landowner with jurisdiction over a captaincy in colonial Brazil

Dote: Dowry

Emboaba: 'Tenderfoot', name applied by the Paulistas in derision to their rivals in Minas Gerais from Portugal and Bahia

Escrivão: Scrivener, scribe, secretary

Escudeiro: Squire

Estado da India: 'State of India'; Portuguese India. Often loosely applied to all the Portuguese fortresses and settlements between the Cape of Good Hope and Japan

Estanco: Monopoly, tax-farm

Estrangeirado: 'Foreignised'; person influenced by foreign culture

Fazenda: (1) Property, whether of land, goods or housing; (2) treasury; (3) farm, ranch, landed estate

Feira: Fair, market

Feitoria: Old English 'Factory'; trading agency or settlement, sometimes fortified

Fidalgo: Nobleman, gentleman

Fragata: Originally applied to small oared vessels equipped with one mast and sail, this term came to be applied to 60- and 70-gun warships in the eighteenth century

Fumo: (1) Fume; (2) smoke; (3) Bantu chief in south-east Africa

Fusta: Foist; a small single-masted vessel, rowed by anything from ten to thirty-five pairs of oars and sometimes mounting three or four very small guns

Homem de Negócio: Businessman, as distinct from a shopkeeper

Irmandade: Lay brotherhood

Irmão de maior condição: Brother of higher status in the *misericórdia*

Irmão de menor condição: Brother of lower status in the *misericórdia*

Juiz de fora: Legally trained district magistrate, but inferior to an *Ouvidor*

Juiz do povo: People's tribune; working-class representative on the municipal council

Juiz dos orfaos: Legal guardian of the interests of orphans and widows

Juiz ordinario: Justice of the peace, with no legal training

Lançado: Exile, fugitive from justice; banished man. Often equated with *degredado* and *tango-mao*, *q.v.*

Lanchara: Bark or boat equipped with a single mast, sail and oars

Lascarim: Native soldier in Portuguese Asia

Lavrador: (1) Peasant; (2) tenant farmer or copyholder on a plantation in Brazil

Limpeza de sangue: 'Purity of blood' from a religious and racial standpoint

Mameluco: Mixed breed of white and Amerindian parentage in Brazil

Manchua: 'Small vessels of recreation used by the Portugals here [Macao], as also at Goa, pretty handsome things, resembling little frigates; many curiously carved, gilded and painted, with little beak-heads', as Peter Mundy described them in 1637

Manso: Tame, domesticated

Mantimento: Subsistence allowance

Matricola: Muster-roll; central registry

Mecánico: Artisan; manual labourer; plebeian

Mesa: Board of Guardians of the *misericórdia*

Mesteres: Working-class representatives or practitioners of a trade or craft

Mestiço: Mixed blood; half-breed, often equated with a Mulatto in Africa and Brazil and with a Eurasian in Asia

Mina(s): Mine(s)

Minas Gerais: 'General Mines' region in Brazil

Mineiro: (1) A miner; (2) an inhabitant of Minas Gerais in Brazil

Minhoto: Inhabitant of the province of Entre Minho e Douro, Portugal

Misericórdia, Santa Casa da: Holy House of Mercy; charitable lay-brotherhood

Moeda: Luso-Brazilian gold coin of 4,000 *reis*, anglicised under the name of *moidore* and valued at 27*s*. 6*d*. in 1720

Morador: Settler; colonist; citizen; head of a household

Morgado: Entailed estate

Morisco(s): Moor(s) left in the Iberian peninsula after the Christian reconquest and nominally converted to Christianity

Mouro: 'Moor', but loosely applied by the Portuguese to all Muslims from Morocco to Mindanao

Náo (Nau): 'Great Ship'; merchant carrack, later applied to large warships

Nobre: Nobleman, by extension, gentleman, or anybody not obviously lower-class

Nobreza: Nobility, aristocracy, often more in theory than in fact

Ordenaçoes: Portuguese code of laws

Ordenado: The pay or salary of an appointment or office

Ordenança: Second-line militia

Orfãs del Rei: Orphan girls of marriageable age sent from Portugal to the colonies (principally to Goa) to be married at the Crown's expense
Ouvidor: Crown judge, circuit judge
Ouvidor da Comarca: District judge
Ouvidor Geral: Senior Crown judge in a *Relacão* or *High Court*

Padroado Real: Crown patronage of the Church overseas
Pai dos Christãos: 'Father of Christians'; priest responsible for the welfare of converts in Portuguese Asia
Palmar: Palm orchard; landed estate in Portuguese India
Pardao (*pardau*)*:* Gold and silver coins struck in Portuguese India with a face value of 360 *reis* and 300 *reis* respectively. Also used for money of account
Pardo: Coloured man; mixed blood, often with the connotation of Negro blood
Pauta: Nominal roll of voters; voting or balloting list
Peça de Indias (*peça*)*:* Standard measurement of classification of Negro slaves, according to age, sex and physical condition
Poderosos: Powerful (influential) people, apt to abuse the superiority of their social status by oppressing their social inferiors
Pombeiro (*pumbeiro*)*:* Itinerant slave-trader in Angola
Povo: 'People'; usually applied to persons of some substance and not to the landless proletariat
Prazo: Landed estate in Zambesia, similar in some respects to a fief. The *prazos da Coroa* were granted on a tenure for three lives, and after *c.* 1675 with the proviso that the succession must be in the female line from mother to daughter
Preto(s): Black(s), Negro(es)
Procurador: Person with power of attorney
Procurador da Coroa: Crown official responsible for watching over the financial and other interests of the Crown
Propinas: Perquisites; rake-offs
Provedor: (1) Comptroller or Superintendent of a bureaucratic office; (2) President of the Board of Guardians of the *misericórdia*

Quartel: Quarterly basic pay
Quilombo: War camp or community of runaway slaves
Quinas: Royal arms of Portugal, representing the five wounds of Christ and the thirty talents of silver for which He was sold
Quinta: Country house
Quintal: Four *arrobas*, corresponding to the English hundredweight
Quinto Real: Tax of the royal fifth (20 per cent) on all gold and silver mined

Raça Infecta: 'Contaminated race'. In practice, someone with Jewish or Negro blood in his or her veins

Recôncavo: Fertile sugar-growing plain around the city of Salvador and the Bay of All Saints

Relacão: High Court of Justice

Regimento: Standing orders; set of instructions; rules and regulations; statutes

Reinól (pl. Reinóis): European-born Portuguese

Reis (pl of Real): A small Portuguese copper coin of low value which was abolished in the sixteenth century, but its multiples were retained to use as money of account

Ribeira das Náos: Royal dockyard and/or shipbuilding yard

Roça: Smallholding; allotment; market-garden in Brazil. In Angola the term often meant a farm, plantation, or a large landed estate

Roteiro: Sailing directions; rutter

São Tomé: The *pardao São Tomé* was an Indo-European gold coin, first struck at Goa about 1548, with a value of 360 *reis*, and the seated figure of this saint on the reverse

Senado da Camara: Municipal or town council

Senhor de engenho: 'Lord of the mill'; by extension, the owner of a sugar plantation

Sertão: Backlands

Sesmaria: Land concession, usually granted by or in the name of the Crown

Siza: Excise

Solar: Manor house

Soldado: Soldier. In Portuguese Asia an unmarried man

Soldo: Basic pay

Sova: Angolan tribal chief or headman

Tangos-maos: Portuguese or Mulattos who 'went native' on the West African (Upper Guinea) coast

Terço: Portuguese infantry regiment, corresponding to the Spanish *tercio*

Trovas: Doggerel verses or rhymes

Ultramar: Overseas. *Conselho Ultramarino*, Overseas Council at Lisbon, 1643–1807

Várzea: Fertile sugar-growing region of Pernambuco

Vereador: Alderman, municipal councillor

Viradeira: Turn-about, reversal

Xerafim: An Indo-European coin, originally of gold and later of silver, with a face value of 300 *reis*, but which varied greatly in weight and consequently in intrinsic value

A note on sources and bibliography

SINCE this book is the product of over forty years' reading, research, reflection and publication on and around its subject matter, it would be as impracticable as unnecessary to give a list of all the original documents and printed works which I have consulted during that time, and which include some 4,000 books and hundreds of unpublished manuscripts in my own library. I enter this caveat lest the reader may think that some of my generalisations in the text are unsupported by any evidence, which is not the case. They may, of course, be wrong for all that. I may have been led astray inadvertently by some of my sources and I may unwittingly have drawn erroneous conclusions from others. Moreover, many (perhaps most) aspects of Portuguese colonial history require much further investigation, research and discussion before generally agreed conclusions can be reached. Even in such well-tilled fields as the development of the fifteenth-century discoveries, and the origins of Brazilian independence, widely differing interpretations and conclusions have been reached by scholars who have spent a lifetime in studying those problems. Still more does this reservation apply to such delicate and controversial topics as race relations and religious attitudes. I would be the last person to claim that the present book has the final word on all or any of the diverse themes of which it treats. But I do claim that none of my statements have been made lightly or irresponsibly. Moreover, I have been able to visit at one time or another most of the places concerned, from the Spice Islands of the Moluccas to the Backlands of the Mato Grosso.

I have also had the advantage of working intermittently in many of the relevant historical archives, including those of Lisbon, Evora, Goa, Macao, Luanda, Bahia, Rio de Janeiro and Belo Horizonte. I am greatly obliged to the directors and staffs of all these (and other) archives for the facilities which they have accorded me between 1928 and 1968. The numerous quotations which pepper my text are taken in nearly every instance from primary sources (whether manuscript or printed) rather than from secondary works. I hope in this way to have retained something of the feelings and the outlook of those bygone generations.

In view of the foregoing explanation, and the fact that this book is not primarily intended for readers who would expect every statement and quotation to be meticulously documented, the list of printed works which follows is limited to a small selection of those which I have found most useful, and which will be of interest to anyone desirous of delving further into the topics discussed in my sixteen chapters. For the same reason, as regards secondary works, I have given preference to those which are well documented and have adequate bibliographies.

General

There is no comprehensive guide to the archival resources of Portugal and her overseas empire, whether past or present, and many of the existing archives are inadequately catalogued. Information about the scope and contents of some of the more important ones can be obtained from the undermentioned books and articles, which likewise contain references to earlier publications. I must again emphasise that this is a purely selective and not a would-be comprehensive listing.

(a) *Portugal.* J. H. da Cunha Rivara, *Catalogo dos manuscritos da Bibliotheca Publica Eborense*, I, *America, Africa e Asia* (Lisbon, 1850); E. Axelson, 'Report on the archives and libraries of Portugal', on pp. 184–229 of his *South-East Africa, 1488–1530* (London, 1940); articles by Virginia Rau and Bailey W. Diffie in *The Proceedings of the International colloquium on Luso-Brazilian Studies, Washington, 1950* (Vanderbilt University Press, 1953), pp. 181–213; Georg Schurhammer, S.J., *Die Zeitgenössischen Quellen zur geschichte Portugiesisch-Asiens und seiner nachbaerlander, 1538–1552* (Rome, 1962), which covers more ground than the limitation in dates implies; A. F. C. Ryder, *Materials for West African History in Portuguese Archives* (University of London, the Athlone Press, 1965), which likewise covers more ground than indicated in the title.

(b) *Goa.* C. R. Boxer, 'A Glimpse of the Goa Archives' in the *Bulletin of the School of Oriental and African Studies* (London), June 1952, pp. 299–324; Panduronga Pissurlencar, *Roteiro dos Arquivos da Índia Portuguesa* (Bastorá-Goa, 1955); V. T. Guné, 'An Outline of the administrative institutions of the Portuguese Territories in India and the growth of their central archives at Goa, 16th to 19th Century A.D.', reprinted from pp. 47–92 of the *Studies in Indian History, Dr. A. G. Pawar Felicitation volume* (1968).

(c) *Macao*. Luís Gonzaga Gomes (ed.) *Catálogo dos manuscritos de Macau* (Lisbon, 1963).

(d) *Luanda*. Preliminary inventories made by Carlos Dias Coimbra in the *Arquivos de Angola*, second series, vol. XVI, pp. 1–183 (Luanda, 1959), and by C. R. Boxer, *Portuguese Society in the Tropics. The municipal councils of Goa, Macao, Bahia and Luanda, 1510–1800* (Wisconsin University Press, 1965), pp. 220–4. Since supplemented by José de Almeida Santos, *Raridades Bibliográficas existentes no arquivo e na Bibliotheca Municipal de Luanda* (Luanda, 1965), and A. da Silva Rego (compiler), *Arquivo Histórico de Angola. Roteiro Topográfico dos códices* (Luanda, 1966), although this *Roteiro* is mainly concerned with nineteenth- and twentieth-century material.

(e) *Bahia*. A comprehensive survey of the principal archives of the city of Salvador is given by A. J. R. Russell-Wood, *Fidalgos and Philanthropists. The Santa Casa da Misericórdia of Bahia, 1550–1755* (London, 1968), pp. 386–93.

(f) *Rio de Janeiro*. Dauril Alden, *Royal Government in Colonial Brazil, with special reference to the administration of the Marquis of Lavradio, 1769–1779* (University of California Press, 1968), pp. 514–20. Cf. also A. J. R. Russell-Wood, *op. cit.*, pp. 393–40.

Of the general bibliographies listing printed and (to a lesser extent) manuscript material, far and away the most useful and comprehensive is the truly monumental *Bibliotheca Missionum*, edited successively by Robert Streit, O.M.I., Johannes Dindinger, O.M.I., *et al.*, at Aachen and Freiburg from 1916 to the present (continuing) date. Twenty-five bulky volumes have been published so far, and long may this impeccable series continue. The contents cover far more ground than the title promises, as the editors and compilers have interpreted 'mission history' in its widest possible sense. They have included thousands of books and articles only remotely or indirectly concerned with missionary endeavours; and anyone concerned with the history of European expansion overseas ignores this bibliography at his (or her) peril. Furthermore, these volumes are all admirably indexed and cross-referenced, thus greatly facilitating their consultation.

The *Guia da Bibliografia Histórica Portuguesa*, edited under the auspices of the Academia Portuguesa da História, seems to have petered out after the publication of one slim volume (Lisbon, 1954), which is helpful as far as it goes, particularly in listing collections of printed documents. Among archival publications and collections or calendars of documents, the following will be found useful:

J. J. de Andrade e Silva, *Collecção Chronologica da Legislação Portugueza* (9 vols., Lisbon, 1854–9). Limited to the period 1603–1702, but contains much material relating to overseas as well as metropolitan Portugal. *Arquivo das Colonias, Publicação oficial* (5 vols., Lisbon, 1917–33). Published by the (then) Ministry of the Colonies in a haphazard and disorderly way, with intervals in 1920–1 and 1923–8, it contains a wide range of documentation, especially for the eighteenth century, and for East and West Africa. António da Silva Rego, *Boletim da Filmoteca Ultramarina Portuguesa* (Lisbon, 1954—in progress). A most useful publication, admirably indexed, which contains material from foreign archives as well as Portuguese. Centro de Estudos Históricos Ultramarinos, *Documentação Ultramarina Portuguesa* (Lisbon, 1960—in progress). Another admirable publication covering all the Portuguese *Ultramar*, although there is some needless repetition and overlapping in the first two volumes, out of the five published so far. J. H. da Cunha Rivara, *Archivo Portuguez Oriental* (9 vols., Nova Goa, 1857–76). This invaluable publication, particularly rich in sixteenth- to eighteenth-century documents on Portuguese India in the archives at Goa, should not be confused with its namesake below.

A. B. de Bragança Pereira, *Arquivo Português Oriental, Nova edição* (11 vols., Bastorá-Goa, 1936–40). Contrary to what is implied in the sub-title, this is not a new edition of Cunha Rivara's *APO*, but is a different work, containing many unpublished documents, especially for the eighteenth century. Unfortunately it is very carelessly edited, and riddled with misreadings and misprints.

Documentos remetidos da Índia ou Livros das Monções (5 vols., Lisbon, 1880–1935). Edited for the Lisbon Academy of Sciences, this publication petered out after publishing an invaluable series of the official correspondence between Lisbon and Goa for the years 1605–19. It is much to be wished that its publication would be continued.

Panduronga Pissurlencar, *Assentos do Conselho do Estado da Índia, 1618–1750* (5 vols., Bastorá-Goa, 1953–7). Particularly valuable for the years 1618–1700, this publication fills, in part, the gap left by the unpublished 'Livros das Monções' above. The originals are in the archives at Goa. *Arquivos de Macau, Publicação oficial* (Macau, 1929—in progress). 1st series, 3 vols., 1929–31; 2nd series, 1 vol., 1941–2; 3rd series, 1964—to date). Particularly rich for the period 1630–44 and for the eighteenth century.

Documentos sobre os Portugueses em Moçambique e na África Central, 1497–1840. Documents on the Portuguese in Moçambique and Central Africa 1497–1840 (Lisbon, 1962—in progress). Edited under the auspices of the Centro de Estudos Historicos Ultramarinos at Lisbon and the National Archives of Rhodesia, the five volumes of this admirable bi-lingual series hitherto published cover the years 1497–1518. *Arquivos de Angola* (Luanda, 1933—in progress). Publication was interrupted in 1940–2 between the first and second series. A synopsis of the volumes published down to October 1954 will be found in the *Guia da Bibliografia Histórica Portuguesa*, I, pp. 22–4.

Documentos Históricos da Bibliotheca Nacional do Rio de Janeiro (Rio de Janeiro, 1928—in progress). Over 120 volumes of historical documents have been published so far in this series, which is particularly rich for the period *c.* 1650 to *c.* 1750 and the early nineteenth century. It includes transcripts from Portuguese archives as well as original materials in Brazil. A synopsis of the contents of vols. 1–110, inclusive, will be found in the *Guia da Bibliografia Histórica Portuguesa*, I, pp. 55–61.

E. de Castro e Almeida, *Inventário dos documentos relativos ao Brasil existentes no Archivo de Marinha e Ultramar de Lisboa* (6 vols., Rio de Janeiro, 1913–36). The documents catalogued here are now in the Arquivo Histórico Ultramarino at Lisbon. After the death of the compiler, an additional 1,343 items pertaining to Rio de Janeiro were published in the *Anais da Bibliotheca Nacional*, vol. LXXI (Rio de Janeiro, 1951). Virginia Rau and Maria Fernanda Gomes da Silva, *Os Manuscritos do arquivo da casa de Cadaval respeitantes ao Brasil* (2 vols., Coimbra, 1956–8). The documents calendared here, often at considerable length, are chiefly of the late seventeenth and early eighteenth centuries, but they include some material of importance from *c.* 1641 onwards.

Cartographical studies do not come within the sphere of social history, I presume; but since the student of Portuguese expansion is bound to have some concern with the historical development of maps and charts, the following should satisfy his curiosity in whole or part:

A. Cotesão and A. C. Teixeira da Mota, *Portugaliae Monumenta Cartographica* (6 vols., Coimbra, 1960–3). A sumptuous and scholarly publication, giving reproductions of the originals, many of them in colour; A. C. Teixeira da Mota, *A Cartografia antiga da África Central e a Travessia entre Angola e Moçambique, 1500–1860* (Lourenço Marques, 1964); Ida Adonais, *A Cartografia da Região Amazonica* (2 vols., Rio de Janeiro, 1961–3); Jaime Cortesão, *História do Brasil nos velhos mapas* (Rio de Janeiro, 1966).

Last but not least, mention must be made of three major works, still in progress at the time of writing, and which are indispensable to the student of Portuguese expansion overseas:

Joel Serrão (ed.), *Dicionário de História de Portugal* (3 vols., Lisbon, 1963–8, with the fourth and final volume in the press). As is the case with all co-operative works, the articles are of varying quality; but the best are very good indeed, such as those by V. Magalhães Godinho, A. H. de Oliveira Marques, Jorge Borges de Macedo, Orlando Ribeiro and Luís de Albuquerque.

Vitorino Magalhães Godinho, *Os Descobrimentos e a Economia Mundial* (2 vols., Lisbon, 1965–8), a richly documented and lavishly illustrated work with new insights on the theme of which it treats.

Studia. Revista Semestral (Lisbon, 1958—in progress). Though no indication is given in the title, this periodical, edited by A. da Silva Rego, Director of the Centro de Estudos Históricos Ultramarinos at Lisbon, is exclusively devoted to the history of Portugal overseas. It frequently prints historical documents *in extenso*, as well as carrying authoritative articles and book reviews. Twenty-three numbers in twenty volumes have been published at the time of writing.

PROLOGUE: THE WESTERN RIM OF CHRISTENDOM

A. H. de Oliveira Marques, *A sociedade medieval Portuguesa. Aspectos de vida quotidiana* (Lisbon, 1964), complemented by his recent *Introdução à História de Agricultura em Portugal. A questão cerealífera durante a Idade Média* (Lisbon, 1967).

Orlando Ribeiro, *Portugal, o Mediterraneo e o Atlantico* (Coimbra, 1945); ibid, *Geografia e civilização* (Lisbon, 1961).

Dan Stanislawski, *The Individuality of Portugal. A study in historical-political geography* (University of Texas Press, 1959).

Virginia Rau, *Subsídios para o estudo das Feiras Medievais Portuguesas* (Lisbon, 1943).

Gilberto Freyre, *Brazil: An Interpretation* (New York, 1945).

António José Saraiva, *História da Cultura em Portugal* (3 vols., Lisbon, 1950–62), Vol. 1, which deals with the Middle Ages.

Fernão Lopes, *Cronica del Rei D. João, 1º*, of which there have been several editions between 1644 and 1949, none of them satisfactory nor adequately annotated.

CHAPTER I: GUINEA GOLD AND PRESTER JOHN

A. J. Dias Dinis (ed.), *Monumenta Henricina* (Coimbra, 1960—in progress). The eight volumes of this magnificent collection of documents published so far cover the period down to 1445.

F. M. Esteves Pereira (ed.), *Cronica da Tomada de Ceuta por El Rei D. João 1º, composta por Gomes Eannes de Zurara* (Lisbon, 1915).

Léon Bourdon (ed. and trans.) *Gomes Eanes de Zurara. Chronique de Guinée* (Ifan-Dakar, 1960). Supersedes the Hakluyt Society translation by C. R. Beazley and E. Prestage (1896–9).

Vitorino Magalhães Godinho, *A Economia dos Descobrimentos Henriquinos* (Lisbon, 1962), and his previous selection of *Documentos sobre a expansão portuguesa* (3 vols., Lisbon, 1943–56). The same author is also responsible for many other relevant books and articles, including his annotated edition of Duarte Leite, *História dos Descobrimentos. Colectanea de esparsos* (2 vols., Lisbon, 1959–62).

Charles-Martel de Witte, *Les Bulles Pontificales et l'expansion portugaise au XVe siécle* (Louvain, 1958).

E. W. Bovill, *Caravans of the Old Sahara* (London, 1933), which some people consider a better book than the author's later and revised edition, *The Golden Trade of the Moors* (New York and London, 1958).

R. Mauny, *Les Navigations médiévales sur les côtes Sahariennes antérieures à la découverte portugaise* (Lisbon, 1960); J. W. Blake, *Europeans in West Africa, 1450–1560* (2 vols., 1941–2, Hakluyt Society, 2nd series, vols. 86–7); P. E. Russell, *Prince Henry the Navigator* (London, 1960).

F. A. Chumovsky (ed.) and M. Malkiel-Jirmounsky (trans.), *Tres Roteiros desconhecidos de Ahmad Ibn-Madjid, o piloto Arabe de Vasco da Gama* (Lisbon, 1960). A. Fontoura da Costa (ed.), *Roteiro da primeira viagem de Vasco da Gama, 1497–1499, por Álvaro Velho* (Lisbon, 1940).

On the technical sides of shipping and finance, the following afford an excellent introduction to some aspects only lightly touched on in my own book:

M. Mollat and Paul Adam (ed.), *Les Aspects Internationaux de la découverte Océanique aux XVe et XVIe siècles* (Paris, 1966).

J. H. Parry, *The age of reconaissance. Discovery, exploration and settlement, 1450 to 1650* (New York and London, 1963), a masterly synthesis, also relevant to Chapters II–V of this book.

CHAPTER II: SHIPPING AND SPICES IN ASIAN SEAS

A. Cortesão (ed.), *The Suma Oriental of Tomé Pires and the Book of Francisco Rodrigues* (2 vols., 1944. Hakluyt Society, 2nd series, vols. 89–90).

Cartas de Afonso de Albuquerque, seguidas de documentos que as elucidam (7 vols., Lisbon, 1884–1935). Published by the Lisbon Academy of Sciences. Elaine Sanseau (ed.), *Cartas de D. João de Castro, 1538–48* (Lisbon, 1954). Jan Huigen van Linschoten, *Itinerario* (Amsterdam, 1596). Frequently reprinted in numerous editions and translations, this work, together with the slightly later *Voyage of Pyrard de Laval*, remains the classic account of 'Golden' Goa and Portuguese Asia at its apogee.

C. R. Boxer (ed. and trans.), *South China in the sixteenth century. Being the narratives of Galeote Pereira, Fr. Gaspar da Cruz, O.P., Fr. Martín de Rada, O.E.S.A., 1550–1575* (London, 1953, Hakluyt Society, 2nd series, vol. 106).

. . . *The Great Ship from Amacon. Annals of Macao and the Old Japan Trade, 1555–1640* (Lisbon, 1959). Chiefly valuable for the documents printed on pp. 173–333.

R. S. Whiteway, *The Rise of the Portuguese Power in India, 1497–1550* (London, 1899). Still the best introduction to the subject.

V. Magalhães Godinho, *Os Descobrimentos e a Economia Medieval* (2 vols., Lisbon, 1965–8). The best and fullest treatment of the topic to date.

Orlando Ribeiro, *Aspectos e Problemas da Expansão Portuguesa* (Lisbon, 1962).

M. A. P. Meilink-Roelofsz, *Asian Trade and European influence in the Indonesian archipelago between 1500 and about 1630* (The Hague, 1962). Fundamental.

D. Lach, *Asia in the making of Europe*, I, *The Century of Discovery* (2 vols., University of Chicago Press, 1965). A masterly analysis of a wide range of sixteenth-century literature.

J. Bastin, *The changing balance of the early Southeast Asian pepper-trade* (Kuala Lumpur, 1960).

CHAPTER III: CONVERTS AND CLERGY IN MONSOON ASIA

António de Silva Rego (ed.), *Documentação para a história das missões do Padroado Português do Oriente. Índia* (Lisbon, 1947—in progress). Twelve volumes of this fundamental work have been published to date.

Josef Wicki, S.J., *Documenta Indica* (Rome, 1948—in progress). Ten volumes of this equally indispensable and even more meticulously edited work have been published to date.

Artur Basílio de Sá, *Documentação para a história das missões do Padroado Português do Oriente. Insulíndia* (5 vols., Lisbon, 1954–8). Covers the period 1506–95, with some additional documents of the seventeenth century.

Georg Schurhammer, S.J., *Gesammelte Studien* (4 vols. in 5, Rome, 1962–5). Fundamental studies in several languages by the most erudite and the most fecund of the Jesuit historians of the Asian missions. Fr. Schurhammer is also the author of a massive biography of St. Francis Xavier (in progress), of which the relevant volume for this chapter is *Franz Xaver. Sein leben und seine zeit, II, Asien 1541–1552, Pt. (1), Indien und Indonesien, 1541–47* (Freiburg, 1963).

Rodrigo de Lima Felner, *Subsídios para a história da Índia Portugueza* (Lisbon, 1868).

Alessandro Valignano, S.J., Josef Wicki, S.J. (ed.), *Historia del principio y progresso de la Compañía de Jesús en las Indias Orientales, 1542–64* (Rome, 1944). E. Maclagan, *The Jesuits and the Great Moghul* (London, 1932). Tikiri Abeyasinghe, *Portuguese rule in Ceylon, 1594–1612* (Colombo, 1966). Pasquale M. D'Elia, S.J., *Fonti Ricciane. Documenti originali concernenti Matteo Ricci e la storia delle prime Relazioni tra l'Europe e la Cina, 1579–1615* (3 vols., Rome, 1942–9).

C. R. Boxer, *The Christian Century in Japan, 1549–1650* (University of California Press, 1951). D. Lach, *Asia in the making of Europe*, I, *The Century of Discovery* (1965).

CHAPTER IV: SLAVES AND SUGAR IN THE SOUTH ATLANTIC

W. B. Greenlee (ed. and trans.), *The voyage of Pedro Álvares Cabral to Brazil and India. From contemporary documents and narratives* (1937; Hakluyt Society, 2nd series, vol. 81).

Carlos Malheiro Dias (ed.), *Historia da colonização Portuguesa do Brasil* (3 vols., Oporto, 1921–2).

A. Marchant, *From Barter to Slavery. The economic relations of Portuguese and Indians in the settlement of Brazil, 1500–1580* (Baltimore, 1942). J. F. Almeida Prado, *Primeiros Povoadores do Brasil* (São Paulo, 1935). Fernão Cardim, S.J., *Tratados da Terra e gente do Brasil* (ed. Capistrano de Abreu *et al.*, Rio de Janeiro, 1925). Cardim was captured by English corsairs and his work was first published in English translation in Samuel Purchas, *Pilgrimes* (pp. 1289–1325 of the 1625 edition). Cf. also Maria Odila Dias Curly, 'Um texto de Cardim inédito em português', in the *Revista de Historia* of São Paulo, vol. XXVIII (1964), pp. 455–82.

José António Gonsalves de Mello (ed.), *Diálogos das Grandezas do Brasil. 1ª edição integral, segundo o apógrafo de Leiden* (Recife, 1962).

F. Mauro, *Le Portugal et l'Atlantique au XVIIe siècle, 1570–1670. Étude économique* (Paris, 1960). Best survey of the subject.

António Brásio, C.S. SP. (ed.), *Monumenta Missionaria Africana. Africa Ocidental* (Lisbon, 1952—in progress). Vols. 1–4 are relevant for the sixteenth century. Ralph Delgado, *História de Angola* (4 vols., Benguela and Lobito, 1948–55). Vols. 1 and 2. D. Birmingham, *Trade and conflict in Angola. The Mbundu and their neighbours under the influence of the Portuguese, 1483–1790* (New York and Oxford, 1966). Jan Vansina, *Kingdoms of the Savanna* (University of Wisconsin Press, 1966). Willy Bal (ed. and trans.), *Description du royaume de Congo et des contrées environnantes par Filippo Pigafetta & Duarte Lopes, 1591* (Louvain-Paris, 1965). K. R. Andrews, *Elizabethan Privateering, 1585–1603* (New York and Cambridge, 1964).

CHAPTER V: THE GLOBAL STRUGGLE WITH THE DUTCH

P. Pissurlencar (ed.), *Assentos do Conselho do Estado da Índia*, vols. 1–4, cover the years 1618–63. The Dutch counterpart to this is W. Philip Coolhaas (ed.), *Generale Missiven van Gouverneurs-Generaal en Raden, 1610–74* (3 vols., The Hague, 1960–8). Alfredo Botelho de Sousa, *Subsídios para a história militar marítima da Índia, 1585–1650* (4 vols.,

Lisbon, 1930–56), which gives the Portuguese point of view of the maritime war in the East, as the Dutch point of view is given by N. MacLeod, *De Oost-Indische Compagnie ale zeemogendheid in Azie, 1602–1652* (2 vols., and atlas, Rijswijk, 1927). Both works are based on archival materials. Fernão de Queiroz, S.J., *Historia da vida do venerauel Irmão Pedro de Basto . . . e da variedade de sucessos que Deos lhe manifestou* (Lisbon, 1689), contains details which cannot be found elsewhere, as does his well-known classic, *Conquista Temporal e espiritual de Ceylão* (ed. Colombo, 1916), of which there is a scholarly English translation by S. G. Pereira, S.J. *The Temporal and Spiritual Conquest of Ceylon* (3 vols., Colombo, 1930). The viewpoint of the rank and file on each side is well expressed by (a) João Ribeiro, *Fatalidade Historica da Ilha de Ceilão*, completed in 1685, but first published in 1835, with an excellent English version by P. E. Pieris (4th ed., Colombo, 1948) and by (b) Johann Saar, *Ost-Indianische Funfzehen-Jahrige Kriegs-dienst* (Nuremberg 1662).

For the war and its repercussions in the Atlantic region, see the following works and the sources quoted therein, which include archival as well as published material:

J. A. Gonsalves de Mello, *Tempo dos Flamengos. Influência da ocupação Holandesa na vida e cultura do Norte do Brasil* (Rio de Janeiro, 1947).

. . . *João Fernandes Vieira, Mestre de campo do Terço de infantaria de Pernambuco* (2 vols., Recife, 1956).

José Honório Rodrigues, *Historiografia e Bibliografia do domínio holandês no Brasil* (Rio de Janeiro, 1949).

C. R. Boxer, *Salvador de Sá and the struggle for Brazil and Angola, 1602–1686* (London, 1952).

. . . *The Dutch in Brazil, 1624–1654* (New York and Oxford, 1957). F. Mauro, *Le Portugal et l'Atlantique, 1570–1670* (Paris, 1960). On the language rivalry, Marius F. Valkhoff, *Studies in Portuguese and Creole, with special references to South Africa* (Witwatersrand University Press, 1966).

CHAPTER VI: STAGNATION AND CONTRACTION IN THE EAST

Manuel Godinho, *Relação do novo caminho que fez por terra e mar, vindo da India para Portugal no anno de 1663* (Lisbon, 1665).

P. Pissurlencar, *Assentos do Conselho do Estado da India*, vols. 4 and 5, covering the period 1659–1750. Germano da Silva Correia, *História da colonização portuguesa na Índia* (6 vols., Lisbon, 1948–58). To be used with caution, as the author often mistakenly, though in good faith, ascribes a European origin to women who were Eurasians. Diogo do Couto, *Soldado Pratico* (ed. A. C. de Amaral, Lisbon, 1790; and, much better, by M. Rodrigues Lapa, Lisbon, 1937).

Felipe Nery Xavier (ed.), *Instrucção do Exmo Vice-Rei Marquez de Alorna ao seu successor Exmo Vice-Rei Marquez de Tavora, 1750* (Nova-Goa, 1856).

E. Axelson, *Portuguese in Southeast Africa, 1600–1700* (Witwatersrand University Press, 1960).

António Alberto de Andrade, *Relações de Moçambique Setecentista* (Lisbon, 1955).

Alexandre Lobato, *Colonização Senhorial da Zambésia e outros ensaios* (Lisbon, 1962).

Humberto Leitão, *Os Portugueses em Solor e Timor de 1515 a 1702* (Lisbon, 1948).

. . . *Vinte e oito anos de História de Timor, 1698–1725* (Lisbon, 1952).

Surendranath Sen (ed.), *Indian Travels of Thevenot and Careri* (New Delhi, 1949).

Alexander Hamilton, *A New Account of the East Indies* (2 vols., ed. W. Foster, London, 1930).

John Ovington, *A voyage to Surat in 1689* (London, 1696).

José de Jesus Maria, O.F.M., *Azia Sinica e Japonica, 1745* (ed. 2 vols., Macau, 1941–50).

CHAPTER VII: REVIVAL AND EXPANSION IN THE WEST

Public Record Office, London, Correspondence of the English envoys at Lisbon, 1663–1756 (S.P. 89/5–S.P. 89/50).

Journal of the purser of H.M.S. *Winchester* in the National Maritime Museum, Greenwich (quoted by permission of the Trustees).

D. Erskine (ed.), *Augustus Hervey's Journal* (London, 1953).

João Lucio d'Azevedo (ed.), *Cartas do Padre Antonio Vieira* (3 vols., Coimbra, 1925–28).

Jaime Cortesão, *Alexandre de Gusmão e o Tratado de Madrid* (9 vols., Rio de Janeiro, 1950–63).

Andrée Mansuy (ed. and trans.) André João Antonil, *Cultura e Opulencia do Brasil por suas drogas e minas. Texte de l'édition de 1711, traduction française et commentaire critique* (Paris, 1968). Definitive edition of this fundamental work first published in 1711 under a pseudonym by the Italian Jesuit Giovanni Antonio Andreoni (1649–1716).

A. D. Francis, *The Methuens and Portugal, 1691–1708* (Cambridge University Press, 1966).

H. E. S. Fisher, 'Anglo-Portuguese Trade, 1700–1770', reprinted from the *Economic History Review*, 2nd series, vol. XVII (December 1963), pp. 219–33.

Gazeta de Lisboa (Lisbon, 1715–50).

Ayres de Carvalho, *D. João V e a arte do seu Tempo* (2 vols., Mafra, 1960–2).

C. R. Boxer, *The Golden Age of Brazil, 1695–1750* (University of California Press, 1962).

Jorge Borges de Macedo, *Problemas de História da indústria Portuguesa no século XVIII* (Lisbon, 1963).

Ralph Delgado, *Historia de Angola*, vols. 3 and 4.

Affonso de Escragnolle Taunay, *Subsídios para a historia do Trafico Africano no Brasil* (São Paulo, 1941).

Pierre Verger, *Flux et reflux de la traite des nègres entre le golfe de Bénin et Bahia de todos os santos du 17e au 19e siècle* (Paris and The Hague, 1968).

CHAPTER VIII: THE POMBALINE DICTATORSHIP AND ITS AFTERMATH

Most of the works cited in the bibliography of Chapter VII above are also relevant to this chapter, with the addition of the following:

PRO, London, S.P. 89/53, for Lord Kinnoull's interview with Pombal, 11 October 1760.

João Lucio d'Azevedo, *O Marquez de Pombal e a sua época* (Lisbon, 1922).

Jorge Borges de Macedo, *A situação económica no tempo de Pombal. Alguns aspectos* (Oporto, 1951).

V. Magalhães Godinho, *Prix et Monnaies au Portugal, 1750–1850* (Paris, 1955).

Visconde de Carnaxide, *O Brasil na administração pombalina* (São Paulo, 1940).

José-Augusto França, *Une ville des Lumières: La Lisbonne de Pombal* (Paris, 1965).

Dauril Alden, *Royal Government in Colonial Brazil. With special reference to the administration of the Marquis of Lavradio, Viceroy, 1769–1779* (University of California Press, 1968). Fundamental for the understanding of eighteenth-century Brazil.

Luiz dos Santos Vilhena, *Noticias soteropolitanas e brasilicas* (ed. Braz do Anaral, 3 vols., Salvador, Bahia, 1921–22).

Jacome Ratton, *Recordaçoens, 1747–1810* (London, 1813).

José António Caldas, *Noticia geral de toda esta capitania da Bahia, 1759* (facsimile edition, Bahia, 1949).

Caio Prado Junior, *Formação do Brasil contêmporeneo: colônia* (4th edn. São Paulo, 1953). Translated by Suzette Macedo as *The Colonial Background of Modern Brazil* (University of California Press, 1967).

Marcos Carneiro de Mendonça, *A Amazonia na era pombalina, 1751–59* (3 vols., Rio de Janeiro, 1963).

Albert Silbert, *Le Portugal Mediterranéen à la fin de l'ancien régime, XVIIIe—début du XIXe siècle. Contribution a l'histoire agraire comparée* (2 vols., Paris, 1966).

C. L. Monteiro de Barbuda (ed.), *Instrucções com que El-Rei D. José I mandou passar ao Estado da India o Governador e Capitão Geral e o Arcebispo Primaz do Oriente no anno de 1774* (Pangim, 1841).

J. H. da Cunha Rivara, *A Conjuração de 1787 em Goa, e varias cousas desse tempo. Memoria Historica* (Nova-Goa, 1875).

Fritz Hoppe, *Portugiesisch-Ostafrika in der Zeit des Marquês de Pombal, 1750–1777* (Berlin, 1965).

José Mariano da Conceição Veloso, *O Fazendeiro do Brasil Melhorado na economia rural dos generos jà cultivados, e de outros, que se podem introduzir, e nas fabricas, que lhe são proprias, segundo o melhor, que se tem escrito a este assumpto* (10 vols., Lisbon, 1798–1806).

Sergio Buarque de Holanda (ed.), *História Geral da Civilização Brasileira, I, A época colonial*, Vol. 2, *Administração, Economia, Sociedade* (São Paulo, 1960).

CHAPTER IX: THE INDIA FLEETS AND THE BRAZIL FLEETS

C. R. Boxer (ed. and trans.), *The Tragic History of the Sea, 1589–1622*, and *Further Selections from the Tragic History of the Sea, 1559–1565* (Cambridge University Press, 1959 and 1968; Hakluyt Society, 2nd series, vols. 112, 132).

James Duffy, *Shipwreck and Empire* (Harvard University Press, 1955).

W. L. Schurz, *The Manila Galleon* (New York, 1939).

Quirino da Fonseca, *Os Portugueses no Mar*, I, *Ementa Histórica das naus portuguesas* (Lisbon, 1926).

. . . (ed.), *Diários da Navegação da Carreira da Índia nos anos de 1595, 1596, 1597, 1600 e 1603* (Lisbon, 1938).

Humberto Leitão (ed.), *Viagens do Reino para a Índia e da Índia para o Reino, 1608–1612; diários de navegação coligidos por D. António de Ataide no século XVII* (3 vols., Lisbon, 1957–8).

. . . and J. Vicente Lopes, *Dicionário da linguagem de Marinha antiga e actual* (Lisbon, 1963).

A. Frazão de Vasconcelos, *Subsídios para a história da carreira da Índia no tempo dos Felipes* (Lisbon, 1960).

Regímento dos Escrivaens das Náos da Carreira da India (these were evidently printed yearly from an unascertained date in the late sixteenth century, but I have only seen those for the years 1611, 1640, 1756 and 1779).

Alberto Iria, *De Navegação Portuguesa no Índico no século XVII. Documentos do Arquivo Histórico Ultramarino* (Lisbon, 1963).

Documentação Ultramarina Portuguesa, Vol. IV (Lisbon, 1966).

Gazeta de Lisboa (Lisbon, 1715–1800).

J. R. do Amaral Lapa, *A Bahia e a Carreira da Índia* (Marilia, 1966).

Gustavo de Freitas, *A Companhia Geral do Comércio do Brasil, 1649–1720* (São Paulo, 1951).

Sebastião da Rocha Pitta, *História da America Portuguesa* (Lisbon, 1730).

António de Brito Freyre, 'Assentos de todas as viagens principiadas no prezente ano de 1727' (Biblioteca Nacional, Lisboa, Fundo Geral, MS. 485), and his 'Livro das Viagens, 1733–1744' (Library of the University of Coimbra, MS.).

Gonçalo Xavier de Barros Alvim, 'Jornal de Varias Viagens, 1719–38', Tomo I (original MS. in the author's collection). I have not been able to locate the later MSS. volume(s), which presumably cover the writer's services in the Brazil fleets from 1738 down to the year 1760, when he became garrison commander at Bahia.

CHAPTER X: THE CROWN PATRONAGE AND THE CATHOLIC MISSIONS

António da Silva Rego, *Documentação . . . Índia* (1947—in progress).

Josef Wicki, S.J., *Documenta Indica* (1948—in progress).

Artur de Sá, *Documentação . . . Insulíndia* (1954—in progress).

António Brásio, C.S. SP., *Monumenta Missionaria . . . Africa Ocidental* (1952—in progress).

J. L. d'Azevedo (ed.), *Cartas de Antonio Vieira* (3 vols., 1925–8).

A. van den Wyngaert and G. Mensaert, O.F.M. (eds.), *Sinica Francisoana* (vols. 2–6 inclusive, Florence and Rome, 1933–61).

Unpublished correspondence of the Spanish Augustinian missionary-friars in South China, 1680–1720 (Indiana University, Lilly Library MSS. 21524 (1)–21524 (2).

Francisco Rodrigues, S.J., *História da Campanhia de Jesus na assistência de Portugal* (4 vols., in 7, Oporto, 1931–50).

Serafim Leite, S.J., *História da Companhia de Jesus no Brasil, 1549–1760* (10 vols., Rio de Janeiro, 1938–50).

M. da Costa Nunes (ed.), *Documentação para a história da Congregação do Oratório de Santa Cruz dos Milagres do Clero natural de Goa* (Lisbon, 1966).

J. Cuvelier and L. Jadin (eds.), *L'ancien Congo d'après les archives romaines, 1518–1640* (Brussels, 1959).

Instrucções . . . ao Governador . . . e Arcebispo Primaz . . . no anno de 1774 (ed. Pangim, 1841).

Carlos Merces de Melo, S.J., *The recruitment and formation of the native clergy in India. 16th–19th century. An historico-canonical study* (Lisbon, 1955).

Eduardo Brazão, *D. João V e a Santa Sé. As relações diplomáticas de Portugal com o governo pontificio de 1706 a 1750* (Coimbra, 1937).

Antonio Sisto Rosso, O.F.M., *Apostolic Legations to China of the 18th century* (South Pasadena, 1948).

H. Chappoulie, *Aux origines d'une église. Rome et les missions d'Indochina au XVIIe siècle* (2 vols., Paris, 1943–8).

J. S. Cummins (ed. and trans.), *The Travels and Controversies of Fr. Domingo Navarrete, O.P., 1618–1686* (2 vols., Cambridge, 1962; Hakluyt Society, 2nd series, 118–19).

G. Schurhammer, S.J., *Gesammelte Studien* (4 vols., 1962–5).

Numerous articles and reviews by Fr. Francisco Leite de Faria, O.F.M. Cap., in *Studia*, passim.

CHAPTER XI: 'PURITY OF BLOOD' AND 'CONTAMINATED RACES'

In addition to most of the works cited in the bibliography to Chapter X, which are relevant to the problems of the Creole, *Mestiço*, and Indigenous clergy:

Gilberto Freyre, *Casa-Grande e Senzala* (Rio de Janeiro, 1943) and its English translation by Samuel Putnam, *The Masters and the Slaves* (New York, 1946) together with his *Sobrados e Mucambos* (Rio de Janeiro, 1936), and its English translation by Harriet de Onís, *The Mansions and the Shanties* (New York, 1963) are representative of his voluminous works in the field of social anthropology.

C. R. Boxer, *Race Relations in the Portuguese Empire, 1415–1825* (Oxford, 1963).

Antonio Ardizone Spinola, *Cordel Triplicado de amor . . . lançado em tres livros de sermoens . . . pregou-os na India na See Primacial de Goa, e em Lisboa na Capella Real* (Lisbon, 1680).

Theodore Ghesquiére, *Mathieu de Castro, premier vicaire apostolique aux Indes. Une création de la Propaganda à ses débuts* (Louvain, 1937).

Conego Alcântara Guerreiro, *Quadros da História de Moçambique* (2 vols., Lourenço Marques, 1954). Sebastião Monteiro da Vide, *Primeiras Constituições Synodais do Arcebispado da Bahia* (Lisbon, 1719). Jorge Benci, S.J., *Economia Cristã dos Senhores no governo dos escravos* (Rome, 1705. Reprinted and annotated by S. Leite, S.J., Oporto, 1954).

Manuel Ribeiro Rocha, *Ethiope Resgatado, empenhado, sustentado, corregido, instruido e libertado* (Lisbon, 1758).

Fernando Henrique Cardoso and Octávio Ianni, *Cor e Mobilidade Social em Florianópolis. Aspectos das relações entre Negros e Brancos numa comunidade do Brasil Meridional* (São Paulo, 1960).

João Lucio d'Azevedo, *Historia dos Cristãos Novos Portugueses* (Lisbon, 1921).

António José Saraiva, *A Inquisição Portuguesa* (Lisbon, 1956).

António Baião, *A Inquisição de Goa, 1569–1630* (2 vols., Coimbra and Lisbon, 1930–45).

A. K. Priolkar, *The Goa Inquisition* (Bombay, 1961).

Arnold Wiznitzer, *Jews in Colonial Brazil* (Columbia University Press, 1960).

I. S. Révah, numerous articles in the *Revue des Études Juives*, and elsewhere, 1955–68.

CHAPTER XII: TOWN COUNCILLORS AND BROTHERS OF CHARITY

Eduardo Freire de Oliveira, *Elementos para a História do Município de Lisboa* (19 vols., 1882–1943).

C. R. Boxer, *Portuguese Society in the Tropics. The municipal councils of Goa, Macao, Bahia and Luanda, 1510–1800* (University of Wisconsin Press, 1965).

Viriato de Albuquerque, *O Senado de Goa, Memoria Histórico-Archeologica* (Nova-Goa, 1909).

A Voyage to the East Indies . . . written originally in French by Mr. Dellon, M.D. (London, 1698).

Balthazar de Silva Lisboa, *Annaes do Rio de Janeiro* (7 vols., 1834–5). Based almost entirely on documents in the municipal archives.

Compromisso da Misericordia de Lisboa (1618).

José F. Ferreira Martins, *História da Misericordia de Goa* (3 vols., Nova-Goa, 1910–14).

José Caetano Soares, *Macau e a Assistência. Panorama médico-social* (Lisbon, 1950).

Fritz Teixeira de Salles, *Associações religiosas no ciclo de Ouro* (Belo Horizonte, 1963).

A. J. R. Russell-Wood, *Fidalgos and Philanthropists. The Santa Casa da Misericordia of Bahia, 1550–1755* (Berkley and London, 1968). An outstanding and richly documented work, received as this book went to press.

CHAPTER XIII: SOLDIERS, SETTLERS AND VAGABONDS

Diogo do Couto, *Soldado Prático* (editions of 1790 and 1937).

A. de S. S. Costa Lobo (ed.), *Memorias de um soldado da India, 1585–98, compiladas de um manuscripto portuguez do Museu Britannico* (Lisbon, 1877). I have also consulted the original MS. of Francisco Rodrigues da Silveira from which Costa Lobo took his extracts (B.M. Add. MSS. 25419).

António Freire, O.S.A. (ed.), *Primor e Honra da vida soldadesca no Estado da India* (Lisbon, 1630).

João Ribeiro, *Fatalidade Historica da Ilha de Ceilão, 1685* (ed. 1835).

Panduronga Pissurlencar, *Assentos do Conselho do Estado da Índia, 1618–1750* (5 vols.).

F. Diniz de Ayalla, *Goa Antiga e Moderna* (Lisbon, 1888).

The Travels of Peter Mundy in Europe and Asia, 1608–1667 (5 vols. in 6, Hakluyt Society, 1905–36).

The Voyage of François Pyrard of Laval (2 vols. in 3, Hakluyt Society, 1887–9).

Nicolao Manucci, *Storia do Mogor or Mogul India, 1653–1708* (4 vols., London, 1907–8).

Antonil-Mansuy, *Cultura e Opulencia do Brasil* (see bibliography to Chapter VII).

Luiz de Santos Vilhena, *Noticias Soteropolitanas* (see bibliography to Chapter VIII).

A. J. R. Russell-Wood, *Fidalgos and Philanthropists* (1968).

António de Oliveira de Cadornega, *História Geral das guerras Angolanas, 1680* (3 vols., Lisbon, 1940–2).

Adolfo Coelho, *Os ciganos de Portugal* (Lisbon, 1892).

Damião de Gois, *Cronica do Principe Dom João* (Lisbon, 1567). Several later editions.

Afonso do Paço, 'A vida militar no cancioneiro popular português', published serially in the *Revista de Etnografia*, Vols. I–III (Oporto, 1963–4).

CHAPTER XIV; MERCHANTS, MONOPOLISTS, AND SMUGGLERS

Many of the works cited in the bibliographies of Chapters I–XIII are likewise relevant to this one, particularly those by V. Magalhães Godinho, Jorge Borges de Macedo, J. R. do Amaral Lapa, and the correspondence of the British envoys and consuls at Lisbon, 1640–1750, in the PRO, London.

Virginia Rau, *A Exploração e o comercio do Sal de Setùbal. Estudo de história económica* (Lisbon, 1951).

. . . , *Estudos de História Económica* (Lisbon, 1961).

. . . , 'Um grande mercador-banqueiro italiano em Portugal: Lucas Giraldi', 35-page reprint from *Estudos Italianos em Portugal*, No. 24 (1956).

. . . , *O 'Livro de Rezão' de António Coelho Guerreiro* (Lisbon, 1956).

C. R. Boxer, *Francisco Vieira de Figueiredo: a Portuguese merchant-adventurer in Southeast Asia, 1624–1667* (The Hague, 1967).

F. Mauro, 'La Bourgeoisie portuguaise au XVIIe siecle', in *XVIIe siecle, Bulletin de la Société d'Étude du XVIIe siecle*, No. 40 (Paris, 1958), pp. 235–57.

J. Gentil da Silva, *Marchandises et finances*, II, *Lettres de Lisbonne, 1563–1578* (Paris, 1959).

Myriam Ellis, *O Monopólio do sal no Estado de Brasil, 1631–1801* (São Paulo, 1955).

. . . , *O Abastecimento da Capitania das Minas Gerais no Século XVIII* (São Paulo, 1951).

. . . , *Aspectos da pesca da baleia no Brasil colonial* (São Paulo, 1959).

Alice Piffer Canabrava, *O comércio português no Rio de Prata, 1580–1640* (São Paulo, 1944).

Huguette and Pierre Chaunu, *Séville et l'Atlantique, 1500–1650* (8 vols., in 11, Paris, 1955–6), contains numerous references to the activities of Portuguese traders, slavers and smugglers in Spanish America besides the allusion to Gramaxo quoted in the text (*op. cit.*, IV, 346–7).

CHAPTER XV: THE 'KAFFIRS OF EUROPE', THE RENAISSANCE, AND THE ENLIGHTENMENT

The quotation at the beginning is from Maxime Haubert, *L'église et la défense des 'sauvages'. Le Père Antoine Vieira au Brésil* (Brussels, 1964).

António José Saraiva, *História da Cultura em Portugal*, vols. 2 and 3. Unfortunately, this excellent work with its wealth of new insights ends somewhat abruptly with the year 1580.

Hernâni Cidade, *Lições de Cultura e Literatura Portuguesas*, II, *Da reacção contra a formalismo seiscentista ao advento do Romantismo* (Coimbra, 1948).

. . . , *A Literatura Portuguesa e a expansão ultramarina* (2 vols., Lisbon and Coimbra, 1943–64).

J. S. da Silva Dias, *Correntes de sentimento religioso em Portugal. Séculos XVI a XVIII* (2 vols., Coimbra, 1960). In progress. Only covers the sixteenth century so far.

Elisabeth Feist Hirsch, *Damião de Gois. The Life and thought of a Portuguese humanist, 1502–1574* (The Hague, 1967).

M. Gonsalves Cerejeira, *Clenardo e a sociedade portuguesa do seu tempo* (Coimbra, 1949).

António Alberto de Andrade, *Vernei e a cultura do seu tempo* (Coimbra, 1965).

Joaquim Ferreira Gomes, *Martinho de Mendonça e a sua obra pedagógica, com a edição critica dos 'Apontamentos para a educação de hum menino nobre'* (Coimbra, 1964).

Maximiano Lemos, *Ribeiro Sanches. A sua vida e a sua obra* (Oporto, 1911).

David Willemse, *António Nunes Ribeiro Sanches, élève de Boerhaave et son importance pour la Russie* (Leiden, 1966).

Raimundo José da Cunha Matos, *Compêndio Histórico das possessões de Portugal na África* (ed. J. H. Rodrigues, Rio de Janeiro, 1963).

Fernando de Azevedo (Rex Crawford, trans.) *Brazilian Culture* (New York, 1950).

Pedro de Azevedo and António Baião (eds.), *Instrucções inéditas de D. Luís da Cunha á Marco António de Azevedo Coutinho* (Coimbra, 1929).
Manuel Mendes (ed.), *Testamento Político de D. Luiz da Cunha* (Lisbon, 1943).

I have not ventured far into the field of art-history, but those desirous of doing so will find excellent guides in the following works, all of which are lavishly illustrated:

Robert C. Smith, *The Art of Portugal, 1500–1800* (New York, 1968); Carlos de Azevedo, *Arte Cristã na Índia Portuguesa* (Lisbon, 1959); Gritli von Mitterwallner, *Chaul. Eine unerforschte stadt an der West-kuste Indiens: Wehr-Sakral-und Profanarchitektur* (Berlin, 1964); Germain Bazin, *L'Architecture Religieuse Baroque au Brésil* (2 vols., Paris, 1956–8); G. Kubler and M. Soria, *Art and Architecture in Spain and Portugal and their American dominions, 1500–1800* (Harmondsworth, 1959); Serafim Leite, S.J., *Artes e Ofícios dos Jesuitas no Brasil, 1649–1760* (Lisbon, 1953), the illustrations relevant to this work being in the author's 10-volume *História* of the Jesuits in Brazil (vide bibliography to Chapter X).

CHAPTER XVI: SEBASTIANISM, MESSIANISM, AND NATIONALISM

João Lucio d'Azevedo, *A Evolução do Sebastianismo* (Lisboa, 1916).

Eugenio Asensio (ed.), *D. Gaspar de Leão, Desengano de perdidos, 1573* (Coimbra, 1958).

Mary Elizabeth Brooks, *A King for Portugal: the Madrigal conspiracy, 1594–95* (University of Wisconsin Press, 1964).

Fernão de Queiroz, S.J., *Historia da vida do Irmão Pedro de Basto* (Lisbon, 1689).

Raymond Cantel, *Prophétisme et Messianisme dans l'oeuvre d'Antonio Vieira* (Paris, 1960).

Ignacio de Santa Teresa, 'Estado do presente Estado da India. Meyos faceis, e efficazes para o seu augmento e reforma espiritual e temporal. Tractado Politico, Moral, Juridico, Theologico, Historico e Ascetico. Escrito na India no anno de 1725'. The author was Archbishop-Primate at Goa, 1721–40. Unpublished, but widely circulated in MS.

Hernâni Cidade, *A Literatura Autonomista sob os Felipes* (Lisbon, 1948).

M. Lopes de Almeida (ed.), *Memorial de Pero Rōiz Soares, 1565–1628* (Coimbra, 1953).

Miguel Leitão de Andrade, *Miscellanea* (Lisbon, 1629).

Euclides da Cunha, *Os sertões* (numerous editions, and English translation by Samuel Putnam, *Rebellion in the Backlands* Chicago, 1944).

R. B. Cunninghame-Graham, *A Brazilian Mystic: being the life and miracles of Antonio Conselheiro* (New York, 1925).

Waldemar Valente, *Misticismo e Região. Aspectos do Sebastianismo Nordestino* (Recife, 1963).

Index